TEMPTING FATE

The Black Angel's teeth clenched. His nostrils flared. He moved toward Rosalind, one slow, measured step at a time until he loomed over her. Rosalind looked up at him, at the chiseled perfection of his features. He reminded her of a statue, pleasing to the eye but stone cold. She turned her face away. The Black Angel took her chin in his hand, forcing her to meet his gaze.

"Again and again you provoke me, mademoiselle." His voice was a silky whisper. "I begin to think you want me to beat you."

He jerked her chin up. Rosalind flinched, expecting pain. Instead, the sudden velvety warmth of his lips on hers stole her breath.

Ship of Dreams

ELAINE LeCLAIRE

LEISURE BOOKS NEW YORK CITY

A LEISURE BOOK®

August 2005

Published by

Dorchester Publishing Co., Inc.
200 Madison Avenue
New York, NY 10016

ISBN 0-8439-5575-9

The name "Leisure Books" and the stylized "L" with design are
trademarks of Dorchester Publishing Co., Inc.

Printed in the United States of America.

Visit us on the web at www.dorchesterpub.com.

To my agent, Carolyn Grayson,
for making this dream come true, and
to my mother, Nilah Merry Chamberlain,
who has always believed in me.

Ship of Dreams

Chapter One

Lady Rosalind Hanshaw stood at the rail of the *Bird of Paradise* and stared out across the sea. Jamaica was still a full day's sailing ahead. This journey might have been a grand adventure if only she were visiting her brother Thomas for a happy reason. The tropical water shone like a blue topaz, sunlight glittering off the crest of every wave. The sea breeze tugged at her skirts and made the black taffeta ripple like the waves below. A wide ribbon of black silk tied her straw bonnet firmly in place, shielding her fair skin from the brilliance of the summer sun. It would have been a relief to free her blond hair from its careful arrangement and let it stream out in the wind. The grim burden of her mourning clothes was made worse by the tropical heat. Rosalind chided herself for such selfish thinking. What did it matter how hot or sticky she was? Far greater would Thomas's distress be once she told him of their father's sudden death.

The only land in view was a small islet off to port. How different it looked from Dover's white cliffs. Despite its lush green foliage, it looked desolate, alone and lonely amid the crashing waves. That was how Rosalind felt these days, lost amid the elemental forces that ruled her life, forces that struck without warning and showed no mercy.

"Lady Rosalind?"

Rosalind turned to see Beatrice hovering behind her. The wind and sun had flushed the girl's cheeks a fresh pink, giving her needed color. How splendid she would have looked in a gown of sky blue satin, instead of the plain gray wool she wore. Practical yes, but far too somber. Rosalind's aching heart yearned for some diversion, something cheerful to lighten the unhappiness clouding her heart.

"You're looking rather pale, my lady." Beatrice laid one fragile hand on Rosalind's arm. "Is there anything I can bring you? Perhaps we should go below."

Rosalind turned her face to the sun, wishing its light could brighten the grief that threatened to crush her. "Just mixing seasickness with homesickness, that's all."

Beatrice nodded. "I shall be so glad to reach land. I feel as if my legs will never stop wobbling!"

Rosalind smoothed a stray curl of Beatrice's fine fair hair behind her ear. At sixteen Beatrice was only two years younger than Rosalind. Yet here Beatrice was, making her way in the world, working for her keep instead of playing the marriage game.

"I wonder if Mrs. Lawrence will send a carriage?" Beatrice fretted with her lace collar, tugging at a spot already frayed from her nerves. "I do hope so. I wouldn't want to appear on their doorstep all windblown and dusty from walking. Governesses have to set a good example for their children."

"Everything will be fine, Beatrice. If the family was kind enough to pay your passage, they'll certainly send a carriage for you."

Beatrice nodded. Anxiety still clouded her expression. "I'm sure I shall miss my sisters terribly. That was the hardest part of deciding to accept this situation." She gave herself a shake and squared her shoulders. "Still, I have nothing to complain about. The Lawrences are quite generous. Mother made inquiries, and we've been assured they're regular churchgoers."

"I admire you, Beatrice. You're so brave and determined."

Beatrice smiled. "I must be, my lady, for Mother's sake. She'll need my wages to help Flora, Rachel, and Lucinda."

Rosalind gave Beatrice's hand a fond squeeze. "The colonies are full of the sons of wealthy men. I'm sure the Lawrences can count among their acquaintances some young man who will find in you everything he could hope for in a wife."

Beatrice blushed prettily. "Wouldn't that be lovely? To meet some kind, decent fellow, a man who works hard yet always has time for his children. . . ." Beatrice looked out over the water with a wistful sigh. "And if we're very lucky, he'll have lots of brothers."

Rosalind laughed. "That's the spirit! We'll see all of your sisters married off before next spring!" She laid an arm around Beatrice's thin shoulders. "I'm told the men of the colonies are a wilder breed than the Englishmen we're used to at home. Perhaps you'll find someone quite dashing."

"I'd settle for a man who's steadfast, faithful, and regular in his habits. A man much like Mr. MacCaulay."

Rosalind glanced back toward the stern. The cheerful, white-whiskered Mr. MacCaulay leaned on the rail. Despite being a solicitor, he looked perfectly at home amid the usual clamor and activity on deck. Mr. MacCaulay was as charming as a gentleman could be.

"You must have your choice of eligible young men, Lady Rosalind," Beatrice said. "Have you found one yet you prefer?"

Rosalind shook her head. "No, I have not. Recent events have made me somewhat less attractive to a number of my prospective bridegrooms."

Beatrice sighed. "Love of money truly is the root of all evil." She brightened. "Surely Mr. Murdock will look after you?"

"He's all too willing, he's made that perfectly clear."

Rosalind contemplated the endless crashing of the waves against the shores of the islet. Their relentless assault put her in mind of Edward Murdock. As her father's business partner, Mr. Murdock's concern for her at this tragic time was both appropriate and touching, yet Rosalind found it as oppressive as the tropical heat.

"He's not—I mean," Beatrice said, "you don't find him to your liking?"

"I'm afraid not. Not only is he over twice my age, he's scarcely a head taller than I am. He spends all his time in coffeehouses talking business. I doubt he'd ever take me to a ball, unless of course it had something to do with business."

"I suppose we all dream of a handsome prince." Beatrice looked out over the water. "Mr. Murdock sounds like a very hardworking man."

Rosalind nodded. "Mr. Murdock excels at making arrangements. He claims he wants to protect me, to keep me safe and secure and far from the drudgery of work."

"How wonderful! He must be the picture of devotion."

"Perhaps." Rosalind moved her shoulders in a fretful gesture of her own. "I'm not altogether certain I want my husband to make all the decisions and relieve me of the burden of running my own life."

"It's difficult to rely on other people, when you've been raised to take care of yourself." Beatrice waved her hands in a helpless gesture. "We can never be sure what the future will bring, can we?" She leaned her head on Rosalind's shoulder. "Especially you, poor dear Lady Rosalind. What a time you've had."

Rosalind made herself answer with nothing more than a dignified smile, even though she longed to pour out her heart to someone who would truly listen and care. That was impossible. Beatrice was poor, seeking work to help support the large family she'd left behind. How could Rosalind possibly complain of the disasters that had plagued her wealthy family, the loss of her father's finest ship the *Dover Lady* to pirates, the financial ruin that followed, and then, not a month ago, the final collapse that saw her father buried in an early grave? As much as she needed Beatrice's comfort, it would be wrong to burden the girl with her worries.

"You are very kind, Beatrice. Kinder than you know." Rosalind turned her face to the wind and let it dry the tears threatening to stream down her cheeks. "Poor Thomas. I finally get to visit him at Jasmine Court, only to bring him such heartbreaking news. We must return to London at once. Mother needs us both, now that—" Her voice caught. "Now that Father is gone."

"Poor, dear Rosalind!" Beatrice clasped Rosalind's hand between hers. Beatrice's hands were small and thin, her fingers callused with the needlework she had no doubt done to help keep her family fed. Rosalind clung to their fragile strength. "Please, try not to—"

Off to port a cannon roared. Something screamed through the air toward them. Rosalind pulled Beatrice down with her, huddling beneath the rail. The cannonball hit the water just below with a loud splash.

"What was that?" Beatrice started to rise.

Rosalind flung both arms around her and kept her down. "Someone's firing on us!"

"But why?"

Rosalind searched for the spare, sunburned figure of Captain Harris among the sailors rushing back and forth across the main deck. She spotted him on the quarterdeck. With him stood the first mate and the quartermaster, pointing to port while they bellowed orders. The bosun's pipe shrilled through the air. Sailors ran to their stations, some swarming up the rigging to unfurl more sails. There was more than simple haste to their movements. There was an edge of panic.

"Lady Rosalind! I say! My lady!" Mr. MacCaulay waved both hands in the air, trying to draw her attention. He hurried toward them across the crowded deck, maneuvering with surprising agility. "Get below, quickly! They must not see you!"

Rosalind risked peeking over the rail. Sailing toward them from around the far side of the islet was a black brigantine with only two masts but far too many cannons. Young men crowded its decks, some dressed in the blue jackets of sailors, others wearing gaudy shirts of brilliant silk and breeches of velvet. Those lined up on the main deck held muskets, cutlasses, knives, and pistols. Other crewmen manned the four smaller guns fixed to the ship's rail. With dread chilling her heart, Rosalind followed the ship's mainmast upward, already knowing what she would see. A black flag rippled and snapped in the wind, showing a death's-head with an empty hourglass lying beneath it. Pirates. Rosalind ducked back down, terror filling her mouth with the taste of bile.

"Rosalind?" Beatrice asked. "What is it? What do you see?"

The first mate, a big redheaded bull of a man named Parsons, came charging toward them. "Captain says best you ladies get below! Don't let those monsters get a glimpse of you!"

"Who are they?" Rosalind asked.

"French pirates, my lady." Parsons glanced out across the water, wiped one hand over his ashen face. "They call their captain the Angel of Death."

Beatrice gasped. On her hands and knees, she started to scurry toward the hatch. Rosalind caught Beatrice's skirt and dragged her back. Sailors on the starboard side pointed at something, shouting warnings at the quarterdeck. Rosalind put a firm hand on Beatrice's shoulder.

"Stay right here!"

Rosalind gathered up her skirts and ran across the deck to peer over the rail there. A single-masted sloop approached from the other side of the islet. It flew another black flag showing an hourglass crossed by a cutlass. Two of its cannons fired. One ball struck the poop deck and the other the rigging above it, raining debris down on Captain Harris and his officers. Rosalind knew little of naval strategy, but she knew good aim when she saw it. This Angel of Death didn't intend to kill the captain, but he had made it very clear how easily he could have. God only knew what torment awaited the crewmen and passengers.

· Musket fire from both pirate ships peppered the deck. Rosalind looked around for Mr. MacCaulay, but couldn't find him amid the rushing sailors. A wounded sailor sprawled across Beatrice, his bloody head landing in her lap. Beatrice screamed. Her voice rose high and shrill above the noise of the cannons and muskets. Rosalind hurried over to ease the sailor onto the deck. She caught Beatrice's arms and pulled her back toward the quarterdeck, praying the pirates turned their fire on the undamaged parts of the ship.

"Rosalind!" Beatrice cried. "What are you doing? We should get below!"

"Not if we want to live through this!"

"We'll be safe!"

"We'll be trapped! Now do as I say!"

Rosalind dragged Beatrice along with her, stepping over fallen spars and tangled ropes until they reached the poop deck and the one clear spot near the starboard rail. The ship's surgeon already knelt by Captain Harris, bandaging his bleeding arm while the captain kept shouting orders. More cannon fire made Beatrice scream. She fell to her knees, hands clapped over her ears. Captain Harris glanced their way.

"Dear God! Lady Hanshaw, hide yourself!" He motioned frantically with his good arm. "Get those women below!"

"Heave to!" The shout came from the larger pirate ship. "Heave to and surrender or die and be damned!"

Beatrice wailed, tears streaming down her cheeks. Rosalind shook her.

"Think of the children waiting for you, Beatrice! We have to get to Jamaica for their sake!"

"*How?*"

"First we swim to that islet." Rosalind worked furiously at the buttons on her gown. "Strip down to your corset and petticoats!"

"Here? Now?" Beatrice blushed scarlet.

"You can save your modesty or your life!"

"But—I can't—"

Rosalind kicked away her gown and flung her bonnet after it. She hesitated a moment over her shoes. The weight of the black kid slippers would slow her down, but they would also provide vital protection. The coral reefs in this part of the world would make wading ashore treacherous. Rosalind looked back to see the brigantine coming alongside to port while the sloop closed in from starboard. The pirates were ready with grapples and boarding pikes, straining like dogs at their leashes in their eagerness to come aboard. Rosalind stared down at the watery depths below. She had no idea what lived in the beautiful blue Caribbean waters, but it would only be hungry, not bent on deliberate mayhem.

Rosalind pulled Beatrice up on her feet and began yanking at her buttons, struggling with the heavy wool. A sharp whistle pierced the air, followed by several more. Raucous laughter and lewd remarks filled the air. The pirates crowding the deck of the brigantine had spotted her. Rosalind glanced across at that quarterdeck. What she saw there made her hands falter at their task.

A man, outfitted in a stylish coat and breeches, stood with his legs spread in a commanding stance. The fine cut of his deep maroon velvet jacket accentuated the breadth of his shoulders. He wore no wig. His black hair streamed back from his face, unpowdered and untamed, not even bound into the typical sailor's pigtail. His feral presence made him stand out even more, darkness itself amid the pirates's carnival colors. Rosalind recognized him as the leader of the pirates, for he could be no one else. He met Rosalind's gaze, holding it. A wolfish smile parted his full lips and bared his fine white teeth, making Rosalind shudder as the force of his marauding intentions focused on her. The *Bird of Paradise* now belonged to him, along with everything aboard. Everything including her.

Grappling hooks hit the rails on both sides of the ship. Rosalind wrenched Beatrice's dress down over her legs.

"We'll have to jump. Take a deep breath, then try to break the water feet first."

More shouts and screams told of violence behind them. Beatrice huddled against Rosalind, quivering with terror. Rosalind spun her around, propelling her toward the rail.

"Jump, Beatrice! *Jump!*"

"I can't! I can't—"

A mob of pirates clambered over the debris toward them, roaring and bellowing and cursing, every one of them grinning like the death's-head on the pirates's flag.

"Now, Beatrice! They're coming!"

Beatrice tumbled over the rail, plummeting down into the water below. Rosalind sat on the rail and swung her legs over. Her petticoats snagged on a nail, tearing as she fell. The shock of the water struck her like a blow to the chest. She clapped her hands over her mouth to smother a reflexive gasp. The tropical warmth at the surface gave way to a tepid layer, then to one of greater cold. The briny taste made Rosalind's stomach churn. She fought her way back to the surface. Her hair hung down around her shoulders like so much seaweed. She swept the heavy golden curtain of it out of her eyes.

Beatrice surfaced, coughing. She flailed at the water, trying to keep her head up. "Rosalind! Help me! *Help me!*"

She went under again. Rosalind caught Beatrice by the arms and hauled her up to the surface. Beatrice coughed and spluttered.

"Can't—can't swim! Tried to tell you!"

"It's all right. I'll do the swimming for both of us."

"You can swim?"

"My mother comes from a long line of captain's wives. She swore she'd never see one of her children drown for lack of knowing how to swim." Rosalind got a knee under Beatrice's bottom and pushed upward so Beatrice lay flat on the surface. "You must be still. The island isn't very far. We'll be there soon."

Beatrice mumbled under her breath, eyes squeezed tightly shut. Rosalind hoped she was praying. Rosalind herself would need all her breath for the swim ahead. From the ship the islet had looked relatively close, but now she saw it was a good mile or more away. Some curse must have fallen on her family. Shipping had been their business for generations. Now it seemed bad luck and pirates followed them no matter where they went.

Rosalind struggled toward the islet. The choppy sea kept lifting them up only to drop them into the troughs between swells. Soon she was so busy fighting to keep Beatrice afloat and herself from going under she lost sight of the three ships. Only the crack of a deck gun firing gave her any kind of bearing. She wished she'd had the sense to shed her petticoats. The batiste was light enough when dry, but now it hampered her kicking and threatened to drag her under. The current itself might be her enemy. As hard as she had to fight to make any distance, she could still be moving out to sea.

After minutes that passed like hours, Rosalind heard a loud splash behind her. She looked back. A ship's boat now sped toward them, rowed by two men in the garish clothing of pirates. In the bow sat a third pirate. The angle of the sun showed her only his dark silhouette. With fear spurring her on, she fought to cover a few more yards. Despite the warmth of the water, her arms were stiffening under the unaccustomed exercise. If she couldn't keep Beatrice afloat, the poor terrified girl would give up and drown.

The boat glided up beside them. The man in the bow was the same one who had stood upon the pirates' quarterdeck. He had come for her himself. Rosalind didn't dare guess what fate that foretold. She tried to face him with her chin up, fighting back her unwilling fascination. Soot streaked one high cheekbone and the stern angle of his jaw. That wild mane of black hair tumbled down over his left shoulder. His

fine maroon jacket gaped open, showing a white lawn shirt
stained with more soot and darkening splotches of blood.
Two pistols were tucked into his belt. He stared at Rosalind
with eyes so dark they looked black. If it weren't for Beatrice, Rosalind would have gladly plunged beneath the surface to escape that insolent, possessive stare. He draped his
left arm on the gunwale, trailing his long, slender fingers in
the water. That gesture of idle playfulness only underscored
the air of danger that hung around him.

"Bonjour, mademoiselle." His deep voice held a trace of
amusement. *"Comment vous appellez-vous?"*

Rosalind shook her head. "Can't remember—French right
now. Speak English!"

"Very well. Please be kind enough to climb aboard."

Rosalind hitched Beatrice up higher on her shoulder and
tried to catch her breath. "We have no intention of surrendering to filthy murdering pirates. You can tell that to your
captain."

The man let one corner of his full lips pull upward in a
sardonic smile. "Tell me yourself, mademoiselle."

So she'd been right. "You are this 'Angel of Death'?"

He sighed, shaking his head. "Stupid English peasants.
They never translate it properly. I am known as *L'Ange Noir.*
My ship is *L'Etoile du Matin.*"

The Black Angel, master of *L'Etoile du Matin.* . . . Two
pretty names for Lucifer, Satan, the Devil himself. In the
dark fires of the Black Angel's eyes Rosalind read her doom.
Sudden fright made her hug Beatrice, sending them both
under the waves. Rosalind fought her way back to the surface, spluttering and gasping. The ducking brought Beatrice
around. She screamed.

"Oh Lord, save us! God help us!"

"Hush! Beatrice, do be still!"

"They're here, the pirates, they'll kill us!"

Beatrice clawed at Rosalind, thrashing in her grip and
shoving her under. Rosalind broke away to surface behind
Beatrice.

"Mademoiselle," the Black Angel said. "Simply come aboard and all will be well."

"Whose idea of well, Captain? Yours, I'd think. Nothing like raping two innocent women to finish off this day's bloody work."

The Black Angel nodded toward the islet. "I take it that's your destination? A barren rock, unfit for any living thing. No food, no water. What will you do there, assuming you reach it?"

"Wait for another ship."

"Only fools travel through waters where I've spilled blood. There won't be another ship within leagues of this islet for weeks."

Rosalind kept the distress off her face. That was utterly, horribly, unavoidably true. Even if she and Beatrice reached that godforsaken rock, they'd be marooned.

Beatrice shrieked. "My leg! Something touched my leg!"

Rosalind looked down into the choppy water. She could see nothing, feel nothing.

"That will be the sharks." The Black Angel smiled. "Do you know much of sharks, mademoiselle? With them you can be sure of only one thing. They will eat you. Perhaps not all of you, but enough to leave you severely indisposed."

Anger overcame Rosalind's fear. The cad was laughing at her! "Am I to believe we'll receive any better treatment from you? A man proud of being called a fiend from hell?"

"Only by the English. To my people I am an angel, sent to punish their enemies."

"Angels stand for mercy and compassion. I doubt you possess a shred of either." Rosalind managed to plant her feet on the boat's hull and thrust with all her strength. Beatrice's limp weight slowed her, cutting the distance gained to only a few feet.

The Black Angel said something to his crewmen. They nodded, sharing his laughter.

"I salute your courage, mademoiselle." His dark brows slanted into a frown. "If I cannot appeal to your sense, then let me appeal to this misplaced charity I see. Your *petite amie* there will not last much longer. Permit my men to haul her into the boat."

"You want me to give her up to pirates?" Rosalind shook her head. "Far better to feed the sharks and benefit some living thing!"

"Your life is yours to throw away, mademoiselle, but you have no right to decide her fate."

Loathe to admit the truth of anything a pirate said, Rosalind looked down at Beatrice's pale, haggard face. She wouldn't reach the islet. Rosalind might not last that long herself, given the ache in her body and the shock dulling her mind.

"Beatrice? What shall I do?"

Beatrice clung to Rosalind's arm, eyes shut tight. The girl was plainly too terrified to speak. Rosalind treaded water, miserably aware she had no options left, yet unwilling to put herself and Beatrice in this monster's power.

"Think of it this way, mademoiselle," the Black Angel said. "Kill yourself and you abandon her to us. Stay with her and you can go on vexing me a little longer."

Tears of frustration mingled with the sea water on Rosalind's cheeks. "Forgive me, Beatrice. I can only hope this is the best thing to do."

She pushed the sobbing Beatrice toward the boat. The pirates each took an arm and lifted Beatrice up, laying her down between them. The Black Angel nodded his approval, then held out his own hand to Rosalind. She stared at the callused palm, at those long fingers. Such a graceful hand, even elegant. How odd that it should belong to a despicable pirate.

"Mademoiselle."

The harsh note in his voice made her glance up at those terrible eyes. The Black Angel's full lips had thinned with displeasure.

"I warn you. I am not a patient man."

Rosalind lifted her weary arms and clasped his hand be-

tween her own. The Black Angel hoisted her upward with
ease. This proof of his superior strength only frightened her
further. His other arm slid around her waist to drag her over
the gunwale and onto his lap. He nodded to his men, who
began rowing back toward his ship.

Rosalind perched on the very edge of the Black Angel's
knees. The breeze turned her soaking wet garments chilly,
raising gooseflesh and making her shiver. She hugged her
arms, wishing for a blanket to wrap around Beatrice. Fever
would be the next stroke of bad luck. The Black Angel's
hands closed on her wrists. He drew her back into the circle
of his arms, against the unwelcome warmth of his chest.
The cold metal of his pistols dug into her back. She stiffened, tried to push away.

"Sit still, mademoiselle. Upset the boat and I will have to
beat your tender English bottom."

He stroked the curve of her hip, barely concealed by her
sodden petticoats. Rosalind slapped at his hand. He caught
her wrist, those long fingers like steel bands. He kept her
hand imprisoned in his grip for a moment, then pressed a
lingering kiss on her palm.

"What an excellent day's fishing. It's been too long since
I've dallied with a mermaid."

Rosalind squirmed, trying to work her way back to the
edge of his lap. The solid hardness of his thighs beneath
hers made her even more anxious to escape.

"Mademoiselle." The Black Angel's breath fanned her ear,
warm and far too intimate. "Are you trying to entice me?"

"No!" Rosalind jerked forward, twisting around to glare
at him. "Why would I ever want to do such a thing?"

"If you don't stop bouncing up and down like that, I
might be persuaded to think you'd welcome more thorough
sport."

A hot blush stung Rosalind's cheeks. She sat absolutely
still, keeping her position no matter how the boat rocked in
the swells. The Black Angel laughed. He held her tight, both
arms around her waist and his cheek pressed alongside hers.

Rosalind shuddered. She could see the *Bird of Paradise* now, caught between the two pirate ships, its rigging damaged and gun ports closed. Captain Harris and his officers stood on the main deck with the crewmen lined up behind them, all surrounded by the Black Angel's well-armed pirates. Rosalind despaired to see them as firmly in the grasp of the Black Angel as she was. More than anything in the world, she wished she was home in the drawing room with Mother, anxious and miserable and safe.

Chapter Two

As they neared the starboard side of the Black Angel's ship, Rosalind caught a glimpse of Mr. MacCaulay standing on the main deck. His spectacles were askew. Blood matted his white side-whiskers. One sleeve of his brown jacket had been torn at the shoulder. Rosalind was overjoyed to see him alive, even in such battered condition. The boat bumped against the brigantine's hull. A rope ladder unrolled from the rail, its ends slapping at the boat's oarlock.

"After you, mademoiselle." The Black Angel leaned around to look her in the face. "I believe the English say, 'Ladies first.'"

Rosalind wanted nothing more than to escape the loathsome intimacy of the Black Angel's embrace. Yet that meant climbing up the ladder and placing both herself and Beatrice in the midst of what must be a hundred French pirates. She looked at the deceptively serene waters surrounding them. Never before had she so appreciated the truth of being caught between the Devil and the deep blue sea. She leaned down to tug at Beatrice's hand.

"Beatrice! You must wake up now."

Beatrice's head turned toward Rosalind. Her eyelids fluttered open. By her glassy look, Rosalind knew Beatrice was in deep shock.

"Beatrice, sit up now. Go with these men up the ladder."

Beatrice pressed herself against Rosalind's knees, clinging to the tattered hem of Rosalind's petticoat. "But you—you're coming too?"

"I'll be right behind you. Go on now."

Beatrice obeyed, face white with fear. One pirate clambered up the ladder, then reached both hands down to Beatrice. She started up the ladder, moving with clumsy haste. The pirate who followed gave her petticoats a playful tug. His coarse laughter made Rosalind's fists clench with fury.

"Stop that!" She snatched up an oar and struck the pirate across his shoulders. The boat rocked. Rosalind drew back to swing again. The Black Angel's hand closed around the oar's handle.

"Calm yourself, mademoiselle," he drawled, speaking now in flawless French. "As much as Pierre sometimes deserves a beating, I would not have you hurt your lovely hands."

Rosalind answered with French so formal it denied any attempt at intimacy. "Spare me your flattery, *mon capitaine.*"

She shoved the Black Angel's arm away and grasped the sides of the ladder. The rough fibers dug into her palms. The motion of the choppy sea made her footing precarious. The ladder swung out, then back, slamming her against the hull. Clamping her lips shut against any sound of pain, Rosalind forced her leaden muscles to propel her up the ladder. She had to get up on deck, to find Beatrice and protect her. Eager hands waited to haul her over the rail. One pirate caught her wrists. The sun had bleached his hair nearly white and burned his face bright red.

"Mind your step, mademoiselle. You don't want to slip."

A short, chubby pirate shoved him away, laughing. He pulled Rosalind over the rail and into his arms. "Here, *chèrie,* let me help you aboard!"

"You fiends!" Mr. MacCaulay lunged against the arms holding him. "Leave her alone!"

"*Libertin!* Take your hands off me!" Rosalind struck at the pirate's forearms, trying to loosen his grip.

"Rosalind!" Beatrice cried.

The note of panic in Beatrice's voice gave Rosalind the strength to fight free of the pirate's arms. She hurled herself across the deck toward Beatrice's wails. Two pirates held Beatrice between them while a third slobbered on her neck. Pure fury burned away Rosalind's fright.

"Let her go!" Rosalind yanked the pistol from the belt of the pirate laying hands on Beatrice and clouted him across the back of the head. He reared back with a curse. His arm swung wide to give Rosalind a smart backhanded slap. The force of the blow sent her staggering backward.

"*Halte!*" The Black Angel swung his legs over the railing and landed on the deck. He glared at the pirates still holding Beatrice. "Did I hear anyone give you leave to molest my prisoners?"

The pirates let go of Beatrice and stepped back. Beatrice ran to Rosalind, burying her face against Rosalind's shoulder. Too dazed to speak, Rosalind gave Beatrice a distracted pat. The Black Angel stood before her, towering head and shoulders over her. The breadth of his shoulders and depth of his chest spoke of an excellent figure beneath his elegant attire. He raked both hands back through his hair, drawing it away from his face and securing it with a length of black ribbon. Those cold dark eyes stared at her.

"Well, mademoiselle? What will you do now?"

Rosalind raised the pistol. "We will leave the same way we came. Mr. MacCaulay, please help Beatrice back into the boat."

Mr. MacCaulay stood rigid in the grip of the pirates who held him. "Please, my dear girl, be very careful."

The Black Angel took one step toward Rosalind. "Listen to him, mademoiselle."

She centered the muzzle on his chest. "I warn you, *mon capitaine*. Stand back."

The Black Angel smiled. "Henri? Is your pistol loaded?"

"Non, mon capitaine," answered the pirate whom Rosalind had struck.

"You're sure?"

"Mais oui, mon capitaine. I left the ball in some pig of an *Anglais* sailor."

The pirates surrounding Rosalind laughed. The Black Angel took another slow step forward. Rosalind held the pistol straight out from her shoulder. She centered the barrel right between those impossibly dark eyes.

"Are you sure, *mon capitaine?* He has another pistol. Perhaps that's the one he fired."

The Black Angel stood very still. "Henri? What have you to say to that?"

"I say I fired both, *mon capitaine*. She can do you no harm."

The Black Angel stared at Rosalind until she thought her frantic heart would burst. The weight of the pistol dragged at her hand, making it shake.

"Surrender, mademoiselle. Your threat is as empty as that pistol."

Rosalind wished she could tell by the weight of the pistol whether or not it was loaded. To shoot the Black Angel point blank, to kill the man who had sent so many English sailors to their graves. . . . The Black Angel's left hand shot out. Rosalind's head turned, following the movement. The Black Angel lunged forward. He seized her right wrist and jerked it upward. The pistol fired, sending its ball through both the main and top sails. The noise of it drove a scream out of Rosalind. Beatrice echoed her. The Black Angel wrenched the smoking pistol out of Rosalind's hand. She wrapped her arms around Beatrice, hiding her face against Beatrice's hair to escape the triumphant gleam in the Black Angel's eyes.

"You do amaze me, mademoiselle." He glared at Henri. "Your pistol, Henri? Or did you plan to let the *jeune fille* keep it?"

The pirate's face reddened. He took the pistol from the Black Angel's outstretched hand.

"Yves!" the Black Angel called out.

"Here, *mon capitaine.*" A thin, rangy man with sandy hair and faded blue eyes stepped forward. Rosalind was surprised to see he dressed in nothing more fanciful than the blue jacket and red kerchief worn by ordinary sailors.

"Take the prisoners below. The ladies you will keep a safe distance from their *grand-père.*"

"*Oui, mon capitaine.*" Yves took Beatrice by the arm and tried to pull her away from Rosalind.

Beatrice strained back from Yves's grip. "Rosalind? What are they saying?"

"It's all right, Beatrice. The captain has ordered us taken below. That's about the best we could have hoped for."

"*Mon capitaine,*" Yves said. "Do you wish the captives put in irons also?"

The Black Angel started to shake his head, then paused, glancing down at Rosalind. One corner of his mouth lifted, revealing a dimple in his cheek. "The little one will be no trouble, but this one is a hellcat. Make sure the chains are thick."

The pirates answered with howls and whistles. Rosalind lifted her chin, speaking with all the hauteur she could manage.

"You'd be wiser to think about ropes, *mon capitaine,* namely the one you'll be hanged with!"

The Black Angel smiled, but his eyes narrowed. "You'd be wiser to bridle that tongue, mademoiselle. You are in no position to threaten me." He ran the backs of his fingers along her cheek. "It would serve you better to show me some gratitude for saving your life."

She slapped his hand aside. "I have no doubt how you'd like that gratitude shown, you perfidious rogue!"

"Really, mademoiselle?" The Black Angel stared at her in wide-eyed wonder. "Do you know so much of men you can size me up just by sitting on my lap?"

Rosalind's cheeks flamed. The wicked gleam in the Black Angel's eye blossomed into a shout of laughter. Rosalind's outrage boiled over. Her hand shot up, ready to slap him. The Black Angel's humor vanished. His black glare impaled her.

"Is this your gratitude, mademoiselle? You would strike me?" The icy calm in his voice matched his eyes. "Provoke me again and I will not stay *my* hand. Is that perfectly clear?"

She nodded.

"I have no more time to suffer your insults, mademoiselle. Perhaps a short stay in my brig will restore your *politesse.*"

Yves barked an order. Two of the pirates holding Mr. MacCaulay hustled him down the hatch. Rosalind watched him go, feeling the last of her fragile courage vanish with him. She lifted her chin and willed her voice to be firm.

"You call me a hellcat, *mon capitaine? Très bien.* Beware my claws."

The Black Angel glared at Rosalind a moment longer. A sudden smile curved his lips, sending a fresh jolt of fear through her.

"Perhaps I will avoid them altogether." He studied Beatrice, that evil smile growing broader.

"Non!" Rosalind pushed Beatrice behind her. The Black Angel snapped an order. Pirates caught Rosalind's arms, dragging her away from Beatrice and pinning her arms behind her back.

The Black Angel took Beatrice's face in his hands and spoke in gentle English. "So, you do not speak French, little one?"

Beatrice stared up at him, eyes wide. "No, Captain."

"Are you of a sweeter nature than your nanny? Can a man hope to find a little peace in your arms?"

Confusion and dawning horror made Beatrice's cheeks flush a deep red. "P—please, Captain. Don't hurt Rosalind."

"What is she to you that the two of you will fight for each other?"

Rosalind held her breath. If Beatrice admitted to being her maid, that would reveal far too much. Rosalind's only hope lay in concealing her title. The Black Angel hated the English, making their ships his favorite targets. Should the Black Angel learn she was the daughter of an English peer, his torment of her would surely double.

"She's my sister, Captain," Beatrice said. "My older sister."

The Black Angel stared at Rosalind, then tipped Beatrice's head to the side. "You are both fair, it is true, but the English blood is so thin English women all look like milkmaids." He looked down at Beatrice's upturned face. "No. I do not believe you."

Beatrice's chin quivered. "We—we have different fathers. There now! Are you satisfied?" She turned her face away from him, sobbing.

Rosalind marveled. She would never have credited Beatrice with the ability to spin such perfect half-truths. She flung herself against the hands of her captors.

"Is this the kind of man France breeds, a killer who amuses himself by torturing innocent girls?"

"I have no intention of torturing her, mademoiselle." The Black Angel ran his thumb over Beatrice's lower lip. "On the contrary, quite the opposite."

Beatrice wailed, flinging up both hands to ward him off. She ran blindly to Rosalind and threw her arms around Rosalind's waist, sobbing against her shoulder.

"Shh, hush now," Rosalind said. "I won't let him hurt you."

The Black Angel arched one brow. "Mademoiselle, I am *capitaine*. My will is law."

"You are an outlaw, *un criminel*."

"Your defiance makes you the outlaw. That's a dangerous attitude this far offshore."

His every word was chosen to drive home the desperate nature of the situation. Tears pricked at Rosalind's eyes. It was all she could do to hold out against the need to collapse.

"What kind of man are you? Or rather what sort do you claim to be?"

"A gentleman, as much as time and fortunes allow."

"Then you will leave this child alone."

"I will do as I please aboard my ship. And you, mademoiselle, will do as I say."

The sudden darkening of his expression silenced Rosalind. The Black Angel was not a patient man, and what little he had was clearly gone. Rosalind tried to compose herself into something approaching dignity. She had few illusions about the chances of both her and Beatrice escaping this ship with their lives, much less their virtue. The strong breeze blew the smell of the Black Angel to her. He reeked of gunpowder, smoke, and the hard sweat of a man who'd just slaughtered his enemies. She shuddered.

"May the condemned prisoners be granted one final request?"

"Within reason."

"A bath."

The Black Angel stared at her, then burst out laughing. "I never thought to find a touch of vanity reassuring. By all means, mademoiselle, you may—"

"For you, *mon capitaine.*" Before he could reply, Rosalind rushed on. "You might at least do us the courtesy of making yourself presentable. 'Gentlemen' do not force themselves on ladies when they are in such a condition as to render the ladies quite horribly ill."

She glared at him, rigid with fright and outrage. The dangerous look of temper in his eyes mellowed into a smile. The Black Angel bowed.

"*Très bien,* mademoiselle. You have challenged me to make good on my claims to gentility. I will scrub until I am pink and shining."

"Oh, pray don't stop there, *mon capitaine.* I imagine a good many people would be delighted to see the color of your blood."

The Black Angel's teeth clenched. His nostrils flared. He

moved toward Rosalind, one slow, measured step at a time. Beatrice whimpered and edged around behind Rosalind. The Black Angel's shadow fell across Rosalind, chilling her. At last he loomed over her. Rosalind looked up at him, at the chiseled perfection of his features. He reminded her of a statue, pleasing to the eye but stone cold. She turned her face away. The Black Angel took her chin in his hand, forcing her to meet his gaze.

"Again and again you provoke me, mademoiselle." His voice was a silky whisper. "I begin to think you want me to beat you."

He jerked her chin up. Rosalind flinched, expecting pain. The sudden velvety warmth of his lips on hers stole her breath. He lingered there for an endless moment, just long enough to make her traitorous body betray its pleasure with a sigh. He stepped back, his lips now quirked in an infuriating smirk of triumph.

"Take them away."

Chapter Three

Yves led the way down from the gun deck to the hold. The brig was a row of three cells, each little more than a closet with a barred window in the door. Two other pirates were busy shackling Mr. MacCaulay in the cell on the end. Yves pushed Rosalind up against the bulkhead next to the last cell.

"Stay there." His English was harsh, his accent heavy.

"Who are you?"

"The first mate." Yves pried Beatrice's arms away from Rosalind's waist. Beatrice wailed.

"Please, no!" She clung to Rosalind's hands. "Rosalind!"

"*S'il-vous plaît,*" Rosalind said. "Can't you leave us together? This poor girl is nearly out of her wits with fright."

Yves snapped an order at the two other pirates. One came forward to lift Beatrice off her feet and deposit her in the cell. The other stood before Rosalind, his steady stare a warning against any protest. Yves knelt to fasten the shackle around Beatrice's ankle, then stood back to shut the door on her pleas. Rosalind studied him. In his ordinary blue jacket and red neckerchief, he looked as tidy and clean as if this were an honest ship. His weathered face betrayed nothing, just the grim determination to follow his orders. He beck-oned Rosalind.

"Shouldn't you be seeing to the sails or the wheel?" She dodged his reaching hands, dreading the moment when he'd shut her up in that cramped little cupboard. "Why did your *capitaine* give you such a menial task?"

The pirate watching Rosalind caught her by the shoulders and pushed her back into her cell. As the cold, rusty shackle locked around Rosalind's ankle, the last spark of rebellion still glowing in her dimmed. She sagged back against the bulkhead. The door closed, trapping her completely.

"Mademoiselle." Yves stood watching her through the lit-tle barred window. "If you have any sense at all, you will do whatever *le capitaine* asks."

"Why should I? I was dead from the moment he fished me out of the sea."

"*Le capitaine* is not a happy man. If you could bring him any comfort, any cheer, he would go easier on all of us."

Rosalind was more than willing to fight the Black Angel to protect herself and Beatrice, but to play up to him? To ac-tually encourage the attentions of a vicious pirate?

"How shall I go about doing so, Monsieur Yves?" Her voice heavy with irony. "Have you any suggestions?"

"*Le capitaine* is not a cruel man. Amuse him and he will show his appreciation. Let him be for you the gallant he prefers to be. That is my advice to you."

Sudden fatigue overcame Rosalind, leaving her limp and boneless as a rag. Even if she did as Yves said, that didn't guarantee getting out of this nightmare alive and whole. Weak tears leaked from her eyes. She leaned her head back against the bulkhead. "*Merci*, Monsieur Yves. I will con-sider what you have said."

Yves climbed back up through the hatch, taking the two other pirates with him. Tense quiet descended, broken only by Beatrice's muffled sobs. Mr. MacCaulay coughed.

"I must say, I'm so very glad to see you ladies. When you went over the side, we were sure you were lost."

"I am lost, Mr. MacCaulay," Rosalind said. "I only prolonged my doom."

"On the contrary, my dear girl. My compliments. You fought like a lion." He chuckled. "As long as I live, I will treasure the sight of the Black Angel's face when you pointed out there were two pistols, not just one."

"So you speak French, Mr. MacCaulay?"

"A little. Enough to do business on the Continent."

"What shall we do, Mr. MacCaulay?" Rosalind bit her lip, trying to keep the tears out of her voice. "To be at the mercy of the Black Angel is to have no hope at all."

"First," Mr. MacCaulay said, "we must decide exactly what to tell the Black Angel should he ask who we are and where we're bound."

Rosalind nodded. "I will use my mother's maiden name. If they ask, just tell them I'm Miss Brooks."

"Certainly," Mr. MacCaulay said. "We must keep the Black Angel unaware of your title at all costs. That was a stroke of genius, Miss Henderson, telling him you are sisters."

Beatrice sniffed loudly. "Thank you, Mr. MacCaulay. It was all I could think of."

"It will do nicely. May I further suggest you claim you are both schoolteachers, bound for your posts in the colonies? I require no such pretense. I shall simply pass myself off as an ordinary English subject on my way to Jamaica."

"Rosalind?" Beatrice's voice quavered.

"Yes, dear?"

"You don't think he meant it, do you? That he'd rather—you know, me instead of you?"

Rosalind sighed. The Black Angel might very well prefer the more docile Beatrice. "He said that just to insult me. He knows I'll do everything I possibly can to keep you safe."

The Black Angel also knew they were all completely at his mercy. Why else would he mock Rosalind with that taunting kiss? Recalling the sensation of his mouth on hers brought an unwelcome surge of—what? Excitement? He could have hurt her, could have done far worse. And yet he had chosen to tease her with pleasure instead of pain.

Rosalind sank down until she could wedge herself into the corner at an angle that allowed her to doze. The roll of the ship was soothing. The cell was warm enough, despite her soggy petticoats and shoes. The brig smelled of nothing worse than salt air, damp canvas, and a hint of beer.

Ding-ding! Ding-ding! Ding-ding! Ding-ding!

Four bells. Time for the first dog watch, the short span between four and six in the evening. The fading gold of sunset threw long shadows down the hatch, leaving Rosalind in almost total darkness. She watched the light, hoping to judge the passage of time by it. Leaden weariness overcame her, making her eyelids flutter closed.

Rosalind's mind chased dreamy images of her brother Thomas, his fair hair ruffled by the sea breeze, his bright smile, the quick economy of his movements. He'd sit strong and proud beside Father as they rode their favorite stallions out the gates of Broadmere to spend the day hunting with friends. She and Mother busied themselves seeing to it the pies were baked properly and the linen scrubbed until it was spotless. Father liked nothing better than a beautifully set table groaning under the weight of fine food. Rosalind's empty belly cramped. She would be content to eat day-old bread for the rest of her life if it meant she lived to see Mother again. At the moment she'd even welcome the sight of Mr. Murdock.

Again and again Mr. Murdock had assured her how simple life would be if only she'd marry him. His long-suffering tone left Rosalind even more restless and uncomfortable. He'd take care of everything, help Thomas restore the family business, build it up even greater. At first Mr. Murdock refused to even hear the idea of Rosalind herself traveling all the way to Jamaica to bring Thomas the news of their father's death. He agreed to make the arrangements only after Rosalind promised that upon her return they would talk seriously about their engagement and a wedding date.

Mr. Murdock found a respectable ship, booked her passage, then saw her off at the dock. He'd done everything she could have asked for, yet all the while being so tiresome with his excessive concern for her welfare. How he'd crow over being right in his misgivings! He'd take such pleasure in welcoming poor, distraught Rosalind back into his protection. Now her stomach churned. No matter where she went, there was no escape. She'd avoided Mr. Murdock's efforts to capture her heart, only to face a pirate whose desires were far less refined.

Rosalind smiled, thinking of the shock on the Black Angel's face when she told him he needed a bath. The Black Angel's idea of bathing probably amounted to no more than running a razor over the worst of his beard stubble, then splashing a bit of water over his face and hands. Rosalind shuddered again at the remembered reek of gunpowder. That he meant to touch her, to fondle her, to force on her the agony that must surely be her fate. . . . She shook her head. She was a fool to worry about her virtue when her very life was at stake. What sense was there in fretting over who might have her after this nightmare ended, when she had no guarantee it would end anywhere but in a watery grave?

Rosalind struck the tears from her cheeks. She'd meet her enemy with her head held high, not whimpering and begging like some frightened animal. With her clothing ripped and stained, her hair hanging loose and tangled, and her fury stirring up her color, she might well look as loose and wild as the doxies who waited on the wharves for men like the Black Angel's crew. She stood up and freed the damp mess of her hair, pulling out the remaining pins and untying the white satin ribbon that bound the end. With fingers stiffened by fresh anger, she combed out the worst of the tangles with her fingers until her hair hung down past her hips, then separated three plaits and wove them into a thick braid. She twisted it up above the nape of her neck. The few pins were barely enough to secure its weight, but they'd have to do. She would look every inch the plain school-teacher she'd pretend to be. Perhaps she would be so dull to this magnificent pirate king he'd tire of her before his lust could blind him to anything but gratifying it.

Something nagged at Rosalind. Now that she had a moment to think, she realized these pirates weren't as ragged, as filthy, nor as debauched as she'd heard them to be. They dressed to sport their plunder, wearing plenty of rings and even a few necklaces. Those who didn't dress in garments of silk, satin, and even velvet wore the plain blue jackets and nankeen trousers of everyday sailors. They were reasonably tidy, obeyed orders at once, and clearly respected the Black Angel as their supreme commander. Rosalind frowned. Something was wrong here. These weren't the same pirates Father and Thomas had described when they discussed the trouble Hanshaw ships encountered in the Caribbean. Pirate crews recognized no particular man as captain except when they went into battle. What was more, it was very strange to find an actual brig in a ship as small as a brigantine. Indeed, a brigantine was more truly a boat. That the Black Angel would sacrifice cargo space to have these cells built had to mean he made ransom a regular part of his piracy.

The thud of boots on the wooden rungs of the ladder roused Rosalind from her uneasy rest. Keys rattled in the lock, then her door swung wide. A hulking man stood there, big and bearish and looking ill-tempered.

"Out, girl. *Le capitaine* wants another look at you."

Rosalind hid her fear under a mask of scorn. "Who has *le capitaine* sent to fetch me? The navigator? Perhaps the master gunner?"

"*Je suis le maître d'equipage,* mademoiselle." He made her a mocking bow. "*Enchantée.*"

So this was the bosun himself. Rosalind wondered if she should feel flattered that the Black Angel let no one but his officers attend her. She straightened up, wincing in pain as her cold, cramped muscles protested. The bosun bent to free the shackle chaining her to the deck.

Another pirate knelt before Beatrice, skinny and quick like a weasel. He unlocked Beatrice's shackle and pulled her out of her cell, then looked Rosalind over, licking his lips.

"You go on sassing *le capitaine, chèrie.* Might even be a good idea to swing on him again."

"Justin!" the bosun snapped. "Shut that insolent mouth!"

The bosun prodded her and Beatrice toward the hatch. Beatrice clung to Rosalind in mute terror. Rosalind hugged her, too frightened to take another step toward the fate that awaited them on deck.

"Mr. MacCaulay, I don't know what to do!"

"I say!" Mr. MacCaulay pounded on his cell door. "Let me out also! I want to speak to your captain! You must take me to him at once!"

The pirates ignored him. The bosun took Rosalind by the elbow.

"Go on, *chèrie.* We don't keep *le capitaine* waiting."

"Take heart, dear lady," Mr. MacCaulay called to her. "God will preserve the innocent."

"I hope so." Rosalind stared up at the hatch, fear chilling her. "I truly hope so."

The pirates hustled her and Beatrice toward the ladder. The raucous sounds of drinking songs and the rattle of dice told Rosalind the pirates' victory celebration was well under way. She wondered if the Black Angel meant to make her and Beatrice part of the entertainment.

"Let me go first, Beatrice."

The pirates greeted Rosalind's appearance on deck with howls and whistles. The crew at liberty lounged around the deck, some whittling, some dicing, all of them drinking. Some shouted compliments to Rosalind's lips and skin, while others named far more intimate parts. Rosalind was relieved to know Beatrice couldn't understand French. The pirates' gestures and leers still made Beatrice's cheeks redden with a painful blush. She huddled against Rosalind, who hid her own face against Beatrice's hair.

"*Bonsoir,* mademoiselle!" The Black Angel's deep voice rang out across the deck. "Have you any kind words for me now?"

Unwilling to let the Black Angel think she was hiding from him, Rosalind raised her head. There he stood, up on the quarterdeck beside the ship's wheel. He had indeed bathed. His black hair lay in satiny waves along his forehead and shoulders. The sunset lent it a ruddy sheen and made sparks dance in those dark, fathomless eyes. He wore a loose shirt of white lawn that stretched taut across his broad shoulders, gaping open at the neck to show her the bronzed skin of his bare chest. A sash of blue silk stitched in patterns of black, white, and darker blue girded his hips, the ends hanging down along his left thigh. His leather breeches hugged his hips and the muscles of his thighs and calves before disappearing into the cuffs of his black boots.

The Black Angel came down to the main deck and swaggered toward her. If he was striking while standing still, he was even more impressive in motion. That feral power surrounded him, making Rosalind acutely conscious of his virile appeal. She was by no means blind to his attraction, as distasteful as that knowledge might be. The Black Angel was her enemy. She must remember that.

His men fell back, leaving a wide circle with Rosalind and Beatrice at its center. Rosalind heard the clink of coins passing from hand to hand. Even now the scoundrels wagered on her fate. The Black Angel stopped in front of her and raised his tankard.

"Do I suit you better now, mademoiselle?"

What startled Rosalind most was his face. That same sardonic smile played around those full lips, but a gentler temper moved him now. Wiped clean of the grime, mellowed by the warm glow of the sunset, the hard, merciless pirate captain looked an altogether different man. He was handsome to the point of being beautiful. Rosalind gave herself a mental shake. Of course the Devil could appear beautiful. He'd been the greatest of the radiant archangels until his arrogance sent him to hell.

"Do you really care, *mon capitaine?* I was under the impression you'd had quite enough of my opinions."

"Still haughty, mademoiselle?" The Black Angel shook his head, his expression regretful. Wicked humor danced in his dark eyes. "Does nothing frighten you?"

Knowing he'd use any answer against her, Rosalind kept silent. The Black Angel shrugged, then pulled Beatrice out of her grasp. He spoke softly in English.

"And what of you, little one?"

Beatrice raised her head. Her smile was serene. "What of me, Captain?"

"Will you heap scorn upon my head, or will you allow me the pleasure of your company for dinner at my table?"

Beatrice shook her head. "I'm sorry, Captain. I must decline. You see, I have a previous engagement."

"With whom, may I ask?"

Rosalind's heart lurched. What game was Beatrice playing at? "Beatrice—"

"A moment, mademoiselle." The Black Angel flashed her a stern look. "If you will have none of me, then kindly allow your *petite soeur* the chance to decide for herself." He turned a warm smile on Beatrice. "Now tell me, little one. With whom is this previous engagement?"

"With an authority even you cannot stand against."

Rosalind's panic doubled. What on earth was Beatrice about to say? The Black Angel stepped closer. Rosalind threw her arms around Beatrice and turned, trying to shelter Beatrice any way she could.

"Please, *mon capitaine,*" Rosalind said. "Leave her alone! The shock of all this has unhinged her mind!"

The Black Angel studied Beatrice's smile. "She looks well enough to me." He put one hand on Rosalind's shoulder, applying steady pressure. "Stand back, mademoiselle, before you force me to take her from you."

"There's no need for that, Captain." Beatrice stepped out of Rosalind's arms.

"Now, little one, you will answer my question. How do you mean to keep this previous engagement?"

"I am already keeping it. I have given my soul to the Lord. I have no habit, but the Lord will grant me his armor of light."

The Black Angel looked like he hadn't heard her correctly. His confusion cleared, replaced by a knowing smile. "So you were telling me the truth. You are sisters. You are in fact brides of Christ." His smile grew into a grin. He drank a long swallow of rum, then shook his head in wonder. "English, Catholic, and nuns. The perfect end to a perfect day."

His delight was unbearable. Rosalind pushed Beatrice behind her. "Believe me when I tell you she has gone out of her head. We are schoolteachers, nothing more."

"So you deny you are nuns? I must admit, I can more easily believe it of her than of you."

His smirk ignited Rosalind's temper. He was clearly enjoying himself. "Can't you see? The poor girl is frightened out of her mind! She's simply found a way to make this horrible nightmare go away!"

"And what of you, mademoiselle? Have you found no means of escape?"

"Much to my chagrin I remain perfectly aware of my surroundings."

The Black Angel frowned. "Stand aside, mademoiselle. I will have the truth of this matter from the *jeune fille*." He turned to Beatrice. "Am I right in thinking you are fleeing persecution? The English have no patience with Rome these days."

"You see, Captain," Beatrice said. "You have done a great act of charity in saving us from drowning. God will surely bless you for seeing us safely to Jamaica."

The pirates around them who understood English burst into loud guffaws. Beatrice's fixed smile never wavered. She stared at the air over the Black Angel's left shoulder. He studied her. Rosalind was relieved to see him take in Beatrice's vacant look, nodding to himself.

"Perhaps God has delivered you into my hands for other reasons." His voice became a husky caress. "Perhaps you are not meant for a life among women."

He stretched out his right arm, holding his tankard to the side. A nearby pirate rushed to take it, then dashed back into the circle of onlookers. The Black Angel gathered Beatrice against his chest, smoothing her straggling hair back from her face.

"Tell me, *chèrie,* how can such a charming creature as yourself deprive the male sex of your sweetness?"

"Stop this!" Rosalind cried. "Have you no shred of human decency?"

The Black Angel stroked Beatrice's cheek. "Her safety clearly means a great deal to you, mademoiselle. Why is that, I wonder?"

Beatrice's smile was gone, leaving her looking stunned with fear. Anger overcame Rosalind's own fear. She had to make herself the more amusing target.

"They call you *L'Ange Noir?* Hah! You should be known as *Bête Noir,* for you surely are a beast!"

The Black Angel smiled, thin and cold. "Take care, mademoiselle. You know nothing but what you think you see." He studied Beatrice's features, running his fingertip along her cheek. "She is not your blood sister, *oui?* Then why do you risk yourself for her again and again?"

"Because I am a human being with a heart and a soul."

"Such nobility, mademoiselle. Such charity. How deep, how genuine are these feelings?"

"What—what do you mean?"

"You tell me I am a beast, with no tender feeling. *Très bien.* Teach me, mademoiselle. Show me how far such a fine and superior lady is willing to go to protect this innocent."

Rosalind stared at him. Cold knots of fear tightened within her. He'd called her a lady. Had he somehow learned the truth about her already? "Your heart must be as black as your hair, *mon capitaine*. I believe I stand before the Devil himself."

"*Merci,* mademoiselle." The Black Angel bowed with a mocking flourish. "You are not the first to say that to me." He brushed his lips across Beatrice's forehead. "Such a sweet little beauty. What a pity to waste such loveliness in a life of hardship and sorrow." He put one hand under Beatrice's chin and tilted her face up to his. "I could save you from all that, *chèrie.* I could teach you another way to live that will lift your soul to the very heights of heaven."

Beatrice's eyes focused. Color flooded her pale cheeks. She stared up at the Black Angel.

"Speak to me, little one," the Black Angel murmured. "Will you throw your life away among the wretches of the earth, or will you sail with me as my queen?"

Beatrice's mouth worked. She thrust her arms straight out, trying to shove him away. "Get thee behind me, Satan!"

The Black Angel laughed, sweeping Beatrice up and swinging her around and around until she hung limp and breathless in his arms. He grinned at Rosalind.

"I find this simple piety so much more endearing than your clever rebukes, mademoiselle." He looked down at Beatrice, then nodded. "I do believe I prefer Sister Beatrice. What have you to say to that?"

Rosalind knew he was teasing her, waiting for her to give him the answer he wanted. If she could best him no other way, she could beat him at this particular game.

"I say you disappoint me. I'd heard the dreaded *L'Ange Noir* was great enough to show mercy where mercy was called for. *L'Ange Noir* attacked only those enemies whose defeat would bring him the most glory. Not some defenseless little girl on her way to a convent."

The Black Angel stared at her, as still and cold as marble but for the tempest brewing in the depths of his dark eyes. His stillness spread out to silence his crew. They backed away, to the stern, to the bow, even up into the rigging.

"Mademoiselle, as clever as you are, surely you know

there is only one way to spare your *petite soeur*. If your courage is more than mere words, step forward now and take her place."

"If your reputation is more than lies, let her go."

"So be it." The Black Angel hefted Beatrice over his shoulder and started across the deck toward his cabin.

"Rosalind!" Beatrice flung out her hands. "Help! *Help me!*"

Rosalind fled ahead of the hands snatching at her, racing to put herself between the Black Angel and his cabin door. Her aching muscles betrayed her, making her stumble and fall to her knees in his path. He loomed over her, one black eyebrow quirked. Chest heaving, tears on her cheeks, Rosalind bowed her head before the Black Angel.

"*Oui*, mademoiselle? There was something you wished to say?"

The triumph in his eyes was galling. His arrogant tone suggested a weakness she might use to her advantage.

"This is the measure of my charity, *mon capitaine*. I make myself your hostage. In return you will guarantee the safety of not only Beatrice but the man imprisoned below."

"You are in no position to offer terms, mademoiselle. I insist on your complete submission, or I will amuse myself with the little nun here."

"You will accept my terms with good grace, *mon capitaine*." Rosalind stood up, gathering her strength. "You will yield, and you will see to it Beatrice and Mr. MacCaulay are given food as good as any of your crew. You will permit them an hour of exercise in the morning and the evening."

The Black Angel's brows shot up. He gave a short derisive laugh. "And if I refuse? What will you do then, mademoiselle? Hurl yourself over the rail and take this child with you?"

"I will suffer whatever torments you have planned for me, *mon capitaine*. But I will also have the satisfaction of knowing you have proven yourself no better than the lewdest, most ignorant, most flea-bitten wretch in your crew."

The Black Angel's brow darkened. That dangerous chill came back into his eyes. "Who *are* you? Who are you that you can look death in the face and still keep that hectoring tone?"

"What will it be, *mon capitaine?* Will you accept my terms, as the gentleman you claim to be?"

The Black Angel glared at her, his displeasure like a stormfront sweeping toward her. He swung Beatrice down off his shoulder, trapping her against him with his arms around her shoulders.

"It seems you are delivered, *chèrie.* Of the three of us, I think only you will gain any true relief." He sighed, looking down into Beatrice's face. "Still, it is such a waste."

He bent his head, claiming Beatrice's mouth with his. Rosalind sprang forward to grab a fistful of the Black Angel's silken hair. He fell back with an oath, giving Beatrice a chance to break away. The Black Angel caught Rosalind by her ragged petticoat. She struck at his hand, fighting to tear herself loose. He jerked her to him, his free hand rising, poised to slap her. Rosalind shut her eyes and turned her face away, bracing herself.

"Witch!" The Black Angel glared down at her, his teeth bared as his breath rasped in and out. "I should have you here, right here, with all my men cheering me on!"

Rosalind was beyond terror now, knowing she'd finally pushed him too far. "As you wish, *mon capitaine.* Only do me the favor of knocking me senseless first!"

Moment after moment slipped away in frantic heartbeats. The tension in the Black Angel's arms eased a fraction. He let his hand fall.

"Yves!" he snapped.

Yves came down from the quarterdeck. *"Oui, mon capitaine."*

"You heard mademoiselle's terms? Consider them my orders. Get Sister Beatrice below before she causes any more trouble."

Yves nodded and turned to reach for Beatrice. She shied back.

"Rosalind? What did he say?"

"Go with the first mate, Beatrice. Everything will be all right. I've made the best arrangements possible."

"Oh no." Beatrice saw the way the Black Angel's arms caged Rosalind. Her eyes widened in horror. "No, Rosalind! You didn't!"

"Beatrice, please! Go and tell Mr. MacCaulay we'll be all right."

"Enough." The Black Angel stepped between Rosalind and Beatrice. He spoke over Beatrice's head to Yves. "Have my meal sent in right away. And Yves, you will keep matters in hand while I am occupied. Disturb me for anything short of a typhoon and I will flog you myself."

"Oui, mon capitaine."

The Black Angel spun Rosalind around and shoved her toward his cabin door. She caught her balance and bobbed a mocking curtsy.

"Merci beaucoup, mon capitaine."

He scowled at her. "Don't thank me, mademoiselle. You will live to regret your prissy ways."

As he pushed the cabin door open ahead of her, Rosalind stared through it with a growing sense of dread. She had given herself to the Black Angel to buy Beatrice's safety. Once she crossed this threshold, he would expect to be paid in full. It would be no gentle reckoning.

Chapter Four

The Black Angel pushed Rosalind in ahead of him. Contrary to Rosalind's expectations, the cabin was perfectly in order, almost Spartan in its neatness. An elegant and costly escritoire stood to her left. On it sat an oil lamp, its glass chimney spotless. Instead of the sailor's typical hammock, an actual bed sat against the far bulkhead, lying beneath the row of windows built into the stern. The sight of the Black Angel's bed made Rosalind's heart pound. No other brigantine's captain could boast a private cabin. This was further proof of the Black Angel's strange habits. He must have had *L'Etoile du Matin* built to suit his own tastes. That meant a vast amount of money, but money would be no object to a pirate as lucky and successful as the Black Angel.

Two boys hurried in carrying covered trays. To the right of the door hung a large square of polished mahogany only a few inches thick, bound flat against the bulkhead by cords. The boys unfastened the cords and lowered the square to create a tabletop. On that tabletop they set out plates, filled two silver wine goblets, and arranged a few more dishes. One trimmed the wick in the oil lamp, then lit it. They dashed out as quickly as they'd come.

The Black Angel slammed the door shut. Rosalind flinched, one hand flying to her mouth. He was well and truly angry now. He wouldn't be content with merely ravishing her. She had goaded him to the point of making her pay for her mockery. She pressed her other hand to her lips, trying to trap the sobs that were only moments away from bursting out of her. She had to be calm. She had won a great victory. Perhaps she could maintain her advantage.

The Black Angel circled behind her, the heat of his glare scorching her back. Rosalind stayed where she was, trying to keep her head up and her back straight. He moved around to face her, his expression a mixture of annoyance and fatigue. He opened his mouth as if to speak, then shook his head and stalked over to the cabinet on the far side of the escritoire. He unlocked the cabinet with a little brass key hanging on a peg beside it and poured himself a brandy. He drank one large sip, then another. Normal color warmed his cheeks. He let out a long breath.

"You haven't answered me, mademoiselle. Do I suit you better now after that bath?"

This sudden playfulness caught Rosalind off guard, leaving her speechless. The Black Angel stepped closer. She backed away. He took another step forward, forcing her to move back until she brushed against the door. He laid his hand flat against the wood beside her head, just hard enough to make her jump.

"You are a trial, mademoiselle." He gazed down at her. One corner of his mouth lifted in a wry smile. "I will confess I prefer you this way. I detest women who do nothing but whimper."

He stayed there, leaning on his arm, close enough to let Rosalind feel the warmth that radiated from him. His shirt strained across his shoulders, gaping open to show her more of the lean, tanned muscle girding his ribs. One stray lock of his raven hair hung down between them, nearly brushing her cheek. His nearness was overwhelming. The longer he stood there, simply looking down at her, the more Rosalind's anxiety grew. She found herself staring at the fullness of his lips, recalling their warmth and texture. A bewildering mixture of thoughts and feelings stirred within her, leaving her torn between the need to escape and a deeper need to remain just where she was.

The Black Angel's warm breath fanned her cheek. Only now, when the heat of battle had passed, did Rosalind realize how cold she was. Her damp chemise and petticoats were chilly, hanging on her like so much seaweed. The brandy in the Black Angel's glass teased her with its faint aroma. She sighed. In the horrible days after Father's death, the doctor had suggested small amounts to help with the shock that left her so weak and light-headed. The sips she and Mother had shared made her feel calmer, warmer, somehow closer to Father despite his death. The scent of brandy roused that painful loneliness within her, reminding her of the comfort she needed right now.

"Do words finally fail you, mademoiselle?" The Black Angel leaned a little closer, his voice low and husky. "I hope I can take that as a compliment."

Those dark eyes stared into hers, then moved down to the rise of her breasts above her corset. The creamy skin there burned under the intensity of his gaze. The blush moved up into Rosalind's cheeks. She looked away.

"*Pardonnez-moi, mon capitaine.* I cannot live up to your splendor. Circumstances have left me with few resources to do so." She'd meant it to be stinging, but it came out a little breathless.

"All things considered, you look quite lovely." The Black Angel smiled. "Come sit down. You must be hungry."

He took her hand and led her to one of the chairs the boys had set by the little table that hung down from the wall. The two pewter plates each held a quail, nicely roasted and sprinkled with herbs. A wedge of cheese sat on one side, a loaf of bread on the other. This would most likely have been Captain Harris's evening meal. The sight of it made Rosalind's stomach knot. That upset mixed with her already strained nerves stole her appetite entirely. The Black Angel stabbed one quail on the point of his dagger. Rosalind cried out. She clapped her hand over her mouth.

"What ails you, mademoiselle? Have you no appetite?"

"How—how can I? After all that's happened?"

The Black Angel sliced the bread, then cut away a small chunk of cheese. "The ordeal has left you weak. Try to eat a little."

He bit into the breast of his quail with every sign of enjoyment, sipping at his wine while he ate. Rosalind watched him in astonishment.

"Is this what you do every day, *mon capitaine?* Wake up, find a ship to pillage, kill off the crew, then sit down to a quiet dinner?"

"I am a pirate, mademoiselle. It is what I do."

His casual tone amazed her. The man was utterly shameless. How could Rosalind possibly bring herself to act on the first mate's warning and entertain this monster?

The Black Angel glanced at her. "Do not worry for the lives of your captain and his crew. If I killed every English sailor who crossed my path, I'd soon be left with no ships to plunder." He speared her chunk of cheese on the point of his dagger and offered it to her. "Now eat something. You'll need your strength."

The color drained from Rosalind's face, leaving her feeling weak and empty. She couldn't bear to bite into the poor little dead quail. It reminded her too much of herself, prey to the pirate king's unstoppable appetites. She managed a mouthful of bread along with the bite of cheese he offered her. That woke her hunger. She finished her food, drinking the wine rather too quickly. The Black Angel nodded his approval and refilled her goblet, cutting her another slice of bread and cheese. Chiding herself for gobbling down the first bit, Rosalind ate more slowly.

When he had finished eating, the Black Angel sat back, wine goblet in hand. He studied Rosalind, taking her in with a lazy air of speculation and appraisal.

"Tell me your name."

Why did he need to ask, when Beatrice had been shouting it all day? "Rosalind Brooks."

"*Le nom démodé.* Are you an old-fashioned girl?"

"I am not a girl."

"You're scarcely more than twenty."

"And you, *mon capitaine?* Are you so much older, then?"

"Twenty-six last December. If it matters."

"You're rather young to have such a grim reputation."

"I started earlier than most."

"Really? Then you've always been a pirate? Is it a family trade, like being a silversmith or a cooper?"

His cold stare examined her for any sign of levity. "I was always meant to slay the enemies of France. I am not quite what *mon père* intended me to be."

"So you've become a law unto yourself?"

"Exactly."

"But only at sea, I'd think. Once ashore you're as subject to the laws of the Crown as any of us."

"That, mademoiselle, is why I so rarely go ashore."

"You have everything you need here, then? I find that hard to believe. Staring at the same watery horizon day in and day out would soon drive me mad."

"Ah, but it's not the same. Not from day to day, not even from hour to hour." The Black Angel stared off at some horizon only he could see. "I've heard it said the sea is like a woman. That beggars it. The women I've known are shallow, predictable, possessed of perhaps two or three moods they change like their gowns to suit the moment." He drank, then stared into the depths of his goblet. "*La mer* is so much greater, so much grander than any petty human passion. It is itself, with no apologies and no explanations."

Rosalind found herself caught up in rich music of his voice. "Much like you."

He raised his head. His eyes focused on her. "Are you mocking me?" That dangerous undercurrent lay just beneath his mild tone.

"Mais non, mon capitaine." Rosalind drank a sip of wine. "Still, I find it hard to believe all your needs are met here on one small ship so far out in the middle of the ocean."

He grinned over the rim of his goblet. "Now and then I'm fortunate enough to find some, shall I say, diversion."

"Killing innocent people and sacking their ships? My, what a lovely little hobby."

He shook his head. "That's work. I take my business very seriously." He set aside the goblet and leaned forward. The lamplight illumined his eyes, showing her patterns in the dark brown there, much like folds and swirls in luxurious velvet. "When I say diversion, I mean the occasional passenger who provides me with entertaining conversation." He gave her a wicked smile. "You do entertain me, mademoiselle."

"Really, *mon capitaine?*" Rosalind tried to speak lightly. The sight of him unleashing his considerable charm roused powerful feelings in her. "I received quite a different impression earlier."

The Black Angel leaned his elbow on the table and put his chin on his hand. "I can think of few things that would divert me so well as watching you take down your hair."

Sudden fright shot through Rosalind, making her stomach twist and her hands shake. She clutched her hands together tightly in her lap, keeping her eyes on them.

"Come, Rosalind." The Black Angel spoke softly, reaching across the table to stroke her cheek. "We must begin somewhere. Let it be a gentle beginning."

This show of consideration confused Rosalind, adding to her fear. She rose and started to turn away. The Black Angel's bed lay before her, built long and broad to accommodate him. She turned her back on it, bringing her face-to-face with him again.

"Have you—" Her voice failed her. She coughed. "Have you a comb or brush?"

"Here." The Black Angel rose and moved past her to kneel on the bed. A clutter of personal objects sat on a shelf below the windows. He took up his brush and handed it to her. It was made of mahogany, set with boar bristles. A very fine brush indeed, the bristles still a bit damp from brushing his hair after his bath.

"Merci, mon capitaine."

The Black Angel sat down again and drank another long swallow of wine. He watched her, waiting.

Rosalind reached for the first of the few pins holding her coiled braid in place. She felt as if she were about to peel away her dress and stand there naked before him. Nothing in her life had prepared her for this. Her father's business associates all had sons who were looking for a beautiful, wealthy bride. Or had been, until disaster began to strike Hanshaw Shipping. Even so, the attentions of those young men had gone no further than a shy kiss on her hand or cheek. Never before had Rosalind seen such a man as the Black Angel, so dark, so fierce, so totally in command. He stirred her untried senses, unleashing longings within her whose strength was both startling and exhilarating.

Rosalind held her braid in place with one hand while she tucked the last pin into her corset with the others. The Black Angel sat forward, his face alight with anticipation. Rosalind's hand shook. Her braid slipped free, uncoiling to slap against her hips. She untied the white satin ribbon. Out of habit she stepped toward the table, about to drop it there. The Black Angel caught her hand between his. The wine had put more color in his face and lent his gaze a smoky quality that disturbed her. He turned her hand over to plant a kiss on the inside of her wrist. Again the softness of his lips startled her, caressing her skin with a warmth that sent the blood rushing to her head. He took the ribbon from her fingers and threaded it around his left wrist. A few deft tugs secured it in a beautiful knot.

"I will treasure it."

He thought she was flirting with him! But—wasn't that what she wanted him to think? Her clumsy fingers struggled to loosen her braid into separate plaits. Stiff but wavy from the sea water, the heavy mass of honey-colored hair swished against her thighs. At last she swung the length of it over one shoulder and began to brush out the tangles.

"It's like watching the sun rise." The Black Angel stood up, slipped his fingers back through her hair, cupping her face in his hands. "How absolutely glorious." His lips brushed her ear. "Has no one ever told you how beautiful you are?"

The wonder in his voice. Liar that he was, he sounded perfectly sincere. Rosalind made herself think of all the other women he had flattered this way.

"Merci, mon capitaine, but I'm nothing. I'm just a spinster schoolteacher who works for my room and board. I have no one but my students to look at me."

"I could stare at you from now until forever and still not see enough." The Black Angel gave the torn shoulder of her chemise a playful tug. "And now this, *ma belle.* If you can stir my blood by just letting down your hair, I cannot be denied the rest of your charms."

Rosalind spun away, hugging herself. Her hair fell around her, cloaking her and shielding her from his sight. Behind her, she heard his breath catch.

"Ah, *ma belle. C'est magnifique.*"

He gathered her hair into one hand and laid it over her right shoulder, baring her neck. One arm slid around her waist, pressing her against him, enveloping her in the heat of his presence. He bent his head to plant a kiss, featherlight, on the tender skin of her neck. Rosalind shivered.

"Are you cold?" he asked. "Perhaps a little brandy would warm you."

She shook her head, fighting back the tears. Brandy now, just before this bloodthirsty stranger stole her virtue and left her a whore in the eyes of the world. . . .

"Rosalind."

The Black Angel gently turned her to face him, then touched her chin and tilted her face up to his. She couldn't meet his eyes. He smoothed her hair back, brushing his lips across her forehead.

"It might help."

There it was again, that tone of finality. There was nothing at all Rosalind could do to stop him, short of rushing out of his cabin and flinging herself over the side. He moved away to open the liquor cabinet again. The door lay before her, unguarded. She could run, might even succeed in drowning herself. And when the news got back to London, Mother would be lost to a grief even deeper than the one she suffered now. It would also mean leaving Beatrice to face this nightmare alone.

Rosalind stood still and waited while the Black Angel brought her a small glass of brandy. He closed her shaking fingers around the glass. The sweet bite of the brandy's aroma brought more tears to Rosalind's eyes, reminding her again of her mother's comfort, something Rosalind needed so desperately now. She stared into the brandy's auburn depths, wishing she could drown in it and escape. That would indeed be some help. If she were senseless she wouldn't feel the pain, the agony he would surely make her suffer. For all his pretenses about being a gentleman, he'd turn back into the savage pirate as soon as his lust was sufficiently roused. She drank a large mouthful, closing her eyes against the welcome sting.

"Take care, Rosalind. That's not lemonade."

She ignored him and downed another large swallow, savoring the familiar warmth spreading through her. Mixed with the wine, the brandy would take her away to a place where nothing could touch her. She would sleep, and later she'd wake to whatever awaited her then. The important thing was escaping him right now. She drained the glass, then turned to set it on the table. The ship yawed. Rosalind staggered, the cabin whirling around her. The glass dropped from her limp fingers. She closed her eyes and let herself fall, happy in the knowledge that she wouldn't know when or where she landed.

She collided with the hard muscle of the Black Angel's chest. His arms closed around her. Her hand slid inside his shirt and glided over his bare skin, so warm, fitting so closely over his ribs. Her knees refused to support her. As she sagged, reflex made her other hand cling to his neck, burying her fingers in the silken thickness of his long black hair.

"What possessed you to down it that quickly?" the Black Angel asked. "Another of those and you'll be dead to the world."

Rosalind nodded against his chest. His shirt smelled clean and fresh. The scent of his skin teased her, somehow still faintly smoky, still so male. He wore no scent but his own. That pleased her. Ever fashionable, Mr. Murdock changed the scent for his linen week by week. Mr. Murdock would be furious to know this French pirate had dared to put his hands on her, had even kissed her. Rosalind giggled. The Black Angel compared her to the sunrise. Never once had Mr. Murdock said anything so courtly, so poetic.

Rosalind's head fell back. She looked up at the Black Angel, concentrating on the exact arrangement of his features. His eyes were so dark, darker and more limitless than the night sky. His nose was strong, fine and straight. His jawline showed his determination. His lips claimed most of her attention. The full curve of his lower lip was matched with a well-shaped upper lip. Excellent lips on a man, neither too fleshy nor too thin. Fine and full and most likely tasting sweet from the wine he'd been drinking. Rosalind blinked. Now why on earth had she been thinking that?

"Rosalind." That deep voice was the barest murmur. "You naughty girl, are you still trying to escape?"

She nodded again. Her thoughts whirled. She had to fight him, yet she should play up to him, entertain him. If she made him happy, he would go easier on everyone.

"That was rather stronger than I'm used to." She ran her

fingertips along the hard muscles in his shoulder blades. "But then again, so are you." It wasn't so hard, this pretending.

"Have you ever been kissed, Rosalind?"

"Only—only by you."

The sudden blaze of desire in his eyes made Rosalind shy back. His embrace was gentle but firm, allowing no escape.

"It's very simple. Just close your eyes and lift your chin."

She obeyed, shocked by her own eagerness. His lips met hers in a gentle caress. Deeper need revealed itself in the strain tensing his muscles beneath her fingers. He held her tighter, making her feel the warmth of his bare chest against her breasts. Such a hard man, such a cruel man, yet his hair was like silk and his lips even softer. He was so solid, so warm, so kind and gentle now. The brandy blurred Rosalind's thoughts. Why had she ever thought he was evil? An evil man wouldn't handle her with such care, such restraint. He *was* patient, no matter what he claimed. Catching him in such a sweet lie made her smile against his lips. This wasn't so bad. If it was all so sweet and easy, she could get through it.

The wet heat of his tongue touched her lips. She yielded, parting her lips, sighing into his mouth. Both hands slid up around his neck, his great height making her strain on tiptoe. The Black Angel groaned deep in his chest. His tongue plunged into her mouth, tasting her softness, mingling with her tongue until the new heat within Rosalind blazed up so brightly it left her sagging in his arms. Another groan rose up out of the Black Angel's chest. His hands slid down to her hips, back up into her hair. His tongue thrust deeper into her mouth, filling it with the taste of the liquors and the taste of him alone. A strange longing gathered inside Rosalind, growing stronger.

At last the Black Angel raised his head. His voice was a hoarse whisper. "No plain English schoolteacher could set my blood afire. You must be more than that."

The brandy and his kisses left Rosalind drugged, her thoughts slow and muddled. "I am. I am—" Sudden panic

cut through the haze. Rosalind caught herself. "Your captive." She took a deep breath, sighing against his chest.
"Only a prisoner, at your mercy. Will you have mercy on me,
mon capitaine?" She stroked his hair, drawing a length of it
across her cheek. "On this mermaid, this milkmaid, on this
poor English girl lost at sea?"

A slow, hungry smile curved the Black Angel's full lips.
His mouth claimed hers with a passion so intense Rosalind
feared her very bones would melt. His hands roamed over
her, stroking her hair, kneading her shoulders, sliding down
her back to her hips. He kissed her throat, his tongue tracing patterns of fire across her skin, moving down to kiss as
much of her breasts as the corset allowed him. Caught between fright and this dangerous longing, Rosalind strained
back from him, fighting his iron grip. He bent to catch her
legs up over his arm and carry her to his bed. Freed from the
enchantment of his kiss, Rosalind cried out.

"Please, *mon capitaine!* You can't—I didn't mean—"

"Hush, *ma belle.*" He laid her down on the emerald green
coverlet and stretched out beside her. "I taste such passion
in your kisses. You were made for this, Rosalind. Do not
deny me." He smiled down at her, sweet and tender and
gentle. "Do not deny yourself."

His mouth closed on hers, kissing her so deeply her very
soul shook with the joy of it. Rosalind tried to stir up her
anger, her hatred. She lay in bed with this stranger. This pirate. This killer. Too much pleasure drowned her senses for
any such concern to matter now. She couldn't think, not
with the liquor and the maddening heat of his presence.

The Black Angel pulled his shirt off and flung it aside.
Tanned by his life in the sun, he might have been an exquisite statue molded from bronze. Muscles corded his arms
and shoulders, left his flat belly ridged, his chest solid. He
stretched out again on his side and cuddled Rosalind
against his bare chest, stroking her hair, smoothing it down
over her shoulders. He kissed her, sinking down into her
lips, coaxing her tongue into his mouth. His thigh slid up

along hers, his weight pressing her down into the coverlet. The leather breeches couldn't conceal the rigid proof of his desire. The size of it—Rosalind struggled, trying to roll away. The Black Angel caught her easily, gripping her shoulder and throwing one leg across hers.

"Rosalind." He rubbed his cheek against her shoulder. "Now is no time to turn shy."

Fear stole her voice. She couldn't stop him. He would have her, impaling her on that—that part that would surely rend her in a most ghastly way. She turned her face from him.

"Rosalind? I do hope you're not a tease. That would make me most unhappy."

The return of that stern tone panicked Rosalind further. Anything she did or said now would only anger him, perhaps bring on the very cruelty she'd been trying to avoid. Tears spilled down her cheeks.

"What game are you playing now?" The Black Angel glared down at her. Sudden understanding spread over his features. "*Mon Dieu!* No nun, but still a virgin."

Rosalind spoke in a choked voice. "Let me go. Please, Captain! If you—if you do this, no other man will ever have me."

"To be the first . . ." He kissed her, just touching his lips to hers. "So beautiful, so wild, and yet still a maiden. . . ."

Again that tenderness colored his expression, shadowed by a faint sorrow. Despite her fear, Rosalind found herself captivated. He was so beautiful.

"You have demanded my best from me, *ma belle*. Let me offer it to you here as well. Women call me angel because I take pride in bringing them a taste of paradise."

Rosalind felt her will to resist him slipping away. She was so tired, so frightened and weary. The Black Angel was so warm, so strong and beautiful and gentle now. . . . No! She couldn't just give up. She turned her head to escape his kiss.

"Have you no heart at all?"

"I will have you, Rosalind. I want to hear you cry out my name so the skies ring with it."

"I don't even know your name!"

"*Je m'appelle* Alexandre."

He gripped the torn shoulder of her chemise. She trapped his hand under hers, meeting his eyes for one last plea. Her voice failed before the look he wore, a desire so intense it made his eyes seem molten. Alexandre leaned over her, pinning her beneath the solid wall of his chest. His mouth came down on her throat, leaving a trail of burning kisses. Only her corset protected her now.

His hand slid down her back, finding the ends of the lacings. The salt water soaking them had dried, tightening them into an impossible knot. Alexandre wrapped both arms around Rosalind. With a sudden lithe movement he rolled over, taking her with him. The long waves of her golden hair tumbled down around them. Her thighs fell on either side of the Black Angel's hips, leaving her pressed against the solid strength of his desire. To feel that pressure there, right there, even through the layers of cloth and leather that separated them. . . . The shame and pleasure of it left her breathless. Rosalind tried to sit up. That only ground her hips down against his. Alexandre sucked his breath in sharply.

"You will push me too far, *ma belle*. For your own sake, lie still!"

One arm clamped her against him while the other reached behind his head to slide under the pillow. He brought out a dagger, slim and elegant with a jeweled hilt. Rosalind gasped, staring in horror at the dagger's gleaming edge. Alexandre slid the blade up under her corset lacings, slicing through them. He gripped the dagger's tip, then flung it across the room to land quivering in the cabin door. A loud knocking made the dagger jiggle even more.

"*Mon capitaine!*" Yves called. "*La Fortuna* is three leagues off starboard and closing."

"Vasquez." Alexandre sat up, leaving Rosalind astride his lap. A curse hissed out between Alexandre's teeth. "*Le bâtard Espagnol!* He never knows when to let me be."

"He's flying friendly colors, *mon capitaine.*"

"What does he want?"

"He signaled his desire to come aboard. What shall we do?"

Anger and concern warred on Alexandre's face. "Hail him. Invite him aboard, but only him. His scurvy band of fleas can stay away."

"Oui, mon capitaine."

Alexandre glanced down at Rosalind. "Does this suit you, *ma belle*? I'm called away just at the moment of truth."

His fingers curled over the front of her corset. Rosalind hugged the loose sides tight. Alexandre buried his other hand in her hair, holding her just where he wanted her as their lips met in another soul-stirring kiss. Of their own will, Rosalind's hands came to rest on his naked shoulders, kneading the heavy muscles there. Alexandre pulled the corset down her arms and flung it away. Her full breasts strained against the thin batiste. Still damp, it clung to her, revealing the pink rosebuds of her nipples. Alexandre smiled.

"Kiss me, Rosalind. Kiss me the way you did a moment ago."

She knew what he meant. He wanted her to put her tongue in his mouth. He wanted her to make love to him.

"You—you have to go. That other captain—"

"Kiss me."

His mouth devoured hers, his tongue thrusting deep again and again. Pressing her back on the bed, Alexandre kneaded her breasts, stroking her, teasing her nipples until she tore her mouth from his. A groan gusted out of her, betraying her pleasure and leaving her crimson with shame.

"Speak to me, *ma belle*. Tell me how much you want me." He kissed her breasts through the thin silk. The hot rush of sensation left Rosalind aching, caught between her fear and the wild need for more. Her hands slid up his shoulders, seeking some grip in his hair. She had to make him stop before she abandoned all sense.

"Alexandre. . . ."

"Oui, ma petite fleur?"

The damp silk of Rosalind's chemise gave way under his gentle tugging, baring her breasts to his kisses. The wet heat of his tongue curled around her nipple. He sucked at it, sending a white hot current of desire burning through her. His hand slid under the hem of her petticoat, gliding up along her thigh. Rosalind's back arched as her body offered itself to him. His mouth captured hers. As their tongues mingled, the heat within Rosalind became an inferno, burning away the last of her reason.

Yves hammered on the door again. *"Mon capitaine,* Vasquez is rowing across. Where will you meet him?"

Alexandre sighed and raised his head. "The quarterdeck. Give him enough rum to keep him out of trouble."

"Oui, mon capitaine."

Alexandre laid Rosalind back on the pillows. He gathered the sides of the coverlet together and tucked her in, then took her face between his hands.

"You will stay where you are and make no sound at all, *comprenez-vous?* If you think me a brute, you won't want so much as a glimpse of Ricardo Vasquez."

He eased off the bed, muttering curses under his breath while he snatched up his shirt and pulled it down over his head, stuffing the tails into his breeches. He tied his sash around his hips and tucked two pistols into it, then yanked the dagger from the door and slid it into his boot. Glancing into the small mirror on the shelf beside the bed, he raked both hands back through his hair and bound it with a wide length of black ribbon. He freed Rosalind's white ribbon from his wrist and dropped it beside the mirror. He bent over Rosalind, planting a lingering kiss on her lips.

"Adieu for now, *ma belle."*

After the door shut behind him, Rosalind listened to his footsteps ascend the short flight of stairs that led to the deck above his cabin. A loud voice hailed him in badly accented French.

"Ah, *le Diable Français*! By the looks of the wreckage in the water, you've had another good day."

"What do you want, Vasquez?"

"Got anything you want to be rid of? Too much cotton, too many barrels of salt pork, any *Anglais* we could beat into joining us?"

"What makes you think I have captives?"

"A ship that big must have had passengers aboard. You're still flying the black. That means you couldn't have cut every throat, not yet anyway."

"Clever little vulture, aren't you?" Alexandre said. "I took no captives."

Rosalind sat up. Why did Alexandre lie to Vasquez? New anxiety banished the lingering warmth of Alexandre's kisses.

Vasquez muttered to himself. "Too bad. Nothing like an English girl to scream the knots right out of the rigging!" He banged his tankard on the rail, laughing like a fiend.

The casual cruelty of Vasquez's words rang in Rosalind's ears and brought her to her senses. Here Rosalind lay, carrying on like a strumpet, in the bed of the very pirate who'd killed innumerable Englishmen. She flung aside the coverlet and snatched up her corset. Only the lacings had been damaged. She opened the chest at the foot of the bed. Inside she found Alexandre's shirts and breeches. Digging down farther, she came up with what she sought. A spool of black ribbon, the kind the Black Angel used to tie back his hair.

Rosalind unwound enough ribbon to replace her lacings. Now to cut off the length she needed. Alexandre had taken his dagger with him, but surely there must be at least one other sharp-edged weapon somewhere in his cabin. On the wall across from the foot of the bed, Rosalind spied a sword hanging in its scabbard. It looked to be a very fine sword, one the Black Angel had no doubt taken from some decent man of honor. She fetched it down, letting it drop onto the bed. She bared just enough of the sword to let her pull the ribbon across the edge and cut it neatly.

She fumbled awkwardly with the corset's grommets and the ribbon, trying to tighten it, but at last she'd managed well enough for a quick dash below decks. Once she found Beatrice again they'd put Rosalind's appearance to rights as best they could. Rosalind plaited her hair into a fresh braid, then tied it off with her own ribbon.

She eased the cabin door open a few inches and peeked out through the crack. The victory celebration continued with more drinking and gaming. Three musicians sat near the bow, two sawing on fiddles and another playing a pennywhistle. Some of the pirates cavorted in the crude patterns of a dance. The volume of noise was painful. Even so, she heard the ship's bell toll.

Ding-ding! Ding-ding! Ding-ding!

Six bells. Seven o'clock. The middle of the second dog watch. Rosalind slipped out the door, ducking behind a pile of canvas. She scanned the waters off to starboard and spied Vasquez's ship, *La Fortuna.* It was larger than *L'Etoile du Matin,* its two masts more heavily rigged. Hampered by the darkness, she guessed it to be a large schooner. It had drawn up within hailing distance, but stayed out of cannon range.

"Remy!" Alexandre's voice rang out across the deck.

A young, dark-haired pirate climbed down from his perch in the rigging and made his way toward the quarterdeck. Rosalind ducked down. She wondered why Alexandre didn't call for Yves. Of course. It was the second watch now. Yves, being first mate, took the first watch, so he would have gone below to eat or sleep or amuse himself some other way. That was a relief. So Remy was the second mate.

"*Capitaine* Vasquez will be leaving us now," Alexandre told him. "Kindly tell his men he's coming down."

Remy turned his back on Rosalind's hiding place as he began to call out the necessary orders. Rosalind waited until enough of the pirates had begun to move around, blocking the sight of her hiding place. She dashed to the closest hatch and very nearly slid down the ladder, such was her haste.

"Rosalind!"

Rosalind turned to collide with Beatrice as the younger girl threw herself into Rosalind's arms. Just beyond Beatrice stood Mr. MacCaulay. They had been given what amounted to some privacy near the stern. Several crates and boxes and canvas bags had been rearranged to wall off an area five feet by five feet. It wasn't much, but given the crowded conditions of the ship, Rosalind marveled at Alexandre allowing his captives that much breathing room.

"Are you well, Miss Brooks?" Mr. MacCaulay stepped forward to take her hand. "We feared you paid too great a price for our comfort."

"Not yet, Mr. MacCaulay. It was a close thing, but the arrival of the other pirate must surely have been timed by Providence itself."

"Indeed."

Rosalind looked down at Beatrice. She suddenly realized how warm Beatrice felt, the heat pouring off her skin in nearly visible waves.

"Beatrice! Are you ill?"

Beatrice raised her head to look up at Rosalind. Her blue eyes were dull, her cheeks flushed too bright a red.

"Mother said the tropics would be warm. It's dark out now. Does it never cool off in these waters?"

Rosalind hugged Beatrice, smoothing her hair. She cast one anxious glance over Beatrice's head at Mr. MacCaulay, who nodded his understanding. It was as Rosalind had feared. Beatrice now had a fever, and by the feel of it, one dangerously high.

Chapter Five

Alexandre watched *La Fortuna* glide across the quiet sea. He knew Vasquez hadn't believed him about taking no captives. It scarcely mattered. The vulture might have a schooner with twenty guns, but he was an idiot at tactics with a badly disciplined crew. The ship's boys of *L'Etoile du Matin* could sink *La Fortuna* before the swine that crewed her ran out their first gun. He looked at the masses of clouds gathering on the eastern horizon. A storm, and a nasty one by the look of it. Perhaps come morning Alexandre would enjoy the delightful sight of *La Fortuna* lying wrecked on a reef.

Yves stood at his elbow. "That's one scavenger I would gladly see choke on his own blood."

Alexandre nodded. "If he isn't out of sight by the middle watch, let me know."

"Oui, mon capitaine," Yves said. "And the storm? Should it prove a typhoon, you will wish to be called?"

Alexandre grinned. "Spare me that tone, *mon ami*. It's been ages since I had such an entertaining guest."

Yves looked at the thunderheads massing on the eastern

horizon. "I think we are all in for far more entertainment than we might prefer, *mon capitaine. Bonne nuit.*"

"And to you." Alexandre glanced once more at the sails of *La Fortuna,* dimly visible through the storm's gathering gloom. The way his luck was running, the storm might well rid him of Vasquez. Alexandre put all such tedious matters from his mind and hurried down to his cabin. Rosalind awaited him, swathed only in a few bits of damp batiste, already well on her way to complete surrender. With a smile he pushed open his cabin door.

His bed was empty.

Alexander glared around the cabin, looking for some clue as to where the treacherous little minx had gone. His sea chest had been opened. His naval saber now lay on the bed, beside his spool of black silk ribbon. Alexandre shook his head, seeing no logic in the disarray before him. He struck his forehead with his palm as he caught himself trying to apply reason to the actions of a frantic virgin fleeing the Black Angel's bed. He almost laughed, but the heat of thwarted desire now became anger. He snatched up his saber and hung it back in place, then turned to face the open door.

"Yves!"

Yves jumped down from the quarterdeck. He glanced past Alexandre and saw the empty bed.

"Find her," Alexandre snapped. "She's most likely hiding with her little friend. I want her back here this instant."

With a nod Yves walked over to the stern hatch and disappeared below. Alexandre waited, listening. If the afternoon's uproar had been any indication, Miss Rosalind Brooks would not return to him meek and contrite.

"I tell you she is ill!" Rosalind's voice rang out. The edge of hysteria carried up through the humid air. "If *le capitaine* wishes to see me, he can come down here. I will not leave my sister alone!"

Alexandre sighed. The little English girl had looked to be the sickly kind. The English took chill so easily. Thin blood. Had they the Gallic temperament, the blood that had made

war on England for generations, they would make better enemies. How it would amuse the British naval authorities to
know *L'Ange Noir* was now harried by two English virgins,
one armed with a head cold.

"Yves!" he called. "Bring them both up."

Moments later Rosalind appeared, kneeling beside the
hatch to help Beatrice up onto the deck. Yves followed, his
face set in the stony, colorless expression that concealed his
true thoughts. Alexandre could well imagine what those
thoughts might be. His own temper flared higher as Rosalind came to stand before him, her arms around Beatrice,
her chin up and eyes defiant. The usual noise from the crew
subsided as they looked on with anticipation. Alexandre
scowled.

"Mademoiselle, I told you to stay in my cabin."

"I feared for the safety of my sister, *mon capitaine*. Surely
you can understand that?"

"What I understand, mademoiselle, is that you ran off the
instant my back was turned. Not an auspicious beginning
for our arrangement."

Rosalind waved that away. "*S'il-vous plaît, mon capitaine,* do you have a physician aboard? A surgeon? My sister has a fever."

Alexandre glanced at Yves, who tipped his head down in
the slightest of nods. So, this was no pretense. The little
English girl was ill. Alexandre looked more closely at Beatrice. She was flushed, her eyes dim and unfocused. He
reached out, not quite touching her. Her skin gave off unnatural heat.

"*Très bien.* Send for Gingras."

A tidy little man in a proper set of brown coat and
breeches appeared, dabbing at his thin moustache with a
square of linen. He had bright, intelligent blue eyes. His
mouth was quirked in a permanent half-smile.

"You called, *mon capitaine?*"

"*Monsieur le Docteur,* Mademoiselle claims the little one
is ill. I would prefer a more qualified opinion, *s'il-vous plaît.*"

"Mais oui, mon capitaine." Monsieur Gingras put one finger under Beatrice's chin and tipped her head up, looking into her eyes. He laid the back of his hand against her forehead, then took out his pocket watch and studied it while he grasped Beatrice's limp wrist between his fingers. He nodded to himself and replaced Beatrice's hand gently at her side. "Exhaustion, exposure, a digestion most likely unaccustomed to shipboard fare. Slight congestion and a fever."

"What do you recommend?" Alexander asked.

Monsieur Gingras turned a practiced eye to the eastern horizon. "Shore leave, *mon capitaine*. Two days, perhaps three, out of the wind and wet, preferably before the storm makes all things worse."

This plan suited Alexandre well enough, but he kept a stern look on his face. He could not permit Rosalind to think she'd forced him to agree to her demands yet again. Any more of that and his own crew would be laughing at him behind his back.

"Impossible. I have no time to be taking *l'invalide Anglaise* ashore when the naval patrols are lying in wait."

"A gentleman would find the time, *mon capitaine*." Rosalind looked him in the eye, still defiant. Her nervous hands betrayed her anxiety, patting Beatrice as if she were a fretful baby.

"You would do well to keep silent, mademoiselle." Alexandre gave her a dark look. "After all, what is the life of one little English girl to *L'Ange Noir?*"

Rosalind said nothing. Alexandre studied her. All he saw in her eyes was uneasiness, a watchful cunning, and desperation. If she would show even one sign of true fear, he would yield. Frustration drove him to bait her.

"What's this? Can it be, Mademoiselle *Anglaise* has at last done as she was told?" Alexandre waited, letting the silence between them grow into a yawning chasm.

Rosalind looked at him with fresh dislike. "We are at your

mercy, *mon captaine*. With your permission, I will take my sister below to rest while you decide our fate."

"She may go, but you will abide by the very terms you yourself set." Alexandre stood aside, leaving the doorway to his cabin open. "Come along, mademoiselle. Yves will see the little one below."

Rosalind bent to murmur in Beatrice's ear. A slight nod of the head was all the response Beatrice gave. Rosalind hugged her and pressed a kiss to her fevered brow, then stepped back to let Yves guide Beatrice back down the hatch. Head up, face composed, Rosalind walked past Alexandre. He watched her go, amused to see his black ribbon threaded through the white lacings of her corset. A bold girl, to simply take what she needed where she found it, making him pay for the damage he had done.

Rosalind took a seat on the foot of his bed. She waited, hands folded in her lap, face composed. Alexandre closed the door on the curious faces outside. He took three slow, measured strides, moving to stand directly before Rosalind.

"I see you found the means to mend my handiwork."

"If only I could mend *The Bird of Paradise*. Then perhaps I could make port in Jamaica safe and sound."

Alexandre smiled thinly at her impertinence. "It would take more than a yard or two of silk ribbon to mend the damage *L'Ange Noir* can do."

"*Mais oui, mon capitaine*. That I can easily believe."

Her careless tone didn't fool Alexandre. He saw her knuckles whiten as she clenched her hands together. That unknowing display of fright eased his temper a little. What he longed for above all else was to bring Rosalind back to that breathless state of swooning rapture. But first, he had to make one thing absolutely clear to her.

"You see how I keep my end of our arrangement, mademoiselle. As soon as you made me aware of your *petite soeur's* distress, I summoned my ship's physician."

"*Merci, mon capitaine.*"

"You can thank me by obeying my orders. I am *le capitaine*, mademoiselle, and you will do as you are told. Disobey me again and I will consider our arrangement at an end. I will do with the old man, Sister Beatrice, and yourself whatever it pleases me to do." He took her chin in his hand and made her look up at him. "*Comprenez-vous*, mademoiselle?"

Rosalind jerked her chin out of his hand. "*Oui, mon capitaine.*"

"Oh, mademoiselle, look at how you pout. You make the little moue with those sweet lips." Alexandre let himself sprawl backward across the length of the bed. He pulled Rosalind down beside him. "I am only a man, only flesh and blood. How can I resist such exquisite temptation?"

Before Rosalind could recover, Alexandre caught her hands and pinned them to the mattress above her head, the weight of his chest pressing her down into the bedclothes. He stared down into her eyes, feeling the hot rush of desire course through his veins. She was so beautiful, so wild, and yet untouched.

Alexandre lowered his head and pressed his lips to hers, savoring their silky warmth. After a moment's resistance, Rosalind sighed beneath him, her tense muscles relaxing under the heat and weight of his body. She returned his kiss, moving her lips against his in shy, gentle caresses that stirred his blood until it thundered through him. His tongue sought hers, stroking, mingling, building a fire that left her melting in his arms. Alexandre broke the kiss, staring down into the azure depths of Rosalind's eyes.

"In deference to your wishes, mademoiselle, I must plot a new course."

Much to his secret delight, a hint of disappointment crossed Rosalind's face. Her expression changed to one of relief, prompting Alexandre to taunt her again.

"Abandon any hope of sleep, *ma belle*. For you this night will be a dream, one that many women have longed for."

Rosalind's shoulders shook with faint laughter. "I am sure

you must think so, *mon capitaine*. How could you think otherwise?"

Alexandre chose to ignore the trace of irony he heard in her voice. "I am very good at what I do, *ma belle*. At everything I do."

"Pardonnez-moi, mon capitaine. In England we hear nothing of you but violence. Decent people do not tell a young woman such as myself how well a notorious pirate ravishes innocent victims of his displeasure."

Alexandre smiled, deliberately refusing to rise to her bait. "Perhaps, *ma belle,* you will be the one to carry the glad news back to your sisters in England."

Conflicting emotions warred on Rosalind's lovely features. Her lips parted in a gasp, her delicate brow furrowed with confusion, while hope and fear struggled in her eyes. Satisfied, Alexandre stood up.

"Be ready, *ma belle.*"

With that he quit the cabin, awarding this round to himself.

"There now." Alexandre laid aside his charts and rubbed a weary hand over his face. "Put Adolphe at the wheel. Call me only if we're forced to tack."

"Oui, mon capitaine." Yves took up the charts showing their new course. "I wish you a good night."

Alexandre hurried down the steps to his cabin and stepped inside, closing the door softly behind him.

Rosalind lay beneath the bedclothes. The regularity of her breath and the deep peace that graced her features told Alexandre she was fast asleep. He glanced down to see the remnants of her corset, petticoats, and chemise lying in an untidy pile beside the bed. Had he put the fear of himself into Rosalind so well she had even stripped herself naked to await his pleasure? That thought filled Alexandre with a hot burst of desire. It was good to be obeyed, and even better to be obeyed in such a provocative manner.

Alexandre took off his shirt and tossed it aside, then bent

to pull his boots off. He cast his breeches alongside his shirt and reached back to pull the ribbon from his hair. Naked, Alexandre folded back the blankets, the last barrier between him and the beauty that awaited him.

Rosalind lay on her side with her back to him, wearing one of his own shirts. Her long braid trailed across the pillows. She sighed in her sleep and turned over, arching her back in a luxuriant stretch that pulled the crisp white lawn taut across the full curves of her breasts. Alexandre's breath caught in his throat. With something like wonder he reached out to trail his fingertips over the warm sweet weight of one breast. As he'd hoped, the soft bud of her nipple grew firm and upright. He stroked her other breast, delighting in the feel of her delicate skin responding to his touch.

Alexandre knelt on the bed and gathered Rosalind up in his arms, lifting her up and making room for himself in the middle of the mattress. He stretched out, cuddling her against him with her back against his chest and the tempting curves of her bottom rubbing against the urgent hardness of his manhood. Rosalind stirred, fumbling at his arm around her waist. A vague smile touched her lips. She snuggled back against Alexandre, fitting her legs along his. Slow molten yearning burned through Alexandre's veins, a hunger almost painful in its intensity. He kissed the curve of Rosalind's neck, moving up to brush his lips against her ear.

"*Ma belle,* I have come back to you."

Rosalind slept on, her breathing steady and deep.

"Rosalind. Wake up, *chèrie.* I promise you will be glad that you did."

Still nothing. She couldn't possibly be faking such a profound slumber. Alexandre cuddled her closer, feeling a sharp pang of disappointment alongside the absurd impulse to laugh. Rosalind bested him even when she had no fight left in her. Her fatigue and the brandy had done their work, delivering her from him after all. Alexandre settled down, tucking one hand between Rosalind's plump sweet breasts and settling his head on the pillow so he might drink in the fragrance of her golden hair. He had time. He had all the time in the world. This enchanting English schoolteacher would become his pupil in the arts of love. Thinking of a tutor who had forced the young Alexandre to recopy one lesson a dozen times, Alexandre grinned and let himself drift off to sleep.

It seemed he had scarcely shut his eyes when a frantic hand came pounding on his cabin door. As Alexandre began to wake, the instincts that made him the most feared pirate in tropical waters took stock of the sounds around him. The rigging was singing with the tension of the wind in the sails. The yaw and pitch of the ship spoke of choppy or storm-tossed waves. The roar of the wind vied with the slap of the sea against the hull. The storm was upon them.

"*Mon capitaine!*" Remy's voice. "We're approaching the reefs! We need you at the wheel!"

With a muttered curse Alexandre eased Rosalind out of his embrace and padded barefoot to the door. "I ordered Adolphe to the wheel! He knows the reefs as well as I!"

"*Mon capitaine,* one great gust carried away a jib! It caught Adolphe a nasty one across the back of the head!"

Alexandre shut his eyes and listened to the rhythm of *L'Etoile du Matin*. In the orderly symphony of his rigging, there were notes out of tune. The waves struck the hull with such vigor because they were sailing against the current. Alexandre snatched up his shirt and breeches.

"Does he yet live?"

"*Oui, mon capitaine,* but we cannot wake him."

"Tell Gingras to do as much as he can. I'll take the wheel presently."

"*Oui, mon capitaine.*"

Alexandre pulled on his boots and cast one last look of longing at his little milkmaid who slept on in her apparently permanent innocence. Reminding himself that she was his until he decided otherwise, Alexandre went out on deck to fight the storm.

* * *

Rosalind opened her eyes. The bed swayed slightly beneath her. Outside sailors sang out from their places in the rigging. The long, broad figure behind her stirred, turning toward her and throwing one arm around her waist, cuddling her against his bare chest as a child might cling to a favorite toy. Rosalind glanced back over her shoulder and gasped. Alexandre was naked! She was lying in the same bed with a naked pirate! Rosalind took a careful grip on Alexandre's wrist, readying herself to fling back his arm and make her escape. Then she realized Alexandre lay between her and the cabin door. With his great height and long, well-muscled legs, she could not escape the bed without the risk of jarring him awake. Far better that he slept on than woke to pursue his advantage.

By moving only a little at a time, Rosalind achieved a more comfortable position on her back. Now the heavy arm lay draped across her waist instead of curved tight around her. Alexandre stirred again, rubbing his cheek against her hair. Rosalind glanced up at his face. Composed in sleep, free from his stern or sardonic expression, Alexandre looked peaceful, almost happy. Rosalind studied the shape of his lips, the long black lashes, and the silky black hair that spilled down over his shoulder. One thick black tress slipped down inside the open neck of the shirt Rosalind wore, its silkiness caressing her breasts.

Rosalind couldn't help smiling. The fierce pirate king looked like an overgrown boy, tired of his games and napping soundly. He did indeed look tired. Now Rosalind noticed the shadows beneath Alexandre's eyes. Here and there his hair was streaked with white, the drying sea spray leaving its salt behind. His shirt had been flung across the end of the bed. Rosalind extended one leg and touched her toe to the sleeve. The shirt was soaking wet. What had happened to Alexandre? Had he fallen over the side? That was so unlikely as to be ridiculous. How then did he come to be soaked in sea water?

Rosalind slipped her fingers into the palm of the hand that still lay across her. Alexandre's skin was rough, abraded, and even cracked. Rope burns, perhaps? Had he been laboring alongside his men in the rigging while the storm raged outside? Rosalind felt a curious surge of admiration. Alexandre must have left his bed to go out on deck and battle the storm with his crew. Instead of asserting his rank and leaving them to it while he took his pleasure with his captive, he had gone out and passed some sleepless, probably painful hours. And when he returned, he did nothing more than lie down beside Rosalind, cuddling close to her while he slept.

"Bonjour, ma belle," Alexandre murmured drowsily. "Is that smile for me?"

"What—what happened last night, *mon capitaine?"*

Alexandre ran one fingertip down her cheek. "Do you mean here, or out on deck?"

"On deck, *s'il-vous plaît."*

"My best helmsman took a knock on the head from some rigging that fell. I had to steer the ship a while." He smiled, propping his head on his hand. "Did you miss me?"

He looked so sweet, so playful. Rosalind couldn't hide another smile. *"Pardonnez-moi, mon capitaine.* I'm afraid I can't recall when you joined me or when you left."

Alexandre nodded. *"Ma pauvre fleur.* You did need your rest. Are you better?"

Rosalind started to agree, then paused as she realized where he might be leading her. "A bit, *mon capitaine, merci.* I have not been altogether well for some time."

Alexandre lifted his hand from her waist and brushed his fingertips along her braid where it tumbled down across her breasts. "I can make you feel much better, *ma belle.* Will you let me try?"

Rosalind tried to speak, to shake her head, to somehow deny him. The flame of desire burned in those dark eyes. His hand moved from her braid to her hip, smoothing the lawn of his shirt down along her thigh. When it moved up again, Rosalind felt the rough skin of his palm stroking her bare thigh, sliding up under the shirt, moving higher.

"Mon capitaine!"

Alexandre leaned over her, planting a soft kiss on her temple. "This is no time for formalities, *ma belle*. You know my name."

"L'Ange Noir."

He nodded, his lips tracing the line of her cheekbone. His voice became a seductive whisper. "It's time you knew why women call me that."

He kissed her, his lips lingering on hers with soft, sweet power. Rosalind raised her hands, caught between the fear of letting him go any further, and the growing need to return his kiss. Her hands settled on his bare shoulders. Alexandre planted one hand on the far side of her, then shifted his weight across her, covering her like a great warm blanket. Rosalind gasped, frightened and pleased and confused all at once. Alexandre made it all worse by tracing the soft fullness of her lips with his tongue. Overwhelmed by sensation and conflicting needs, Rosalind groaned aloud.

"Mais oui, ma belle," Alexandre murmured against her lips. "Call out to me. Tell me what you need."

While Rosalind's mind fought itself, arguing propriety against a rising tide of yearning, her body made its choice. Her hands slid up into Alexandre's thick black hair. Her mouth opened under his, inviting the hot sweet sensation of his tongue twined with hers. Alexandre's arms closed around her, one hand sinking into her hair while the other slid up her ribs to cover her breast, stroking it, kneading it, his thumb rubbing her nipple to a hard peak. His knee slid between hers, pushing her thighs apart. Rosalind gasped, tensing. Alexandre caught her fear in his mouth and banished it with a deeper kiss, his tongue plunging between her lips again and again, every thrust sending a fresh surge of heat through Rosalind.

Now Alexandre groaned. He tore his lips from hers and

panted in her ear. *"Ma fleur. Ma belle divine.* Do you want me?"

"Yes. Yes. . . ."

"Mon capitaine!" Yves's voice, just outside the cabin door. Rosalind flinched.

"Ignore them," Alexandre said. "They can wait."

He kissed her, filling her mouth with his tongue just as she wished he'd fill that other part of her with himself.

"Mon capitaine! Vasquez is still with us! He makes for Isla la Veche as well!"

Alexandre growled with more displeasure than passion. He rose up on his elbows and turned his head to bellow at the door. "Keep the island between us! Return no signals! If he comes too close, fire a broadside to warn him off!"

"Oui, mon capitaine."

Rosalind shrank from the loudness of the strange French voices. The warm spell of pleasure was broken. Abruptly she came to herself. Looking down, she saw she was on the brink of wrapping her legs around this pirate! In the struggle between desire and propriety, propriety gained the upper hand. As if he felt her sudden change of mood, Alexandre looked down at her.

"What is it, *ma belle?* I told you to ignore this. A moment's distraction, nothing more."

"Mais non, mon capitaine." Rosalind turned her face away. "You must do what pirates do. That includes this, I presume."

Alexandre looked at her with a perplexed expression that rapidly gave way to anger. "You want me, Rosalind. Even now your body cries out for the relief that only I can give you."

"But my heart cries out against you taking what is mine alone to give."

His expression wavered, momentary confusion replaced by bitterness. "I thought you wanted me to have it."

Rosalind hesitated, caught by the melting look in those

depthless eyes. "I—I no longer know what I want, *mon capitaine*. I am an innocent, and you use my ignorance against me."

That stern mask crept over Alexandre's features, concealing the sorrow that dulled his eyes. He moved to one side, then sat up with his back to her. Rosalind pulled the sheet up to cover herself. Alexandre glanced back at her and frowned.

"Yves!"

"*Oui, mon capitaine!*"

"How fares Adolphe?"

"Gingras says he sleeps now. He should wake by afternoon."

"*Très bien.* I will take the helm."

"*Merci, mon capitaine.*"

Alexandre rose and flung open the lid of his sea chest, snatching out a fresh shirt and new breeches. He yanked the shirt down over his head, muttering under his breath. Thunder clouded his brow again, more intense and forbidding than the storm outside.

"Mademoiselle, you would do well to decide what you want. I see in you a longing for greater things, deeper feelings, hotter passions. I cannot believe a dull, spiritless life of perfect manners and precise etiquette suits you."

He finished dressing and went out on deck, slamming the door behind him.

Chapter Six

Toward noon *L'Etoile du Matin* navigated into a little cove on the southwest side of Isla la Veche. The *Diabolique* skimmed in alongside it, dropping anchor in the shelter of the larger ship. The weather was still disagreeable and damp. Brooding thunderheads dumped buckets of rain down at unpredictable intervals. Rosalind sat in Alexandre's cabin, occupying herself with putting her baggage to rights.

One of Doctor Gingras's first instructions had been the fetching of Beatrice's baggage. Alexandre ordered both women's possessions found and taken to his cabin. Beatrice now wore a lovely gown of pale blue muslin, sprigged with little white flowers. Rosalind smiled, thinking of the love and pride shining in Beatrice's eyes when she brought out the gown. Beatrice's mother had made four, to be worn by the bridesmaids in the eldest sister Coralie's wedding. Beatrice already looked much better, her cheeks flushed with nothing more than sun, the plain relief of the lighter clothing raising her spirits. Beatrice now took the air in the stern under the watchful eye of Doctor Gingras.

Rosalind plucked at the skirt of her own gown. With her

black clothing lost, she had little that was suitable for mourning. She'd been forced to fall back on a gown of dark blue taffeta, its white underskirt and stomacher trimmed with taffeta ribbons and lacings of the same blue. Another difficulty that caused Rosalind additional discomfort was the loss of her pocket panniers. She and her mother agreed full panniers were ridiculous aboard ship, and impractical as well in the tropics. Far better to minimize her silhouette with pocket panniers. Now she had none at all, leaving the extra yardage of taffeta sagging around her ankles. She was forced to roll a white lace shawl into a belt and tie that around her waist, hitching up her skirts enough to prevent tripping on them. The result was positively medieval. Still, even though Rosalind might not present the most fashionable appearance, it was an immense relief to be fully dressed again, wearing whatever protection the appearance of propriety might afford her.

Now Rosalind sat on Alexandre's bed, folding handkerchiefs and gloves and stockings, just to keep herself busy and avoid dwelling on the painful scene that ended with Alexandre storming out to take the ship's wheel. She'd seen nothing of Alexandre since he left his cabin so abruptly. Rosalind wondered why the great *L'Ange Noir* should be forced to hide from the likes of Vasquez. To hear Alexandre tell it, Vasquez hardly knew port from starboard. She was beginning to understand how typical it was of Alexandre to think he knew better about other people's lives than they themselves knew. Monstrous arrogance. How very French. As if Rosalind could ever pursue a life as wild and lawless as his, no home to return to, no friends but his officers, no wife or children. . . .

Rosalind suddenly realized just how little she knew about the Black Angel. Perhaps Alexandre did have a wife somewhere, one who'd given him children. Perhaps he'd run from that responsibility as well. She could not envision Alexandre content with managing his estate while his wife gave exquisite little soirées featuring the crème de la crème of Parisian society. How strange that once again Rosalind should think of Alexandre as a nobleman. It was scarcely conceivable that *L'Ange Noir* could be a renegade farmer.

Rosalind flung aside the lace cap she held and marched to the cabin door. Just as she reached for it, the door swung inward. In the doorway stood Doctor Gingras. He made her a little bow.

"Mademoiselle. *Le capitaine* asks you to make ready to go ashore." He looked up at the turbulent sky. "I fear we will have little opportunity for *la petite* Beatrice to enjoy a dry spell, but we will do what we can."

"*Merci, Monsieur le Docteur.* You are very good to be so attentive to her."

With a smile, Doctor Gingras shrugged. "One must obey *le captaine,* must one not?"

Rosalind gathered up a heavier shawl to wear against the breeze onshore. She stepped out through the doorway, doing her best to control her trailing skirts. Doctor Gingras escorted her to the rail. Just above it hung a curious contraption. A rectangle of canvas had been slung between ropes that were in turn all gathered to a wooden crossbeam that hung from more ropes. It looked like a makeshift swing.

"*Voila!*" Doctor Gingras said. "*La chaise du maître d'équipage.*"

The bosun's chair, used for going up into the rigging. Now it would lower Rosalind to the ship's boat. What a profound relief to know she didn't have to struggle down a rope ladder with six pirates staring up her skirts. Beatrice sat toward the bow between two younger pirates clearly pleased with their luck. Mr. MacCaulay sat in the stern, flanked by burlier pirates. Rosalind smiled and returned Beatrice's wave.

"How kind of *le capitaine* to allow us such a dignified descent."

Doctor Gingras's steady gaze told her he'd caught the slight irony in her tone. "*Oui,* mademoiselle. I suggested it to *le capitaine* to spare *la petite* Beatrice the strain of the ladder."

Of course. If not for that suggestion, Rosalind wouldn't have been at all surprised to see Alexandre order his men to simply drop her over the side like a bag of dirty linen.

"Will *le capitaine* be joining us?"

"*Non,* mademoiselle."

Rosalind glanced toward the quarterdeck where Alexandre stood with his back to her, listening to a short, thickset man who held a hammer and gestured with it as he spoke. The ship's carpenter, perhaps? Clearly Alexandre was preoccupied with the upkeep of his ship. All at once this shore leave took on the feeling of a temporary exile. If Rosalind had at last succeeded in driving Alexandre away, why then did she feel a sense of loss?

Some of the crew standing by lowered the chair to deck level. Rosalind took her seat. The pirates hoisted her upward with slow, gentle tugs on the ropes. As she rose into the air, the chair turned toward the quarterdeck. Alexandre now watched her ascent. Some imp of mischief prodded Rosalind.

"*Merci beaucoup, mon capitaine!*" she cried gaily. "How kind of you to see to my comfort!"

Alexandre scowled. He started to turn away, then glanced back at her. Rosalind smiled, kicked her feet, tilted her face up to the sun, doing everything she could think of to make Alexandre believe she was enjoying the jerky, dizzying ride. She hung just above the hands reaching to help her down when Alexandre's voice rang out.

"*Halte!*"

Alexandre appeared at the rail, glaring down at Rosalind. "You seem entirely too pleased to be leaving my ship, mademoiselle. Now why is that, I wonder?"

"Do you really need to ask, *mon capitaine?* Escape has been my only thought since I first laid eyes on you."

"It might have been your first, mademoiselle." Alexandre gave her a thin, knowing smile. "But not the second, or the third."

The pirates around him hooted and jeered. Rosalind realized what a fool she must look, hung out in the wind like more laundry left to dry. She did her best to mimic Alexandre's hauteur.

"*Vraiment, mon capitaine.* My first thought was escape. My second, death at your hands. My third, death at my own."

"Rosalind!" Beatrice clapped both hands over her mouth.

"Beatrice," Rosalind said. "Please be still. Do not excite yourself."

Beatrice kept her hands over her mouth, her blue eyes wide with fright.

"'Death before dishonor,' mademoiselle?" Alexandre shook his head, mouth quirked in a sneer. "How very British."

"And you, *mon capitaine?* Terrorizing innocents. How very French."

Mr. MacCaulay cleared his throat. "Miss Brooks, really, this won't do."

"Oh please," Alexandre said in English. "Do not attempt to restrain *La Belle Dame Sans Merci.* If more of your captains had even half her courage, I'd take fewer of your ships."

Mr. MacCaulay's face reddened, not with embarrassment but anger. He gave Rosalind a pointed look, but said nothing else.

Alexandre stared down at Rosalind, his face impassive. "I see I can expect no quarter from you today, mademoiselle."

Did Rosalind hear the slightest upward inflection? He could not show her any tenderness in front of his men, but perhaps Alexandre hoped she'd relent? How ironic that the Black Angel looked for mercy from her. Mindful of Mr. MacCaulay's warning, Rosalind held her tongue.

Alexandre continued to regard her steadily. "*Eh bien,* it's for the best. Enjoy your liberty, mademoiselle. You return here at sunset."

Alexandre started to turn away. Rosalind had a sudden premonition of disaster. She could not let him walk away like this. Angry, yes. Amorous, perhaps. But not this stone-cold disregard.

"Tell me, *mon capitaine,*" she said. "Is this intended for our comfort, or yours?"

Doctor Gingras started to speak. Alexandre silenced him with a raised hand. He turned back to the rail and looked down at Rosalind with dark eyes full of some old pain.

"A man does tire of being nagged and scolded."

So. He didn't want her anymore. Wasn't that the victory she'd wanted? Rosalind smiled, cold and brittle. He'd given her just the opportunity she needed to show him for the complete blackguard he was.

"Is that the great secret of *L'Ange Noir?* He makes war on English shipping just to escape his wife and children?"

Rigid silence descended. Once again the pirates near Alexandre drew back. Alexandre closed his eyes. Moments passed before he spoke.

"I have no wife, mademoiselle," he said. "Nor any children. Should *le bon Dieu* see fit to grant them to me, I will treasure them always and defend them with my last breath."

It was the answer Rosalind might have secretly hoped for. She never imagined such a weight of pain would come with that admission. She wanted to speak, to ask Alexandre's pardon for intruding on this private sorrow, but no words came to her. She cast a pleading look at Mr. MacCaulay, who could only shake his head.

Alexandre tapped his fingers on the rail, then let out a long breath. He swung one long leg over the rail, got his footing on the rope ladder, and started down it. He stopped halfway down and reached out to give Rosalind's skirts a tug, sending her spinning around like a top.

"Mon capitaine!" she cried. "What are you doing?" She clung to the ropes with her eyes tight shut while the pirates roared with laughter.

"Once again, mademoiselle, you remind me that I was about to act very poorly as your host. A gentleman would be at your side every moment to protect you from what dangers may await us." As soon as Alexandre stood in the boat, he called out, "Lower away!"

His crew obeyed, letting out more rope until Rosalind's feet almost touched the boat's deck. Before she could make a graceful exit from her seat, Alexandre scooped her up, then sat on the bench in the center of the boat.

"Make for shore, Louis."

"Oui, mon capitaine."

Once again Rosalind found herself sitting on the Black Angel's lap, trying to keep some semblance of propriety while the rising swells made her rock back and forth across the marble hardness of his thighs. His right arm still lay around her waist. His left he draped across her thighs, his hand tightening on her knee now and then to keep her firmly anchored on his lap. After the events of the morning, Rosalind had no idea how she should deal with this familiarity. Despite the indignity of her position, Rosalind couldn't help liking the feel of his arms around her. The stiff breeze blew his long hair over his shoulder, spilling it down across her cheek. The tickle of it made Rosalind smile, drawing Alexandre's attention back to her.

"Something amuses you, mademoiselle?"

Rosalind gathered the black silken streamers into one hand so she could lay them back over his shoulder. She resisted the urge to smooth his ponytail down across his broad, muscular back.

"Not a thing, *mon capitaine*. Nothing at all."

He cocked one brow, his disbelief plain, but a shade more warmth colored his smile. He had enjoyed her touch as much as she enjoyed touching him. Rosalind didn't know whether to cry or scream. He was a French pirate; she was an English lady. The ordinary rules of drawing room flirtation simply did not apply here. What was she to do?

The boat's keel hit bottom with a loud scrape. Four of the pirates abandoned their oars, rolling over the sides into the breakers. They grabbed the gunwales and hauled the boat farther up the beach. Before Rosalind could make any effort to get to her feet, Alexandre simply stood up, holding her like a large, flustered doll.

"*Mon capitaine,* really, this isn't necessary."

"But of course, mademoiselle. A gentleman would never permit you to ruin your gown wading through sea water."

Alexandre stepped down into the sea foam. He glanced back to where Beatrice still sat. "And what of you, little one? Six of my finest stand ready to carry you ashore. Which one will you favor with that privilege?"

Seeing all the pirates looking at her hopefully, Beatrice blushed to the very roots of her hair and held out her hands to Mr. MacCaulay. He sprang forward to take them and pull her into a fatherly embrace. She clung to his waistcoat.

Alexandre laughed. "Very well. Do as the little one prefers."

Rosalind offered up a silent prayer of thanks. Mr. Mac-Caulay gathered Beatrice up in his arms and followed Alexandre through the breakers and up onto the beach. The pale sand was strewn with driftwood, seaweed, and broken pieces of seashells. Above the high-water mark, the beach gave way to the tree line that marked the beginning of the jungle. A canvas pavilion had been set up in the shade. Alexandre made straight for it and set Rosalind down on the Persian carpet spread out over the sand. He kept his hands on her waist and looked into her eyes.

"Listen to me, mademoiselle. You will stay here, right here, *comprenez-vous?* On no account do you leave your little salon."

He was neither punishing her nor warning her, but speaking in deadly earnest. Rosalind nodded.

"*Oui, mon capitaine.*"

"*Très bien.* Someone will bring you some refreshment."

Mr. MacCaulay set Beatrice on her feet beside Rosalind. Rosalind promptly sat her down in the darkest part of the shade. Beatrice curled up obediently with Rosalind's shawl bundled under her head for a pillow.

Alexandre studied Mr. MacCaulay. "I would not think a man of your years capable of carrying a young woman this far."

Mr. MacCaulay smiled. "The constitution runs quite strong in my family."

"Truly? Then perhaps you would not object to lending a hand with the water barrels." Alexandre stared up at the murky clouds. "Time is not with us."

"Certainly, Captain, but the ladies might feel more comfortable if I remained."

"The ladies will be perfectly safe," Alexandre said, "as long as they remain on this spot." He gave Rosalind a stern look. "My crew is vigilant. If any trouble should befall you, simply call out for help."

Rosalind smiled. "*Merci beaucoup, mon capitaine.* Your concern is touching."

Alexandre said nothing. He looked at her for a moment longer, then turned and beckoned Mr. MacCaulay along with him back down the beach. Rosalind watched them go, wondering at this sudden civility on Alexandre's part.

One of the ship's boys came running up the sand carrying a basket and a bottle. He pulled to a breathless halt just past the edge of the carpet. He was perhaps seventeen, with dark brown hair streaked almost tawny by the sun. Rosalind took the basket from his outstretched hand.

"*Merci.* Please tell *le capitaine* we are grateful for his kindness."

"*Oui,* mademoiselle."

Just then Beatrice turned over toward them. She sat bolt upright. Rosalind laid a soothing hand on her shoulder.

"It's all right, Beatrice. The captain has sent us a picnic basket."

Beatrice frowned. "I don't understand any of this, Rosalind. They take us prisoner, yet they're kind to us. They won't let us go free, yet the Captain takes us ashore and gives us a picnic basket."

"I don't know what to make of it. One moment they're pirates yelling for blood," Rosalind mused, "and the next you'd think we were in some fashionable Parisian salon."

She unwrapped the bread and spread the cloth out between them, then laid on the feast. The food was quite good for shipboard fare. Even the wine was light and refreshing.

Beatrice reached out beyond the edge of the carpet to pick up some damp, wilted flowers lying on the ground nearby. "These would make a lovely daisy chain. Wouldn't that be fun? Perhaps there are even more colors than these. We might press one or two of the flowers and save them," Beatrice went on. "Mother would be delighted."

Rosalind thought of her own mother, pale, drawn, and sad, sitting in the drawing room busying herself with embroidery. It was very likely a floral pattern, something for Rosalind's hope chest or possibly the child she might one day bear. Mother would take such pleasure in seeing a new kind of flower. It might be the only bright spot in the endless hours of grief. Rosalind buried her face in her hands.

"Rosalind?" Beatrice struggled to her knees. "What is it? Why are you so sad?"

Rosalind scrubbed the tears from her cheeks and forced herself to smile. "Beatrice, if you want flowers, then we shall fill up my shawl with every color we can find."

Rosalind rose just beyond the edge of their pavilion and looked around. To her left, perhaps two or three yards away, glimpses of purple and red showed through the dense greenery. "There we are. Almost within arm's reach."

"Oh, but Rosalind," Beatrice said. "Do we dare go even that far? I'm sure the captain expects us to stay right here."

"The captain." Rosalind took a deep breath and squared her shoulders. "His Eminence the Captain deserves to be hung by the heels from any one of these trees."

She made for the purple and red flowers with such a determined stride Beatrice had to hurry along to keep up. Rosalind pushed aside the thick foliage and held it out of Beatrice's way.

"There, you see? Only a few steps away."

Beatrice stepped through the shrubs cautiously, glancing down around her feet with trepidation. "Is this safe, Rosalind? Who knows what might live on this island."

"We'll only be a moment. Come along, Beatrice. I think I see some yellow blossoms as well."

That turned out to be nothing more than a trick of the pallid sunlight, but even so Rosalind was pleased to discover two shades of pink, a deeper red variety, and more of the royal purple flowers. She knotted the ends of her shawl together and gave Beatrice the makeshift basket to hold. Together they circled the flowering bushes, plucking blossom after blossom until the flowers kept spilling out in a brilliant cascade.

"I think that will do." Rosalind reached for the branches and ferns she had moved aside earlier. Instead of sand leading the way to their pavilion, Rosalind saw only more greenery. "Beatrice, how many times did we walk around the bushes?"

"Once, surely, then back again to the spot with all the red flowers."

"Around once, then a quarter back." Rosalind murmured this to herself over and over like a magical formula. She reached the spot she thought was the one she wanted. Nothing looked familiar. "Beatrice? Can you hear the waves striking the shore?"

"No, not at all!" From the far side of the bush, Beatrice's voice soundly oddly muffled. "Rosalind, where are we? We must find the way back!"

Somewhere nearby a man's voice shouted something. Rosalind listened, eyes shut and ears straining, but she could make out neither the words nor the direction from which they came.

"Call out, Beatrice," she said. "I will gladly suffer the captain's displeasure as long as it means getting out of this jungle!"

Together they raised such a din they drove colorful birds from their perches in the trees around them. Rosalind held up her hand for silence. From far off they heard shouting, male voices raised in anger and confusion. From another direction, possibly closer, Rosalind heard that single voice again.

"Once more, Beatrice! I think we have their attention!"

Rosalind cried for help in English and French. Beatrice imitated her, mimicking the sounds of the foreign language with such a ponderous look of determination Rosalind forgot her fear and started to laugh.

"This is not one of England's finest moments."

Beatrice managed a sheepish smile. "What now?"

"Now we must wait. Someone heard us, we know that much." Rosalind leaned against the gnarled trunk of a nearby tree. "I'm sure the captain will have his men searching the area all too thoroughly."

A crashing in the underbrush caused Beatrice to dash to Rosalind's side. Rosalind patted her hand, but stayed between Beatrice and whatever made the noise. Man or beast, it plowed its way through the jungle with little hesitation.

"Mon capitaine?" Rosalind asked. "Is that you?"

A moment of unnatural quiet slipped by. The bushes around Rosalind and Beatrice suddenly exploded with swarthy, bearded men dressed in the colorful rags of pirates. To her horror, Rosalind realized these men were not of Alexandre's crew. Despite their flamboyance, the crew of *L'Etoile du Matin* was clean, tidy, and presentable. This lot looked more like mangy curs circling a single bone. One tall, rail-thin pirate stepped forward to bark at Rosalind in a language she didn't know. She could only shake her head and shrug helplessly.

"Inglés?" the pirate snapped. Rosalind nodded. "You go with us. Now."

"Where?" she asked. "Who are you?"

The pirate seized her by the wrist and jerked her forward. "Walk or be carried!"

The impatient glare on his villainous face told Rosalind it was not a choice but a threat.

"Not while I live!" From out of the bushes hurtled Mr. MacCaulay, brandishing a tree branch almost as thick as his arm. His sudden rush caught two of the pirates unprepared. The branch cracked against their skulls, felling them. Mr.

MacCaulay struck one more with the backswing, then spun around to plant himself between Rosalind and the pirate giving orders.

"Run!" Mr. MacCaulay thrust the tree branch at the pirate, making all four remaining pirates duck back. "On your lives, ladies, turn right around and keep running until you strike sand!"

Two of the pirates moved to flank Rosalind. She snatched her shawl out of Beatrice's hands and flung it in their faces. They swatted at the mass of yarn and flowers with their swords, slicing her shawl open in a burst of color that blinded them momentarily. Rosalind seized Beatrice's arm and dragged her along as they dashed ahead through the foliage that began to thin out. The thunderous crack of a pistol tore through the air. Rosalind ran on, sick with the horrible certainty that Mr. MacCaulay now lay dead or dying.

Beatrice jerked backward out of her grip. Rosalind spun around to see Beatrice fighting to free herself from some thorny bush that had snagged her skirt.

"Tear it, Beatrice! Now!"

"I will not! Mother made these, for Lucinda and Abigail and Mary and me."

Rosalind caught her by the arm and tried to drag her onward, but it was too late. Three of the pirates came rushing out of the green gloom. Two grabbed Rosalind's arms. The third jerked Beatrice up against him with one sinewy, tattooed forearm around her throat. The tall thin pirate came walking toward them through the trees. Giving Rosalind a pointed sneer, he blew on the smoking muzzle of his pistol.

"Yo maté al hombre viejo."

The words meant nothing to Rosalind, but the smoking muzzle told her the worst had happened. Mr. MacCaulay was dead. The pirate jerked his head back the way he'd come.

"Traiga las mujeres. Capitán Vásquez quiere que las dos estén en buena salud."

Rosalind felt true despair swamp her soul. Yves had warned Alexandre Vasquez followed them to the island. Vasquez would think he had captured the Black Angel's captives. His playthings. Whatever resentments Vasquez held toward Alexandre would surely be vented on Beatrice and herself.

Chapter Seven

Alexandre stared up at the stormy skies. An hour, perhaps less, and they would have to seek what shelter could be found in the jungle or face spending a wet night aboard the brigantine packed together like fish in a net. After one more boatload of water barrels had been shipped, he'd order his men back to *L'Etoile du Matin* to batten down every single piece of ship's gear that wasn't already fixed in place. The isle would protect them from the worst of the storm's fury. Once it passed, they could resume their usual trip back to Martinique. Alexandre had nothing pressing to do, nowhere in particular to be. At the moment that suited him very well. Rosalind was growing accustomed to the comfort of his cabin. What better place to spend the evening, keeping themselves amused?

A furious shrieking split the air. Alexandre spun around and raced up the beach, heading straight for the pavilion. It was empty. The screaming stopped, then began again. Alexandre's heart thudded with a mixture of worry and rage. Remy and a handful of the crew came running after Alexandre.

"Mon capitaine! What are we to do?"

"Find them! They can't be far!"

Alexandre plunged into the bushes to the left of the pavilion. The ground was so littered with pebbles, twigs, and leaves he could make out nothing of a trail. Off to his right, somewhere ahead, he heard Mr. MacCaulay shouting. Other voices joined in, harsh with the accent of uncouth Spanish. Alexandre lunged toward them, praying he got there in time. Something crashed through the undergrowth, moving away from him.

"Rosalind! To me! To me!"

"Alexandre!" The terror and desperation in that cry made Alexandre fight his way through the jungle with even greater force. She was there, somewhere just ahead. . . .

Pistol shots to his left made Alexandre throw himself flat on the ground. When no more shots were fired, he scrambled to his feet and broke into a small clearing. Before him lay two of Vasquez's men, sprawled in that unmistakable posture of death. Mr. MacCaulay had fallen a few yards away. Blood ran down the right side of his face. More stained his left shoulder in a spreading patch. What was left of Rosalind's shawl lay across his legs, nearly burying him in a rain of spilled flowers.

"Mon Dieu. . . ."

Remy burst in from the opposite side of the clearing. Chest heaving with exertion, he licked his lips and tried to speak. *"Mon capitaine,* we cannot find them. We cannot even hear them now."

Alexandre scowled. "They might outrun us ashore, but they'll never do so at sea! Back to the ship! All hands! Back to the ship!"

"What of the *Anglais, mon capitaine?"*

"Take him back aboard."

Remy looked puzzled. *"Pourquoi, mon capitaine?* He can die here as easily as he can in the hold."

"Just do as you're told. Take him to Gingras."

Remy ducked his head in a placating nod and whistled for

two pirates to join him. Together they bundled Mr. Mac-Caulay up and hustled him toward the ship's boat. Alexandre followed them, silently cursing himself for a fool. He could have made the dangers of the isle perfectly clear to Rosalind, but that would have distressed the little one and spoiled the entire purpose of this outing. Now Rosalind and Beatrice had fallen into the hands of Vasquez. There could be no doubt about it. At this very moment they were being dragged across the isle to whatever cover Vasquez had slunk into, sitting there biding his time like an eel waiting to bite.

Alexandre cast one last furious glance at the empty pavilion, then ran down the beach to the boat. He rolled over the gunwale and took his seat in the bow. The rowers worked hard, propelling the boat across the water to *L'Etoile du Matin.* Alexandre looked up at the lowering skies. The storm was blowing up again, with black clouds and bad wind. They'd be lucky to get out into the current. As they neared the *Diabolique,* Alexandre cupped both hands to his mouth.

"Etienne!" he shouted. "Etienne, make for the far side of the island! Vasquez has taken the women!"

Etienne Duchard waved his red kerchief in reply. His crew jumped to it, swarming up the mast and changing the sails to take greatest advantage of the uncertain wind.

As soon as the boat touched the hull of *L'Etoile du Matin,* Alexandre climbed up the rope ladder, shouting for Yves. "Take us out! I want the ship out into the current before this storm breaks."

Yves looked perplexed, then gave the helmsman a few terse orders. *"Mon capitaine,* has something happened? I thought you wished to ride out the storm here."

"Vasquez did follow us. He made for the far side of the isle, then sent his bilge-swilling swine to make a surprise attack." Alexandre slammed one fist against the rail. "I should have killed him years ago!"

Yves frowned. He glanced around, then over the side at the ship's boat. "You have ordered the ladies to remain ashore?"

"Imbecile! Would I do that here, on Isla la Veche?" Alexandre shook his head. "Vasquez's vermin were waiting for their moment. Stubborn little shrike that she is, Mademoiselle Rosalind provided it for them."

"Morbleu!" Yves sighed and put his hand over his eyes. "What has she done now?"

"Wandered off. To pick flowers, from the look of it. We heard her screaming, but we couldn't get to her in time." The anger within Alexandre seethed, leaving a scorching pain in his chest. "Both women are gone. We found the *Anglais* half-dead from his wounds." His lips curved in a wolfish smile. "It's him we have to thank for knowing who our enemy is. He killed two of them with nothing more than a tree branch."

"I wonder who that old man is," Yves said. "Never yet have I met a solicitor who was worth anything in a fight."

Alexandre nodded. *"Vraiment.* That will have to wait. We must catch Vasquez's scow before he can ride the storm and leave us behind."

"Oui, mon capitaine."

A quarter of an hour later, it was plain to Alexandre there was no hope of besting the storm. The contrary wind kept giving out just as the sails were set to catch it. The *Diabolique* fared little better. She managed to slip out of the cove, but the force of the growing stormfront left her all but pinned against the isle's coastline. *L'Etoile du Matin* rode the choppy waves with an uneasy rolling. Alexandre knew the feel of his ship. He understood she was not pleased. This was not what she had been made for. Hunting down Vasquez was an acceptable reason, but not this mad flight to recapture two captives who'd given him nothing but trouble.

Sharp gusts of wind now assaulted the masts. Alexandre heard a cry of alarm and spun to face the bow. Two of his crew wrestled with the jib sail. One lost his grip and tumbled back over the bowsprit to hit the water with a splash. Men farther astern threw him a line and dragged him back aboard. All through the rigging, the men were clamping on to whatever was nearest and sturdiest. The evening ahead would see much use of the old sailor's rule, "One hand for the ship and one for yourself." A cloudburst broke over the deck, soaking Alexandre to the skin in mere moments.

"Mon capitaine!" Yves shouted above the rising wind. *"C'est impossible!* She cannot clear the cove without the risk of heeling over or breaching on the rocks!"

Alexandre shook his head. *"C'est incroyable! L'Etoile du Matin* has outrun inshore patrols in worse than this!"

"That was in the open sea, *mon capitaine.* With a strong wind behind us."

"That he stole my prisoners is insult enough. That *le bâtard Espagnol* could claim he outran my ship— It is not to be borne!" Alexandre ran up to the quarterdeck and seized the wheel, shouldering the helmsman aside.

Yves followed him. "You have a plan, *mon capitaine?"*

"We tack back and forth, gaining only inches if we must, until we are able to get out into the current. Every moment is precious now. Make them jump to it!"

Chapter Eight

Rosalind stood on the main deck of *La Fortuna,* the twenty-gun schooner captained by Ricardo Vasquez. The wind whipped at her braid, snapping it against her cheek. Cold spray drenched her. Beatrice held her so tightly around the waist she could scarcely breathe. They were both terrified, scratched and bruised, and driven to exhaustion. Their pirate captors had marched them through the jungle to the far shore. The instant Rosalind and Beatrice were both aboard, *La Fortuna* had shot out into the current, riding the incoming stormfront westward.

As word of their arrival spread, pirates came boiling up out of the hatches both fore and aft. The unholy glee on their faces struck a chill deep into Rosalind's heart. They jabbered at each other in Spanish, pushing and shoving to get closer to Rosalind and Beatrice. The tall, skinny pirate with the voice like a whip drove them back again and again. All at once he gave Rosalind a shove toward the stern. She almost lost her footing on the slippery deck. Righting herself, she shepherded Beatrice along, ignoring the many hands waiting to paw at her.

A man stood on the quarterdeck hunched up inside a scarlet redingote, looking less like a human being than a gargoyle squatting there in the worsening weather. Ricardo Vasquez was only a little taller than Rosalind. The face he turned toward her froze her blood. He was young, might once have been handsome, but a deep scar split his left cheek. He raised one hand to his mouth and drew on his cigar.

"Quíen está?" He blew out a cloud of foul smoke. *"Habla Español?"*

With a helpless shrug, Rosalind shook her head.

"Parlez-vous Français?" he asked.

She flinched again at the coarseness of his accent. *"Oui."*

His hand cracked against her cheek. "You will address me as *mon capitaine.*"

Rosalind forced the words out through the stinging pain. *"Oui, mon capitaine."*

"So that primping whoreson lied to me. He meant to keep you for himself." Vasquez hooted with laughter, sharing the joke with his men. *"L'Ange Noir,* terror of the Caribbean, and he can't even keep one little English girl in her place. The shame of this will gnaw at his liver forever!"

Vasquez barked an order. More lanterns surrounded Rosalind. Rough hands yanked Beatrice away from her. Vasquez looked Rosalind over, pinching the ripped and stained taffeta of her sleeve between his thumb and forefinger. He laughed again, making his scar wrinkle with his devilish pleasure.

"This is too good, *chère. L'Ange Noir* will spend this dirty night in a cold and empty bed. That alone will enrage him." He seized Rosalind's chin, glaring into her eyes. "But that you fell into my arms, now that will drive him mad."

Vasquez caught the tail of Rosalind's braid and wrapped it around her throat, jerking her up on her toes. He thrust his face close to hers. "Your life is mine! Be happy you are worth more to me alive than dead. The two of you will bring a good price at Port Royal."

Rosalind shut her eyes against his leer. This was what she had expected from Alexandre. Yet he had yielded to her terms, tried to make some show of playing the gentleman. Here there would be no pretenses at all.

"El Capitán!" One of the pirates from the gun deck stepped forward, speaking a rapid stream of Spanish. He could have been Vasquez's younger brother, dressed up in a soiled white shirt and tight black trousers, his face as grim and depraved. Other pirates nearby nodded, moving to stand with him. More pirates were rushing up from belowdecks, gathering into a noisy mob.

Vasquez laughed. "Shall I tell you what they want, *chèrie?* They want you."

Rosalind swallowed painfully beneath the pressure of her braid. She shivered, eyes shut against the mass of jeering pirates.

"My men insist I hand you over to them. I have told them we'd be much wiser to sell you and divide your price among us. They don't believe you'll bring enough to make that the better choice."

Vasquez unwound Rosalind's braid from around her throat. He tugged the ribbon free then fumbled at the plaits, tangling her hair as he tried to loosen it. At last the damp mass hung down around her, blown about by the furious winds. Vasquez jerked Rosalind around to face his crew.

"It is up to you, *chèrie,"* Vasquez hissed into her ear. "You must show them how much you are worth. Only you can convince them how high a price you will bring."

"And how am I to do that, *mon capitaine?"* Rosalind spoke in a cold, clear voice, giving no sign that she was drowning in despair.

Vasquez replied by seizing the shoulders of Rosalind's gown and splitting the taffeta down her back, then tore the gown down to Rosalind's waist. Gripping her wrists, Vasquez held her arms out at her sides. Rosalind fought his grip, shaking her head in an effort to make her hair fall down over her breasts. The pirates roared their approval, whistling and slapping their hands together. Vasquez called out to them. They answered with nods and more shouting.

"Well done, *chèrie*. We are all agreed." He licked her ear, his breath hot and foul. "Remember this: If not for me, they'd be swarming over you like flies on a dung heap. I doubt you would have lived long enough to amuse more than a dozen of them."

He marched Rosalind back down the stairs and shoved her through a doorway. She stumbled farther into the cabin, then sank down onto the deck, gathering her hair over her breasts and crossing her arms tight. The cabin reeked of unwashed flesh and rotting food. Roaches scuttled among the remains of a meal left on the little table in one corner. A hammock had been slung along the starboard bulkhead, covered by a tangled mess of stained blankets.

The tall, skinny pirate carried Beatrice in, slung over one shoulder like a sack of grain. He muttered a question at Vasquez. With a jerk of his head, Vasquez indicated the hammock. The pirate dumped Beatrice into it. She made no sound, her arms flopping limply over the side. Rosalind prayed Beatrice had merely fainted, instead of slipping into a lethal coma. She didn't dare do anything to draw Vasquez's attention to the helpless girl.

Vasquez took a knife from the clutter on the table. He stood directly in front of Rosalind and tapped the tip of her nose with the flat of the blade.

"You will find me a hard master, *chèrie*." He turned away to root inside a crate shoved up against the bulkhead. He threw a pile of red cloth onto the bed. "Put those on."

Rosalind hesitated. Vasquez's hand cracked against the back of her head.

"Move, you stupid slut!"

Rosalind wobbled to her feet, stars flashing behind her eyes. She lifted one corner of the cloth. It was silk, a red so dark it reminded Rosalind of garnets, or blood, with a cascade of tiny flowers embroidered in gold and silver thread. Old stains and stale tobacco smoke had dulled the costly fabric. A long rope of fat pearls spilled out of the bundle, tangled in two heavy gold bracelets. She stared at the whorish costume, wondering how many other women had worn it, and what had happened to them. Rosalind dropped the cloth, wiping her fingers on her skirt.

Vasquez sat down at the table and grabbed a half-empty bottle. He yanked the cork out with his teeth and spat it aside, then poured himself a full tankard. "Make yourself pretty for me, *chérie*."

Rosalind forced herself to look at him. In the better light Vasquez's scar was even more revolting. His eyes were a muddy hazel, his black hair greasy, his hands grimy and blunt-fingered, his broken nails encrusted with dirt and worse. She shuddered.

"*S'il-vous plaît, mon capitaine.* My sister is sick. A fever, I think. She needs attention."

"So do I, *chérie*. Make me happy and we'll see about your sister."

Rosalind felt a mad sense of déja vu. Again she faced the same terms, but this time in a much cruder form. With trembling hands she freed what few fastenings still held her gown together, then let it fall.

"And the rest of it as well," Vasquez snapped.

Rosalind obeyed, casting aside her corset and petticoat bloomers. Shame stained her cheeks a deep red. Only the heavy curtain of her hair shielded her now.

Vasquez whistled. "What a pretty picture, an *Anglaise* dressed in nothing but her shoes and stockings. Look at me, *chérie*."

Rosalind didn't move. If she raised her head, her hair might swing back. She wondered if it was possible to literally die of shame.

Vasquez stabbed his knife into the scarred tabletop. "I said look at me!"

Rosalind straightened. Her hair slipped back over her shoulders, leaving a few golden tresses like garlands across her breasts.

Vasquez nodded. "I like that. I like that very much."

Moments of silence crawled past. Rosalind could feel the slimy touch of those muddy eyes all over her body.

"Now put on the dress."

Rosalind fumbled with the unfamiliar garment, recoiling at the suspicious nature of the stains on it. She found the holes for her arms and pulled the gown down over her head. The silk hugged her breasts and hips, draping over her in a way that made her look something worse than naked. The skirt was slit so high that with every step she'd bare her leg to the hip. Her painful blush deepened, bringing fresh tears to her eyes. She struggled with the gown, trying to tug it into some semblance of modesty. Vasquez laughed.

"You'll make a fine whore, *ma fille*. Ripe and sweet and ready for plucking." He smothered a belch against the back of his hand. "Now the jewels."

Rosalind fitted a bracelet onto each wrist. The gold warmed against her skin. She'd be much happier to feel the rusty iron shackle that had bound her in Alexandre's brig. She dropped the pearls around her neck. They hung in the silken valley between her breasts, weighing the fabric down and pulling it tighter.

"Good. Very good. Now come here." Vasquez slapped his knee.

Rosalind kept her eyes on the deck. Her vision blurred as more tears flooded her eyes. Alexandre meant to have her, but he claimed he took pride in making sure his women enjoyed themselves. Had she not turned away from him, he would have taught her even greater pleasures. . . . She shook her head against the peculiar longing within her, a longing that defied all reason or sense.

Mistaking that for refusal, Vasquez grabbed her wrist and jerked her down onto his lap. In the lantern light he looked all the more like a gargoyle as he grinned at her with tobacco-stained teeth. Fright and exhaustion made Rosalind feel faint. She swayed. Vasquez threw one arm around her waist, crushing her against his chest.

"To take a woman from that poxy peacock's bed, to have her here with me while the great *L'Ange Noir* rages at the loss of her. . . ." Vasquez shook his head. "It is too much. I have waited for such a day, dreamed of it, even prayed for it. And here you are."

He pulled his knife free from the tabletop and sighted along the edge, then began stroking the flat of it up and down Rosalind's bare arm. Rosalind held still, denying him the reaction he so obviously wanted.

"What color is your blood, *chèrie*?"

"Wh-what?"

"I asked you the color of your blood."

"Red, *mon capitaine*. Like anyone's."

"Mais non. My blood is red. The blood of my men is red. I have seen enough of both to know. But the English, and the French, God curse them all. . . ." Vasquez dropped the knife. He snatched up his tankard and drank deeply, thumping the tankard on the table. "Their blood is finer, purer, more worthy than the blood of my people."

He flung aside the tankard and grabbed the knife, pressing down not quite hard enough to cut Rosalind. Tears spilled down her cheeks, tears of fright and despair.

"Will I see your blood, *chèrie*? Or has that arrogant bastard bcatcn mc to that treasure as well?"

Rosalind shook her head, confused. *"Non, mon capitaine.* He did not hurt me."

"I mean this treasure!" His hand slid down her belly. Rosalind clamped her thighs together and wrenched herself out of his grip. Vasquez leveled the knife at her.

"Get back here!" A scowl darkened Vasquez's hideous features. He rose slowly. "Well? Did he have you or not?"

Rosalind faced him, breathing hard. She didn't know which was wiser, to deny Alexandre had raped her or to claim her virginity was gone. Those bleary eyes bored into her, watching for a lie. Not trusting her voice, Rosalind shook her head.

"Still a virgin? Damn it to hell." Vasquez cursed in a low grumbling stream of Spanish. "Be thankful I need the money, *chèrie,* or you'd be on your back already."

"You mean—you won't—"

He tossed his knife aside and stepped up behind her, jerking her hips back against his. He ground himself against her, chuckling into her ear.

"I can use you as I like and still leave you a virgin. The whorehouses will pay even more for a girl who knows a few tricks." His hands slid up to her breasts, rubbing them together, grinding the pearls into her skin. "I might make enough on your sister to keep you for a while. You'd like that, wouldn't you?" He squeezed harder, making Rosalind cry out in pain. "Tell me you'd like that!"

"*Oui, mon capitaine.*" The words came out in a strangled whisper.

"*L'Ange Noir* kept you from me." Vasquez breathed the words into her ear. "That means you're worth something to him. How much, I wonder?" He spun her around and shoved her up against the port bulkhead. Those muddy eyes narrowed as he studied her. "Who are you, little English girl?"

"Rosalind Brooks. I—I'm a teacher."

Vasquez stared down at her for a long moment, then grinned. "Don't lie to me." He ran a stubby forefinger down her throat. "You want to stay pretty, don't you?"

Rosalind fought to keep her voice steady. "I am Rosalind Brooks. I teach English to the native children on Jamaica."

Laughing, Vasquez shook his head. "It doesn't matter, little Rosa. *L'Ange Noir* will come for you. To do anything else would mean living with the knowledge that I took a woman away from him." He stared off into the distance, an evil smile on his face. "He will come. And then I will kill him."

Vasquez snatched up Rosalind's ruined gown. "But first, I will teach him what a fool he was to cheat me. He'll see this flying from my main mast." He gripped the rope of pearls, twisting it around his fist until Rosalind started to choke. "My new red flag, soaked in your pretty English blood!"

Rosalind screamed, fighting against the bite of the pearls. The roaring in her ears became a thundering darkness that smothered her.

Chapter Nine

The worsening weather matched Alexandre's mood. He stood in the bow, straining to see ahead through the blackness. Cold mist soaked his shirt. It clung to him like a clammy second skin. The wind shrieked through the rigging. Heavy clouds covered the moon, promising more rain. He'd been chasing *La Fortuna* for four hours and had come no closer to catching her. *L'Etoile du Matin* was as fast as a brigantine could be, but with the wind against her and her hold full of cargo from the *Bird of Paradise,* she couldn't keep up with *La Fortuna*. Alexandre slammed a fist down on the rail, cursing the turn of luck that gave Vasquez every advantage.

Yves appeared at his elbow. "If we cannot catch him before he passes the reefs, we've got to let him go."

"We'll catch him. God and the Devil can't both be against us. One of them will see us through."

"Even if that puts us in sight of land? Only the price on our heads will force the naval patrols to try taking us alive."

Alexandre scowled. "You talk too much, *mon ami*. Trim the sails."

"As you wish. The *Diabolique* would have been the better choice for chasing him."

"For speed, *oui*, but not for sending that thieving scum to the bottom."

Alexandre glared out into the night. Vasquez's presence in the Caribbean was something he should have dealt with long ago. The swine harassed French and English shipping with equal incompetence. It was a wonder Vasquez's own crew hadn't thrown him to the sharks. Alexandre cursed the lust for Rosalind that had made him so impatient. If he'd had a single clear thought in his head he could have satisfied Vasquez with the Englishman and kept the two women for himself. That would have shown Rosalind he wasn't the monster she claimed.

Beneath his anger churned cold dread. As much as he longed to beat Rosalind's sweet bottom until she begged for mercy, he'd be satisfied to see her safely bundled up beneath his blankets. This unwelcome surge of tenderness annoyed him. What madness possessed him that he was willing to risk a battle with a twenty-gun schooner over one troublesome English girl? The English were his sworn enemies, just as they had been ever since the day those English privateers had the gall to attack the *Eugenie*. Bad weather and the Devil's own luck turned the battle in their favor. Alexandre cursed as the memories rushed in to fill him with their endless pain. Lieutenant Sans Souci, that perfect example of why God forbade bestiality, taking the helm and turning a minor skirmish into a losing battle. Damn him! Thanks to his impeccable family connections, he sat drinking fine wines with the *crème de la crème* in Paris, while Alexandre skulked among the scum of the earth too far from home.

He spun away from the rail, hands clapped to his ears. The screams still haunted him, the cries of his shipmates dying because he hadn't had the courage to shoot Sans Souci when the opportunity came. Eighty lives lost, the *Eugenie* so much splintered wood, and all because he hesitated a moment too long. He lifted his head to the rain that now began to fall, hoping the drops streaming down his cheeks might douse the pain twisting like a knife in his heart. He never hesitated now. Not now, when the sight of an English vessel made those screams echo in his mind. The sound of cannon fire could drown them out, but only for a little while. And then he'd have to find some other target and begin again.

"*Mon capitaine?*" Yves stood nearby, watching him with a wary eye.

Alexandre tried to keep his voice level, to hide the fury boiling within him. "What is it?"

"The *Diabolique* has taken on all she can. We'll need the wind behind us. Otherwise—"

"It will turn." Alexandre yanked the knife from his boot and spun around to hurl it into the face of the storm. "*Vive la France,* damn you! For France! For the glory that should have been ours!"

Yves laid a hand on his shoulder. "*Mon ami,* go inside. I will bring you any news."

Alexandre glared up at the turbulent skies. "I can hear them, Yves."

Yves patted his shoulder. "I know." They stood together, surrounded by old ghosts. "Go on, *mon ami*. Think about how you will sink *La Fortuna*. Vasquez is an animal, but even rats can be clever."

The voice of reason told him Yves was right as usual. If he insisted on taking such risks for this little milkmaid, he should at least prepare his strategy. With a nod he walked back to his cabin through the driving rain. Inside, he pulled off his boots, then stripped away his sodden shirt and breeches and reached for dry clothing. He stopped, thinking of the silly *Anglais* frock Rosalind had been wearing. Did she still wear it even now? Or had Vasquez already destroyed it, along with Rosalind's virtue, her spirit, perhaps even her life? Even she couldn't be clever enough to turn Vasquez from his depraved purpose.

Alexandre flung himself down on his bed, wishing Rosalind lay beside him, wishing he hadn't hesitated that morning, but had taken her, leaving her deaf to any voice but her own as she cried out to him in ecstasy. Jade! She'd defied him, laughed at him, nearly struck him, had in fact pulled his hair, and all in defense of that thin little mouse who would surely have fainted if he'd kissed her a moment longer. No, Sister Beatrice would have given him no real pleasure at all. Relief, yes, but no satisfaction. He would have that satisfaction once he had Rosalind at his mercy again.

And yet . . . And yet . . . Despite his fury, Alexandre could not deny a grudging admiration. There was no end to the courage of his little milkmaid. Unfortunately for her, courage was not a virtue Vasquez appreciated in a woman. How long would she manage to hold off the stinking bilge rats Vasquez called his crew? Filth like that saw such golden perfection once in their blighted lives, if ever. They would all want a turn at her, to say nothing of what would surely befall poor little Beatrice. Rosalind's only hope lay in making Vasquez stand between her and his crew.

Alexandre pulled on a fresh pair of breeches, then sat down with a bottle of rum and tried to think. *La Fortuna* had more guns and more sail, but Vasquez was a slow, clumsy tactician. His men were badly disciplined and too lazy to move with the speed that would save their lives. Come daybreak *L'Etoile du Matin* would be clearly visible, giving Vasquez all the time he needed to prepare. Alexandre mulled over the possible strategies. Two things had to happen, and in precise order. He must get Rosalind off Vasquez's ship, then send that ship to the bottom. He rose to pace around the cabin, his thoughts turning again and again to Rosalind, to the way she'd attacked and even disarmed Henri, her delight in baiting Alexandre, and the cold precision in her voice when she'd accused him of cowardice in preying on the girl Beatrice. Who was she? No common schoolteacher possessed such a fearless, defiant spirit.

Alexandre carried the bottle to his escritoire and turned

up the flame in his oil lamp. Inside the top drawer were the ship's papers taken from the *Bird of Paradise*. He thumbed through the documents, searching the tidy lines of Captain Harris's handwriting for any mention of Miss Rosalind Brooks. A sheet of fine stationery fell out, fluttering down to the deck. He picked it up and studied it.

> *"My dear William,*
>   *You will see to it Lady Rosalind Hanshaw reaches Jamaica in complete safety. Understand that she is my fiancée and I will be most displeased if any harm should come to her. Upon your successful arrival in Jamaica, you will see Lady Rosalind to the very door of Jasmine Court. My agents will be in touch with you regarding compensation for this additional effort on your part.*
> >   *Your obedient, etc.,*
> >   *Edward Murdock"*

Alexandre read the note again, then once more, his eyes wide with astonishment. Laughter rose up inside him, gaining strength until he threw his head back and roared with delight. A simple schoolteacher indeed! He'd known that was nonsense from the very first. Rosalind was far too lovely, far too elegant even in her *déshabillé*. He sat back, the warm glow of victory spreading through him. What a coup, to know what Rosalind had gone to such lengths to conceal from him! The little nun must know nothing. But why? Why was Rosalind hiding her true identity? What business sent her alone and unguarded into the perils of the Caribbean?

As if all that wasn't mystery enough, she was in fact to be married to none other than Murdock himself! It was too much to believe. His flagging spirits soared with the wild burst of excitement that presaged another glorious triumph. Now there was no question at all. He must retrieve Rosalind. Knowing her secret would give him just the advantage he needed to conquer the last of her resistance. He would make such love to Rosalind she would belong to him, body and soul. And then he would make Murdock pay handsomely for her return.

Alexandre grinned down at the note. The safe return of Murdock's fiancée would rank as the greatest of favors, one that would cost Murdock far more than any of the others. Up to now it had merely been a matter of sinking Murdock's rivals and keeping the spoils. Now it was Rosalind herself. Alexandre chuckled with wicked delight. Murdock might still treasure her, might really believe *L'Ange Noir* wouldn't be foolish enough to touch his fiancée. Come the wedding night he'd learn the truth, that the jewel of Rosalind's virginity had already been stolen by *L'Ange Noir*.

Alexandre tucked the papers away in his escritoire, then hurried out on deck. Yves stood on the quarterdeck. When he caught sight of Alexandre's satisfied expression, one corner of his mouth lifted.

"Good news, *mon capitaine?*"

"*Mais oui.* Good news indeed." Alexandre swaggered over to him. "Our little schoolteacher is in truth Lady Rosalind Hanshaw, who has the bad luck and worse taste to be the fiancée of none other than Edward Murdock himself."

A look of relief mellowed Yves's reserve. "*Très bien.* We can give up this mad chase and leave Vasquez to Murdock's tender mercies."

"You lazy fool! Can't you see the opportunity here? Murdock will be in our debt forever once we rescue his bride-to-be."

"And that is a good thing, is it?"

"*Certainement!* It's high time that arrogant *Anglais* shopkeeper was reminded of how much he owes me."

"The true good fortune here lies in letting Murdock know who has his little *chèrie amie.* Murdock can risk his men and his ships taking her back. Vasquez will hang and that problem will be solved with no cost to us."

"No cost? Is that all this means to you? A few pistoles or doubloons here and there?"

Yves shrugged. "I am a pirate, *mon capitaine*. That is what matters to me."

Alexandre stared out across the heaving waves. The anger always simmering in him threatened to ignite into pure rage. To kill Vasquez, to put Murdock under such an immense obligation to Alexandre, and best of all, to have Rosalind back aboard his ship, at his mercy, knowing who she really was. . . .

"I will have her back. I will see Vasquez dead by sunset. And you will have the pleasure of stripping Vasquez's ship of every single pistole or doubloon."

Yves shook his head. "You know I will do as you say, *mon ami*. One last thought, *s'il-vous plaît*?"

"It's not like you to beg."

"And it's not like you to throw away time and supplies chasing after one girl who's more trouble than she's worth." Yves put his hands on Alexandre's shoulders. "You cannot bring our dead shipmates back to life by getting even more killed this way. Vasquez is not worth one single drop of French blood. Neither is Murdock. Neither is she."

Alexandre's mouth set in a grim line. "Continue on course. If the wind favors us, we'll halve the distance by dawn."

Yves's expression hardened. He saluted. *"Immediatement, mon capitaine."*

Alexandre turned away from Yves's silent disapproval and stalked back across the deck to his cabin. Out of habit he reached for the key to the liquor cabinet, then scowled. No brandy. That would remind him of the taste of that minx's lips. He sprawled backward across his bed, arms flung over his eyes. Yves's entirely sensible warnings left him nettled. He'd much prefer to have Yves share his enthusiasm than simply carry out his orders.

A faint scent teased him, a lingering sweetness mixed with the tang of brine. He raised his head from the pillow. Her hair. It had to be the scent of Rosalind's magnificent golden hair. He recalled the sight of it, the waves of lustrous honey flung across his pillow. What he would give to see that same sight now, to have Rosalind in his arms once again. He sat up with his back against the bulkhead, gathering the pillow against his chest. Now just the thought of her made his blood pulse hotly through his veins. Little did he need the extra vexation of thwarted desire, yet he was reluctant to let go of this link between them.

Never had he met an adversary so well-armed to do battle in the arena of lovemaking. So clever, so shapely, her virgin senses alive now to the pleasure that awaited her in his arms. What a victory, to make this proud, fierce, wild beauty yield, to make her love him beyond all sense or reason. Alexandre smiled. Now his course was set. His thoughts were clear. He would take Rosalind back from Vasquez. And then he would dedicate himself to her total enslavement.

Chapter Ten

Rosalind woke to the sound of a horrible clanging that made her temples throb with pain. Just opening her eyes hurt. Sunlight streamed in through the cabin's one stern window, so bright Rosalind covered her eyes with her hands. Her dry throat forced her to swallow, bringing more pain. She touched her neck and winced. The pearls had left a ring of bruises. She still wore them along with the gold bracelets and the indecent dress. She struggled to sit up, tugging the soiled red silk into place over her legs. Every muscle ached from spending the cold hours slumped on the hard wooden planks of the deck. Her hair hung down around her in a tangled mass.

Rosalind glanced around the empty cabin. No sign of Vasquez. That was some mercy at least. She frowned, rubbing at her aching temples. It was so difficult to think through the haze of pain and fatigue. Yet she had to think, to come up with some kind of plan. Did she try to arm herself against Vasquez's next attack, or would that simply provoke him into greater brutality? Her only advantage lay in reminding him the more marks he put on her, the poorer a price she'd bring when he put her up for sale in Port Royal. The very idea left her ill with fright. To think she must now use her future worth as a prostitute as the means to keep herself alive and whole. . . .

Where was Beatrice? Rosalind turned to look at the hammock. Beatrice lay there, just as she'd fallen when the pirate dumped her into it. Rosalind got to her feet, wincing as every joint complained. She hobbled over to the hammock and laid the back of her hand against Beatrice's forehead. Still hot. The poor child would need water at the very least.

A sudden series of explosions outside made Rosalind cry out with the pain of her headache. Now she became aware of all the shouting out on deck, many voices yelling in Spanish above the roar of what must be the cannons. The cannons. Alexandre! Last night Vasquez seemed certain Alexandre would pursue them. She could only pray that was true. Alexandre might be no more honorable than Vasquez, but at least he didn't rave like a madman while brandishing a knife.

Rosalind tottered to the cabin door and pulled it open. The burst of sunlight made her cry out again, clutching the door jamb for support. She peered through slitted eyes at the ship off the port bow. A merchantman, with the upper third of its mainmast shot away. Rigging tumbled down across its deck. Rosalind searched the two remaining masts for some ensign, some flag that would tell her whose ship that was. There on the mizzenmast flew Mr. Murdock's colors. This was a ship of his personal fleet! If only she could get to that ship and tell the captain who she was, perhaps then she might truly be delivered. The agony threatening to split Rosalind's skull argued against any hope of a frantic swim. *La Fortuna*'s cannons fired again. Two balls struck the merchantman at the waterline. Another demolished still more of the mainmast. Rosalind hung her head, dismally certain who the victor would be.

"*Bonjour, chèrie.*" Vasquez appeared above her, walking down the steps from the quarterdeck. "You bring us luck. A fine fat English ship, full of rich cargo. My men will be a little happier now. *Gracias a Dios!*"

Vasquez gripped her arm and dragged her out into direct sunlight. Rosalind flinched.

"Are you sick, *chèrie?*"

"*Oui, mon capitaine.* My sister—"

"Then you'd best get well quickly. The whorehouses won't pay for girls who can't work." He pushed her back inside. "Clean my cabin. Do it well enough and we'll see about your sister." He pulled the door shut with a bang.

Rosalind fumed. Her thoughts veered one way then another, trying desperately to avoid thinking about the fate of the English sailors aboard the merchantman. A new thought struck her, one so horrible the wooden dish she held fell from her hand to clatter on the deck. Vasquez had convinced these pirates they'd turn a better profit by selling her and Beatrice to a whorehouse. Now they had captured an English merchantman. They were rich, possessed of a new ship and everything on it. Instead of sparing Rosalind and Beatrice for the sake of a few extra ducats, these vermin would be thinking of nothing but slaking their grotesque appetites on unwilling victims. Rosalind's fear of dying aboard *L'Etoile du Matin* was nothing to the cold terror gripping her now.

The noise on deck quieted. Rosalind heard Vasquez shouting in Spanish, then a trembling voice speaking English. Rosalind pressed her ear to the cabin door. Another English voice answered, sullen and terse. Heavy footsteps approached the cabin door. Rosalind sprang back just before it flew open. The short bearded pirate named Pedro grabbed her by the arm and dragged her through the mass of pirates crowding the main deck.

Vasquez leaned against the mainmast, puffing another foul cigar, watching the frenzy of activity aboard the merchantman. His prize crew had gone aboard to take control of the vessel. Rosalind turned away from the spectacle to find Vasquez now staring at her.

"Chèrie," Vasquez said. "Do you know this English dog?"

Two of his men dragged a third man forward and flung him down on his knees before Vasquez. An older man, he wore the brown wool coat and breeches of a gentleman. Blood matted his gray hair. One eye was already beginning to blacken. Gyves hung from his wrists.

Rosalind shook her head. *"Non, mon capitaine."*

"What was the name of your ship? The name of her captain?"

"The *Bird of Paradise, mon capitaine.* The captain's name was Harris."

At the mention of that name, the Englishman on his knees raised his head. "Did she say Harris?"

Vasquez turned and spoke in rapid Spanish to the skinny English sailor who stood trembling between two of Vasquez's men. The sailor nodded.

"Cap'n Bellamy, sir, Cap'n Vasquez says ours ain't the first English ship he's taken this week. He says he took a ship named the *Bird of Paradise* just yesterday."

Captain Bellamy's face flushed a deep red. He looked away, but not before Rosalind caught the glint of a tear in his eye.

"Seamen Walsh, you tell this scabrous gull dropping he's as good as dead. I happen to know one of the passengers aboard that ship was Edward Murdock's fiancée, as pretty and sweet as God ever made a woman. Mr. Murdock will hunt this scurvy excuse for a bottom feeder to the ends of the earth."

Rosalind's heart thudded painfully. Fiancée? Mr. Murdock's fiancée? A sudden fierce disorientation struck Rosalind, making nonsense of the voices around her. How could this Captain Bellamy, this total stranger, know that she was Edward Murdock's fiancée, when Mr. Murdock had yet to make a formal proposal? More to the point, when she hadn't yet accepted it? Confusion gave way to mortifying certainty. There could be only one explanation. Mr. Murdock had the absolutely breathtaking presumption to make his intentions known publicly before the object of those intentions had given her consent!

Rosalind wrenched her mind back to the scene before her. Her immediate peril demanded attention. She had to keep Vasquez from realizing who she was. Seaman Walsh looked from Captain Bellamy to Vasquez and back. He clearly didn't relish the notion of conveying Captain Bellamy's sentiments to Vasquez.

"I was on that ship!" Rosalind's shout made all heads turn. She spoke in English, hoping Seaman Walsh and Captain Bellamy would understand what she was really trying to tell them. "She died. A cannonball hit the mast and a spar came down on her head."

Captain Bellamy stared at her. His eyes widened. The recognition there gave way to dawning horror.

"En Français," Vasquez snapped.

Rosalind repeated herself in French. Vasquez eyed her, then studied Captain Bellamy. He spoke to Seaman Walsh.

"Cap'n Bellamy, sir, Cap'n Vasquez wants to know how many women were aboard that ship."

Captain Bellamy said nothing. Vasquez barked an order at Pedro, who stepped forward and looped a length of cord several times around Captain Bellamy's temples. Pedro jerked hard on the cord, pulling it tight and driving a gasp of pain out of Captain Bellamy. Rosalind wanted to scream, to grab a pistol and put an end to Vasquez's evil.

"Please, Cap'n Bellamy, sir," Seaman Walsh said. "He'll take his time killing you!"

"He will anyway, lad."

Vasquez gave Pedro another order and stepped away from the mainmast. Pedro hauled Captain Bellamy up onto his feet and shoved him up against the mast.

"Stop!" Rosalind caught Pedro's arm and dragged at it. "Please, Captain Bellamy, just tell them what they want to know. I can't bear to see you tortured!"

Captain Bellamy looked at her with the deepest sorrow. "Is it true, my lady? Did these scum kill Captain Harris?"

Pedro tried to shove Rosalind away. She ducked around him and clung to Captain Bellamy's jacket. "No! The *Bird of Paradise* was attacked by the Black Angel."

"Oh dear God. That's even worse!"

"Captain Harris is alive! The Black Angel doesn't believe in killing the goose that lays the golden eggs."

Relief flooded Captain Bellamy's face. "God bless you, dear lady. You have no idea the comfort you've given me. William Harris is my brother-in-law."

A fist closed in Rosalind's hair and jerked her backward. Vasquez forced her down onto her knees. A malevolent smile spread across his scarred face. "Tell me, *chèrie,* about your sister. Which of you was meant to marry the grand Edward Murdock?"

Rosalind's heart sank. The only way to spare Beatrice was to tell him the truth. *"C'est moi, mon capitaine."*

Vasquez let out a howl of laughter. He staggered over to Pedro, shaking his head as he thumped Pedro on the shoulder. He gasped out a stream of Spanish, laughing all the while. Pedro and the other pirates joined in, looking Rosalind over with evil grins.

"What is it, my lady?" Captain Bellamy asked.

"Nothing, Captain. Nothing he wouldn't have learned anyway. I can only hope I've spared you some suffering."

"No! My lady, you didn't tell him?"

"Only that I am the fiancée, nothing more. There is another girl onboard, stricken with fever. My one hope now is to see her back to land alive and well."

"Chèrie." Vasquez wiped his eyes and flung one arm around her. "You have brought me luck beyond my wildest dreams! This Englishman Murdock, he is wealthy?"

"Oui, mon capitaine."

"He will pay a fortune to see you again?"

"I believe he would." Of course he would, since marriage to her meant control of her interest in Hanshaw Shipping.

Vasquez turned to his crew and shouted to them in Spanish. By their cheers Rosalind guessed he was telling them about the fat ransom they could look forward to.

"Now *chèrie,* you have brought me such luck I'm feeling generous. I will grant you one request. You may have anything you like, other than your liberty. What shall it be?"

Rosalind hesitated. Beatrice had to have some medical attention, or she might well perish. And yet, Captain Bellamy stood a far greater chance of dying within the next few minutes.

"*Mon capitaine,* let Captain Bellamy go. You will ransom me, *oui*? Let him take the news back to my fiancé. *Capitaine* Bellamy has seen me with his own eyes, and can assure my fiancé I am well."

Vasquez scowled, glaring from Rosalind to Captain Bellamy and back again. At last he nodded. "*Trés bien.* You may tell him yourself."

"*Merci beacoup, mon capitaine.*" She turned toward Captain Bellamy. Vasquez jerked her back to him, pinning her against his chest.

"Little words, *ma fille.* They mean nothing. Show me your thanks."

He ground his mouth against hers. Rosalind kept still, concealing her disgust. She was willing to endure even this rather than risk angering Vasquez now. Vasquez pushed her away, a frown of displeasure puckering his forehead.

"You'll have to do better than that." He shoved her at Captain Bellamy. "Get on with it. I'll have time enough to teach you what I want."

Rosalind swayed on her feet, dizzy from the pain of her headache and the monstrous prospect of Vasquez's "teaching." She reached up to free the cord still wrapped around Captain Bellamy's head. She flung it aside, wiping her bloodied hands on her skirt.

"Captain, it seems I've won you a reprieve. You will take the ransom demand back to Mr. Murdock."

"But, my lady, I can't possibly leave you—"

"Please, Captain, this is no time for chivalry. Go, as fast as you can."

Captain Bellamy slumped against the mast, his breath gusting out. "My lady, there are no words fine enough to express the depth of my gratitude."

"You can thank me by seeing to it the families of the other passengers aboard the *Bird of Paradise* are made aware of the situation. Beatrice Henderson is here with me. Lionel MacCaulay. . . ." Rosalind bit her lip, then drew a shaky breath. "I fear Mr. MacCaulay may be dead of wounds he suffered while trying to save us from these pirates."

"You have my word on it. But tell me, my lady, if the Black Angel captured the *Bird of Paradise,* how came you to be in the hands of these pirates?"

"That, Captain, is a very long story. God willing, you will join me for tea in London one day and we can laugh together over the whole appalling tale."

"It would be an honor and a privilege." Captain Bellamy bowed. Pedro and another pirate stepped up to hustle Captain Bellamy away. He called back to Rosalind over his shoulder. "God keep you, my lady! You will be delivered!"

Rosalind gave him a wan smile. She watched while pirates rowed one of the boats from the merchantman across. Pedro waved Captain Bellamy into it, then threw in what Rosalind hoped was a sack of provisions. Captain Bellamy set off toward the west, rowing strongly. Rosalind stared after him, wishing with all her heart she manned the second oar. That was one life saved, or at least saved from Vasquez.

Chapter Eleven

Alexandre stood in the fighting top high up the mainmast. The small circular platform gave him an excellent vantage point for using his spyglass. It was a glorious morning. The storm had blown itself out by dawn, leaving the skies clear. The sultry tropical air seemed to shimmer with the clarity of the sunlight. He scanned the horizon in every direction. Aside from the *Diabolique* sailing off the portside stern, there was nothing to be seen but the beautiful blue Caribbean waters stretching away on every side. Nothing at all. Not a gull, not a dolphin, and not a single sign of Vasquez.

Alexandre lowered his spyglass and rubbed at his weary eyes. It had taken all the skill he possessed to keep *L'Etoile du Matin* and the *Diabolique* together through the night. Had they lost each other, their only hope would have been to sail for Martinique and pray the other ship arrived in due course. The Caribbean was not the largest sea on earth, but it was easily large enough to get lost in when a storm made it impossible to take bearings and then blew each ship several miles off course.

They were heading toward the southern tip of Jamaica,

sailing farther and farther away from Alexandre's preferred waters off the southeast coast of Martinique. The longer *L'Etoile du Matin* lingered in the common shipping lanes, the nearer she sailed to one of the more popular harbors, the greater her chances of encountering British naval vessels. Alexandre would gladly show any British commander the speed and accuracy of his gun crews, but he did not relish risking a broadside from a ship of the line. Taking fire from the three gun decks on a British man-o-war would carry away *L'Etoile du Matin*'s two masts and rake her hull to splinters. With every passing hour the likelihood of Rosalind suffering at Vasquez's hands increased. By sunset at the latest Vasquez would reach his precious coral reefs and the numerous little islets they surrounded, burrowing into their safety like a rat into its favorite sewer. If Alexandre couldn't catch him up by then, Rosalind was lost to him forever.

Alexandre climbed down the mast, feeling an urge to work his way around the ship line by line. There was a certain relief in taxing the muscles of his shoulders and back. He needed activity, action, physical exertion, not this damned endless waiting. He stepped down onto the main deck and made his way straight to the quarterdeck. The ship's navigator stood there, sighting through his sextant at the sun. Beside him stood the ship's clerk, making notes. Yves waited there as well. Alexandre took the sheet of paper from the clerk's hands and looked it over. The readings closely matched those he himself had taken shortly after sunrise. He handed the paper back to the clerk and spoke to the navigator.

"Well, Maurice? Have you any idea where we might be?"

Maurice folded up his sextant and cleared his throat. "*Mon capitaine,* it is my belief we have gone astray some few miles to the south. Setting a course north by northwest should bring us to the reefs by noon."

"What are our chances that Vasquez was blown off course as well?"

Maurice shrugged. "Impossible to say, *mon capitaine*. If

he managed to run ahead of the storm, he might have escaped it entirely."

"That is not what I want to hear, Maurice."

"If he was blown south as we have been, *mon capitaine,* then there is a chance we will cross his wake."

Alexandre glared up into the rigging, at the bare yards and mast tops where his royals and topgallantsails should be spread. "How long until the sails are ready?"

"Within the hour, *mon captaine.*" Yves nodded toward the men seated in the forecastle stitching away with the great iron sailmaker's needles.

Alexandre stared at the empty horizon. Too slow. Too damned slow! Frustration threatened to boil up into rage. He calmed himself with an effort. His men were tired, having spent a long night battling a storm for no better reason than this fool's errand. Fatigue and pessimism washed over Alexandre, leaving him on the very brink of calling off the chase. He raked both hands back through his hair. It was entirely possible they would overtake Vasquez only to learn Rosalind escaped Vasquez in the only way possible, by throwing herself over the side to drown. If that proved to be the case, then Alexandre would look the perfect fool.

He found himself standing at the rail, looking down at the water as it rushed by. The very idea that Rosalind might have drowned filled him with an unwelcome sense of loss. She was maddening, she was insolent, she was plainly more trouble than she was worth, yet at the same time she was so lovely, so commanding, and so fragile. . . . Alexandre turned his face to the west. She must be alive. If she had succeeded in living through the night, she was still out there, somewhere, at the mercy of Vasquez and his crew. And a virgin, no less. Rosalind was worthy of the most artful seduction, of the greatest care a man could take in seeing to it her deflowering was accomplished with the utmost pleasure. Vasquez was incapable of such consideration. He would hurt Rosalind, and take great delight in doing so. The very idea offended Alexandre to a depth that startled him. To permit Vasquez to touch Rosalind would be akin to stabling farm animals in the Louvre. Alexandre welcomed the anger that ignited within him once again. It drove off the dismal sense of hopelessness. Rosalind was out there. He would find her. And then she would be his, body and soul.

Alexandre breathed deep, filling his lungs with the same power that filled his sails. The trade winds had finally come to his aid, blowing strong from the northeast. That decided him. He turned to his officers.

"Set course north for Jamaica. As soon as we sight land—"

"On deck!" cried the lookout. "*Mon capitaine*! Sail ho! Sail to port!"

Off to port a column of smoke smudged the horizon. Now the noise of cannon fire reached across the choppy water. Alexandre shut his eyes, concentrating on the rhythm of the explosions. The first volley had been a broadside. Would the ship under attack return fire? The answering volley thundered out, weaker than the first. The upper gun deck, lightly manned. So, some guns damaged, too few crew to run them all out, or a slow crew tangled in its own preparations. If the attacker pressed his advantage— Three cannons fired, one after the other. The attacker must have been aiming to cripple the ship rather than sink it.

"Andre!" he called to the lookout. "Whose colors are they flying?"

Andre stared hard at the horizon. Alexandre could make out sails, but nothing in the way of ensigns. Another blast of cannon fire and the rising wind stole Andre's reply.

"Again, Andre! Who are they?"

"Pirates, *mon capitaine,* flying the black. As to the other, I cannot see. The sails of the first block my view."

"It could be a French ship, then." Alexandre turned to Yves. "Fly English colors until we see who Vasquez is hounding now."

Alexandre faced the stern. There sat the *Diabolique,* some leagues off but still following *L'Etoile du Matin* under full sail. Her crew was as weary and hard-pressed as his men. That could make a crucial difference when it came time to fire the guns. Alexandre banished his worries.

"Yves! Signal the *Diabolique*. Tell them to keep the prize crew occupied. We will engage the pirate vessel." Alexandre scanned the deck, spotting the next officer he required. "Claude! A word, *s'il-vous plaît*."

The master gunner came running, eyes alight at the prospect of the coming battle. *"Oui, mon captaine?"*

"Man the guns. Our usual strategy may serve us here, but we must be prepared to change tactics at a moment's notice."

"Black or red, *mon capitaine?*"

Claude referred to the color of flag Alexandre chose to fly. Red meant no quarter would be given, regardless of how the vessel under attack might choose to cooperate. Alexandre frowned, wishing he knew exactly whose ship he raced toward.

"Black for now, Claude. We must be very sure of ourselves before we fly the red."

Claude nodded and turned to dash below, calling for his gunner's mates.

Alexandre strode to his cabin. His steward Christophe had been in to tidy up. He'd laid out Alexandre's burgundy velvet coat and breeches on the foot of his bed, nicely brushed and ready for the next attack. Alexandre stripped off his shirt and breeches and cast them aside. The burgundy velvet was a far cry from his French naval uniform, but it would serve. When the enemy saw *L'Ange Noir* coming, dressed in bloody colors with his black hair streaming out in the wind, then the terror began. Alexandre snatched his saber from its rack on the wall and belted it around his waist. He stuffed two pistols in his sash and tucked knives in his boots. His blood sang through his veins. This was all that was best in life, the ceremony of preparing for battle. He missed the formality of the French navy, missed its order and routine and the honor of serving his Crown. He still served, although to ordinary eyes he was nothing more than a pirate. Today he would serve the greater cause of humanity in general. If the ship ahead was indeed *La Fortuna,* Alexandre would put an end to Vasquez's despicable mayhem once and for all.

He stood for a moment in the doorway, watching his crew swarm up and down the rigging, setting the sails to bring *L'Etoile du Matin* as close to the wind as possible. They were his men, many of them his former shipmates, every one his brother-in-arms. They followed him, and he made very sure he always led them somewhere worth their while. One day he would lead them back to France. They would return as heroes, not as criminals to be spat upon and hanged.

"Mon capitaine!" Andre's voice rang out. *"La Fortuna* two leagues off starboard! Her mainsail took two shots and her mizzen lies athwart the deck! She's low in the water and looks ready to heel!"

Alexandre grinned. Relief surged through him, followed by the wild joy of the chase. He sprang up onto the quarterdeck. When he saw the glee lighting up Andre's face, he threw his head back and laughed. It roared out across the water like his own personal cannon fire. The mad mirth of it spread from one face to the next until the whole crew was roaring out their delight and defiance.

"Make for *La Fortuna*!" Alexandre shouted. "May God have mercy on that Spanish bastard's soul!"

Rosalind stood on the quarterdeck, huddling between some rigging and the ship's rail. She had wedged herself into a corner shaded by the spanker sail. Vasquez had insisted she join him on deck, claiming he needed his "little good luck charm." Vasquez stormed back and forth, a cigar in one hand and a brimming tankard in the other. He shouted to his men in slurred Spanish. They cheered, their voices growing louder, cruder, and less coherent thanks to the rum taken from Captain Bellamy's ship.

Rosalind watched the drunken merriment with increasing dread. Vasquez was every bit the fool Alexandre called him, to let his men range so far out of control. Much as she loathed him, Rosalind stayed close to Vasquez. As long as he thought he could make the greatest profit from keeping her alive and unmarked, he would defend her from any man aboard. She had to keep him thinking that. Vasquez spun around and staggered toward her, weaving across the deck as the ship yawed. Rum sloshed out of his tankard and spilled across his breeches. He cursed, then burst out laughing.

"More where this came from, eh *chèrie?*" He gulped it down. "Ah, good. Good rum. No thin-blooded grog for my crew." He thrust the tankard at her. "Drink to our luck, English lady. I could have sold you for a whore, but now I'll sell you for a queen's ransom!"

An evil grin bared his stained teeth. "But your sister's no lady, is she, *chèrie?*" He nodded to himself, jerking his head up and down with a violence that made him stagger against the rail. "I can afford to lose some money on her." Licking his lips, he bottomed his tankard and started toward his cabin.

Rosalind flung herself forward and caught Vasquez's arm, dragging him back. He swung at her, spinning himself around. Rosalind ducked underneath his arm, darting back as Vasquez staggered into the ropes called shrouds. He was so close to the rail—a quick shove would send Vasquez over the side. Louder shouts on deck reminded her of the seething mass of unwashed, drunken, lawless animals who had looked on gleefully while Vasquez tortured Captain Bellamy. Where was the frying pan, and where was the fire?

"My sister has a fever, *mon capitaine*. For all you know it could be ship's fever." She was relieved to see Vasquez turn pale beneath his swarthy coloring. "Would you run the risk of catching it, of having it spread throughout your crew? It will kill every man aboard before you can reach any port that might offer you medical assistance."

Fear of speaking more truth than she realized lent Rosalind's voice a firmness that made Vasquez hesitate. Ship's fever was nothing to be trifled with. She doubted Vasquez had anything like a ship's surgeon aboard, more likely some butcher with a rusted saw and a minimal knowledge of human anatomy. Vasquez tried to drink from his empty tankard, then cursed. He thrust it at her again.

"Go get me more rum!"

"*Oui, mon capitaine.*"

Rosalind took the tankard and searched among the riotous pirates for the one called Pedro. He seemed most willing to play the loyal follower to Vasquez. Better he should fight his way through the crowd to the casks of rum. Nothing on earth would make Rosalind take one step down off the quarterdeck.

From the rigging above her came a voice shouting frantically. Vasquez shoved Rosalind aside and trained his spyglass on the horizon. A whoop of laughter burst out of him. He grabbed Rosalind's arm and dragged her up beside him.

"Look, *chère*. Here comes that French bastard now." His lips peeled back from his stained teeth in a ghastly smile. "He thinks to fool me, flying that *Anglais* rag." Vasquez shook his head. "I know his sails too well."

He jerked Rosalind up against the rail, pushing her far out over it.

"He's coming for you, English lady. He'll overtake us in two hours."

Rosalind clung to the rail so tightly her knuckles whitened. "You sound like you want him to catch up, *mon capitaine.*"

"Oh, I do, *chère*. I do." Vasquez grinned, belched, then laughed. "I have that English dog's powder and shot. I have his rum. I have his fiancée." He flapped one hand at the sails on the horizon. "That swaggering French peacock lost his luck when he lost you, little Rosa." He laughed again, babbling to himself in Spanish. "Today I am king of the Caribbean! Today I tear the wings off *L'Ange Noir!*"

He shoved Rosalind away and stepped up to the edge of

the quarterdeck. Putting both hands to his mouth, he bel-
lowed· in Spanish. The drunken pirates answered Vasquez
with hoarse shouts and jeers. Vasquez roared at Pedro, who
snatched up a coil of rope and charged down across the
deck. He lashed the pirates left and right, snapping the end
of the rope across faces, necks, and arms. By the time he
reached the bow, the mood on deck was one of sullen attention. Rosalind could not imagine why the pirates hadn't simply turned on Pedro and flung him over the side.

Vasquez shouted in Spanish, pointing off to starboard
and speaking with more urgency than temper. The pirates
shuffled themselves into some semblance of order, manning
the guns on deck and disappearing below to form gun
crews. All this activity confirmed Vasquez's certainty about
Alexandre catching up to *La Fortuna*. Knowing Alexandre,
he wouldn't be satisfied with anything less than blowing *La
Fortuna* to kingdom come. That meant Rosalind had to get
Beatrice up and on deck. If Alexandre was really intent on
taking Rosalind back from Vasquez, then the safest place
for Beatrice was right beside her where no cannonball
would be allowed to strike.

Vasquez and Pedro were busy shouting orders and getting
the pirates to their battle stations. Vasquez stood there, his
face flushed as dark as the redingote now slung across his
shoulders. He drew on his latest cigar and blew out a cloud
of stinking smoke.

"Your champion is making better time than I thought.
Will you welcome him, *chèrie*? Will you be happy to see the
man who will sell you to a whorehouse as soon as he tires
of you?"

Rosalind marched past him to stand at the rail, letting her
silence and rigid back be her answer.

Vasquez chuckled. "Don't let him fool you, *chèrie*. He's a
pirate, a black-hearted bastard, some nobleman's get on a
dockside whore. In the end he'll hang from a rope the same
as the rest of us."

Rosalind ignored him. How strange to think that only yesterday she had watched the Black Angel approach her ship with the keenest dread. Now the sight of Alexandre standing tall on his quarterdeck, dark and dangerous in his finely cut coat, meant salvation. Rosalind twisted the rope of pearls around her fingers, wishing she could stretch it out between *La Fortuna* and *L'Etoile du Matin,* making it a lifeline that Alexandre could use to drag Vasquez into range of his guns.

The sails of *L'Etoile du Matin* moved closer. Alexandre's consort boat, the sloop he called the *Diabolique,* had veered to starboard and was angling to cut *La Fortuna* off. Now that both of Alexandre's ships were in sight, the tension aboard *La Fortuna* became visible in the wide eyes and frantic movements of the crew. The rum they'd swilled had become their enemy, slowing their movements and muddling their thoughts. Facing the prospect of almost certain death, the formerly boisterous mob manned their stations with unnatural silence.

Sick with fright and confusion, Rosalind took herself firmly in hand. She had to get Beatrice out of Vasquez's cabin. That was her immediate difficulty. To that she would apply herself. Taking advantage of Vasquez's distraction, Rosalind crept down the stairs to his cabin.

Chapter Twelve

Alexandre stood in the bow, savoring the taste of the salt spray as *L'Etoile du Matin* closed in. With his spyglass he searched among the press of bodies on Vasquez's deck, finding Rosalind on the quarterdeck with Vasquez. Gone was the matronly blue gown with all its fussy little bows. In its place Rosalind wore a few scant yards of brilliant red silk that bared her arms and clung to every curve. The sun blazed down on her, calling out the shine of her golden hair, painting honeyed highlights along her silk-covered breasts and thighs. Desire surged through Alexandre, raw and primal. Rosalind was everything a man could possibly want. This little milkmaid stirred the need in him like no other woman he'd ever met. That she remained alone but for Vasquez was a testament to Rosalind's cunning.

Alexandre studied Rosalind, unable to take his eyes off the arousing spectacle she presented. This prim and proper English lady, stripped of her dignity only to become this silk-wrapped goddess, the very essence of a lonely sailor's dream. He ached to reach out and stroke the soft skin of her thigh, bared by an errant gust of wind. Rosalind knotted a long rope of pearls around her fingers. Gold bracelets hung from her wrists like gyves. Restless and fretful, for a moment it seemed Rosalind looked right at him. That look of desperation, of longing. . . . Alexandre's heart thudded, his blood rushing hot and wild through his veins. Rosalind would welcome him, he was sure of it. And not merely for delivering her from the foul attentions of Vasquez.

Alexandre turned to his officers waiting behind him. "*Monsieur le Docteur.* Hail the swine and tell them they will hand over the girl at once. Any defiance and we will slaughter them to a man."

Gingras hailed *La Fortuna* and repeated Alexandre's terms in Spanish. Vasquez's crew replied with insults in several languages. Vasquez flung aside his cigar and caught Rosalind by her braid. He coiled the braid around her throat and jerked her up on her toes.

"You want her, you poxy French peacock?" he roared out in his abominable French. "Come and take her back! It will cost you every man aboard!"

Alexandre smiled. Now was the time to fire his guns, to put so many holes into the hull of *La Fortuna* she'd sink like a stone. He raised his spyglass. Rosalind's cheeks were flushed, her chin raised high as she fought the garrot of her own braid. In those magnificent blue eyes there showed a little fear, yes, but far more anger and defiance. Vasquez hadn't broken her yet.

Alexandre's own men were watching him, the gun crews waiting with lit fuses in their hands. At his nod they would light the slow matches and put an end to *La Fortuna*. What was it the little milkmaid had said to him when she all but called him a coward? She'd heard *L'Ange Noir* was great enough to show mercy when mercy was called for. So be it. Let Rosalind see *L'Ange Noir* live up to his fame.

"Monsieur Gingras," Alexandre said. "Be kind enough to tell the men aboard that scow I will stand by my terms. If they hand the girl over to me now, I will show mercy. This is their last chance."

Gingras translated. Now some of Vasquez's crew were looking uncertain, casting dark looks at the quarterdeck. Alexandre kept his delight off his face. If he could push the dogs into mutiny, he might take Rosalind back without a single shot fired.

Vasquez bellowed in frantic Spanish, brandishing his pistol.

"He tells them you are the Devil," Monsieur Gingras said, "and French at that. You will cut their hearts out no matter what they do."

Alexandre laughed.

La Fortuna's stern guns fired, sending cannonballs arcing over *L'Etoile du Matin*'s bow. Had Vasquez waited for the natural roll of the waves to bring their ships even, he might have nicked a yard or some rigging. Now he'd opened fire first, putting Alexandre in the position of defending himself.

"Soak his guns. Carry away his masts. Leave him adrift and helpless."

The orders passed from man to man, raising a cheer from the gun crews. Guns on the lower deck spoke, firing weakened charges that sank their balls along Vasquez's waterline. Salt water fountained up, splashing into the gun ports and down the mouths of the ready cannons. Wet powder and damp fuses left them useless. The *Diabolique* might have to return some cannon fire on the port side, but *L'Etoile du Matin* was now in no danger. All that was left was to come alongside and send the boarders across.

"*Mon capitaine!*" Monsieur Gingras cried. "Look!"

He pointed to *La Fortuna*'s mainmast. Alexandre raised his spyglass. Six of Vasquez's men were ranged up the mainmast, working in pairs. The pair nearest the deck handed Rosalind up to the next pair who took her by the arms and hoisted her farther up the mast. The highest pair held Rosalind's wrists above her head and lashed them to the mainmast. The other four pirates did the same with ropes at her waist and ankles.

Alexandre cursed. "Cease fire! *Now,* damn you!"

The *Diabolique*'s lighter guns loaded with grape and chain shot were meant to shred that very mainsail. Alexandre had to stop them before they shredded Rosalind as well. He ran to the quarterdeck and snatched the signal flags from the waiting crewman. It was no use. The *Diabolique* couldn't see straight through *La Fortuna*'s tattered sails.

L'Etoile du Matin drew up alongside *La Fortuna*. Vasquez's crew was waiting with their pistols and cutlasses. They knew this was a fight to the death. The stony looks on their faces said their ship might as well be burning under them already.

"Boarders!" Alexandre shouted. "I want that girl! Fifty ducats to the man who brings her to me alive and well!"

His own men crowded up to the rail, armed and eager. Alexandre took one precious moment to scan their faces, wondering as he always did which ones would not return.

"Bonne chance, mes amis," he murmured. It was time to give the order that would send some of them to their deaths. "Boarders away!"

Rosalind's arms ached. The coarse ropes dug into her wrists. Her own weight dragged at her shoulders. The mast swayed with the motion of the ship, adding nausea to her woes. And now, with Alexandre's cannons firing, she could only wait until he chose the mainmast as his target. She remembered all too well the accuracy of his aim.

All at once *L'Etoile du Matin*'s cannons stopped firing.

"Chèrie!" Vasquez stood at the foot of the mast, laughing up at her. "You are the best good luck charm I've ever found! See how *L'Ange Noir* trembles at the very thought of hurting you?"

Sick as she was, frightened as she was, Rosalind struggled to focus on Alexandre. As best she could tell, the look on his face was grim. Gone was the self-assured poise he'd shown while issuing his terms. The Black Angel looked genuinely distressed. Could it be true? Was Alexandre really worried about her getting hurt? That would make sense if he intended to ransom her as Vasquez did, but Alexandre still had no idea who she really was. Why then would her safety matter so much to him?

"I must be sure to keep you!" Vasquez barked an order. Pedro and a dozen other pirates lined up around the mast, armed with cutlasses and pistols. Vasquez did mean to keep her. The horror of that prospect left her nearly overcome with dizziness and fright.

Rosalind watched as *L'Etoile du Matin* came alongside. Alexandre's men hurled themselves across the watery gap, straight into the faces of Vasquez's waiting crew. Steel clashed as cutlasses met. Vasquez's pirates struggled with Alexandre's men, hoisting some up and flinging them back over the side. Alexandre's men broke Vasquez's line first, pushing hard straight for the mainmast. The fighting raged from bow to stern, the rival crews packed shoulder to shoulder across the deck. Pedro and his crewmates held their ground, slashing and hacking at Alexandre's men, doing their best to drive them off. With military precision Alexandre's men surrounded the pirates, leveled their pistols, and fired. Four of Vasquez's men fell. Cutlasses and daggers in hand, Alexandre's men pressed in.

Pedro and three other pirates dropped their weapons and raced up the rigging like spiders in a web. Pedro clenched a dagger in his teeth. One of the other pirates held Rosalind in place while Pedro cut her free. As much as she loathed them touching her, Rosalind kept still. Now was not the moment to fight them. If they dropped her, she'd fall straight down onto the blades of the pirates below. With luck she might go overboard, but striking the water from such a height could be fatal as well.

The remaining two pirates had fashioned a harness out of more rope. They slid it up Rosalind's arms, snugging it tight across her shoulders. They looped the end of the rope around one of the heavier lines that ran down toward the stern. Pedro growled at her in Spanish, making swooping motions with his free hand. Rosalind didn't know if he was giving her instructions or merely a warning. Rough hands pulled her arms around a thick neck. The pirates argued in harsh Spanish, then the ropes around Rosalind's shoulders jerked sharply. The wind rushed past as she slid down the heavier line, clinging to the pirate who led the way.

Their feet hit the deck. Before Rosalind could get her bearings, the pirates hustled her onward. Shouts and screams and pistol fire raged all around her. The air reeked of gunpowder and the coppery smell of blood. When the pirates finally set her on her feet, Rosalind opened her eyes to find herself on the quarterdeck. Vasquez stood waiting. His shirt was torn, streaked with powder burns and stained with blood. More blood ran down his face from a cut over one eye.

"L'Ange Noir may take my ship, but he will not take you. I will rob him of this treasure once and for all!" Vasquez faced *L'Etoile du Matin.* "Hear me, you fancy French dog! She is mine!" Vasquez yanked her out away from Pedro. "This fine English lady is *mine!"*

Rosalind gasped. Mindful of nothing but silencing him, she slapped Vasquez across the face. His eyes bulged. He seized her by the throat with both hands, screaming at her in Spanish. Rosalind fought him, desperate to continue the distraction even though Vasquez was painfully close to strangling her. Pedro pulled at Vasquez's arms, gesturing madly. Vasquez snarled at him, then flung Rosalind down on the deck. He pulled a knife from his boot and grabbed a fistful of her hair, jerking her up onto her knees. He bent low to hiss in her ear.

"L'Ange Noir will take back nothing but a corpse with the name of Vasquez carved on your English heart!"

"Alexandre!" Rosalind shouted. "Help me! *Help me!"*

The battle was now a bloody riot. Bodies littered the deck. Smoke from the cannons and pistols hung in murky streamers above the men still fighting. The gaudy pirate garb worn by both crews made it impossible to tell which side was winning. Rosalind screamed and slapped at Vasquez's hands.

"Rosalind!" Alexandre's voice boomed out across the deck. He stood near the bow, a sword in his right hand and a pistol in his left. "Bring me the girl!"

Alexandre shoved his way through the throng of pirates still fighting on the main deck, making his way toward her as fast as the battle allowed.

A man, built broad and solid like a heavy oak door, lunged at Vasquez, cursing in molten French. Vasquez seized a pistol from one of his men and shot the big man, who staggered and fell. Before Rosalind could get out of reach, Vasquez caught her by the rope of pearls and dragged her to him.

"Rosalind!" Alexandre struck aside the Spanish pirates who tried to block his way.

"Alexandre!" Rosalind twisted and strained against Vasquez's grip on the pearls, trying to break the rope.

"Too late!" Vasquez shouted over her shoulder. "You'll be too late, *L'Ange Jaune!*"

Vasquez dragged Rosalind back inside his cabin. She slumped against the wall beside the hammock where Beatrice still lay, feverish and silent. Fumbling at his breeches, Vasquez grabbed Rosalind by the arm and jerked her up against him, biting at her neck and shoulders. Shrieking with fury and disgust, Rosalind struck out at him, kicking and slapping. With a bestial growl Vasquez kicked Rosalind's feet out from under her. She landed flat on the deck. The back of her head struck the planks, leaving her stunned. Vasquez pounced on her, pinning her beneath his weight.

The cabin door slammed open. Alexandre stood in the doorway, a pistol in each hand. His eyes blazed like dark stars. His fine burgundy clothing hung on his tall frame like the very robes of righteousness. *L'Ange Noir* had become an avenging angel.

Vasquez grinned, the madness of it absolute. He snatched

the knife from his belt. Alexandre's pistols fired. In the confined space their noise was deafening. The force of the pistol balls slammed Vasquez back against the bulkhead. He toppled over and lay still.

Rosalind clapped her hands over her ears. She curled up into a ball, shaking and sobbing. No more. No more! No more noise, no more blood, no more dead bodies. Tears poured out of her, all the grief she'd been holding in mingling with this new horror to break the last of her self-control.

Gentle hands lifted her up and wrapped her in something heavy and warm and soft. A deep voice murmured soothing words. Slowly the shock and terror faded. Nestled in the comfort of Alexandre's burgundy velvet coat, Rosalind looked up into those dark stars, the somber jewels of Alexandre's eyes.

"I am here, *ma belle*," he murmured. "You are safe."

Rosalind clung to Alexandre. He was here and he had saved her. For one precious, shining moment, nothing else mattered. He was still a pirate, still her enemy, but at that moment she was more than happy to accept the lesser of two evils. Looking up at him through the blur of her tears, she could not think of him as evil. So beautiful, so kind and gentle now. In front of his crew he was the hard pirate captain, but alone with her he was a different man.

"Can you stand, *ma belle*?" he asked. "I am sorry to hurry you, but the ship is sinking."

"Beatrice. . . ." Rosalind lifted a limp hand toward the hammock in the corner.

Alexandre eased Rosalind up onto her feet, keeping his arm around her waist to steady her. After looking Beatrice over, Alexandre leaned out through the doorway.

"Eric," he called. A tall, burly pirate stepped inside. "You will take particular care with Mademoiselle Beatrice. She is ill."

"*Oui, mon capitaine.*" Eric bent and lifted Beatrice in his arms as if she were no more than a baby.

Alexandre led them out on deck. *La Fortuna* rode low in

the water, low enough to cover her cannons. With increasing haste Alexandre's men brought up the cargo from below and moved their wounded shipmates across to *L'Etoile du Matin*. Eric shepherded Beatrice along with the others. When Rosalind started to follow, Alexandre drew her back with a gentle arm around her waist.

"And now for you, mademoiselle." Alexandre smiled down at Rosalind, a hint of mischief in his eyes. "After all this effort to reunite us, I insist on escorting you aboard myself." He swept her up in his arms. "Hold on, *ma belle*. This is no time for another swim."

Rosalind was only too happy to obey. She wrapped her arms around his neck and pressed her cheek against his chest. Alexandre called out to the men aboard *L'Etoile du Matin*. They ran out a plank from rail to rail. Alexandre walked across, balancing easily despite the roll of the two ships. He carried her to his cabin and laid her down atop the emerald coverlet.

"Now." Alexandre took her face in his hands. "You will rest."

She gripped his wrists. "Please, *mon capitaine*. Beatrice's fever is worse. She may be very ill. I beg you, ask *monsieur le docteur* to spare her a few moments."

"*Immediatement, ma belle.*" He bent to kiss her forehead. "Now I must go. I will look in on you later."

He straightened and turned to leave. Rosalind clung to his hand. He looked down at her, one black brow raised, a slight smile playing on his lips.

"*Oui, ma belle?* What is it?"

Rosalind wanted to say something to him, to give voice to the profound relief she felt at having been delivered from Vasquez and his plans for her. More than that, she wanted to find some words to express the way her heart had leaped when the cabin door slammed open and Alexandre stood there with pistols drawn. Too much. It was all too much to think about, too much to feel.

"I would count it the greatest of favors if you would be

kind enough to allow me a little fresh water." Rosalind brushed at the stained red silk with distaste. "I must make the best toilette I can."

She waited, eyes fixed on a stain near her knee. Would Alexandre take this opportunity to avenge himself for the way she'd baited him over taking a bath?

He touched her cheek lightly, trailing his fingertips down along the line of her jaw. "To me you are as fresh and lovely as the first rose of spring."

Rosalind raised her eyes to his. On that normally stern face was a look of such tenderness. For once those full lips were curved in a smile without sardonic meaning. Those dark eyes, so often stormy, were tranquil. Rosalind felt an overwhelming desire to wrap her arms around his waist and take refuge within his embrace. She held his hand to her cheek, then sank back on the pillow with a weary sigh.

"Merci beaucoup, mon capitaine."

Chapter Thirteen

Alexandre stood outside his cabin door feeling quite pleased with himself. *L'Etoile du Matin* had suffered little damage, and that was due entirely to the storm. Between the cargo from Vasquez's hold and the goods taken from the *Bird of Paradise,* he'd turn a pretty profit for only two day's work. Last but far from least, Lady Rosalind Hanshaw now lay safely asleep in his own bed. Alexandre's lips curved in a wolfish smile. She'd need her rest. He could scarcely keep his mind on overseeing the disposition of the cargo, so eager was he to enjoy a more leisurely reunion.

The sails of the *Diabolique* were already growing smaller as she sped north by northeast toward Jamaica. *L'Etoile du Matin* followed a similar course, one that would ride the currents and the trades winds around Jamaica, bringing her east again to Martinique. There both ships could lie up in safety and make further repairs. Alexandre looked out over his crew still lashing down cargo and the others occupied with sailmaking. They were tired, in need of some refreshment. He owed them a celebration for taking back Rosalind with so few hands lost.

Alexandre watched the *Diabolique,* wondering at the reaction his message would cause. Murdock's agents in
Kingston would never expect Lady Rosalind Hanshaw to
fall into the hands of *L'Ange Noir.* Oh, to see the looks on
their fat English faces when they realized the man they'd
treated as some hired servant, some negligible lackey, now
held the very life of their employer's fiancée in his hands.
There could be little doubt about their response. They
would reply immediately, confirming the amount he required and the site of the rendezvous. Alexandre had allowed himself a few extra days, always a wise precaution.
Weather could be an obstacle, along with the presence or
absence of the key agent who would be the one to count out
the necessary number of pistoles. More important, this allowed him just that many more days to enjoy Rosalind's
company, to draw her ever closer to him, to bind her virgin
senses with the silken bonds of newly discovered rapture.
No sweeter vengeance had he ever contemplated than this
most exquisite achievement.

He had to make the most of those few days. Once the
date of the rendezvous arrived his little milkmaid had to be
sent on her way. Alexandre knew Rosalind was already too
much of a distraction. He should be closeted with Yves,
planning the division of the cargo and how best to dispose
of it through his father's shipping agents. It was high time
they took shelter on the wilder side of Martinique, lying up
in his favorite cove while the cargo brought him wealth that
didn't have to be paid for in blood and powder. He should
be attending to the business of piracy, but he had no head
for it at the moment. Right now he could do nothing but
revel in his victory, over Vasquez and over the little *Anglaise*
milkmaid who thought she could escape *L'Ange Noir.*

Alexandre let his mind linger on the taste of Rosalind's
mouth, on her hair like streams of gold pouring through his
fingers, on his longing to see her transfigured at the peak of
her ecstasy. The more Alexandre contemplated their reunion, the more impatient he became. Common sense and

common decency dictated he leave Rosalind in peace to get some sleep. Strong as she was, stubborn as she was, she had pushed herself far beyond the endurance some men could claim. She would be no fit companion for the reunion he had in mind if she couldn't stay awake long enough to appreciate it. Alexandre frowned, torn between different strategies. All at once he saw himself standing there, stalled by indecision. The little chit had him dithering like a fool outside his own cabin door. With an oath he thrust out one hand and shoved the door open.

Rosalind lay across his bed, dressed in a typical English nightgown, made of yards and yards of linen wholly unsuitable to the tropical climate. Its very modesty stirred Alexandre's desire, prompting him to recall the soft skin and sweet curves that lay beneath its chaste folds. Alexandre took a step toward her. The toe of his boot struck one of the golden bracelets and sent it skittering across the deck. He bent to examine the other bracelet and the pearls. The bracelets were fine enough, but the pearls were inferior, dull and chalky without the luster that made them so prized. Typical of Vasquez to have such trash. The silk dress stank of old tobacco and spilled rum, just like the whores who wore such things. Alexandre's jaw clenched. If Vasquez weren't already dead, Alexandre would take exquisite pleasure in killing him again. What a pity the swine had forced him to end the matter so abruptly. Keelhauling would have been a proper punishment for such degradation, to say nothing of the way Vasquez nearly strangled Rosalind with her own braid.

Alexandre eased his weight down on the bed beside Rosalind, leaning on one elbow and propping his head on his hand. In sleep Rosalind's expression was calm, tranquil, freed from the cares that burdened her and the wariness that she wore like a shawl wrapped tightly around her. Her fair skin had taken the sun well these last few days, adding a rosiness that suited her. Delicate brows of golden silk curved above the thick lashes framing those entrancing blue

eyes. Her nose was straight, the tip tilted just a trifle upward. Alexandre's gaze lingered on her lips, a deeper shade
of rose, full and more than full. The line of her cheek and
the angle of her jaw were all that beauty could demand.
Rosalind would look well on a cameo, in a portrait, in any
work of art rendered by a master. She was beauty itself, and
valor, and all the maidenly virtues.

Alexandre was startled to realize Rosalind was even
younger than he had guessed. Perhaps eighteen, yet with a
gravity that became her and lent her the air of a woman
twice that age. Lady Rosalind Hanshaw, betrothed to Edward Murdock by bad luck and adroit scheming. She'd be
wise to seize the moment and allow *L'Ange Noir* to teach
her the heights of joy a woman could reach in the arms of a
man who appreciated her. She'd get no such consideration
from Murdock. To be the first man to taste the full flowering of her passion, to see the fury of her proud temperament
transformed into the wild delight of complete surrender. . . .

He ran a fingertip along the curve of her cheek. What had
she endured aboard *La Fortuna*? Sister Beatrice seemed no
worse, other than the fever that made her all the more frail
and silent. How had Rosalind sheltered her from the least of
the abuse any woman might expect aboard such a ship?
Alexandre frowned, thinking again about Rosalind's talent
for spinning clever lies. Whatever lies she told Vasquez
must have been a masterpiece of cunning to keep even him
at bay. Vasquez was a stupid brute, but even he had somehow discovered Rosalind's presence aboard *L'Etoile du
Matin*. Knowing therefore that Alexandre had kept her
presence a secret, Vasquez would rightly interpret that as
meaning Alexandre meant to keep Rosalind for himself.
That alone should have driven Vasquez into an orgy of
vengeance.

And yet, the milkmaid had triumphed once again. She
had apparently preserved not only her own virtue but that
of Beatrice as well. Instead of bringing Alexandre comfort,

that knowledge left him uneasy. Rosalind was dangerous, in so many ways. She had inspired *L'Ange Noir* to kill for her, and on only a day's acquaintance. The truth of that struck Alexandre. Vasquez needed killing, had for some time, but not until Rosalind came into it had Alexandre cared to finish Vasquez once and for all. That uneasiness grew, filling his mind with forebodings. Yes, Rosalind was an English lady, and yes, she was fiancée to Murdock, that arrogant swine. Was she clever enough to be even more than that? The English would do anything to be rid of *L'Ange Noir,* even to the extent of sending spies after him. It was remotely possible Rosalind was a very clever form of bait in a trap set by Murdock himself.

For the moment Alexandre banished all such dismal thoughts. Rosalind was here with him, safe and whole and lovelier than ever. The bow at her throat teased him, inviting him to regard her as a gift meant just for him. He took one end of the ribbon between thumb and forefinger and slowly pulled it free, baring the slender column of her throat. Alexandre's breath hissed out. The creamy velvet of Rosalind's neck, so recently a favorite target for his kisses, now bore a ring of welts and bruises. That sight confirmed his fears and caused his blood to boil anew. What other signs of savagery would he find?

Rosalind stirred. Her eyes opened. She looked up at Alexandre with the blank incomprehension of one still asleep. She looked so much like a rumpled kitten. Enchanted, Alexandre bent to brush his lips over hers.

"Bonsoir, ma belle," he murmured. "Will you go back to sleep, or shall we talk a little?"

Rosalind sat up, rubbing at her eyes. "I think it best if we talk, *mon capitaine.*" She yawned, covering her mouth with her hand. "First, I must know if Beatrice is all right."

"Let me assure you your *petite soeur* is in good hands. *Monsieur le Docteur* tells me her condition is due largely to fatigue and lack of water."

"How bad is it?"

"Nothing that cannot be remedied with fresh water and rest. She will be well enough shortly."

Alexandre was glad to see Rosalind's shoulders sag with relief.

"Where is Mr. MacCaulay?" she asked.

This was the moment Alexandre had hoped to put off. "He is no longer aboard."

Rosalind's head came up. "What have you done with him? Did you abandon him on that island?" She glared at him, those entrancing blue eyes brilliant with anger. "He tried to save us! He stood between us and those filthy, evil animals who dragged us away to Vasquez! Where were you, *mon capitaine*? Where were you when we needed you?"

Alexandre sighed. He should have known rescuing Rosalind wouldn't be enough. Now he had to win his way back into her good graces as well.

"Where were *you,* mademoiselle? Did I not order you to remain within the safety of your pavilion?"

"My whereabouts is not the issue, *mon capitaine.* Where is Mr. MacCaulay? What have you done with him?"

"Monsieur Gingras removed one pistol ball and stitched up the shoulder wound. We put him aboard the *Diabolique,* which even now sails for Jamaica. He will receive further medical assistance there."

Rosalind stared at him, speechless. Alexandre smiled. He smoothed a few stray golden tresses back over her shoulder.

"Are you so surprised, *ma belle?*"

"*Mais oui, mon capitaine.* Mercy is rare enough in a pirate, but compassion. . . . That is unheard of."

"Perhaps your stay aboard *La Fortuna* has made you realize there is more than one kind of pirate."

"In the end all pirates are the same, *mon capitaine.* They make their living by preying on the innocent."

"The English are not innocent in their dealings with France, nor have they been for some time now."

Rosalind put her head to one side and looked him over.

Alexandre had the uncomfortable sense of being weighed and found wanting.

"Tell me, *mon capitaine,* do you ever run out of ways to excuse yourself for what you do?"

Alexandre's jaw clenched. "I need no excuses, mademoiselle. I need only a fast ship and the open sea."

"Surely there is one more item you are forgetting, *mon capitaine.*"

"And what would that be, mademoiselle?"

"An enemy so far beneath you that by comparison you seem heroic."

A slow, molten anger began to grow within Alexandre. Rosalind had insulted him time and again since coming aboard *L'Etoile du Matin,* but this surpassed all previous scorn.

"Have a care, mademoiselle," he said softly. "There are many men who would fear to take that tone with me."

Rosalind stared at him. Anger, distress, scorn, even sorrow all faded from her expression, leaving her pale and exhausted.

"*Pardonnez-moi, mon capitaine.* Some rest, *s'il-vous plaît,* and I will resume my role in this comedy."

She turned over, putting her back to him. Alexandre sat there looking at the golden coil of her braid. How could he possibly explain himself in terms that Rosalind would not only believe, but even accept? Yves would mock him for a colossal fool if he knew what Alexandre was about. This battle required more strategy than taking his last three prizes. The success of his entire plan hinged on regaining Rosalind's favor. Given the cleverness of his milkmaid, perhaps the truth would serve him best.

"Mademoiselle, you have every right to think the worst of me. I have seized you and your friend, disrupting your lives and imposing my will on you." He stood up, pacing, his long legs taking him across the cabin in only three strides. "I am a pirate. I am known to be very good at what I do. Should I show my face in any but a few particular ports, the hangman will greet me."

Alexandre waited, hoping curiosity would prompt Rosalind to face him. The bedclothes rustled. Alexandre turned, fixing Rosalind with an intense stare. To his secret delight, she blushed beneath his gaze, clasping the open collar of her nightgown. He lowered his voice, turning contrition into seduction.

"Any ship I choose for a prize should simply strike its colors and surrender. There is little chance of any authority capturing me."

He sank down on his knees beside the bed.

"I am not a fool, and yet my only excuse is to claim the greatest foolishness. When Vasquez arrived, my blood was afire and my mind so addled by the glory of your beauty my wits had vanished." He took Rosalind's hand, rubbing his cheek against it. "In my impatience, I simply wanted to be rid of Vasquez and any other distractions."

He paused, trying to gauge her response. Her pulse beat against his fingers. The warmth remained in her cheeks. He lowered his voice to a passionate caress.

"I wanted you, *ma belle*. More than anything. I was blind to any consideration but that."

Rosalind tried to pull her hand back. Alexandre held it fast, planting a kiss on her palm.

"Do not judge me too harshly, *ma belle*. I came for you, did I not? I allowed nothing to stop me, not even a storm that threatened to tear the very sails from my masts."

Rosalind studied him. Her lips thinned to a stubborn line. "Am I to believe you think doing the honorable thing in rescuing us cancels out the first outrage?"

Alexandre held himself in check with an effort, making his voice even softer. "Let this be proof of my refinement, *ma belle*. Only a fool would have chased *La Fortuna* to the far side of Jamaica and attacked in the face of Vasquez's twenty guns. Any other pirate would have left you to Vasquez and laughed about it."

"And yet you didn't. Why not, *mon capitaine?* Could

L'Ange Noir really be such a fool over one English milk-maid?"

Alexandre rose and turned his back on her before he lost his temper completely. As much as he'd love to see the righteous indignation on Lady Rosalind Hanshaw's face wiped clean away, now was not the moment to reveal his knowledge of her true name. Perhaps the greater vengeance against Murdock would be sending this fishwife back alive and well. Alexandre forced himself to keep to his strategy. He would win her. He would conquer Rosalind so thoroughly she would be devastated when the time came to send her home.

"I could not abide the thought of you in that fiend's clutches, so I risked my ship and my crew to save you." He stood with his head bowed. "Does that win me no reprieve in your eyes, *ma belle?* Am I to be damned forever, no hope of redemption?"

Silence. He waited, keeping still in his posture of repentance. Finally Rosalind spoke.

"I find it odd to hear the Devil himself begging for mercy."

Something in Rosalind's tone made Alexandre raise his head and meet her gaze. Her expression was as wary as it had been when he hailed her from his own quarterdeck, telling her he'd offer her more personal terms of surrender. Alexandre knelt beside the bed again, bringing them closer together, capturing her hand between his. He raised it to his lips.

"I have admitted my foolishness, Rosalind. No man has ever heard me say as much. Will you not relent?"

Rosalind sighed. Her hand in his was weakening, growing limp with fatigue. Alexandre knew he was being cruel to tax her like this, but he had to wring some mercy from her, some sign of truce.

"The way to win my mercy and forgiveness is to make port in Jamaica, preferably Kingston, and let us go free."

"Would you rob me of your company so soon, *ma belle*? And after all I've done to bring us back together?" Alexandre gave her the smile that had once caused a barmaid to swoon on the spot.

Rosalind closed her eyes and turned her face away. "Please, *mon capitaine*, I am too tired for flirtation."

"Then I shall not waste your strength on minor pleasures."

Alexandre leaned forward and planted a lingering kiss on the silky column of Rosalind's throat. His lips moved downward, following the open neckline of the nightgown. His cheek brushed her breast, making her gasp. The heat of the day had left the linen molded to Rosalind's figure, clearly showing him the tender pink rosebuds of her nipples. His mouth closed over one. Having bathed, Rosalind tasted of fresh water and her own skin. The scent of lilacs surrounded her. The hunger in Alexandre grew so intense he longed to lick her, to devour her as he might consume some sweet marzipan.

Alexandre slid his hands under her calves, drawing Rosalind down across the bed, making her nightgown slide up along her thighs. The linen bunched up along her smooth belly, baring the treasure he longed to seize, the soft thatch of golden curls that shielded her tender depths. Before he could taste her virgin honey, Rosalind twisted away, rolling out of his grip. She backed up against the bulkhead, cheeks flushed and breasts heaving.

"I'm not so exhausted I cannot defend myself, *mon capitaine*."

Alexandre clenched his fists in the coverlet, willing down the throbbing need to tear the nightgown off her and hear nothing more from her but her cries of pleasure. Even more difficult to ignore was the ferocious temptation to show her just how helpless she really was. He knew he could easily kiss her into submission, then bring her back to a new world of hunger and need. In the end she would cry out his name, begging him to give her the ultimate joy she had yet to taste.

Rosalind huddled into the corner, knees drawn up and nightgown tucked securely in around them. "I congratulate you on the handsome profit you've made. The cargoes of three different ships, the satisfaction of killing Vasquez, and now whatever your final reward once you've disposed of us."

Alexandre glanced at her sharply. What had she overheard this time? "You mean ransom, mademoiselle? By your own claim you're worth nothing. Why would I ransom you?"

"Why indeed, *mon capitaine?*" She gestured to the pearls and bracelets where they lay scattered on the floor. "You'll want those as well."

"Oh no, mademoiselle," Alexandre said, rising. "Those are yours by right."

"What right?"

"You were first aboard the prize ship. By what few laws I recognize, those are yours." Alexandre gathered up the pearls and bracelets, holding them out to her on his cupped palms. "You are an amazing woman, Rosalind. I have never met such courage."

Tears spilled down Rosalind's cheeks. She struck the pearls and bracelets from his hands, flinging them across the deck. "I don't want them!"

Startled by her sudden emotion, Alexandre reached out to pick up the pearls. As his fingers closed over the smooth, round shapes, his glance went to the bruises on Rosalind's throat, now hidden as she clutched her collar tight around them.

"*Mon Dieu—*" Cold rage seized him. "Hear me, Rosalind. With all my heart I wish I could kill Vasquez again. I would make him pay with fifty lashes for every mark he put on you!"

Scrubbing the tears from her cheeks, Rosalind scrambled off the foot of the bed and bent to snatch up the bracelets. "You say these are mine. Very well, *mon capitaine.* I offer them to you as payment for the passage of myself and my companion Beatrice. Surely there is enough gold here to compensate you for whatever stores we consume before we reach Kingston."

Alexandre marveled. No matter how great her exhaustion or distress, Rosalind was determined to preserve some semblance of dignity. "And what of our original agreement, mademoiselle? What of those terms you so clearly set?"

"As for Beatrice's care, the terms are the same. All that has changed is the method of payment."

Alexandre stood, rising to his full height. He towered over Rosalind, who could barely stand upright, and yet she maintained her challenging pose. The bracelets were of sufficient value to make her new terms acceptable. Perhaps it would suit him to yield now. They were still on his ship, in the middle of the Caribbean. He fully intended to take shelter off Martinique before going anywhere near Kingston. That meant he had days before him, as many days as he chose. Allowing Rosalind this victory might mellow her temper and grant him greater headway with his plans.

"As you wish." Alexandre held out his hand for the bracelets. A wry smile tugged at the corner of his mouth. "You understand, mademoiselle, I accept these with the greatest disappointment."

"You are a rogue, *mon capitaine.*"

"I've been called worse, *ma belle,* and by you yourself."

Alexandre bent to scoop up the pearls. The sight of them made Rosalind blanch and turn away. A sudden longing seized Alexandre, a deep desire to wipe away all memory of Vasquez and the harm he'd done to Rosalind. Some of the blame lay on Alexandre as well. His first mistake had been in underestimating the magnificent woman who stood before him.

If only he could see Rosalind dressed up in her finest for a ball, perhaps one at his father's house. How his mother, the light-hearted Veronique, would delight in Rosalind's quick wit and stubborn ways. Sudden sorrow seized Alexandre, that bitter longing for everything he'd been forced to leave behind. He closed his mind and heart to such thoughts. If he let such grief take hold, it would torment him for days.

"And now, *ma belle,* I have kept you awake far too long." His instinct for tactics warned him to make a graceful retreat. He pressed his lips to her forehead in a gesture of reassurance. "Rest as long as you wish."

"But—I can hardly stay here."

"These are the best accommodations I can offer a lady who pays in gold. Unless you would prefer a hammock down below?"

When she still hesitated, Alexandre swept her up in his arms and deposited her on the bed. "Must I start giving you orders again, *ma belle?* And just when we were getting along so well."

Rosalind clung to his shoulders for a moment, giving him a fleeting hope of joining her. "May I see Beatrice later?"

"Of course. Sleep now. All will be well."

She smiled and snuggled beneath the covers. Alexandre stood looking down at her until her breathing deepened and he knew her to be fast asleep. The notion of what Veronique might think of Rosalind lingered in his mind, teasing him with impossible possibilities. He shook his head. He had other plans, plans that must be fulfilled. These days his life could be lived for nothing but revenge.

Chapter Fourteen

When Rosalind woke, the sunlight slanting through the stern windows painted reddish gold streaks across the bulkhead. The heat had begun to taper off. Late afternoon, then. The first dog watch? She'd slept a good many hours, warm and safe and undisturbed, not even hearing the ship's bell. She lay there, clinging to these few moments of peace. She turned her mind to the amazing puzzle presented by the sudden change in Alexandre. How different he had been, calling himself a fool and going down on his knees before her, very nearly begging her to have mercy on him. What a contrast to the mighty pirate king who made sport of her in front of his entire crew.

Alexandre had accepted the bracelets, appeared to accept the new arrangement, but the bitter events of recent months had taught Rosalind to be realistic. She was still trapped aboard *L'Etoile du Matin* miles from any friendly port. Alexandre was the Black Angel, enemy of the English, and he would do as he pleased aboard his own ship. At the moment it pleased him to let Rosalind think he was a gentleman, capable of being bound by his word.

She had her duty also to Beatrice. Waves of guilt banished the last of her comfort. She should have been up long ago, making sure Beatrice was getting the best care Dr. Gingras could provide. Rosalind threw back the bedclothes. If nothing else, she could regain some semblance of propriety by being dressed as a lady should be. That thought gave her a moment's panic. Her clothes would surely reveal her social class. Why would a spinster schoolteacher be dressing as a young lady of fashion? Alexandre would notice and comment on that. Rosalind made a face at the cabin door. She would tell him they were hand-me-downs from a wealthier sister-in-law.

She opened her trunk and took out a dress of peach satin, laying it out across the bed. Corset, petticoats, stockings, and white kid shoes followed. What a pity she had no maid on hand. Even Beatrice would have been helpful in putting her hair up. Alexandre had seen her at her worst, fetched up from the sea in the torn remnants of her lingerie. He'd seen her dressed up in the despicable costume Vasquez had demanded. Let the Black Angel now see her as Miss Rosalind Brooks, a young woman of dignity and purpose.

It was a great comfort to be fully dressed again in clean, dry clothes. With every garment she put on, Rosalind felt her command of herself returning. The heat was doubly oppressive, but with evening coming on there should be some respite. Rosalind freed the end of her braid and unplaited it. She hunted in the depths of her trunk until she found the ivory comb Thomas had brought back to her from one of his voyages abroad. A few stray hair pins came to hand. She sat on the bed and leaned over, letting the golden curtain of her long hair fall free. She worked the comb through it, patiently separating the tangles. The rhythm of her strokes soothed her ragged nerves. First she would see Beatrice. Then she would seek out Dr. Gingras and hear his opinion of Beatrice's condition. Armed with that knowledge, she would appeal to Alexandre again to make haste for Jamaica. Vasquez had been sailing parallel to the island rather than away from it. They might still be only a day or two out of port.

The cabin door opened. Alexandre stood there, dressed in one of his loose white shirts and a pair of light cotton breeches. Even his boots were gone in deference to the heat of the day. His long hair was drawn back from his face. He looked so young, so carefree. Embarrassed to realize she'd been staring, Rosalind sprang up. Habit made her swing the length of her hair back over her shoulder. It fell heavy and loose in a golden wave, breaking against her hips and curling forward around her thighs. Alexandre stared at her. Those dark eyes took in every inch of her appearance. His lips parted, as if longing for a taste of her. His normally stern expression softened into wonder and delight.

"Oui, mon capitaine?" Rosalind asked.

Alexandre stepped forward. His fingertips touched Rosalind's temples, sliding back into her hair, moving down her neck. The tenderness, the wonder, the reverence in Alexandre's touch. . . . Rosalind stood still, powerless to resist the look of total fascination in Alexandre's eyes. His hands came up again, sinking down through her hair, cupping her face in his hands. He bent his head and claimed her lips with his. She leaned into him. His thinner clothing let her enjoy the contours of his muscular frame.

Alexandre's hands sifted through her hair, stroking it, caressing it, just as his lips caressed hers. He touched her as if he treasured her. Such a man, such a beautiful, passionate, thrilling man. . . . Her lips parted beneath his, her hands rising of their own will to embrace him. Alexandre sighed. His tongue caressed hers, curling around it, coaxing her into his mouth. He tasted rich and sweet and potent, a mixture of rum and his pipe tobacco and the salt spray on his lips. Those long, elegant fingers kept gliding through her hair. Rosalind waited, expecting him to take further liberties. He simply held her, stroking her hair.

"You are a vision, *ma belle.*" Alexandre pressed a kiss to

her temple and let a handful of her hair spill through his fingers. "Never have I seen such radiance."

"*Merci, mon capitaine.*" Rosalind moved back, putting a little safe distance between them. The look on Alexandre's face, the tone of his voice, disturbed her. They spoke more loudly than all the pretty protestations he'd made earlier. "I believe you were about to say something?"

"Whatever it was, it can wait."

Alexandre shut the door and took Rosalind's hands, holding them out at arm's length as he turned her around. Rosalind almost laughed. They were very nearly dancing, just as she had imagined earlier. Alexandre watched her twirl, then spun her around again in the opposite direction. Her hair flew out, catching the sun. When he reached for her again, Rosalind staggered back out of reach, one hand to her head.

"Please, *mon capitaine!* You are like a little boy with a top, spinning me around."

Now the wonder and admiration in Alexandre's expression were replaced by that wicked charm. "And you, *ma belle,* are the kind of toy only bigger boys are allowed to play with."

Rosalind tried to muster some dignity. "I am not a toy, *mon capitaine.*"

"You say that only because you've never been properly played with."

Alexandre caught Rosalind up in his arms, whirling her around. She could do nothing but cling to him. When the cabin stopped spinning around her, she was chagrined to discover they lay on his bed.

"I'm not one for playing with dolls," Alexandre said, "but I think I would enjoy dressing and undressing you." He gave the lace at her bosom a playful tug.

Rosalind swatted his hand. "*Mon capitaine!* Must I tell you to act your age?"

Alexandre grinned, a slow, hungry curve of those full lips, causing Rosalind a thrill of both fear and desire.

"As you wish, *ma belle.* I will stop making nursery jokes and do what a man my age would do."

He swung one long leg over hers, then planted his hand on the far side of the pillow beside her head. His weight came down on her, trapping her beneath him. The breath gusted out of Rosalind in a squeak of outrage. Her hands were caught between their bodies. She jerked them free, ready to shove him off her if need be. Alexandre caught both wrists in his left hand and pinned them over her head. His free hand settled over her breast, the heat of his palm sinking down through the satin and batiste to her bare skin.

"Tell me, *ma belle,* just how many layers of your fine English linen do I have to wade through before I land on your virgin shores?"

Rosalind looked away, feeling hot and flustered and very much afraid he wasn't joking anymore. She put on an expression of cold hauteur. "*Mon capitaine,* I must insist you remove yourself at once. You are creasing my gown."

"Am I?" Alexandre stared at his hand in mocking amazement. "I would have thought it would take much more to crease satin. Like so, perhaps?"

He squeezed her breast, a slow, gentle, sensuous movement. Confusion, frustration, and desire warred within Rosalind, emerging in a low groan.

"I cannot hear you, mademoiselle. You will be kind enough to speak up." He squeezed harder, a rolling movement of his hand that made Rosalind's back arch. Another groan gusted out of her.

"*C'est bon.* Now we continue." Alexandre lifted his hand from her breast. "I see no creases here, mademoiselle. Perhaps it is the little points of great pressure that do the damage." His thumb and forefinger closed on her nipple, rolling it back and forth.

"Stop that!" Rosalind struggled beneath him, trying to gain some leverage.

Alexandre made a low sound in his throat. "Take care, mademoiselle. As I said the day we met, if you persist in rubbing your body against mine in this wanton fashion, I may take that as an invitation."

Rosalind lay still, furious at knowing he'd trapped her in more ways than one.

"Perhaps mademoiselle is worried about her skirt." Alexandre gathered a handful of the satin, baring Rosalind's right thigh. "What are we to do about mademoiselle's skirt?"

Alexandre's weight suddenly left her. Before Rosalind could move, her skirt and petticoats came flying up over her face. She shrieked with embarrassment and fury and struck out at the mass of cloth, trying to fight her way clear.

"Mademoiselle is worried about her gown." Alexandre murmured the words against the last thin layer of linen that protected her. "I must then avoid it." The sudden heat of Alexandre's breath on the sensitive skin of her inner thigh made Rosalind hold very still. "Mademoiselle has taken such pains with her toilette, I cannot bring back her *déshabillé*."

The tropical heat was nothing to the heat burning inside Rosalind, a slow liquid yearning that left her breathless. She struggled free of her skirts, pushing them down far enough to glare at Alexandre. He rested his head on her thigh. His face was flushed, his dark eyes bright beneath his half-closed lids. One corner of his mouth pulled up in a lazy smile.

"Unless," he said, "mademoiselle herself asks me to do so."

" 'Mademoiselle' has no intention of doing so," Rosalind snapped. "Now kindly get off me!"

Alexandre rubbed his cheek against her thigh, moving slightly higher each time he turned his head. He looked so smug, so sure of himself. That alone was enough to infuriate Rosalind. Worse still was the knowledge that her traitorous body was responding to him, to the feel of him pressed against her in such an intimate place.

"I warn you, *mon capitaine*. Remove yourself at once!"

"And if I do not?" Alexandre touched a fingertip to a tiny satin bow nestled amid the lace on this last petticoat. He stroked the bow's loops, trailing his finger back and forth over them in a slow, lazy gesture. Rosalind quivered beneath his touch.

"Very well, *mon capitaine*. You leave me no choice."

Rosalind planted her right foot against Alexandre's chest. Before she could shove him away, his hand came up to catch her ankle and push it up over his shoulder. Too late Rosalind realized her mistake. She fought, trying to jerk her leg free. Alexandre held her thigh clamped to his shoulder. He took the hem of her petticoat in his teeth and dragged it higher up her thigh, baring more of her naked skin. The heat of his breath teased her, its caress making her long for more. He kissed the tender skin high on the inside of her left thigh, soft little kisses that stirred her to a new height of longing. Her body ached for more, but her mind refused to surrender.

"No! Please, I beg you!"

"What's this? My Lady Hellcat begging me for mercy?"

Alexandre planted a lingering kiss on that soft cluster of curls fair as cornsilk. He teased her, darting his tongue into her soft, moist depths. Rosalind cried out, torn between the need to escape him and the powerful need to yield. She tried to twist away. Alexandre held on, using her struggles to help him as his tongue explored her. Rosalind fell back against the pillows, dizzy from the wild heat raging through her.

Alexandre ran one fingertip lightly over the flaxen curls so damp from his kisses. "Will you beg, *ma belle?* Will you beg me to love you, to make love to you, to be the first man who feels you tremble beneath him as you taste the rapture this will bring?"

Rosalind lay still, every nerve in her body focused on the light brush of his fingertip. His voice was hypnotic, wrapping her in its rich music just as she longed to be wrapped up in the velvet darkness of his eyes.

"Nothing to say, *ma belle?*" Alexandre sighed in mock distress. "Very well. If I must torture you, I will."

Rosalind drew breath to speak. His lips touched her, his tongue thrusting deep. He kissed her there as thoroughly as he'd kissed her mouth, exploring every hidden fold. Rosalind's breath gusted out in a groan. His tongue touched that tiny nub of flesh, teasing her until the breath caught in her lungs and she feared she'd choke.

"Alexandre! Please, I can't—can't breathe—"

Hot waves of pleasure washed over her, drowning her. Her body took over, her hips moving, her breath shallow. Her back arched. Her head fell back against the pillows. All the sensations Alexandre roused in her gathered into one hot, tight knot. Rosalind let out a cry, hands fisting in the bedclothes. Her world shattered in a sudden brilliant implosion of joy. The glory of it raged through her again and again, leaving her gasping in the wake of such hot pulsations. She sagged back against the pillows, breathing hard. Alexandre gently brought her legs together, drawing down her petticoats and skirt. He stretched out beside her and leaned on one elbow, resting his head on his hand.

Rosalind floated in a cloud of pleasure, feeling a delicious lassitude fill her as the echoes of her joy faded away. Lost as she was in her rapture, she turned her head to look at Alexandre. "Will you not—not press your advantage, *mon capitaine?*"

"Would you like that, *ma belle?*" His voice was a husky whisper. "Do you want me, even as I burn for you?" He took her hand and guided it to his hips, pressing her palm against the hard strength of his desire. "You are ready, my sweet rose. There will be a moment's hurt, true, but it will be quickly forgotten." He brushed his lips over hers. "You will remember nothing but paradise."

Paradise. The Black Angel prided himself on giving all his women a taste of paradise. How many women were there? How many had there been? Rosalind snatched back her hand and sat up, shaking back her hair.

"No thank you, *mon capitaine*. This rose refuses to become just another withered blossom in your pirate's vase."

She swung her legs off the bed and stood up, cold indignation chasing off that sinful heat. In a further effort to regain her composure, she moved away from the bed and began to wind the length of her hair into a golden rope. She bound it into a hasty bun atop her head, securing it with those few precious hairpins. She turned to find Alexandre watching her with an expression somewhere between bafflement and vexation.

"You are a fool, Rosalind. These could be the happiest moments of your life."

Something in his voice disturbed her. Gone was the joking tone, the mockery, even the stern captain's command. Alexandre spoke plainly, almost as if he gave her some kind of warning. He rose, circling around behind her, speaking so that his breath fanned her neck.

"Will you let your prissy English ways stand between you and true happiness?"

"You are confused, *mon capitaine*. Not everyone equates satisfying his lust with finding true joy."

"Perhaps not, *ma belle*. But it is an excellent beginning."

He took her by the shoulders and turned her to face him. Rosalind was startled to see the intensity of his expression, the determination there. "You have tasted the merest sip of the joy I plan to bring you."

"Please, *mon capitaine*." Rosalind turned her face away from the passion blazing in the depths of those dark eyes. "I must see to Beatrice. The poor child needs me."

"What of your needs, *ma belle*? You give no thought to yourself. Even now your body cries out for greater fulfillment, yet you would dash off to play nursemaid."

"You will excuse me, *mon capitaine,* if I value duty above self-indulgence."

Alexandre blew out his breath, ran one hand back over his hair. "*Très bien,* mademoiselle. You will play the cold, proud lady no matter how much it costs you."

Rosalind flinched. Again he called her a lady. Did he know? Had he somehow guessed? She put on a stubborn face, hoping Alexandre would mistake her reaction for hurt at his rebuke.

"I believe I have done very well so far, *mon capitaine.* Now. Beatrice needs me."

"*Mais oui.*" Alexandre dropped his hands from her shoulders and stepped back. "Your *petite amie* calls for you. That was what I came to tell you."

"I will go to her at once."

"Of course."

Rosalind raised her head and met Alexandre's steady gaze, searching the depths of those dark eyes, hoping for some glimpse of the truth. Alexandre could be charming, to the point of stealing her wits and leaving her defenseless. Even now, standing this close to him was dangerous. His tall, broad presence, the warmth of him, the pulse beating in his throat, even the scents of salt spray and pipe tobacco on his clothing. She longed to touch him, to be gathered up in his arms again, to lose herself in the joy of his embrace. He had brought her an ecstasy far beyond anything she'd ever known. Having discovered it, her newly awakened senses taunted her, making her think about the greater pleasure Alexandre could give her.

She was so tired. Her whole being ached for a safe haven, for someone to make everything all right again. To be free of the anguish that was her constant companion. Here before her stood a man who could offer her all that, were it not for the inescapable fact that he was a pirate, and not just any pirate. He was the Black Angel, enemy of English shipping and brother to the pirates who had destroyed her family.

Alexandre smiled. "You are so beautiful, Rosalind. I cannot look at you enough."

Again that tender simplicity. Speechless, Rosalind bowed her head against the sight of what smoldered in the depths of Alexandre's dark eyes. There was no denying the reality of his desire, whether or not she chose to believe his reasons for it.

"May I go now, *mon capitaine?*"

"*Oui.* At the suggestion of my surgeon, the *jeune fille* now sits on the quarterdeck. You may join her there." He opened the door for her and stood aside.

Chapter Fifteen

Beatrice sat on a low stool on the windward side of the quarterdeck, fanning herself with a fan woven of palm fronds. Thinner, pale, and haggard, she looked the picture of misery, despite the festive style of her pale blue bridesmaid gown.

"Beatrice!" Rosalind rushed forward to embrace her.

"Rosalind!" Beatrice hugged Rosalind as tightly as she could. The very weakness of the embrace pained Rosalind. "I was so worried for you, when that evil man made you put on that horrible costume. How are you?"

Rosalind looked away. "I am well enough."

Beatrice clasped Rosalind's hands in her own. "Poor Rosalind. You've suffered so much, and all for my sake. I owe you a debt I cannot possibly repay."

"Nonsense, Beatrice. You owe me nothing. What I've done I've done out of common human decency."

"Not so common." Beatrice sat back, a happy smile shining through her obvious exhaustion. "You are so grand, Rosalind. So clever, so strong. I hope I will see more of you once we reach Jamaica."

Rosalind shut her eyes against the hope and faith in Beatrice's voice. She had to be strong, to hold on, to keep her fear and grief in check until she had accomplished some better long-term solution to their predicament.

"Where is Mr. MacCaulay?" Beatrice said. "I've asked for him, but no one will answer me."

"The captain has sent him to Jamaica aboard the smaller pirate ship."

"Then . . . he's safe?"

"Or shall be, very soon."

"I didn't know what to believe," Beatrice said. "Eric claimed the Black Angel had chased that other pirate ship halfway around Jamaica, and all because he wanted you back! Is that true?"

"Yes, apparently it is."

"But why? Why would the captain go to such lengths to take you prisoner again?"

"I don't know, Beatrice. I've been wondering that myself."

Beatrice leaned forward and spoke in a whisper. "There's something very strange here. Mr. MacCaulay thought this isn't really a pirate ship at all."

"Had he any idea what it is?"

"Mr. MacCaulay said the captain and crew behave as they might aboard a regular merchant ship, or on one of those navy ships that escorts merchant vessels through dangerous waters. What do you think, Rosalind? Are these men really pirates?"

Rosalind fretted, wishing she could put the pieces of this puzzle together. There were gaps—large, tantalizing gaps in the picture. Who was the Black Angel? What had he been before he took to piracy? Surely a man so elegant and commanding hadn't grown up aboard ship. He had the manners of a gentleman, if not the sensibilities.

"Eric said the captain was crazy to attack the other pirate ship. He thought the captain must know something about you that made it worth his time to take you back." Beatrice dropped her voice to a whisper again. "He doesn't know, does he? Who you are?"

"There's no way he could have found out. Except . . . Oh no." Cold terror shot through Rosalind. She had stopped Vasquez before he could shout out her title and the news that she was engaged to Edward Murdock, but she recalled how Vasquez had gleefully tortured Captain Bellamy to find out all he knew. Perhaps Alexandre had done something similar to Captain Harris. "Only Captain Harris knew my full name. The Black Angel might have learned it from him."

"Do you think that's what happened? That he does know?"

Rosalind concentrated, calling to mind everything Alexandre had said, all those flowery phrases of apology and desire. Why would Alexandre try so hard to win her, to convince her of his honorable side? He might have been exercising his charm on "a little English milkmaid" just to satisfy his arrogance and amuse himself. If he did know her to be the daughter of an English peer, wouldn't the Black Angel count it a glorious revenge to hand her over to a monster like Vasquez? Alexandre himself had said any other pirate would have left her to Vasquez and laughed about it.

"No," Rosalind said. "No, I am sure he does not know. He would not treat me half so well if he did."

"Then it will all be over soon? He'll take us to Kingston and we'll go ashore and everything will be all right?"

Despite her own misgivings, Rosalind smiled. "Yes. Just a little longer now, and all will be well."

For a moment Rosalind's heart lifted. Things might be all right after all. She simply had to persuade Alexandre to put into port at Kingston as soon as possible. One look at Beatrice's pale face, thin cheeks, and haggard manner should convince him how necessary that was. A sudden weariness dulled Rosalind's relief. They were still a long way from home. She had never been one for cards, although she played piquet well enough when Mother coaxed her into a game. Now she found herself counting her cards, calculating her plays, and hoping with all her heart she could somehow manage to trump the Black Angel himself.

"I think it's time you rested," Rosalind said. "Does Dr. Gingras have a place for you?"

"He told me to take the air up here. The sick berth is full of men, some of them badly wounded."

Rosalind gasped. Of course. As madly as Vasquez's crew had fought, there had to be wounds. Perhaps even deaths. She turned away before Beatrice could see her anguish. The ship's bell struck four times. Rosalind tried to count the pirates as they swarmed over the main deck and up into the rigging, taking their places for the second dog watch. As many as there were, it was hard to tell if there were fewer than yesterday. The second mate, Remy, stood by the helmsman. Nowhere did she see the tall, lean figure of Alexandre.

Even as she thought of him, Alexandre's voice rang out above her. Rosalind looked up to see him seated on a yard well up the mainmast. Alexandre called down to someone on the deck, his impeccable French booming through the warm air. After giving a final tug on one of the ropes, Alexandre rolled forward off the yard with practiced ease and planted his bare feet in the ratlines below him. He climbed down to the deck, moving with graceful ease. Rosalind could not take her eyes from the play of muscles in his shoulders and back, their rhythmic bunching and flexing. Her hands tingled with the memory of stroking the hard muscles girding his ribs and shoulder blades. She knew only too well how strong he was, strong enough to hold her captive while he'd—while he'd kissed her in that indecent manner. Her body still savored the fading languor of that wild blazing joy. The sight of Alexandre stripped to the waist did nothing to cool the heat ready to flare up within her. Alexander landed lightly on the deck, presenting her with the view of his bare chest. He laughed at something one of the pirates said, his white teeth gleaming. He was at ease, master of his vessel. Victory had lightened his saturnine manner, bringing out more of his natural charm. He was indeed a charming man, when he chose to be.

Rosalind turned back to Beatrice and held out both

hands. "Come, Beatrice. We should go below. This tropical sun is too much for us."

Beatrice rose obediently. Rosalind led the way toward the hatch. It lay beyond Alexandre. He saw them coming and watched as they approached. Rosalind's heart began to pound, sending warmth rushing through her. Alexandre's smile broadened. The scoundrel! He knew the effect he was having on her. He flexed his shoulders, pretending stiffness when all he wanted was an excuse to flaunt his figure. Rosalind looked straight ahead as they passed him.

"A moment, mademoiselle."

Rosalind kept moving, gently herding Beatrice on ahead of her. Alexandre's hand closed on Rosalind's elbow.

"Such hurry, mademoiselle. One would think you don't wish to speak to me." Alexandre looked Beatrice over, then spoke in English. "All is well, little one? You are recovering?"

Beatrice blushed scarlet, her eyes fixed on her tightly clasped hands. "Yes, Captain. Thank you."

"How soon will we make Kingston, Captain?" Rosalind asked, also in English. "As you can see, Beatrice requires more thorough medical attention to fully recover from this ordeal."

"We are perhaps two days from Kingston at this point."

"Wonderful! How soon will we dock there?"

Alexandre's brows drew together. "We will not dock there, nor in any common port. There is a rather high price on my head, as I'm sure you can appreciate."

"Then how can Beatrice possibly receive the care she must have? Really, Captain, you must—"

Alexandre held up one hand. "Dr. Gingras is one of the finest in the Caribbean. He tells me the little one needs fresh air and good food. Both are available here."

"But surely you mean to put us ashore at some point, Captain?"

" 'At some point' I do. Until then, you must permit me the pleasure of your company. It is not often I enjoy such entertaining passengers."

His mocking attempt at gallantry sparked Rosalind's temper. "So. We are captives of your will, if not your irons."

Annoyance flashed in Alexandre's eyes like lightning before a storm. "Please, mademoiselle. You are my guests." He drew her away from Beatrice. "And now, little one, perhaps you should rest until dinner is served." He scanned the horizon. "By the look of the clouds, it should be a most delightful sunset."

Beatrice gave Rosalind an anxious glance. "Please, Captain, may Rosalind go with me? Eric is very kind, but I'd prefer the company of another woman."

"I prefer her company as well, little one. You shall see her again at dinner." Alexandre's tone was pleasant but final.

Beatrice made her way to the hatch. Two pirates appeared beside her, attending her like bearded, scruffy maids. Eric himself stepped forward and went down the hatch first, his big hands reaching up to steady Beatrice.

"Your orders, *mon capitaine?*" Rosalind asked.

Alexandre nodded. "We don't want the *jeune fille* to come to any harm. She is weak and ill and not to be left alone."

He drew Rosalind along with him to his private area on the quarterdeck. The lowering sun bathed him in its rich light, gilding his bronzed skin and making him seem all the more fierce and powerful. He took one step toward Rosalind, then another. Rosalind backed up until her shoulders touched the network of ropes called the shrouds. Alexandre reached up to grasp a rope in each hand. He leaned on them, his arms making a little alcove that trapped Rosalind. He was so close to her the sun lit his eyes, changing the dark brown there into a bewitching cinnamon.

"Perhaps you are not quite so eager to return to this life I interrupted?"

"Really, *mon capitaine.*" Rosalind fought to steady her voice. "You cannot imagine I want to do anything more than get off this ship and go home again."

"Shall I tell you what I think, *ma belle?*"

Alexandre reached back to pull the ribbon from his hair. He shook it out then leaned forward, making his hair spill down around his face and hers, cloaking them in its ebony satin.

"I think you no longer know precisely what you want." His lips brushed her temple. "Here in the Caribbean you've found life to be wild and dangerous and full of all the things you've been warned against." He trailed tiny kisses down her cheek until he just touched the corner of her lips. "You've survived a shipwreck and eluded the sharks and known the triumph of seeing your enemy fall dead at your feet." He kissed her throat, moving up to whisper against her ear. "Most of all, you now know the pleasure a proper English girl should never admit to feeling."

Shame and anger and the need to surrender fought within Rosalind, bringing hot color to her cheeks. She had to escape this dangerous truth before she was lost completely. She planted both hands on Alexandre's chest, about to push him away. His arms slid round her waist, one hand moving down to her hips and the other up into her hair. He pressed her against him, making her feel the hard strength of his body. She stood rigid within the circle of his arms.

"Release me, *mon capitaine*."

Alexandre clucked his tongue. "You cannot pretend to be as innocent as you were, *ma belle*. I have brought you to heights of pleasure you never knew existed. Once such a fire is roused in the blood, it cannot be denied."

"It most certainly can," Rosalind said. "There are some people who can restrain themselves, *mon capitaine*. There are even those who take pride in doing so."

"It is easy to avoid what you've never known." Alexandre ran his fingertips over the golden wealth of Rosalind's hair. "But you, *ma belle*. You have tasted the merest sip of that heavenly nectar that awaits those who savor true passion. Can you tell me you have no thirst for more?"

He touched her chin and forced her to meet his gaze. His dark eyes glowed with that inner fire, that molten longing she'd seen when she lay in his arms. Those arms, bare now, every muscle defined beneath the bronzed skin stretched taut over sinew and bone. A sudden wild urge seized Rosalind, a mad longing to run her hands down his back, then up into his hair. How glorious to lose herself in its blackness, to wrap herself in its silky length and hide forever from the present that tormented her and the future she dreaded.

"You are fortunate, *mon capitaine.*"

"And why is that, *ma belle?*"

"Some of us who long for wine must make do with water."

Alexandre stared at her for a long, silent moment. The playfulness faded from his expression, replaced by puzzlement. "Nonsense, *ma belle.* A woman as glorious as you can command the rarest vintages."

"You don't understand!" Rosalind twisted in his grip, fighting him until he released her. "You know nothing of me or my life, *mon capitaine.* I'll thank you to spare me your flattery. As for this precious nectar you speak of, you may go and drown yourself in it!"

She ran down the few steps to the deck, rushing past the startled faces of the pirates. The hatch lay before her. Her foot came down on a coil of rope lying in front of the hatch. She stumbled forward, about to fall headlong down the hatch. Strong hands caught her skirt and arms and hauled her upright. To her chagrin, she found herself looking up into the pale eyes of Yves.

"Have a care, mademoiselle. You might hurt someone."

Rosalind gathered up the shreds of her dignity. "*Merci,* Monsieur Yves."

"*Le capitaine* has ordered dinner on the quarterdeck, mademoiselle. He will expect you and your *petite soeur* in half an hour."

"Is that so?" Rosalind glared at the quarterdeck. "I believe I've provided *le capitaine* with quite enough entertainment for one day."

"Mademoiselle, you cannot refuse to attend."

"Oh yes I can." Rosalind planted one foot on the first rung of the ladder leading down the hatch. "Be kind enough to remind *le capitaine* I've paid for my passage in gold. If he wants jesters or dancing bears, he's in for disappointment!"

Chapter Sixteen

Beatrice rubbed her cheek. "Mr. Lawrence lives on a plantation. Acres and acres of fields. How quiet it shall be there." She cast a rueful look at the constant uproar above them, then nestled her head against Rosalind's shoulder. Her eyes closed. After a moment, she began to nod off.

They sat near the bow of the ship on a pile of canvas that made the softest seat available. Their current quarters were airy enough, with the breeze blowing down the forward hatch. Given how tightly packed *L'Etoile du Matin*'s hold was with the accumulated cargo, it was a wonder they found any empty deck space at all.

Rosalind eased Beatrice down across her lap, stroking the girl's fine hair. Beatrice curled up like a child. Rosalind winced a little at the feverish heat still flushing Beatrice's skin. There had to be more this Monsieur Gingras could be doing for her! Rosalind made a fretful noise.

Loud voices approached their little sanctuary. Two pirates appeared, cleaner and neater than most of the men aboard, led by none other than Yves himself.

"Mademoiselle." Yves wiped a weary hand over his face.

"You told me you intended to take my advice. Kindly do so now."

Rosalind looked away. "I have since told you I do not intend to provide *le capitaine* with any more entertainment this evening. Of any sort," she added.

Yves considered her for a moment, then squatted down beside her. "Mademoiselle, shall I tell you what will happen if I carry your refusal to *le capitaine*? He will come down here himself, throw you over his shoulder, carry you up to the quarterdeck, and order you lashed to your seat."

Rosalind crossed her arms tightly and fixed her gaze on the deck before her. "I invite him to try."

Yves's expression darkened. "Mademoiselle, do you know how many men of *L'Etoile du Matin* died today?"

Rosalind flinched. She shook her head.

"Twenty. In a battle such as that, so few must be counted as a small loss. I do not count them so." Now Yves's voice became pure ice. "Those were men, mademoiselle. Frenchmen. My shipmates and my friends."

Rosalind hugged her arms tighter around herself, trying to shut out the agonizing knowledge. Yves was making it personal, making her see and feel every single death.

"Those men gave their lives to save you, mademoiselle. All because they were loyal to *le capitaine*, who believes you are worth such a price."

"It's plain you do not share his belief."

"I'll tell you what I believe, mademoiselle. If you have any decency in you, you will honor the memory of the men who died today. You will get yourself up to the quarterdeck this instant. You may think nothing of *le capitaine*, but you might at least show your gratitude to the rest of us."

For the first time Rosalind saw Yves as a man, a fellow human being, someone's son, brother, perhaps even father. She looked at the two pirates with him. They too were men, and they had fought among the other men who saved her from Vasquez. By now she knew they weren't simply pirates. She'd seen true pirates aboard Vasquez's ship, vile curs who were human only in appearance.

"Thank you, *messieurs*. I owe you my life. I am truly sorry for your loss."

"Prove it, mademoiselle," Yves said. "Keep *le capitaine* in a good mood. Do not provoke him again."

Rosalind stood. "You have made your point, Monsieur Yves. Kindly stand aside and let me show this gratitude you demand." Head held high, Rosalind led the way up through the hatch and onward to the quarterdeck.

Alexandre stood at the rail, staring out at the horizon. A few masses of clouds floated against the deep blue of the tropical sky. They caught the rays of the setting sun and showed them like solid bars of light spearing upward. Rich pinks and oranges glowed against the bellies of the clouds. The changing light made the waves flash almost silver.

Alexandre turned. Rosalind's breath caught and her heart raced. Gone were his casual working clothes. Now he wore green velvet, a coat and breeches cut as fine as his burgundy attire, glittering with gold lace. His crisp white shirt bore both a cravat and jabot. White stockings outlined the muscles in his calves, their pristine state made all the more dramatic by his black leather shoes with bright silver buckles. As ever, Alexandre scorned both a hat and a wig. The sleek blackness of his hair accentuated his cheekbones and the stern line of his jaw. Silhouetted against the glorious sky, Alexandre cut a dramatic figure, fierce and imposing. He held Rosalind's gaze for a long moment. A smile curved those full lips, bringing out the beauty of his features.

"*Bonsoir,* mademoiselle."

"*Bonsoir, mon capitaine.*" Rosalind glanced back at Yves who stood just behind her, his expression once more impassive. She moved a few steps closer to Alexandre, lightly placing her hand in his. "I take it this is a victory dinner. We must salute the courage of your crew."

"It is indeed, mademoiselle." Alexandre pulled her hand through the crook of his arm.

"Mademoiselle." Yves stepped up beside Beatrice and offered her his arm.

Beatrice hesitated, clearly unwilling to allow him this familiarity. At Rosalind's encouraging nod, Beatrice took Yves's arm and followed him to her place across from Rosalind.

Eight finely carved wooden chairs had been positioned around a rectangular table. Dr. Gingras and three officers stood waiting, each behind the chair set at his particular place. The table was laid with porcelain plates, sterling cutlery, and linen napkins. Shining silver goblets sat at each place. Upon Rosalind's arrival, they all fell silent and stood at attention.

"Ladies." Alexandre spoke in English, giving Beatrice a smile. "Permit me to present to you the officers of my ship. Our fine doctor you already know."

Dr. Gingras bowed. Alexandre gestured toward the round little man on Rosalind's right.

"As a reward for his brilliance in keeping us on course despite the storm, mademoiselle, I have placed on your right hand *Monsieur le Navigateur*."

"Monsieur." Rosalind held out her hand. The navigator bowed over it in the proper fashion.

"Next to him you will find the clever rogue who sent *La Fortuna* to the bottom. May I present *Monsieur le Cannonier*."

Rosalind made a careful nod at the master gunner, the man responsible for the Black Angel's impressive record of prizes taken with such speed and devastating accuracy. Despite her annoyance with the farcical nature of this charade, Rosalind gave him a genuine smile.

"Your precision saved my life, particularly when *Capitaine* Vasquez had the bad taste to make me a secondary figurehead."

Alexandre and Dr. Gingras chuckled. The navigator

smiled briefly. The master gunner thought for a moment, then laughed.

"*C'est bon,* mademoiselle! I am glad to see you once again aboard *L'Etoile du Matin,* where you belong."

Rosalind wondered at his choice of words. Before she could give it further thought, Alexandre turned her to face the man who stood to the left of Dr. Gingras. His jacket hung oddly across his torso, pushed out of line by what had to be a mass of bandaging around his lower ribs. It was the same enormous bear of a man who had tried to put himself between Rosalind and Vasquez.

"You!" Rosalind cried. "But—but I saw Vasquez shoot you! I was sure you were dead!"

"Ah," Alexandre said. "Of all of us, you have won Mademoiselle's regard. Well done, *Monsieur le Maître d'E-quipage.*"

The bosun. Of course. When he tried to shrug off Alexandre's praise, he winced a little. This proof of blood shed in her name made Rosalind hurry around the table.

"*Merci beaucoup, Monsieur le Maître d'Equipage.* I am sorry for your pain."

The bosun smiled down at her. "You have nothing to apologize for, mademoiselle."

Rosalind held out her hand. He bowed, wincing only a little, and brushed his lips across her fingers.

"If I cannot die in the service of my country, I would be content to die in the service of such a beautiful and courageous lady."

"*Messieurs.*" Rosalind faced them all. "This contretemps I find myself in has been most educational. I now realize a pirate can be many different things, and many different sorts of men may become pirates. You yourselves I cannot but think of as *chevaliers du mer.*"

The officers looked suitably pleased. Alexandre moved around the table to take Rosalind's hand back from the bosun, flashing him a friendly grin.

"*S'il-vous plaît,* mademoiselle. Praise my men much higher and their heads will swell so big not one of them could climb down a hatch!"

He spoke with a touch of his usual irony, but when Rosalind looked up at him, she saw only that tenderness, that sweet, boyish charm. She had done more than merely please him. Somehow she had made him happy.

Pirates arrived bearing dishes of fresh fish, poultry, and shellfish, each in its own unique sauce. One of the ship's boys brought a bucket that held three bottles of wine. Alexandre chose one and inserted a slender dagger into the cork. With one adroit twist he pulled it free, then poured a generous amount of wine into each silver goblet. He rose, holding his goblet so it caught the light of the setting sun. The other men rose as well.

"*Messieurs.*" Alexandre smiled on all of them. "What shall we drink to?" His gaze came to rest on Rosalind. One corner of his mouth quirked with gentle mischief. "Ah, I have it. Let us drink to courage, that most admirable of virtues."

Rosalind met this display of flattery with that other admirable virtue, sangfroid. Alexandre clearly intended to put on another of his performances. As he gazed at her, the heat in his eyes lent his smile a shade of intimacy that made Rosalind's heart pound. To look away would be an insult, but to go on meeting that hungry stare would make her lose her wits completely.

"*A courage, ma chère* mademoiselle."

"*A courage,*" Yves said.

The other officers echoed him, raising their goblets to Rosalind. Her peach satin suddenly felt as hot and constricting as heavy wool. She made herself sit perfectly still, betraying none of her discomfort.

The men drank. When Rosalind took a token sip from her goblet, Beatrice did the same. Beatrice made a face at the taste of the wine, bringing an involuntary smile to Rosalind's lips. The excellent Madeira was quite strong. She would take care not to drink more than a minimal amount. She did her best to ignore everything Alexandre said until she heard the familiar sounds of English being spoken.

"Tell me something, little one."

Beatrice jerked back in her chair. "Me, Captain?"

"What is it you teach?"

Beatrice fumbled nervously at the napkin lying in her lap. "Well, Captain, I teach reading and writing, some sewing, a little embroidery."

"You are but a child. How is it your parents have not kept you at home?"

"I chose to leave home, Captain." Beatrice spoke in a voice of quiet dignity. "I must do what I can to support my family."

Alexandre's clever smile mellowed for a moment into something kinder, more genuine. "I see Mademoiselle Rosalind is not the only lady here who can claim her share of courage."

An icy chill swept over Rosalind. Again he referred to her as a lady! She laid her fork aside, suddenly unable to bear another bite. Alexandre couldn't know. He couldn't. A man like him, with his wild temper, wouldn't play this kind of waiting game. He'd trumpet his knowledge and mock her to the very skies.

Beatrice glanced at Rosalind. "No courage, Captain. Just what has to be done."

Rosalind held back a smile. How well Beatrice answered Alexandre! Sweet, brave, honest girl!

"Perhaps you would be kind enough to tell us about your field of expertise, mademoiselle."

Rosalind found herself the object of Alexandre's steady dark stare. Confronted with such a direct question, she could think of nothing to say. The noise of cutlery gradually subsided as the officers gave her their attention. Alexandre leaned his elbow on the table and rested his chin on his hand, arching one black brow. He would wait until she gave in and spoke. With a sigh, Rosalind resigned herself to breaking her silence.

"I teach music, Captain."

"What instrument do you play?"

"The piano, the harpsichord, and a little harp."

"I should love to hear you play. Do you sing?"

"Not well, I'm afraid."

"Nonsense. The force and grandeur of your ordinary speech must surely be matched by the loveliness of your singing voice."

Once again the irony was missing from his voice. He sounded sincere, perhaps even wistful. For some reason that upset Rosalind even more. As the color flooded her cheeks, she stabbed a scallop and drowned it in its creamy sauce.

"You mock me, Captain."

Alexandre inclined his head. "Perhaps a little."

He turned his attention to his meal, freeing the rest of them to do the same. When that course was finished, the ship's boys came again to clear away. They set out a variety of smaller dishes filled with cheeses, nuts, oranges, and limes.

" 'Eat, drink, and be merry,' is that it, *mon capitaine?*" Rosalind asked.

Alexandre nodded. "Our very motto here, mademoiselle. We might die tomorrow, it is very true. So today must be savored, to the very last drop of joy that may be wrung from it."

The rich music of his voice disturbed Rosalind, stirring up needs that she'd only just become aware of, needs that refused to be denied, demanding satisfaction. Alexandre was right. Rosalind was no longer what she had been when she began her voyage aboard the *Bird of Paradise*. Perhaps the pirates' lawlessness was contagious, giving her an excuse to escape all the sorrow and turmoil she'd left behind. Alexandre regarded her with an open, gentle expression, a look that might almost have been sympathy. Rosalind turned away and found Yves watching them. Oddly enough, he looked displeased.

"Do you agree, Monsieur Yves?" she asked.

"That we may die? Surely, mademoiselle. Every day we go looking for death." Yves glanced at Alexandre. "Every day we do not find it is a good day."

Rosalind puzzled over that. "I am afraid I do not understand."

"No, mademoiselle, you do not."

"Don't mind him." Alexandre sat back, a glass of brandy clasped in his long, elegant fingers. "Yves was gloomy in the cradle."

Rosalind wondered what Yves knew, what he might tell her about Alexandre if only she could find the right way to approach him. She looked at the sunset rapidly fading into warm twilight. The muted colors made her sad. Such glory earlier, and now with a trick of the light it all vanished. The darkness would last much longer. The sorrow she kept at bay by force of will rose again within her, making her eyes sting and her breath catch. She wanted to get off this ship, to find Thomas and enjoy at least a little of his cheerful company before she had to tell him the news that would surely break his heart.

"Mademoiselle? Rosalind? Are you still with us?"

At the sound of Alexandre's voice, Rosalind turned her attention back to the table and found them all staring at her.

"Are you well?" Alexandre asked.

The desperate need to cry put a brittle note in Rosalind's voice. "*Mais non, mon capitaine,* I am not. I would like very much to be excused." She rose. Chairs scraped back as all the men rose with her.

"You have eaten very little," Alexandre said. "Perhaps that accounts for it. Sit down, mademoiselle, and take a bit more. You must recover your strength."

Rosalind remained standing. "*S'il-vous plaît, mon capitaine.* As you say, I must recover."

"You will do so far better up here in the open air, than down below where there is scarcely room to turn around." Alexandre nodded at her chair. "Please be seated, mademoiselle."

Rosalind remained standing one defiant moment longer, then sank down onto her chair, letting her rigid back show her displeasure.

Alexandre turned to his officers. "*Messieurs,* perhaps you would be good enough to allow Mademoiselle Rosalind and myself some privacy. *Monsieur le Docteur,* I trust you will provide suitable escort for Mademoiselle Beatrice."

Beatrice wavered for a moment, then squared her shoulders and spoke. "Captain, if you please, Miss Brooks has worn herself out watching over me. I beg you, let us go below together."

Rosalind smiled. Now there was courage. Alexandre pursed his lips, considering Beatrice for a long moment, then spoke.

"At this point I do not believe Mademoiselle Rosalind knows what is best for her." He spoke over Beatrice's head to Dr. Gingras. "She is in shock, she is exhausted, and I will not allow her to go mooning about below decks. Yves tells me she nearly fell down a hatch earlier today."

Alexandre's courteous mask had slipped. The Black Angel now sat there, master of his ship and all he surveyed. Beatrice looked to Rosalind for guidance. Rosalind raised her shoulders in a minimal shrug. There was nothing to do but obey.

"If you require anything," Alexandre said to Beatrice, "tell the Doctor here and he will see to it. I wish you good night."

"Thank you for dinner, Captain. It was very good."

Alexandre smiled. "If I have pleased you, little one, that is all I could hope for."

"Good night, Captain." Beatrice turned an anxious look on Rosalind. "Don't be long, please?"

"I'm sure the captain will be mindful of my fatigue." Rosalind gave Alexandre a smile whose sweetness was entirely false. "He understands only too well what we've all suffered."

With Dr. Gingras shepherding her along, Beatrice left the quarterdeck. One by one the officers bade Rosalind a good evening. She watched them go back to their stations, wishing she could free herself from the invisible chains that bound her to her seat.

"Shall I check on the repairs, *mon capitaine?*" Yves asked.

"*Oui.*" Alexandre studied the skies with a practiced eye. "We should be able to keep this course for another two hours. The wind seems steady enough."

With a slight bow to Rosalind, Yves made his way back to the main deck. Rosalind folded her hands in her lap and resigned herself to her role of dancing bear.

Chapter Seventeen

Alexandre stretched his long legs out in front of him and crossed one ankle over the other. Eight bells struck, the first watch took their stations under Yves' strict eye, and all was well. This was Alexandre's favorite time of day. The harsh sunlight gave way to the gentler shades of evening. It had been a marvelous sunset, everything he might have hoped for, but this warm, tropical twilight suited him best. He drank his brandy, enjoying its bracing sting, and contemplated Rosalind. Just as he could read the mood of his ship by the tension in her rigging, he could read Rosalind's mood in the lines of her body. Gowned in the color of a fresh, ripe peach, with the weight of her long golden hair straining at her hair pins, somehow she sat there so stiffly, hands primly folded.

The truth blazed in those brilliant blue eyes. Alexandre read her defiance there. Beneath it he suspected a turbulence of emotions that would blow up into a fine gale. Within the prim schoolteacher Rosalind pretended to be, there burned the heart of a pirate queen. She could accept the way she'd nearly shot him. She could accept the dangerous game she'd played aboard *La Fortuna*. Yet she could not allow herself to accept the rightness of the pleasure he could give her. If only Rosalind would accept the chance Fate had given her. She'd already gone too far to ever return to what she had been. Her every effort in that direction only caused her pain.

Alexandre roused himself from his reflections. The fine meal and excellent liquor had mellowed him. Pleasant conversation with such a beautiful woman would suit him very well. Perhaps he could get Rosalind to talk to him without drenching every word in disdain.

"The little one looks better already," he said. "A good night's rest, my cook's best work, and she will be better than when we found her."

" 'Found' her? Is that how you think of it, *mon capitaine*?"

"It is. You were not taken off the *Bird of Paradise* at gunpoint, mademoiselle."

"We would have been, *mon capitaine*, had we not dived overboard and risked the sharks."

"You think so?"

She turned her head and looked straight at him. Her blue eyes narrowed. "Can you really sit there and tell me you would not have taken us captive and made sport of us for your amusement?"

"Of course not. I will tell you I do not allow my men to handle female prisoners as if they were trollops to be hidden below decks."

"Not when you intend to hide them in the captain's cabin."

Alexandre let his head fall back. He stared up at the first few stars glimmering in the darkening sky. "Mademoiselle, you are determined to spoil my enjoyment of this evening. I asked for quarter earlier and you consented. Kindly sheath that wicked tongue before you strike a vital organ."

He sat up and drained his brandy, then reached for the bottle. Rosalind glanced at the bottle, then down at her hands. He took a fresh glass off the tray and poured a bit into it, then set it before her. She turned her face away.

"Surely you cannot expect me to drink that, not after— after what happened before."

Her prissy tone roused Alexandre's temper. He checked it with an effort. "Rosalind. Look at me."

That tone of command never failed. She turned to face him. He read the wariness in her eyes, the defiance in her stiff back. Pitching his voice low and gentle, he reached out to stroke her cheek.

"Let there be peace between us, if only for this evening. Please, Rosalind. Just sit and talk with me."

She glared at him a moment longer. Her expression softened. She picked up the brandy glass and stared into it.

"There's a toast my father was fond of." Her voice was so quiet Alexandre had to lean closer to hear her. She looked him in the eye and raised her glass. "Confusion to the enemy."

Alexandre laughed and touched his glass to hers. They drank, Rosalind taking the smallest sip. He watched the way her lips fitted against the glass, recalling the taste of brandy in her mouth. How sweet she had been, how soft and warm and willing. If only he could bring her to that state again, lying languid in his arms, stroking his hair and murmuring his name. She was but a young girl, an innocent, for all her ferocious ways. Seducing her would be a simple matter. Now that she had savored the ultimate joy lovemaking could bring, her wild heart could not refuse him a third time.

A sudden bitterness made Alexandre frown. This was Murdock's doing, that Alexandre should be forced to treat this magnificent woman as nothing more than a pawn in his endless game of vengeance against the English. Had he met Rosalind some ordinary way, perhaps at one of Veronique's tedious garden parties, they might have traded *bon mots* instead of verbal broadsides. He could draw Rosalind away to the flower gardens, to the gazebo hidden by a flowering creeper whose blossoms gave off a sweet and heady scent. That was an ideal spot for innocent embraces.

"What takes you to Jamaica?" he asked.

"Family business." The curtness of her answer warned against asking anything else.

"I am amazed to find even one young *Anglaise* traveling alone, and here I find two aboard the same ship. What fools dwell in England these days that two innocents were sent into the Caribbean alone and unprotected?"

"Captain Harris and his men were our protection."

"You saw how well that served you."

Rosalind glared at him. "*Pardonnez-moi, mon capitaine.* We were not expecting *L'Ange Noir* to attack us and carry us off. If we had, I assure you we would have sailed with a man-of-war and at least three frigates!"

Alexandre thrust back his chair and marched around the table, seizing Rosalind by the arms and lifting her up onto her feet. "Hear me, Rosalind. I have tried to play the gentleman for you. I have tried to make the polite conversation and show you and your little friend all the kindness my life permits. This is what you asked of me. Is that not so?"

Rosalind started to speak, faltered. Looking away, she nodded.

"Answer me, mademoiselle. Have I not met your terms?"

"*Oui, mon capitaine.*"

He stared at her, his frustration so intense he wanted to shake her. "Why must you insist on playing the shy little schoolteacher? We both know you're far more than that!"

Beneath his fingers the muscles in her arms tensed. He'd seen her face turn pale each time he referred to her as a lady. She must be wondering if he knew, how he could know, who she really was. Little wonder she was so flighty and nervous. Then Rosalind looked him squarely in the eye.

"What am I, *mon capitaine?*" Her voice shook only a little. "What exactly do you think I am?"

Was this the moment to end her charade? No. To bed her,

to conquer her completely, then to reveal his absolute victory, that would be the greatest triumph.

"I think you wear your righteousness like a mask to hide that wild streak. I think there's no room in your proper little English life for all the things you've had to do these past few days. Fortune has shown you a side of yourself you never dreamed existed, and now you try to remain what you were!"

Rosalind let out her breath, sagging a little in his grip. "Well said, *mon capitaine*. There is no room in my life for shipwreck, pirates, or clever seduction. I am a plain, ordinary Englishwoman with a plain, ordinary life."

There was sorrow in her voice, hinting at some profound grief. While Alexandre didn't know the cause, he understood the symptoms all too well. What had broken Rosalind's heart? What had left her so defeated, so lost to whatever forces shaped her life? Having seen her fight so hard to protect Beatrice, Alexandre doubted anything could conquer Rosalind's spirit. His hands moved from her arms down to her waist. He held her lightly.

"Tell me, *ma belle*, is that what you want?"

Rosalind closed her eyes. A tear slid down her cheek, then another, and a third. "Please, *mon capitaine,* do not ask me such questions."

"How can a woman like you abandon yourself to whatever this is you dread so? You have pitted two of the Caribbean's greatest dangers against each other and emerged the victor! What is this thing you fear?"

Rosalind shook her head. Tears streamed down her cheeks, striking the fine lace of his jabot.

"If you will not tell me what it is, I can only guess." Alexandre held her at arm's length, considering her. "It must be marriage. It so often is. Perhaps there is no man. I cannot believe that. Even if you have no money to your name, you are too beautiful not to draw the eye of some rich lord."

Rosalind pushed at his arms, trying to escape. Her struggles were so weak they prompted Alexandre to draw her closer to him, enfolding her in his arms.

"Therefore it must be a man, but he is the wrong one, *non?* He does not suit you. Perhaps you do not suit him, but he will have you anyway." Dampness soaked his shirt, dampness that came from Rosalind's tears. He could have no greater proof of how right his guesses were. "Do you sail to Jamaica to meet this man, *ma belle?* Or to escape him?"

Murdock was still in England at this point, so it had to be the second reason. Alexandre grinned over Rosalind's head. How delightfully convenient, that Murdock's fiancée should flee right into his arms. He stroked Rosalind's hair, toying with the temptation to pluck out those few hairpins and watch the golden rope uncoil in a great shining sweep to Rosalind's hips. He became aware of Rosalind's hands caught between their bodies. He pulled her arms up around his neck. Rosalind leaned against him, shaking with silent sobs.

"Forget him, *ma belle*. If he was enough of an imbecile to let you sail into these waters alone, he surely doesn't deserve you." Alexandre kissed her hair. "How could you possibly become engaged to such a fool? Of course, a woman like you is far too hot-blooded for some *Anglais* burgher. You need a man of the Continent."

Rosalind leaned back to look up at him. "A man like you?"

The soft twilight, her melancholy, and the shining trails of her tears combined to bring Rosalind's beauty to the height of perfection. For the first time Alexandre found himself helpless before the tenderness that filled him, the need to comfort and protect this woman. Rosalind had risked death time and time again in the last two days, yet she trembled with despair before the thought of this unwanted marriage. Why couldn't she see her own strength?

Moved by a depth of feeling that engulfed him like the very ocean itself, Alexandre touched his lips to hers. It was the lightest of kisses, the intimacy of his breath mingling with hers. Rosalind's chin rose a fraction, deepening the kiss just enough to set his very blood ablaze. The faint taste of brandy in her mouth called to mind the satiny skin of her bare breasts. That stole the last of his control. His arms tightened around her, one hand sinking into her hair. Rosalind shuddered, leaning into him, parting her lips to welcome the onslaught of his kiss. The shyness, the sweetly timid nature of her caress drove Alexandre wild. It took every ounce of his will to move slowly as he sought out each hairpin and flung it aside. Rosalind's hair spilled down over his hands, a gleaming torrent that made him long to fling aside his garments and wrap his naked body in all her silken glory.

Rosalind's head fell back. She turned her face from his, trying to catch her breath. Alexandre pressed his lips to her throat, feeling her heartbeat in the blood racing beneath her skin. He had roused her desire, had awakened her to an ecstasy she'd never known. It was her master now, making her body respond to him, making her cling to him and return his passion in her own untutored way. He brushed his lips across hers, outlining their sweet curves with the tip of his tongue. The fury of his desire compelled him to plunge into the honeyed depths of her mouth. What exquisite bliss awaited him as the first man to complete her fulfillment.

Alexandre tore his mouth from hers. "*Ma belle*, can you still deny me?"

Rosalind blinked up at him, then shook her head. For a moment Alexandre thought the battle was over. Rosalind's hands slid down his chest. Her arms stiffened, pushing him back. She swept her hair out of her eyes and turned away.

"You don't understand."

Alexandre could scarcely think for the thunder of his blood. His hands slid around Rosalind's slender waist, bringing her back against him.

"I understand that I want you more than I have ever wanted any woman. I understand that you have chained yourself to some mad notion of honor, one that prevents you from pleasing yourself. Do you not owe yourself some kindness, *ma belle?* After all you have suffered, can you not recognize succor when it is offered to you?"

She stood rigid in his arms. "I am responsible for the settling of greater debts."

"*Je ne comprendre.* Whose debts must you pay?"

"Beatrice and I have a great deal in common." Rosalind bowed her head. "I too must help support my family. This man who wants to marry me, whom you mock with such perfect ignorance, is the answer to my family's distress. I must marry him. That will make everything right."

Alexandre frowned. What had Murdock done to Rosalind's family that she should become such a hostage? That the monster had worked his evil on Rosalind made Alexandre's hatred of him blaze up all the hotter. Revenge would still be his, but of a sweeter nature. He would show Rosalind all the joy and kindness he could possibly arrange not just to spite Murdock but to honor her as a woman deserving of such consideration.

"That cannot be true." He held her tighter, rubbing his cheek against her hair. "If this man was the man he should be, you would not be here, in my arms."

"It's true." A sob burst out of Rosalind. "All too true."

"Ah, Rosalind, you were not meant to play this game of marriage and advantage. You were meant to run along a sunny beach with flowers in your hair. You were made for joy, *ma belle,* not this horrible proper dignity you try to affect."

"There is no joy for me, *mon capitaine.* Not now."

"Why not?"

Rosalind shook with sobs. When she could speak, her voice was so quiet with leaden certainty Alexandre almost shuddered to hear it.

"My father is dead. My mother is heartbroken. My brother knows nothing of this yet. My family is ruined, my future is bleak, and my wants and needs mean nothing." She wiped the tears from her cheeks. "So you see, *mon capitaine,* the source of what some might call my suicidal bravery. I have very little left to lose."

She turned in his arms. The moon threw enough light to show Alexandre her face. It might have been carved from the purest white marble, the very model of stoic defeat.

"Meeting *L'Ange Noir* has put the finishing touches on my demise. Should I live to see England again, my fiancé will surely cast me off, confirming the ruin of my reputation. *Merci beaucoup, mon capitaine,* for destroying what was left of my life."

The bitterness in her voice left Alexandre speechless. She saw him as the culmination of her misery! He took his hands from her and stepped back, making an ironic little bow.

"I would offer you my most humble apologies, mademoiselle, if I thought I had done you any real harm. Had you met any other pirates in these waters, I assure you there would be nothing left of you or little Beatrice worth calling human."

He was glad to see the anger leap into Rosalind's eyes, bringing color to her ashen cheeks.

"Yes, I took your ship," he went on. "You did not know that *L'Ange Noir* never tolerates the torture of women, so you dived overboard. I rescued you, mademoiselle, and as soon as I realized you'd been taken captive by that fiend Vasquez, I rushed to your aid then as well."

"Am I to thank you again, *mon capitaine?* Am I to go on thanking you for this farce, this nightmare, this endless waiting to know if we will live to see our homes again?"

Alexandre drew a slow, deep breath, struggling to keep his temper in check. "Tell me this, mademoiselle. Why have you condemned yourself to misery? Here you are, on the deck of a magnificent ship, sailing in the Caribbean. Even now you might be enjoying the moonlight with a man who admires you, who desires you, and who knows you far better than this fiancé of yours."

Rosalind turned her back on him. "You know nothing."

Alexandre smiled, tempted once again to reveal just how much he did know. Not yet. He had to coax her back into his arms, into his very bed. Only after she had willingly given up her virginity to him would he seal the triumph with calling her by her true name. He stepped up behind her, close enough to make her feel the heat of his presence.

"You have defied me, *L'Ange Noir,* when you thought it could mean your death. You have bested a loathsome monster who might easily have tortured and killed you within an hour of taking you aboard his ship. You have staked everything on preserving not yourself but the safety of that little girl down below."

He laid light hands on her shoulders. Rosalind stood still, her arms wrapped tightly around herself.

"I know who you really are, *ma belle.* I know what fury, what passion, what amazing strength lie within that heart of yours. Does your fiancé know any of this? Would he credit it if anyone told him?"

"No," Rosalind whispered. "No. He would not."

"Forget him! Such a man is not a man. He is a bloodless beast, counting you among his possessions as if you were no more than a carriage or a pocket watch." Alexandre's growing hatred of Murdock sharpened his voice to a razor edge. "Ugly, stupid, brutish, no sense of the finer feelings. As a lover you may discount him entirely. Such a man has nothing in his veins but ice water, nothing in his loins but dust."

A painful blush reddened Rosalind's cheeks. She jerked away from him, hands clapped over her ears.

"No more!" she cried. "No more!"

Alexandre grasped her wrists and pulled her hands down, determined to make her yield this time. Rosalind fought him with frenzied strength, yanking her hands free. She thrust one slim forefinger at him like a sword.

"*You* have no right to speak of anyone in such terms!" She ran to the table and snatched up a silver goblet. "You know how to set a table like a gentleman." She slammed it down and held up her brandy glass. "All the courses, all the liquor. Where did you learn it all?" She marched up to him and jabbed him in the chest with that same forefinger. "What were you, *mon capitaine?* What were you before you threw it all away and turned pirate? You say you know who I am? I know who you *were*."

The usual noises that filled the deck had died away. Alexandre scowled. Every man aboard had stopped his work to listen, to hear this little English milkmaid mock *L'Ange Noir* with barbs all too close to the truth.

"Careful, mademoiselle," he growled. "You are on very dangerous ground."

With all the courage he had come to expect from her, Rosalind stood her ground. "I listened to your guesses, *mon capitaine*. Now you can hear mine. You were born to the upper classes. You were meant for greatness. Something happened, something so terrible it made you turn against the English with this insane hatred. You must have done something that forced you to flee to the Caribbean. Now you vent your rage against English shipping under this absurd *nom de guerre*."

"That's quite enough, mademoiselle." Alexandre turned away to pour himself more brandy, hoping to show the watching crew how little Rosalind's damnable insight affected him.

"Or what, *mon capitaine?* Will you beat me? Chain me up again? Finally throw me over the side?" Growing outrage steadied Rosalind's voice. "We all know about your dreaded temper. If not for that I imagine you could go anywhere, be anyone you chose. But no. *L'Ange Noir* must be allowed to throw his tantrums whenever and wherever he chooses."

The brandy glass shattered in Alexandre's hand. Liquor and blood dripped onto the deck. He turned a glare on Rosalind that should have made her faint with fright. Instead she lifted her trembling chin.

"Tell me, *mon capitaine*, do you keep a supply of Englishmen on board just in case you wake up in the night and feel like throwing a fit?"

Now Alexandre's blood was boiling, with a desire not for lovemaking but violence. Only by a supreme effort did he keep still, reminding himself again and again of all he stood to lose if he did throw this shrieking little harpy to the sharks.

In a final gesture of contempt, Rosalind coiled up her long hair and held it in place behind her neck, restoring her veneer of propriety. "You have no right to judge any man, nor any woman. Whatever you were, *mon capitaine*, you chose to throw it all away."

The fury churning within Alexandre burst free in a bellow of pure rage. He swept his arm across the table, hurling the last of the plates and brandy glasses aside to shatter on the deck. Rosalind backed away, fetching up against the rail. Now she was afraid. She'd learn what fear really was, the presumptuous little chit. He'd done his best for her, risked his life for her—

Someone darted past him. Yves. He stepped in front of Rosalind, shielding her with his body. Even in the madness of his rage, Alexandre knew better than to raise a hand against his most treasured friend. He stood shaking with the force of his unspent temper.

Yves pushed Rosalind toward the main deck. "Get below, mademoiselle. Right now!"

Without a word Rosalind fled. Alexandre watched her go, still seething. Only Yves could have stopped him. Anyone else he would have flung over the side. Had Rosalind been a man, he'd have struck her down where she stood. The milk-maid had brought him low in tones loud enough to carry to the very end of the bowsprit. Because she was a woman, not just any but Rosalind herself, he had stayed his hand, leaving himself sick with the knowledge that he could not seek satisfaction for this insult, this gross insult to his honor and his prestige.

Alexandre flung himself into his chair and grabbed the bottle of rum. He pulled the cork out and drank a long swallow. Only then did he notice Yves still standing nearby.

"What is it?"

"Shall I send the boys to clear away, *mon capitaine*?"

"Be quick about it."

In minutes the mess was gone. Yves set a fresh bottle of rum down within Alexandre's reach.

"You think I'm a fool, don't you, *mon ami?*" Alexandre asked.

"Only a fool would answer that question, *mon capitaine.*"

Alexandre stared up at the sky now agleam with stars. "I tried, Yves. I tried to do as she asked."

Yves sighed. "What has she done to you now?"

"Only named the sin on my soul. Only used those eyes like mirrors to show me what I've let myself become."

"She's a little girl with a sharp tongue. Bed her, give her a few pretty trinkets, then show her the back of your hand."

Alexandre shook his head. "That won't work with this one."

"Then clap her in irons or feed her to the sharks. Don't let her do this to you!"

Alexandre downed another long swallow of rum. "Peace, old friend. A few more days and we'll be rid of her. I can't just fling her overboard, not when the great Lord Murdock will owe me forever for saving her pretty skin not once but twice over."

"That *Anglais* bastard will be the death of you. You really think you're using him? He already has you patrolling the coasts like his private errand boy. Now you're picking up strays for him! Where will this end?"

Alexandre glared at him. "*Sacré Dieu!* Will you cease that carping? Bad enough I have that little baggage flogging me. What need have I of a wife when you nag me like this?"

Yves folded his arms across his chest, scowling. "Is it time we went ashore? Have you at last had enough of this life?"

Alexandre shut his eyes and leaned his head back. "No. I cannot go back. Not yet."

Yves made a noise of disgust. "Listen to me, Alexandre. You want her only because she refuses you. Once you've had her, you'll forget her. The chase will be over. Do us all a favor and end the chase."

Alexandre shook his head. "Ah, Yves. She told me I'm cold-blooded, but you are made of ice." He drank again, then flung the empty bottle overboard and reached for the rum Yves brought. "I am going to sit here and drink until I stop wanting to kill something, then I'll retire to my cabin. She is at liberty to return there when she pleases. Just keep her out of harm's way."

"I sent her below to keep her out of harm's way, *mon capitaine*."

Alexandre sighed. "Your point?"

Yves leaned closer to him, lowering his voice. "What would you have done to her, if I had not intervened?"

Alexandre drank another long swallow. "That is on par with asking me what I would have done in battle if the wind had blown from another quarter."

"Impulse is far different from strategy carefully considered."

"There is a strategy at work here, *mon ami*. Of that I can assure you."

"Once again you believe you have your enemy in the palm of your hand? Take care, Alexandre. This *coquine* has been full of surprises from the very start."

Alexandre stared into those cold gray eyes. The depression that always followed his temper rose to engulf him, drowning him in its black depths. "You are entirely correct, as always. This is a most annoying habit, *mon ami*. I do wish you'd allow me some measure of confidence in myself aboard my own ship."

He stared up at the stars, at the many familiar constellations. Only they remain fixed. Only they were always in their proper places, ready to help him find his way. He took another long drink, wishing it was brandy, wishing he could share the mouthful in a kiss that would leave Rosalind swooning in his arms.

"She is a worthy adversary, Yves. She rouses in me such passion. I have never felt so much, not in love, not in war."

"Perhaps now that mademoiselle has seen you at your

worst, she'll listen to me the next time I tell her not to provoke you."

"You sound like you don't believe that."

"I don't, *mon capitaine.*" Yves stood. "I can only hope your strategy succeeds. Take the queen. End the game. This is more than just another dalliance. She matters too much to you."

As Yves walked away, Alexandre nodded to himself. The rum couldn't blunt that stark truth. Rosalind mattered to him, far more than any little English milkmaid should.

Chapter Eighteen

Rosalind huddled in a miserable heap. The hammock that would be her bed for the night made her feel like a sack of laundry. The heavy folds of her peach satin skirt lay twisted round her legs. Her petticoats had bunched up under her hip. There was no room at all to stretch out, much less stand up and shake out her clothing. Beatrice lay in another hammock beside her, curled up with her hands tucked under her cheek like a child.

Adding to Rosalind's discomfort was the presence of Eric on the other side of the wall of crates, snoring loudly enough to make the rats flee the ship. Sleeping so late into the afternoon also left Rosalind wakeful. She remembered with reluctant clarity how comfortable she'd been in Alexandre's bed, as long as he was elsewhere. She could scarcely draw a breath of decent air down here, crammed in among the cargo. As much as she longed to escape to greater space and fresher air, she didn't dare show her face on deck again. Having roused the full fury of the Black Angel, the last thing she wanted to do was cross his path again this night.

Rosalind's mind churned with a thousand questions. What did that horrible scene tell her about Alexandre? That she was right about his past. Alexandre's rage confirmed the truth of her instincts. She lacked the details of his downfall, but she could see much more of that elusive picture.

Yves had warned her not to provoke Alexandre. Being first mate, he knew the limits of the Black Angel's temper better than anyone else aboard. What did it say of Yves that he would protect a woman, an Englishwoman, from his precious *capitaine*? If Yves's appearance on deck wasn't mutiny, it was close to it.

Beatrice made a faint noise in her sleep, bringing Rosalind's attention back to the present moment. She reached over to smooth Beatrice's hair. The fever had eased a little. Rosalind sighed, giving silent thanks. Her uppermost concern now was convincing the Black Angel to put Beatrice ashore as soon as possible. Beatrice was an innocent victim, caught in the wrong place at the wrong time. If the Black Angel insisted on carrying out his vengeance against the English, let it be on Rosalind alone. Perhaps it was time to let Alexandre think he had cowed her a little by his show of temper. From what she'd observed so far, nothing put him in a better mood than thinking he'd won. And so she came full circle, back to Yves's original suggestion. Frustration made her want to kick the planks beside her.

Beatrice turned over. Her eyes opened. She saw Rosalind and her face lit with a wan smile. "You're here. I thought he wouldn't let you stay with me."

Rosalind patted her hand. "I think the captain has had enough of my company for one evening."

"Did something happen?"

"He thought he'd amuse himself by mocking me and my marital prospects. I made it clear to him how little such talk amused me."

"I don't understand. The captain acts like he can't live without you, yet he talks like you mean nothing to him. I imagine Mr. Murdock can't wait to see you again."

Rosalind almost laughed. "He'll be more concerned about the *Bird of Paradise* and the loss of her cargo."

"Oh, Rosalind, you can't mean that. He wants to marry you!"

"No," Rosalind said, thinking of the way Captain Bellamy had believed she was already Mr. Murdock's fiancée. "He wants me to marry him."

"Poor Rosalind." Now it was Beatrice's turn to pat Rosalind's hand. "He doesn't suit you?"

"That doesn't seem to matter. I suit him, and it suits everyone else to see us suit each other." She fretted with the lace at her bosom. "If only Father were still here. He was more than happy to have me at home as long as I chose to stay. He'd seen too many young girls married off too early."

"It's all so very sad."

"I had hoped for more out of marriage."

Rosalind wasn't sure if she actually spoke the words aloud. That wasn't important. What mattered was finally admitting the truth to herself. She *had* hoped for more. Edward Murdock might be eminently eligible, but he was not what she wanted in a man. He left her cold, bored her to tears, and treated her like a featherhead without an ounce of sense. He would never credit her with the courage to snatch a pistol from a pirate's sash and strike him with it, then hold the Black Angel himself at gunpoint. Should she be foolish enough to tell him of these exploits, Mr. Murdock would pat her hand and say something patronizing.

Rosalind stared upward, through the deck to the captain's cabin above it. Was Alexandre still up there, nursing his wounded pride? She had hit him hard, that was plain. What a pity she couldn't be sure which of her guesses was closest to the mark.

Eric shifted in his hammock. A moment later the earsplitting rasp of his snore filled the little space around them. Rosalind groaned aloud.

"I think I will take the air on deck."

"Oh Rosalind, is that wise?" Beatrice asked.

Moving with great care, Rosalind managed to slide out of her hammock without jostling Beatrice too much. "He won't hurt me."

"How can you be sure?"

"If he meant to hurt me," Rosalind said, "he would have done so by now."

Another snore tore through the darkness.

"I cannot bear being cramped up down here a moment longer. Please, Beatrice, don't worry. I'll be fine."

Rosalind climbed up the ladder onto the main deck. The first watch greeted her arrival with murmurs of surprise. One voice spoke in a loud whisper, the words a muddle but the tone of mockery all too clear. A crack like a whip and a hastily muffled curse followed. Rosalind turned to see the bosun standing over a pirate working near the starboard rail. The bosun held the length of rope that had just laid a nasty welt on the offender's bare back. The bosun made Rosalind a proper bow.

"Bonsoir, mademoiselle."

"Bonsoir, Monsieur le Maître d'Equipage."

The bosun turned his baleful glare on all the pirates watching. Every face turned back to the task at hand. Rosalind gave the bosun a hesitant smile. A glance at the quarterdeck showed her the helmsman at the wheel, with Yves and the navigator conferring over some papers the navigator held. There was no sign of Alexandre. Rosalind glared at the closed door of his cabin. Was he sprawled out on that great bed even now, wallowing in his bad temper, planning some horrible means of ridding himself of his captives?

Rosalind hurried to the bow. It was most convenient, the way the pirates avoided her. She took care to keep herself out of their way as well, minding her footing on the crowded deck. Mutters followed in her wake, smothered laughter, here and there a noise of disgust. Rosalind wondered how much money had been won and lost as the pirates watched her dress down their beloved captain. She stood as far forward in the bow as the crates and barrels and rigging allowed, wishing she could climb out to the very end of the bowsprit.

She took a deep breath of the fresh sea air. With that her thoughts seemed to clear as well. The Black Angel was a thief and a blackguard and a killer of innocent men, but he was also entirely correct about one thing. Returning to her life in London would have been difficult enough after breaking the news to Thomas. Life had to go on, no matter how painful, no matter how awkward it would be to face Mr. Murdock again. All that would have been simplicity itself compared with the rumors that would spread after it became known she survived a meeting with the notorious Black Angel. Everyone knew what pirates did to women. No one would believe she'd been spared, ransom or no ransom. There would be smirks and titters. The best people would drop the Hanshaws as a family disgraced both financially and socially. Things would only continue to get worse. Rosalind might well have to seek a position as a teacher or governess just to keep a roof over her mother's head.

She shuddered with the violence of her grief, pressing the heels of her hands against her eyes to stem another flood of tears. She glared up at the multitude of stars glittering overhead. Here, beneath these strange constellations, she had become a different person. No longer Lady Rosalind Hanshaw, careful and correct daughter of a noble house. Here she was Miss Rosalind Brooks, a schoolteacher not afraid to swim with sharks, disarm pirates, and even yank the glossy mane of *L'Ange Noir* himself! How could she be both of these women? More important, how could she ever go back to being the proper, dignified young woman who had boarded the *Bird of Paradise*?

Rosalind leaned on the rail, staring out at the moonlight where it fell on the waves. *L'Etoile du Matin* sailed along, quiet and brisk. The sea was calm enough to show the reflections of the stars here and there. Behind and above her, the crew went about their business, still carefully avoiding her. Rosalind closed her eyes and felt the rhythm of *L'Etoile du Matin* through the wood beneath her. The ship was a living entity, with flesh and bones giving life to the wood and canvas. That life stemmed from one heart: Alexandre's. How strange that she should think of him as the heart of *L'Etoile du Matin*, not its brain. Alexandre was an intelligent man, but in him passion ruled intelligence. He would act from his heart first and his reason second. All she had seen of him proved that.

What a pity they could not have met at a ball in London. How well the tall, dashing pirate king would wear all the finery of a French nobleman, the lace and gold embroidery and sleek satin. Russet, perhaps, or midnight blue. Alexandre would surely dance with surpassing grace, his life at sea lending him a fluid style that would put all the landsmen to shame. Yet no matter how his tailors dressed him up in fancy formal attire, Alexandre would still have that air of danger, that molten heat simmering in the dark jewels of his eyes. How marvelous to meet him on a dance floor, knowing that beneath the careful speech of polite company there lay the iron will that would pursue a rival pirate through a storm to take back the woman he had claimed for his own.

That thought startled Rosalind out of her daydreams. Was that not exactly what Alexandre had done? He considered Rosalind to be his woman. All his, to the point of killing the man who had taken her away from him. Even as she pondered this, a warm glow spread through her, something akin to the heat of the brandy but deeper, richer, more compelling. How absolutely grand Alexandre had looked, standing there on Vasquez's ship like the very wrath of God. Just a little while later he had been gentleness itself, cuddling her in his arms, soothing her. Rosalind hugged herself, caught between two very uncomfortable ideas. Even if Mr. Murdock did want her for more than business reasons, he'd never so much as kissed her hand. Alexandre wanted her enough to kill for her.

And she wanted him.

That was the most dangerous truth of all. Alexandre insisted Rosalind had a wild streak. He had brought it out in her. Passion after passion he hurled at her, whether rage or scorn or desire. The only way to meet him was to respond with equal fury. Now that this wildness had been unleashed, how could Rosalind dismiss it, lock it away, pretend these days with the Black Angel had never happened? After tasting the explosive joy of his kiss, after being swept up in his arms and carried from the deck of one pirate ship to another, after having the Black Angel on his very knees declaring his desire for her, how could Rosalind possibly tolerate the tedium of being Mr. Murdock's wife?

"So thoughtful, mademoiselle. What are you thinking, I wonder?"

Rosalind gasped and whirled around. Alexandre's voice reached out to her much like his long, elegant fingers, caressing her with its warmth. It took a moment for her eyes to find him in the moonlit darkness. She finally sighted his tall, broad-shouldered silhouette leaning up against the mainmast. Where had he come from? Surely she would have heard some noise from the crew hailing his approach. Rosalind looked up into the rigging.

"*Exactement,* mademoiselle. You sent me to the masthead, so to the masthead I went."

He was teasing her again, referring to the traditional naval punishment for minor infractions. All the way to the top of the mainmast? Rosalind marveled. That a man of his height and breadth could move through the rigging silently, and then sit atop the yard at the very top of the mainmast. . . . Yet she had seen him do something similar that very afternoon.

"I do not recall giving you leave to come down." She turned her back on his charm. She'd had quite enough of his mercurial temper.

Alexandre laughed, soft and low. "I could not resist. You stand here like a living figurehead, bathed in the moonlight, torturing my crew with your loveliness."

"I am sorry to cause your men such distraction."

"You are not." His footsteps approached until he stood just behind her. "No woman dislikes being told how beautiful she is."

Rosalind turned to look directly at him and imitated his sardonic tone. "I take it you are no longer angry with me, *mon capitaine?*"

His face was hidden in shadow. He spread his hands in a gesture of peace. "Shall we agree on a cease-fire, *ma belle?* I've found to my cost your guns are double-shotted."

What game was he playing now, that he wanted to banter with her? Still, if Alexandre wanted to be pleasant, she'd best play along, all the better to talk him into making port in Kingston as soon as possible. She put her hand on his.

"Very well, *mon capitaine.* Peace."

He'd laid aside all the finery he wore at dinner in favor of the simple white shirt and cotton breeches he'd worn earlier. To the masthead, and now this plain appearance. . . . It might almost be taken for humility.

Alexandre leaned on the rail beside her, looking down into her eyes. "So formal. You know my name, *ma belle.*"

"*L'Ange Noir.* How did you decide on that?"

"It's not a story one normally tells to ladies."

"But I am not a lady, *mon capitaine.* I'm an honorary pirate."

"So you are." Alexandre looked out over the dark waves. "The doxies in Port Royal saw *L'Etoile du Matin* warping in one day, and they all started calling out to each other. They said I have the face of an angel, and they love my long hair."

Rosalind tried to look scandalized, but her own laughter overcame it. "The English fear you as the Devil himself, when you got your name from a mob of trollops who think you're pretty?"

Alexandre's mouth quirked in annoyance. "You rob the story of its charm, but yes."

"How delightful. To think you were known first as a lover, not a—" The harsh word caught in her throat.

"A what, *ma belle?*"

"A pirate."

His look told her he knew that was not the word she was about to say. They both knew men died as a result of what he did, but for the moment the bloodier aspect of his calling was banished by the moon's silver light and the sound of the waves splashing against the gunwales.

"What were you meant to be, *ma belle*? Before your life became so difficult."

He asked the question so softly, in such a delicate tone. Rosalind considered the different ways she might answer it.

"I was meant to be happy. To be married to a man I could love and respect, whose children I would be proud to bear. I was meant to lead a decent, respectable life, to grow old content with having done so."

Alexandre nodded. *"Très bien, ma belle.* A good life, one many women would envy."

"I suppose so."

Alexandre looked at her more closely. "And yet you have some doubts?"

"I can't help thinking such a life has been lived over and over again. It is what's done, and that is all there is to it."

"Vraiment. And yet perhaps you dream of another kind of life?"

She hadn't, not until fate had thrown her into the arms of the Black Angel. *"Mon capitaine,* I believe you would call that question sailing too close to the wind."

"I call that answer no answer at all."

"Then perhaps, *mon capitaine,* you might take the hint."

Alexandre stared down at her for a long moment, then drew a fingertip down her cheek. "You will not even ask yourself the question, will you? Is it so painful, *ma belle,* the thought of a happier life?"

Rosalind longed to lean into his touch, to be gathered into his arms and rest her cheek against his chest. As if he read the longing in her eyes, Alexandre opened his arms to her. Rosalind stepped forward into his embrace. Her arms slid around his narrow waist. She settled her head just under his chin, her cheek against the warmth of his bare chest. His heart beat steady and strong, lulling her.

"I know, *ma belle,* I know. When you have a wild heart, you cannot live a quiet life."

"I didn't know I had a wild heart."

"You do, *ma belle,* you do indeed." Laughter rumbled in his chest. "Ah, the look on Henri's face when he realized you'd struck him with his own pistol!"

His fingertips traced the shape of her brow, moving down the curve of her cheek and along her jaw. He rubbed his thumb across her lower lip. The softness of that touch, the unthinking way he followed the curve of her lip from one side to the other, was almost hypnotic.

"You would be wasted in the role of some English burgher's wife," Alexandre said. "A woman of your panache with nothing to occupy her but dinner parties and trips to her dressmaker and finding a nanny who can be relied upon? Bah!" He struck the air with the back of his hand, knocking the idea away. "You deserve more than that, *ma belle.*"

The richness of his voice washed over Rosalind like a warm wave, making her cling to him as much as to his words. An alarm rang somewhere in her mind. "One little English milkmaid? Now it is you who mock me, *mon capitaine.* How could I have such a life?"

Alexandre's hand beneath her chin tipped her head back. He gazed down at her. "I speak, *ma belle*, of what you deserve. I think you deserve far more than what you've chosen."

Rosalind stared up at him. "*Merci*, Alexandre," she whispered. "*Merci beaucoup.*"

They stood together watching the moonlight play on the waves. Rosalind shut her eyes and clung to the moment, trying to catch every impression and save it. The crisp linen of Alexandre's shirt stretched taut across his back and shoulders. The night air moved across her skin, the warmth of the day finally giving way to cooler hours. The smells of salt air and damp canvas, of tobacco and brine. Most of all, the heat of Alexandre's skin and the faint scent of rum on his breath.

"And you?" Rosalind asked. "What were you meant to be?"

Alexandre tensed. Rosalind felt rather than saw the frown gather on his face like a thundercloud. Sudden panic swept over her as she realized her mistake. She tried to back out of his embrace.

"*Pardonnez-moi, mon capitaine.* I did not mean to renew our earlier quarrel."

When he would not release her, she turned her face aside, bracing herself for the coming outburst. Alexandre's arms tightened around her, gently drawing her against him. After a moment, he let out his breath. When he spoke, his voice was little more than a hoarse whisper.

"I was meant to follow my father in the family business. I would have had my own ship, a ship of the line." He tensed again, his breathing becoming uneven. His heart thudded hard within his chest. "All that was lost the day three pirate ships attacked the ship I served aboard. Only a handful of us survived."

"How terrible!"

Rosalind leaned back to look up at him. He stared out into the night, his beautiful face cold and stony as a marble mask. He had withdrawn, from her, from his ship, from the world he had built for himself. With that thought, another piece of the puzzle dropped into place. Rosalind gasped.

"The pirates. They were English, weren't they?"

Alexandre nodded. "They should never have defeated us. It was madness, the worst luck, sheer blind raving stupidity—"

He thrust Rosalind away from him and turned his back on her, clinging to the heavy ropes running down from the mainmast to the bowsprit. His back heaved with frantic breaths.

Rosalind grabbed the rail to steady herself. Was it grief or rage that stirred Alexandre's temper now? She looked around to find herself alone but for Alexandre. His crew had withdrawn from the forecastle, treading no closer than the middle of the main deck. As much as she'd hate doing so, she wished she could call out for Yves. He seemed to know how to deal with Alexandre's peculiar moods.

"Perhaps—" Rosalind began.

Alexandre raised his head.

Fear choked off Rosalind's voice. She swallowed, tried again. "Perhaps I should go below."

Before Rosalind could take another step backward Alexandre turned, reaching out to catch her by the wrist.

"*Mais non,* mademoiselle." Again shadows hid his face, concealing his expression. "You were brave enough to call me out before my crew." His voice was cold, precise, aloof. "Will you turn coward now, just when you might hear the truth?"

Still gripping her wrist, Alexandre turned to glare out at the sea. "That was the worst day of my life. That was the end of my life. Now here I am, far from home, chasing little *Anglais* boats and scaring schoolteachers." He shook his head, muttering to himself. "I too deserve better. But that time has not yet come."

He raked his fingers back through his hair, jaw clenched and eyes tight shut. He was such a picture of misery Rosalind laid a hesitant hand on his shoulder.

"How strange that we should have something so tragic in common. Pirates sank the ship that held the key to my family's finances. When that ship went down, my future went down with it." She looked at the water racing by. "The *Dover Lady* was on her way to Jamaica." She laughed, cold and bitter. "I think the Caribbean must be bad luck for my family."

Alexandre turned to look at her. On his face was an expression she couldn't read. It might have been apprehension, or embarrassment, or something darker and more complex.

"It is good luck for mine," he said. "But only because I have made it so." He ran one hand over his face, and with it seemed to wipe away his distress. He managed an uneven smile and raised her hand to his lips. "Perhaps you have broken the bad luck, *ma belle*. Twice now you have braved pirates and emerged triumphant."

Rosalind's heart suddenly lifted. She had survived. She had kept Beatrice safe. She had lived through another day without losing either her virtue or her life. Her senses sharpened again, bringing the night alive in all its sultry splendor. She was aboard *L'Etoile du Matin,* standing in the bow with the Black Angel himself. She was seized by a mad urge to let her hair stream loose in the breeze and laugh until she was breathless.

Beside her Alexandre stared up at the skies. Moonlight shone down on his face, the pale silver light chasing off the shadows that hung about him and showing her the carefree youth he must have been before tragedy changed his life. She had seen him angry, amused, tender, and furious. Now, in this pensive mood, his beauty was beyond breathtaking. She drew a careful breath, letting it out in a little sigh of wonder.

"They say the third time is the charm."

Alexandre turned to her, regarding her with that same stillness. His eyes searched hers. Rosalind wondered if he saw what he hoped to see. He smiled, one corner of his lips lifting to reveal the dimple in his cheek.

"Come, *ma belle*. It's time we were both abed." He let go of her wrist and stepped away from the rail. "I offer you the comfort of my cabin. If your sense of decency demands that you sleep below, so be it."

The warmth and softness of Alexandre's bed would be far preferable to the unstable hammock and Eric's unbearable snore. Rosalind hesitated, torn between fatigue and reluctance to follow him into the lion's den.

"What is your idea of 'comfort,' *mon capitaine?*"

His smile broadened. "A good mattress, fine linen, enough blankets, and a pillow stuffed with down. Whatever did you think I meant, mademoiselle?"

He was being playful again. She knew better than to trust him in that mood. "And where will you be? On the floor?"

"Hardly. But have no fear, *ma belle.* Think of me as a rather large warming pan."

Rosalind laughed. It spiraled out of her, rising up in waves of musical sound. Perhaps her hair wasn't streaming, but by the time the laughter emptied out of her she was indeed breathless. Alexandre watched her with a grin, then held out his hand to her. She caught his hand and dropped him another curtsy.

"I accept your most gracious offer with pleasure, *mon capitaine.*" She hung back a moment. "But not too much pleasure."

Now it was Alexandre's turn to laugh. He led her across the deck to his cabin door. Around them Rosalind could sense the relief sweeping through the pirates on deck. They grew noisier, laughing and singing out at their stations. Yves was right. The entire crew went in fear of Alexandre's temper. Now that she had brought his good spirits back, they were all that much happier. At the cabin door Alexandre paused.

"Do you require any assistance with your gown?" His smile was as intimate as a kiss. "I make a poor ladies' maid, but I have some little practice with such fastenings."

The very sweetness of the offer sent Rosalind's pulse racing. She shook her head. *"Merci, mon capitaine.* I can manage on my own."

"As you wish." He opened the door, standing back so she could step inside. "I will be just outside. Knock when you are done."

With that he shut the door. Rosalind stared at the oak planks, amazed. The Black Angel, notorious pirate, enemy of her people, was apparently intent on sharing his bed with her for nothing more than sleeping. He even offered to help her change her clothes, then left her to do so in privacy. What could it mean? Was Alexandre simply trying to lull her into trusting him so he could ambush her later? Rosalind shook her head. That wasn't like him. It was just possible he did mean to conduct himself as a gentleman and honor their agreement after all.

Chapter Nineteen

A small oil lamp on Alexandre's desk threw out a cozy light. The cabin had been tidied, with the bed remade. Rosalind hurried out of her gown and corset, hiding her petticoats beneath the pile of rumpled peach satin. She slipped her nightgown on over her head. Once her hair was combed out and freshly plaited into a loose braid hanging down over her shoulder, she folded back the bedclothes. She rapped on the door three times, then slipped under the covers before the door opened.

The lantern light made Alexandre seem taller, broader, and darker. Even his voice seemed deeper. "Are you comfortable, *ma belle?* Is there anything you might want before we retire?"

Rosalind listened for that sardonic tone, but he regarded her with what seemed to be the most innocent concern. *"Non, mon capitaine."*

He arched a brow. "Perhaps, *ma belle,* now that we are in the privacy of my cabin, you might call me by my given name."

"If that pleases you," she said. "Alexandre."

"The sight of your lips speaking my name gives me a great deal of pleasure." He spoke with deceptive calm. The sudden heat in those dark eyes told another tale. "A moment, *ma belle,* and I will join you."

Alexandre turned away to strip his shirt off and throw it on the chest at the foot of the bed, then bent to pull off his boots. Rosalind watched the play of muscles in his shoulders. He reached back to untie the ribbon that bound his hair. The heavy black mass of it fell loose, spreading out across his shoulders to hang halfway down his back. He padded barefoot to the foot of the bed, climbed onto it and pulled back the bedclothes, still wearing his cotton breeches. Rosalind was about to wonder aloud about that when she realized it was another gesture of reassurance. Alexandre kept well to his side of the bed, lying on his side with his head propped on his hand. Big as he was, he still managed to leave a narrow strip of empty mattress between them.

"Make yourself comfortable, *ma belle.* You cannot sleep well huddled up like that."

Rosalind released her tight grip on the blanket. Now Alexandre's smile was faintly teasing. That fire still burned in his eyes, but he seemed to have it under control. She stretched out more comfortably, then snuggled down into her pillow. Alexandre was true to his word about acting as a large warming pan. Heat radiated from him, quickly turning the bedclothes into a warm cocoon. This late at night it was cool enough to make that warmth delicious and relaxing. Rosalind sighed. She knew she should remain on her guard, but it was impossible. She was still so tired, so worn out by all the upheaval.

"Have you ever seen a dolphin?" Alexandre asked. "Sweet creatures. Playful, always smiling. They follow ships, riding the bow wave. Sailors believe they bring good luck."

Rosalind smiled. The timbre of Alexandre's voice was one with the warmth surrounding her now. "Do they bring good luck?"

Alexandre shrugged one shoulder. "Sailors have as many superstitions as trees have leaves."

"My father always carried one of my mother's cameos with him when he went to sea. He told people it was his way of making sure he came home again." Rosalind smiled at the memory, even as her heart ached. "Now my brother does the same."

"Yours is a loving family."

"They are." She looked him in the eye. "They will miss me."

"Not for long, *ma belle*. When we reach Jamaica, you must try the conch chowder. It is a wonderful dish. There are many hazards to living in the Caribbean, but the food is often superb."

Rosalind smiled. Her eyelids were growing heavy. "Goodnight, Alexandre."

She started to turn over. Alexandre stopped her with a touch on her shoulder. He leaned over her. The ebony silk of his hair spilled across her bosom.

"Perhaps, *ma belle,* you would allow me to kiss you good night?"

His eyes held her, the heat in them calling out her own hidden fires. The force of her desire left Rosalind both frightened and exhilarated. Alexandre took her hesitation for fear and laid a fingertip against her lips.

"That is all I ask."

Rosalind raised one hand to stroke Alexandre's hair, brushing it back from his cheek. He turned his head to kiss her palm, then bent to touch his lips to hers. He lingered there, prolonging the velvety sweetness, seeking nothing more. The very act of his holding back seemed to draw Rosalind forward, fanning the fires within her. His nearness was overwhelming, making her long to wrap her arms around his shoulders, to feel the hard solid weight of his chest against her breasts. Her hand touched his naked shoulder. She stroked the smooth bronzed skin, enjoying the sense of leashed power in the muscles beneath her fingertips. Her fingers moved upward, along his neck, sinking into his hair.

As her lips parted under his, Alexandre raised his head. In his eyes shone the unmistakable glow of desire. Rosalind held her breath, her skin alive with impatience for his touch. Alexandre saw her need and smiled, slow and hungry and hot.

"Bonne nuit, ma belle. Sweet dreams."

He lay back against the pillows and turned his face away. Now a different kind of outrage made Rosalind want to cry out. How like him to make her want more, no matter how much she had insisted on the terms of their agreement. He was a devil indeed! She stared up into the darkness, disappointment a sharp stabbing pain. She wanted Alexandre, longed for him, yet every shred of propriety within her cried out against the wrongness of allowing this pirate to seduce and deflower her. A quiet voice deep within her argued against the greater disappointment of saving herself for a husband who didn't love her, didn't even want her for herself.

Loneliness consumed Rosalind. Death had taken Father away. Distance cut her off from Mother, Thomas, and her friends. The increasingly complicated nature of her relationship with Alexandre had separated her from Beatrice. Now, thanks to a sense of decency that continued to cause her nothing but grief, Rosalind was cut off from the man whose bed she shared. A man whose life had been ruined in much the same way hers had. How strange, to have that in common. To be brought together by such different chains of events, both started by a pirate attack. Rosalind didn't believe in anything as intangible as destiny, but her meeting with the Black Angel was surely due to something stronger than mere coincidence. She thought over their conversation, alone in the moonlight with all the stars shining down on them. They had been just a pirate and schoolteacher, just two people, lost in the Caribbean. Two strangers, drawn to each other, sharing a few mild jokes. How sweet it had been. How dear. Clasping those thoughts to her like a favorite toy, Rosalind drifted off.

In the depths of her restless sleep, Rosalind obeyed an overwhelming compulsion, searching, running, looking everywhere. One moment she rushed through the quiet avenues of London's Grosvenor Square, racing past her own front door. Next she ran along the waterfront, searching every deck of every ship for one particular face. Where was he? She had to find him before it was too late.

Two unwelcome faces kept appearing: Mr. Murdock and Vasquez. Mr. Murdock was speaking. Rosalind couldn't make out the exact words, but the tone was far too familiar. Patient, understanding, excruciatingly polite, and considerate. Rosalind stood frozen while Mr. Murdock looped coil after coil of rope around her, tying her up like a spider binding its prey. On and on Mr. Murdock talked. As the words grew clearer, a horrible feeling of dread crept over her. Mr. Murdock was more than a little put out over not getting as much for her as he'd hoped, and after all the trouble he'd gone to making all these arrangements. It was for her own good. In time she'd become the kind of wife he really needed, the kind who did as she was told. If only she'd listened to him, if only she'd stayed at home and let him take care of notifying Thomas. . . .

Now Rosalind stood before Vasquez on the deck of *La Fortuna*. He threw a bag of coins to Mr. Murdock who waited nearby, wearing Vasquez's redigote and smoking one of Vasquez's foul cigars. Vasquez grabbed Rosalind by her braid and started dragging her down to the bilges. He was going to clap her in irons and let his entire crew have a go at her. To her horror, Rosalind realized Vasquez was still dead. All of his crew came creeping over the ship's rails, soaking wet, bloated, showing their bloody wounds. All grinning their dead grins right at her. Rosalind screamed. She thrashed against the ropes that bound her, fighting against Vasquez's hold on her braid.

"Rosalind!"

The horrible dead pirates were grinning and bleeding and reaching out for her.

"Rosalind!"

She was shaking all over, shaking from terror, shaking from the cold, shaking—

Rosalind's eyes opened. Alexandre held her, pinning her arms to her sides. They lay in his bed, aboard *L'Etoile du Matin*. The blankets were twisted around her legs. She heaved a great breath of relief and burst into tears, burying her face against Alexandre's chest. Holding her against him, he lifted her up and freed her braid where it was trapped beneath her shoulder.

"Shush, *ma belle*. Hush now. All is well."

Rosalind shook her head frantically, dragging her breath in with great gulping sobs. "They were dead! All of them! They meant to attack me, every single one of them!"

"Who was dead? Can you tell me?"

"Vasquez. His men. All dead!"

Alexandre held her tighter. *"Ma petite fleur.* Poor sweet girl. Of course. You have never witnessed such a battle."

"Mr. Murdock—he *sold* me! To them! So they could— could—" Her voice failed her. She shook her head against the lingering horror.

Alexandre rocked her, kissing her forehead, murmuring soothing words in French and English. "Who is this Mr. Murdock?"

"The man I'm supposed to marry."

"Ah yes. Your fiancé."

Despite her fading terror, something in Alexandre's tone got Rosalind's attention. She leaned back against his shoulder until she could look at him. He was trying to keep a neutral expression, but by now she knew him well enough to see the tension in his jaw, the slight narrowing of his eyes. He looked like he hated Mr. Murdock. Even though his features had hardened with dislike, Alexandre kept his voice gentle.

"Would he do such a thing?"

"Sell me? To pirates? Of course not!"

"And yet he did not save you from them, did he?"

"No." Rosalind clung to Alexandre, to the warmth of his skin and the solid muscle beneath it, to the beating of his heart and the comfort of his arms around her. Rosalind looked at Alexandre, seeing not this pirate façade he chose to assume but the man behind it. The man who had yet to hurt her, who didn't ignore her, who spoke to her as if she was capable of rational discourse. The man who proclaimed his desire for her in words as charming and seductive as he was. She reached up to touch his cheek.

"Twice now you've saved me from them." A sudden vision struck her, a new nightmare of the emptiness stretching before her. Days and nights without end, filled with polite conversation, pleasant little dinner parties, card games. Perhaps even children. Somehow Rosalind couldn't see Mr. Murdock having anything to do with something as messy as a baby. He would want heirs, but their conception would be as cold and bloodless as all his business deals. Sudden harsh sobs wracked Rosalind.

"Please, Alexandre! Save me! *Save me!*"

Alexandre held her away from him and took her face in his hands. "Hush, hush now! Look at me."

Rosalind bit her lip against further sobs and blinked away the tears streaming down her cheeks. Alexandre looked down at her, the stern cast to his features sharpened by genuine worry. He was truly concerned about her.

"How can I save you? Tell me what I must do."

That rich voice, those eyes like dark jewels, the beauty of his face, and the majesty of his figure. . . . She would never meet a man like Alexandre again. That wild streak rose in her. This once, just this once, she would fling caution to the winds for her own sake. There would be a price, one she had no idea how to reckon, but that didn't matter. All that mattered was claiming this night for her own. Slipping free of his embrace, Rosalind lay back against the pillows and took hold of the ribbon that tied the high collar of her nightgown closed. She pulled it free, letting her collar fall open.

Alexandre stared down at her. When he spoke, his voice

was hoarse with wonder. "Are you sure, Rosalind? Is this truly what you want?"

Rosalind stared up at Alexandre, at the sympathy and concern in his expression. Never had she seen a fraction of that in Mr. Murdock's face, nothing beyond a polite interest or patronizing attentiveness. Here was genuine concern, genuine regard. She laid her hands on Alexandre's chest, feeling the heat of his skin and the beat of his heart. Her hands moved slowly upward, around his neck and into his hair. She closed her eyes and ran her fingers down through the raven silk.

"This is the third time," she murmured. She opened her eyes and looked up at Alexandre. The fire burned there in the depths of those dark jewels, hotter now with his enjoyment of her touch. "First you saved me from drowning. Second, you saved me from Vasquez. Third—"

"Third, *ma belle?*" Alexandre's hands slid down her arms to rest just beneath her breasts.

Rosalind took a deep breath. "And third, you will save me from myself."

Alexandre gazed down at her, reading the strength of her resolve in her eyes. He bent to kiss the tears off her cheeks. His lips moved across her skin, following the damp trails down to her throat. This was no dream, no idle fantasy. Alexandre was maleness itself, all that feral energy caged within his magnificent figure. Rosalind sighed, making it a gesture of submission as she surrendered herself to his embrace.

Alexandre claimed her mouth in a fierce kiss. His fingers freed the ribbon that bound her braid and began separating the plaits, working upward with a deliberate slowness that made Rosalind's body come alive with sensation. When her hair spilled loose across the pillow, Alexandre sank both hands into it and held her still while his tongue glided along her lips, coaxing them apart. Rosalind melted against him, doing her best to return the passion of his kiss.

His hands slid down her back to her bottom. He gripped

her, kneading her flesh, pressing her hips against his. The loose cotton breeches did nothing to hide the strength of his desire. Made bold by her recklessness, Rosalind returned his caress, tracing the outlines of his manhood with her fingertips. Alexandre groaned into her mouth. His hands pressed her closer, rubbing her against him. A hot thrill burned through her. To feel such delicious pressure there, right there, where her ache for him went deepest and the memory of his kiss still made her tingle. . . .

"You astound me, *ma belle*. So cold, so sensible, and yet such a fire waiting within." Alexander's cheeks were flushed, his eyes glittering, and now he wore that wicked grin. "Do you remember how I kissed you, *ma belle?*"

His other hand settled on her hip, gathering up the folds of her nightgown until her thigh was bare. The heat of his palm caressed her inner thigh, drifting upward. He twined his fingers in her delicate silken curls. Now Rosalind drew her breath in sharply, every muscle taut with anticipation.

"Oh yes. . . ."

"You remember how I kissed you there, just as I kiss you now?"

His mouth covered hers, his tongue parting her lips with a slow thrust. One long finger slid down through her wet heat, gliding over that one perfect spot. Rosalind arched against Alexandre, her breasts heavy and warm with the pleasure surging through her. He teased her, circling that spot even as his tongue circled hers, catching her up in a whirlwind of pleasure. Alexandre's tongue thrust deep into her mouth. His finger slipped inside her, gently, slowly. Rosalind stiffened, overwhelmed by the new wave of sensation. Where was the pain she knew must be part of this? She felt only pleasure, this sweet tormenting bliss. She tore her mouth from his, gasping.

"Remember, *ma belle*," Alexandre whispered, "the softness of my tongue here inside you?"

Rosalind nodded, cheeks burning, heart pounding, scarcely able to breathe.

"Isn't it better, this hardness, this length, sinking deeper, giving you so much more?" He turned his wrist. His finger sank all the way in. His thumb lay against that perfect spot, making Rosalind stiffen again. Too much. It was too much. She fell back against the pillows, too weak to protest.

"*Mais non, ma belle.* You cannot give up now."

He quickened his movement, stroking her most secret places, touching her there where no other man had ever ventured. His thumb matched the pace, sending hot spirals of joy roaring up through her. Just when she feared she'd faint dead away, the final glory struck her. She threw back her head and let it out in a cry of rapture.

When she came back to herself, Rosalind was startled to see an expression on Alexandre's face of such tenderness, such simple happiness.

"Now, *ma petite fleur, mon ange Anglaise,* let me see you in all your beauty."

He slid both hands up her thighs, raising the hem of her nightgown higher and higher. He drew it off over her head and tossed it aside. Rosalind shook her hair back, showing him everything he wanted to see. His eyes drank her in while his fingertips followed the curve of her shoulder, the line of her collarbone, the swell of her breast down to her nipple, pink and hard like a furled rosebud. The slightest touch made Rosalind moan, aching for more.

"You are more than beautiful, Rosalind." That deep voice spoke in a hushed, reverent tone. "You are divine."

Shyly, feeling every inch a wanton, Rosalind took Alexandre's hands in hers and pressed them to her breasts. The heat in Alexandre's eyes was cold ash to the inferno that blazed up now.

"I see your wild streak shows itself here as well, *ma belle.*"

"*Oui, mon cher capitaine.*"

Seized by a delicious sense of abandon, Rosalind brushed her fingertips along the rampant proof of his arousal. Alexandre caught her hand and trapped it between his own.

He drew a long, shuddering breath, then brought her hand up to his lips.

"You offer me a great honor, Rosalind. I will do my best to be worthy of it."

Rosalind smiled. Alexandre moved back to the edge of the bed and stepped onto the deck just long enough to strip off his breeches. Rosalind stared at him, lost in the wonder of his naked beauty. The long muscles in his thighs, his trim hips, and, most of all, the object of her exploration, the virile length of his manhood. If he called her divine, then surely he was godlike as well.

Alexandre knelt again on the bed and moved to the center where she lay. He bent to kiss her thighs, turning his head back and forth, gently urging them apart. His long black hair fell across the tender skin of her inner thighs. The faint tickle only added to Rosalind's excitement. She opened her thighs to him, both eager and fearful.

Alexandre glanced up at her. "I see worry clouding the clear skies of your eyes, *ma belle*. You have nothing to fear from me."

"Not true, *mon capitaine*."

Rosalind smiled, intending it as a joke. A shadow crossed Alexandre's face, something like regret. Before she could ask him what troubled him, he reached the juncture of her thighs. His tongue added to her wetness, bearing her up on a new tide of pleasure. A long breath, part sigh, part moan, eased out of her.

Taking his weight on his hands, Alexandre slid his body up the length of hers, moving slowly, letting her feel his skin, his breath, the weight of muscle in his arms and torso. At last he lay against her, her bare breasts against his chest, his naked belly against hers, the hard length of his desire pressing into her there, where the ache for him went deepest. Rosalind sighed again, her body relaxing into complete surrender. She was Alexandre's captive, his hostage, entirely at his mercy. Could anyone blame her for being unable to resist him, this fearsome pirate king? She ran her hands up his arms, stroking his shoulders, caressing the glorious black silk of his hair.

"Have mercy, Alexandre. When you take this treasure, it's gone forever."

"All the more precious, then."

He kissed her, his mouth hot and sweet and gentle. His hands slid down her hips to her thighs, bringing them up along his waist. He slipped one hand between their bodies to touch that perfect spot, coaxing Rosalind into another breathless frenzy. He pressed in, bearing down slowly until she winced. Earlier that very evening Alexandre had toasted her courage. Nothing else Rosalind had done up to now required as much courage as lying still beneath him, trusting him. And yet she could not lie still. To feel that hard silky thickness poised to fill her ignited sparks that raced along every nerve. Her thighs gripped his waist as her hips rocked, seeking completion, fulfillment. Alexandre groaned. He buried his face in her neck and brought her once again to that devastating peak of rapture. At the height of the glory sweeping through her, Alexandre bore down, flexing his hips. There was a moment's stinging resistance, then he sank into her. The fullness, the exquisite pressure of him filling her, sent Rosalind whirling up to a new plane of ecstasy.

Alexandre nuzzled her breasts, suckling her, nipping at her. He thrust deep, driving cry after cry out of her. Every new peak made Rosalind tighten up around him, forcing him to plunge even deeper with each thrust. Only when her hands fell away from him and she lay back in utter exhaustion did he raise his head to look down into her eyes.

"This is my mercy, *ma belle*. I have told you I am not a patient man. For you I have made myself wait."

Rosalind brushed her fingertips along his cheek, then drew his head down to kiss him. His tongue thrust between her lips even as he drove into her. She clung to him, nearly delirious with the joy of it as she rode out the fury of his passion.

"*Ma belle, ma petite fleur—*" His hips heaved once, twice, three times. His head fell against her shoulder.

Slowly the tension eased out of Alexandre's arms and back. He lay against her, the broad length of him a warm and comforting weight. He raised his head to give her a lazy, lopsided smile. She had never seen him look so sweet, so charming. She kissed him lightly. His mouth opened over hers, answering her with a deep, slow kiss that proclaimed his satisfaction louder than any words could. He shifted his weight to her side and tugged at the rumpled bedclothes. She wriggled under them, grateful for the warmth.

"You look quite satisfied, *ma belle.*" Alexandre slid in beside her and opened his arms to her. Rosalind snuggled down against his chest. "Are you well?"

She was stiff from the exertion, but only a little soreness remained. That amazed her. Given his size, she'd been sure all her fears were justified. How kind of him to take such care to make her ready. She nodded sleepily. He chuckled, stroking her hair back from her face.

"Give me a little time to rest, *ma belle,* and we'll see just how much of this new pleasure you can stand."

"What, all that *again?*"

Alexandre smiled, eyes half-closed. "*Mais oui, ma belle.* For you I think I could go on forever."

Rosalind turned her head to kiss his shoulder, then let the rhythm of his heartbeat lull her. There couldn't be many hours left before dawn. The sun would rise, another day would begin. She was no longer a virgin. This was the first irrevocable step she'd ever taken. She sighed fretfully.

"Don't think, *ma belle.*" Alexandre's voice was soft, muffled by his drowsiness. "Let today be today. Tomorrow will come all too soon."

She nodded again, eyes closing as she drifted off.

Chapter Twenty

Rosalind floated in a world of contentment. Eyes closed, breathing peacefully, she drifted in that sweet state between sleeping and waking. As she turned over, the sheet slipped down, making her gasp. She lay there stark naked, clothed in nothing but her own long golden hair. He'd won. The Black Angel had won! Even after the way she'd dressed him down on his own quarterdeck, he had mastered himself enough to switch tactics and maneuver her into his bed. She snatched up the sheet, covering herself. How would the mighty Black Angel regard her now, having conquered her as he had conquered so many women before her?

Rosalind squared her shoulders. The thing to do was carry on as if nothing had happened. That was a ridiculous thought, but appearances were all she had left to preserve. She must wash, and dress, and see to Beatrice. She must try to learn how much closer the ship had traveled to Martinique in the course of the night. She must do all she could to keep the Black Angel steering the course he promised to set.

A few minutes of vigorous scrubbing saw Rosalind as

clean as she could be short of full immersion in a proper bath. With the intensity of a warrior arming for battle, Rosalind carefully chose her petticoats, fresh stockings, and a gown made of lightweight green muslin. It was a summer frock, hardly the thing for a daughter in mourning, but it was plain and comfortable and would stand shipboard wear far better than the peach satin.

Decently gowned, hair braided and pinned up, dignity mended as best it could be, Rosalind took a deep breath and stepped out on deck. The first thing she noticed was the sun in the wrong place. It was behind the ship, still rising toward its zenith. That meant *L'Etoile du Matin* was sailing west. Martinique lay to the northeast, a good many sea miles behind them. Jamaica itself was a green smudge on the northern horizon, visible off the stern. Rosalind felt a rising sense of panic. Alexandre was not making for Jamaica. He was not even headed toward Martinique! Where had his capricious temper decided to lead him this time?

As Rosalind turned and moved down toward the main deck, a piercing whistle split the air behind her. She glanced back to see the helmsman with two fingers in his mouth. The noise on deck subsided. Every face turned her way. Rosalind met the pirates' stares with a look of disdain, keeping her bearing stiff and proud. It was just possible they didn't know Alexandre's latest attempt at seduction had succeeded.

Remy, the second mate, suddenly dropped out of the rigging before her. Looking breathless, his dark curls mussed by the wind, Remy jerked his blue jacket into tidier lines, wiped a hand over his mouth, then made Rosalind a slight bow.

"*Bonjour,* mademoiselle. Is there anything you need?"

"*Mais oui.* I need an answer. Why are we sailing away from both Jamaica and Martinique? Where on earth has your almighty *capitaine* decided to rush off to now?"

"We are proceeding on course, mademoiselle. Shall I call Christophe? He will fetch you whatever you like from the galley." He turned to shout over his shoulder. "Christophe!"

The bosun and his mates carried the cry down the nearest hatch. Christophe appeared, slapping what looked like flour from his breeches. He gave Remy the shadow of a nod and presented himself to Rosalind with a formal bow.

"*Bonjour,* mademoiselle," Christophe said. "*Le capitaine* regrets extremely his absence this morning, but there is so much ship's business to be attended to." He stepped past Rosalind to open the cabin door. "If mademoiselle would be pleased to wait inside, I will bring a tray from the galley. While you refresh yourself, I will ask *le capitaine* when you might see him."

Rosalind seethed with anger and humiliation. So, the Black Angel had slaked his lust. Now he had no time for her, no use for her until he wished to "play" with his little English doll again.

"Don't bother." Rosalind stepped around Remy and hurried down the steps to the main deck. "I believe I'll have a word with *le capitaine* myself."

Remy jumped down behind Rosalind and caught her by the arm. His grip was light, but definite. "Mademoiselle, *le capitaine* thought it best that you remain in his cabin today."

"Did he?" Rosalind spoke lightly. "And did *le capitaine* say why he felt I needed this rest?"

Remy looked at Christophe, who replied with a sharp shake of his head, warning Remy to say nothing more. So they did know. Rosalind jerked her arm out of Remy's grasp.

"*Messieurs,* you have a choice. You may take me to *le capitaine* or bring him to me. If you try to lock me in his cabin, you will have to carry me there. It will not be an easy task, that I promise you."

"Mademoiselle. . . ." Christophe began.

Rosalind pushed past the two of them and made for the stern hatchway. When Remy's fingers brushed her shoulder, she stopped him with a glare. Holding her skirts out of the way with one hand, Rosalind climbed down the ladder. She paused at the bottom to arrange her skirts and smooth her windblown hair. Just above her, the men began to argue.

"Imbecile!" Christophe said. "Now we've put her in a temper. *Le capitaine* will haze us for a month!"

"And she thinks we're going the wrong way." Remy cursed, mixing French with Spanish and some other throaty tongue. "He had to pick a clever one this time, didn't he? *La Belle Tempétueux.*"

Rosalind glared upward, wishing she could throw them overboard. "The Tempestuous Beauty," they had called her. Or perhaps "The Stormy Beauty." How like pirates to pour salt in a wound! That Alexandre could distance himself from her this way, put a wall of his men between himself and her. . . . That wall was about to come tumbling down. She was a passenger aboard this ship, nothing more. A passenger who paid in gold, and had thus purchased the right to know exactly where they were heading. She hurried forward, into the maze of cargo. Just as she reached the hold amidships, Alexandre's voice rang out.

"Is it so impossible for you fools to keep one *Anglaise* occupied until I have a moment to look in on her? Just give her whatever she wants. I'll be there shortly."

Rosalind stepped around a larger pile of crates. Alexandre stood with his back to her, hands on hips as he harried his men.

"What I want, *mon capitaine,*" she said, "is a word with you. Right now, *s'il-vous plaît.*"

Alexandre hung his head. He ran one hand back over his hair, then hissed something at his men. They scattered. Alexandre heaved a heavy sigh, then turned to face her. He looked shabby and tired, his hands filthy and his shirt streaked with dirt. His hair was mussed, the ribbon that bound it having slipped down to let a few wayward strands fall loose. For some reason the sight of him no more grand than his crew touched Rosalind. He'd been down there in the hold with them, moving crates and rolling barrels and sweating along with the rest. He was no primping fool to pose on his quarterdeck while the real sailors did the hard work.

"Bonjour, mon capitaine." Rosalind kept her tone cool

and her bearing formal. "Why are we sailing in this direction? With every passing hour we leave Jamaica and Martinique farther and farther away."

Alexandre laid light hands on her shoulders, tilting his head to one side. He studied her, smiling. "How are you, *ma belle?* I am sorry I could not be with you when you awoke."

The warm regard in his eyes, the deep resonance of his voice, the affection in his entire manner. . . . Rosalind tried to maintain her aloof posture, but her rebellious body yearned for the feel of his arms around her.

"Please answer me, *mon capitaine.* We must reach Kingston as soon as possible. You know how urgent it is."

"I would hear your answer first, *ma belle.*" He held her at arms length, looking over her gown. "Yesterday you were a tropical blossom. Today you are a sea sprite, lovely enough to shame the most beautiful mermaid."

Rosalind dismissed the flattery. "I am fine, *mon capitaine.* There. Now will you tell me why you've set this course?"

"Will you stop acting like someone's maiden aunt and give me an honest answer?" Alexander enfolded her in his arms, kissing her temple and rubbing his cheek against her hair. "You are fully a woman now, *ma belle.* That is a great change. It can be a little frightening."

It vexed Rosalind still further to know he could see through her so easily. As much as she wanted to take comfort in his embrace, she remained distant.

"Do you make such a habit of deflowering virgins, *mon capitaine,* that you know so much of their moods the next day?"

Rosalind expected Alexandre to frown, to scowl, to take exception to her tone and her manner. Instead he smiled.

"*Non,* I do not. I avoid virgins whenever possible. I do not care for ignorance, on my ship or in my bed."

Before any retort could leave her lips, Alexandre silenced her mouth with his. Rosalind quivered at the sweet tenderness of the kiss. Of their own will her hands slid up his chest and around his neck, freeing the ribbon that held his hair. She combed her fingers through it, spreading the black silk across his shoulders.

He raised his head to grin down at her. "I do make the occasional exception."

"On what grounds?"

"Beauty, passion, courage, a natural ability to enjoy such pleasure and to return it with an open heart."

Alexandre bent to kiss her throat, moving down to the swell of her bosom. His hair fell forward, spilling across her neck and shoulders. That dangerous joy swelled inside Rosalind again, stealing her wits and leaving her breathless. She longed to strip away his threadbare shirt and kiss his naked shoulders. Now that she knew what it was to have him inside her, remembered sensations overwhelmed Rosalind. Her skin burned, her breasts tingled, and that other place so newly discovered throbbed with the thunder of her rushing pulse.

Alexandre lifted her up and set her on a stack of crates. He rained kisses on her breasts, his tongue plunging between them again and again, leaving her nipples taut and aching for his lips. He stood between her thighs, leaning his weight on her there, where her longing went deepest. He kissed her endlessly, leaving her helpless before the force of her own desires. His long slender fingers curled around her ankle. His hand glided up her calf to her knee, pushing her skirts up. The heat of his palm on her inner thigh brought Rosalind to her senses.

"*Non!*" Rosalind jerked her head away and pushed Alexandre back. She glared at him, breathing hard, trying to ignore the hunger he had roused within her. "I will have no more of these distractions!"

Using a crate as a stepping stool, she climbed down to the deck and shook out her skirts, smoothing them back into place. Alexandre stood there, chest heaving, dark eyes glittering. He looked wild and fierce and ready to pounce.

"You say you will have no more distractions, *ma belle?* You have driven me to distraction." He advanced on her, one hand held out. "Let me show you another way, Rosalind. You might enjoy this one even more."

Rosalind took a few steps backward. "You will answer me, *mon capitaine,* and you will do so now. Why are we sailing in the wrong direction?"

Alexandre blew out his breath and wiped both hands down his face. "Mademoiselle, once again you have fallen under the mistaken assumption that you may give me orders aboard my own ship."

"I have paid you in gold, *mon capitaine,* gold I nearly paid for in my own blood." When he winced at that, Rosalind nodded. "I thought we had a new agreement. I thought you were bent on convincing me of your noble sense of honor."

"And I thought I'd finally softened that sharp tongue." Alexandre shook his head. "Yves keeps telling me what a fool I am, and I keep proving him right." That familiar stern mask settled over Alexandre's features. "If you are done shrieking at me, mademoiselle, I will be happy to tell you why we are in fact sailing in the best direction."

Rosalind seated herself on a nearby crate and arranged her skirts primly. "Very well, *mon capitaine.* I am listening."

"You do know something of ships, you've proven that, but you plainly know nothing of navigation. We are in the path of the trade winds. They blow northeast to southwest on this side of Jamaica. When we reach the other side of the island, the trades will carry us around to Martinique. Believe me, mademoiselle, this is the fastest and safest way."

Embarrassment over her ignorance struck Rosalind mute, along with the annoyance of having nothing to rebuke him for. Her sense of being totally powerless drove Rosalind to take refuge in disdain.

"Tell me, *mon capitaine,* has your entire crew congratulated you on your great victory? Have they drunk a toast to your health, celebrating the power of your masculinity in besting *La Belle Tempétueux?*"

"What ship—" Alexandre stopped short. His brow darkened with a thunderous scowl. "Did any of them address you in that manner?"

"*Non*. They were laughing at me behind my back once I escaped them and went below."

"The Stormy Beauty." Alexandre pronounced it in English. "It is a compliment, *ma belle*. A salute to both your beauty and your refusal to be conquered."

"It is nothing of the kind! It sounds like an unlucky name for a ship! Is that what they think of me, *mon capitaine*? That I am bad luck for you, for all of them?"

It was the question of a peevish child, but Alexandre's sudden silence told her the unpleasant truth.

"Does it really matter, mademoiselle, what uncouth French pirates think?"

Again Alexandre spoke in that soft, sad voice. It made Rosalind want to go to him, to wrap her arms around his waist and hold him tight. She didn't care what his crew thought of her. They'd think the worst no matter what, just to amuse themselves. But Alexandre . . .

Alexandre knelt before Rosalind, taking her hands in his. He stared into her eyes, searching their depths as if they held the answer to the greatest mystery of all. At last he smiled. "My poor courageous milkmaid. The loss of your virginity doesn't distress you half so much as this sense of defeat."

Rosalind closed her eyes, mortified at the accuracy of his insight.

"You think you've lost, don't you?" Alexandre asked. "You think that in surrendering to the passion within you, you've given up any advantage you might have had."

Instead of the anger she'd anticipated, Alexandre looked on her with tenderness, with humor, perhaps even with affection.

"You have lost nothing in my eyes, Rosalind. If anything you have gained even greater advantage over me than any you had before." He lightly kissed her forehead, her eyelids, her cheeks, her lips. "I regard last night as a singular honor. I would not defile that for anything in this world."

"*Merci,* Alexandre." Rosalind reached up a shaking hand to brush her fingers along his cheek. She wasn't just another doxy to him. She wasn't just another English girl he'd seduce then abandon. He would remember her. No matter what happened, he would remember her. Thus reassured, she turned to the matter now uppermost in her mind.

"*Mon capitaine,* again I must point out to you the fragile state of Beatrice's health. She cannot languish aboard this ship while you and you crew take days or weeks to refit your ship."

Alexandre's brows drew together in exasperation. "There are few medical men in these waters superior to my ship's physician. She could have no better care ashore."

Rosalind stood up. "Very well. If that is the extent of your compassion, it will have to do." She gathered up her skirts and turned to make her way toward the bow.

Alexandre's arm circled her waist, pinning her against his chest. He nuzzled the tender skin behind her ear. "Take care, *ma belle.* Provoke me with that saucy tone again and I might see fit to make those delicious lips beg for mercy."

"*Mon capitaine.*" Rosalind stood rigid within his grasp. "I am not some waterfront trollop willing to rut like an animal wherever the mood might strike."

"You fool no one with this display of prissy manners." Alexandre spun her around, catching her up in his arms. "You are as hot-blooded as I am, *ma belle divine.*"

"With all possible respect, *mon capitaine,* may I point out that you are filthy, unshaven, and none too fragrant as well. Perhaps your usual *chèrie amies* find you all too manly in this condition, but I find it somewhat less appealing."

Just as she'd hoped, this attack on his vanity left Alexandre speechless. In the moment of his consternation, Rosalind broke free and ran for the nearest hatch, clambering up the ladder so quickly she almost tore her skirts.

Up on deck the pirates avoided her. That suited Rosalind's mood perfectly. She wanted to be left alone, all alone, so alone there wasn't a single human being for miles around. As she crossed the main deck, she heard Beatrice's weak laughter drift back from somewhere near the bow. Beatrice stood at the rail, looking over the side. Eric stood beside her, pointing to something in the water below. Drawn by their happy smiles, Rosalind made her way toward them.

"You look quite cheerful."

Beatrice's cheeks were pink with the wind and sun, her eyes bright. "Oh, Rosalind! We've been watching the dolphins ride the bow wave. They were swimming right along, keeping up with the ship!"

"*Mais oui,* mademoiselle." Eric nodded. "Dolphins bring good luck."

"To whom, I wonder?"

Hearing the dry note in Rosalind's voice, Beatrice's smile faded. "Oh, Rosalind, forgive me. Here I am prattling about fish when I've been so worried about you!" She waved a hand at the ship's bell hanging toward the stern. "Those horrible bells woke me up when it was still dark out. Where were you, Rosalind?"

Before Beatrice could pursue the question, Rosalind broke the unfortunate news she had come to deliver.

"The captain has refused to take us to Kingston. He will not risk the inshore patrols. He tells me we are following the trade winds around Jamaica and back to Martinique."

"But . . ." Beatrice's hands flew to her mouth. "Once the *Bird of Paradise* reaches Kingston without me, the Lawrences will surely find another governess!"

Rosalind nodded. "And my brother will surely think I am lost."

"This is horrible!" Beatrice cried. "I must have that position. It took Mother ages to find one she approved of!"

"Beatrice, please." Rosalind tried to put an arm around Beatrice's shaking shoulders. "Do not distress yourself.

You're too ill for this." She looked up at Eric. "Bring me the doctor now, please."

"*Oui,* mademoiselle."

A few minutes later heavy footsteps crossed the deck behind Rosalind. Dr. Gingras hurried ahead of Eric.

"*Oui,* mademoiselle?" Dr. Gingras asked. "You sent for me?"

"*Merci, Monsieur le Docteur.* As you can see, Mademoiselle Beatrice is looking quite pale."

Dr. Gingras took Beatrice's wrist and watched the timing of her pulse. He looked at her closely. "Mademoiselle, what distresses you? Not a quarter of an hour ago I saw you smiling and happy."

Beatrice refused to speak, hiding her face against Rosalind's shoulder.

"*Monsieur le Docteur,*" Rosalind began. "Is there any way under heaven or on earth to make *le capitaine* understand the need to get this girl ashore at once? He's determined to make port only at Martinique, a good three days away! God only knows what else will happen to us between now and then!"

Dr. Gingras nodded. "You have a point, mademoiselle. Unfortunately, I do not believe *le capitaine* will be persuaded to change course."

"Why not?"

"*Le capitaine* has a great many reasons for docking at Martinique."

Apparently preserving Beatrice's life did not rank high among them. Rosalind turned her back on Dr. Gingras before she lost her temper completely.

"Eric, please see Mademoiselle Beatrice below. She must rest."

"*Oui,* mademoiselle." Eric put his arm around Beatrice's shoulders and gently steered her toward the forward hatch.

Rosalind looked down into the blue-green waters, past the white foam that raced away along the ship's hull. Just beneath the surface, two and then three sleek shapes appeared, their gray bodies moving in smooth ripples as they easily kept pace with the ship. One cleared the surface, shooting ahead a few feet before plunging in again.

"Such bright eyes," Rosalind said. "And the way they smile so. . . ."

"You see, mademoiselle?" Dr. Gingras smiled. "How easily they can be mistaken for mermaids!"

"Landsmen think us sailors lonely fools, that we should mistake every other fish in the sea for a lovely woman."

Rosalind closed her eyes. Alexandre's voice, just behind her. Where had he come from this time? Her fingers tightened on the rail.

"Ah, *mon capitaine*," Dr. Gingras said. "Mademoiselle has discovered the dolphins."

For a moment Alexandre was silent. Rosalind braced herself. When he did speak, his voice was oddly subdued.

"I would have gladly shown them to mademoiselle, had she but asked."

"They are lovely, *mon capitaine*," Rosalind said. "They are everything you said they were."

"I am gratified, mademoiselle, to discover that at last we agree on something."

That cold, aloof tone made Rosalind's temper flare again. "*Mon capitaine*, please hear what *Monsieur le Docteur* has to tell you about Mademoiselle Beatrice's present state of health."

"Be good enough to face me when you address me, mademoiselle."

Rosalind took herself firmly in hand and turned to face Alexandre. He stood there bare-chested, dripping wet, rubbing the sea water from his long hair with a towel. All traces of dirt and grime were gone. He wore those light cotton breeches again. The water left them molded to his hips and thighs, enflaming more than just her imagination. Her cheeks burning, Rosalind quickly turned back to the rail.

Dr. Gingras cleared his throat uneasily. "Shall I, *mon capitaine*?"

"By all means."

"The *jeune fille* is now in a state of nervous prostration, which will delay her recovery somewhat."

"Mon capitaine." Rosalind tried to keep her breathing even, her voice steady. "You say we will not make port in Martinique for three days. I say to you, Beatrice could be dead by then."

"Not a pressing concern, *mon capitaine.*" Dr. Gingras gave Rosalind a look of stern disapproval. "In all honesty I must tell you that due to the *jeune fille's* fragile constitution I can rule out no possibility. But death, sir, does not seem likely."

"Merci, Monsieur le Docteur." Alexandre turned that stern look on Rosalind. "Very well, mademoiselle. I have heard what *Monsieur le Docteur* had to say. His word on this is final. You will nag me no further."

Rosalind stared at him. That was the end of it? Alexandre refused to give the health and welfare of a female captive the concern common human decency required? Nothing could have been a sharper reminder that he was the Black Angel, sworn enemy of England.

Chapter Twenty-one

Two days later *L'Etoile du Matin* rounded the easternmost point of Martinique and anchored in *L'Anse du Paradis*. Paradise Cove was aptly named. Gentle waves rolled up onto a smooth, serene beach dotted with palm trees and smaller shrubs. Even the noise of the wind quieted. Rosalind stood with Beatrice in the bow, taking in the air and keeping out of the way. The pirates dashed about, bringing up a few particular barrels and boxes from the hold and lowering a boat.

Rosalind looked on with growing anxiety. At sea the Black Angel was acknowledged as supremely dangerous. How much more so would he be here, in French waters, on French soil? She turned her attention to Beatrice. Beatrice's color was steady and her eyes brighter and more alert. She was still a trifle feverish, but Dr. Gingras assured them the worst was certainly past. That might be true of Beatrice's illness, but Rosalind was in no way confident the worst of their ordeal was over.

Heavy boots thudded toward them. Eric presented himself, making a small bow. "The boat is ready, mesdemoiselles. *Le capitaine* has given you leave to go ashore."

"Is this to be another picnic on the beach?" Rosalind asked. She nearly winced at her own sarcasm. The unnerving prospect of plunging even deeper into the unknown put a sharp edge on her tongue.

Eric glanced back at the quarterdeck where Alexandre stood with Yves and the ship's carpenter, then took a step closer to Rosalind. "Mademoiselle, *s'il-vous plaît.*"

Rosalind hid her embarrassment by turning to look at the quarterdeck. Alexandre stood there, gripping a line in each hand, leaning into the wind that blew his long black hair back from his face. The two days of chilly distance between them had brought back the stern pirate captain who had lifted her one-handed from the sea.

Rosalind led Beatrice to the rail where the rope ladder once again hung in readiness for their descent. The sight of it made Rosalind shy back, all too mindful of what had happened to the two of them the last time they'd set foot on dry land. What unforeseen torment awaited them now?

A long shadow fell across her. "Is there some trouble, mademoiselle?" Alexandre asked. "You look as pale as milk."

Rosalind tried to steady herself. "Forgive me, *mon capitaine,* if I do not relish the idea of being taken to a den of pirates like so many Spanish doubloons."

"Such a long face, *ma belle!*" Alexandre scooped her up in his arms. "No coin of Spain could ever match your worth, no matter how pure its gold."

The sunlight danced in his dark eyes, bringing a shade of warmth to his stern expression. Rosalind acknowledged his flattery with a cool smile.

"*Merci, mon capitaine.* As ever, you have a very nimble tongue."

Alexandre bent his head, the caress of his breath warm on her neck as he murmured in her ear. "*Ma belle fleur.* Who would know that better than you?"

Rosalind closed her eyes against the knowing look in his. A blush stung her cheeks even as her blood pulsed in hot waves. If she hadn't had a wild streak inside her before meeting the Black Angel, she surely had one now.

Alexandre set her on her feet, then swung over the rail and down the rope ladder. He waited for her at the bottom, his hands up to steady her. "To me, *ma belle*. We must catch the tide."

Rosalind made her way down the ladder one cautious step at a time, relieved to feel Alexandre's hands close around her waist. He steadied her while she found her footing, then took his seat, pulling her down onto his lap. His arms tightened around her. Out of sight beneath his other sleeve, one hand covered her breast. His fingers caressed her, teasing her nipple. The sudden rush of sensation made Rosalind clamp her lips together for fear of making some sound that would betray her. She could do nothing more than lean back against Alexandre, helpless in his embrace. The smile he wore told her he knew it as well.

When the boat grounded on the beach, the pirates sprang out to haul it farther ashore. Keeping Rosalind cradled snugly in his arms, Alexandre stood up and stepped down onto the sand. Driftwood lay here and there, the occasional clump of seaweed stretched across it. Sea birds wheeled overhead. The breeze teased the tops of the palms. Alexandre drew a deep breath and smiled.

"Here we are, mademoiselle. The one place that scoundrel *L'Ange Noir* now calls home."

He set Rosalind on her feet. Keeping one arm around her waist, he led her up the beach toward the wall of dense greenery that marked the beginning of the jungle. Rosalind looked back to see Beatrice following along, leaning on Eric's arm with her face turned up to the sun. Sudden anxiety made her hesitate, resisting the gentle pull of Alexandre's arm.

"Forgive me, *mon capitaine,* if I hesitate to follow France's most notorious pirate into a jungle infested with all sorts of dangers."

His stern expression didn't alter. "Have patience, mademoiselle. You will soon see our destination."

The path led upward for some time, into a range of hills. A small tower stood at the summit, topped by a flagpole.

"Your watchtower, *mon capitaine?*"

Alexndre nodded. "I'm told smugglers used this cove before we made our home here."

"Do your neighbors consider you an improvement?"

"Hard to say, *ma belle*. Many miles lay between us."

After the summit, the path dipped down, leading them into a small valley tucked into the island's hills. When the trees gave way to thinner foliage, Rosalind looked down into the little valley with a sudden gasp.

"*Merci, ma belle.*" Alexandre smiled. "Welcome to my home. We call it *Chez Jardin.*"

Rosalind stood still, amazed at the magnificence of the estate that spread out below her. Its fields had been sown. In farther meadows cattle grazed, separated from the flock of sheep by sturdy wooden fences. A fine stallion trotted around the paddock near the stables. The house itself was beautiful, a mansion built of shining white trimmed here and there with dark blue. Flowers surrounded it, tropical blossoms laid out in rows to make a rainbow of brilliant colors. Great terra cotta pots with more blossoms lined the flagstone walk leading up to the front door. Another stony path led around the front of the house to the porch on the northeast side, a verandah where one might take the evening air while sipping a cordial.

Beatrice stepped up beside Rosalind. "How wonderful! Oh, Rosalind, isn't it magnificent?"

Rosalind nodded, too surprised to say any more. Alexandre laid his hands on her shoulders.

"You thought I was taking you to some filthy cave, didn't you? Some horrible little hole strewn with bones, the very air inside alive with bats?"

"*Mais non, mon capitaine*. Nothing quite that bad."

Alexandre led the way down the path. Two boys ran out

from the stables. With much shouting and waving of arms, they hailed Alexandre, then ran back inside. Scant moments later people began spilling out of the mansion through the front door and the verandah and from around the back. French voices filled the air, shouting a welcome and thanking God that *le capitaine* had returned safely once again. Some of the crew behind Rosalind broke into a run, straight into the open arms of several serving women. There was a great din of happy, laughing voices. Rosalind drank it all in. How long had it been since she'd witnessed such happiness, such relief?

Standing in the open doorway like a squat black statue was a mulatto woman. Much of her dark hair had turned silvery. She wore a dress of dull calico, stained and patched, marked with soot and flour and grease. Only her hands were clean.

"Maître de la maison." The mulatto woman greeted Alexandre with a voice like hoarse tropical music. *"Bienvenu. Grâce à Dieu, mon seigneur."*

The mulatto woman held out her arms. Her lips parted to reveal two rows of straight white teeth, gleaming with delight at seeing Alexandre home again safe and sound. Alexandre bent to embrace her. Rosalind observed all this with mounting wonder. She never thought to see the mighty Black Angel paying his respects to a mulatto cook.

"Madame LeFevre," Alexandre said. "May I present to you Miss Rosalind Brooks, who happened to fall into my hands on her way to Jamaica."

Madame LeFevre looked Rosalind over. *"Bonjour,* mademoiselle."

"Bonjour, Madame."

Madame LeFevre turned a startled look on Alexandre. *"Anglaise?"*

"Oui, Madame. The lady is English. And so is her companion."

Alexandre turned to beckon Eric forward. Eric led Beatrice to Rosalind's side.

"Madame," Alexandre said, "allow me to make known to you Miss Beatrice Henderson, who was aboard the same ship."

Madame LeFevre looked Beatrice over with a knowing eye. *"Ma petite!"* She held out both hands to Beatrice. *"Ma pauvre jeune fille! Entrez-vous!"*

She caught Beatrice's hands in hers and pulled her across the threshold, making Beatrice follow along as she hurried off into the interior of the mansion.

"Rosalind!" Beatrice cried. "Where is she taking me?"

Rosalind turned an anxious look on Alexandre. Before she could speak, he pressed one long forefinger against her lips.

"Peace, *ma belle*. Next to Dr. Gingras, there is no better healer in the islands than Madame LeFevre."

Alexandre's hand on her waist pressed Rosalind forward, toward the threshold. Rosalind hesitated. As lovely as this mansion appeared, she recognized her presence here as captivity of another sort. There was no way to so much as guess when she might leave this valley again.

"Mon capitaine."

"Oui, ma belle?"

Rosalind drew close to Alexandre, toying with a fold of his shirt. "I wonder if I might take advantage of this happy moment to make a small request."

Alexandre took her hands in his and kissed them both. "Whatever your heart desires, *ma belle*. You have only to ask."

Rosalind drew her breath in slowly, willing her heartbeat to remain quiet and even. She looked up into Alexandre's eyes.

"Grant me permission to send word to my brother in Kingston. Let me tell him I am alive and well, so he and my mother can be spared that much grief."

"Cunning little milkmaid." Alexandre retained his good humor, but there was a distinct hardening of his eyes. "Is this is some trick? Some way to tell him where you are?"

"Mais non, mon capitaine!" Rosalind shook her head. "You may read the message I shall write. You may dictate its

every word yourself. *S'il-vous plaît, mon capitaine*. I only want to spare my family pain."

Alexandre called out to the happy milling throng. Two maids freed themselves from the pirates they embraced and hurried over to drop respectful curtsies.

"Adele, Sophie, you will see Mademoiselle to her rooms. Her trunks have already arrived?"

"*Oui, mon seigneur.*" The pale, freckled one called Adele replied.

"*Bien*. See to it Mademoiselle has a bath and perfect quiet until it is time to make ready for dinner."

"*Oui, mon seigneur.*"

Alexandre turned to Rosalind. "Go with them, mademoiselle. They will bring you whatever is needed."

"But—*mon capitaine!*" As he made to walk back out into the garden, Rosalind caught his sleeve. "You have given me no answer!"

Alexandre glared down at her from his great height. "Nor shall I, mademoiselle, until I have considered the matter at some length."

Her heart heavy with reluctance and resignation, Rosalind had no choice but to follow the maids as they led her away.

Alexandre allowed himself a few moments to enjoy the happiness of his people, both his crewmen and the household staff, which he thought of as his land crew. It was good to be in safe harbor once more, good to be home, as much as this house would ever be his home. He chose a patch of shade under an apple tree and sat down with his back against the trunk. He plucked a fallen apple from the grass and set to peeling it with his boot knife.

As one familiar figure detached itself from the happy mob, Alexandre settled on a neutral expression to disguise the many concerns preying on his mind. He had chosen his course; now he must accept the winds that came. Yves approached him, wearing the slight scowl that promised winds of gale force or worse.

"Mon capitaine."

"Oui, mon ami?" Alexandre looked up. "How is it that you can look so out of countenance on a day such as this?"

"There is something we must discuss."

Alexandre tapped the ground beside him with the hilt of his knife. "Be seated."

Yves hunkered down beside him. "I fear we may never see a day like this again."

"Exactement!" Alexandre bit into the apple. "All the more reason to enjoy it while we have it."

"All the more reason to make sure we live to see another."

Alexandre dropped all pretense of merriment. "Out with it, then. If you must ruin my good mood, do so before dinner rather than afterward."

"Merci beaucoup, mon capitaine." The dry note in Yves's formal tone brought his irony within a breath of insubordination. "The *Diabolique* arrived two days ahead of us. Etienne brought Murdock's answer."

"The usual arrangements, I take it?"

Yves shook his head. *"Mais non, mon capitaine.* He demands that you return *L'Anglaise* at once."

"He 'demands'?" Alexandre laughed. "Does he think to frighten me into obedience? Or to provoke me into some act of defiance that will bring me within the reach of the British navy?"

"It is as I feared, *mon capitaine,*" Yves said. "The girl means nothing to him. The insult, the trespass, must be acknowledged and apologies made, or he will see to it we all hang before winter."

Alexandre scowled. He took a savage bite out of the apple and chewed it, thinking. "The day I beg forgiveness from any *Anglais* is the day I am condemned to the madhouse."

"Alexandre, the time has come. Send the little milkmaid home, and her sickly sister with her. You told me you intended to do so."

"Must we talk of that now?"

"Mais oui, Alexandre, we must. Have you lost your

mind? Bringing two *Anglaise* here, to the refuge it's taken us years to create?"

"What are you afraid of? Two little English girls can't do us any harm."

"The one has caused us considerable harm, in shot spent and lives lost."

"She did not cause that. I had reasons aplenty for sinking Vasquez and his wretched crew."

"But she was the reason that made it worth doing at last."

Alexandre nodded. He leaned his head back against the tree trunk and closed his eyes. Soon Rosalind would be in her bath. He pictured the lazy slide of soap suds along the heavenly curves of Rosalind's naked breasts, down her smooth belly. . . . He smiled.

"Peace, old friend. *La Belle Tempétueux* might know her way around a ship, but she knows nothing of navigation. She could no more bring the British navy to my door than she could fly to the moon."

"The question remains, what are we to do with her and the little one? The longer they are here, the more of a danger they become."

Alexandre blew out his breath in an impatient sigh. "*Eh bien,* Yves. You know best, tell me what to do."

"You should give both of them back to Murdock. His men will not abandon the little one to us, not with *La Belle* shrieking at them to bring her along."

"I cannot abandon her to that man."

Yves shook his head. "She has blinded you to all reason, hasn't she? Don't you understand, *mon ami?* You have left us few alternatives."

Alexandre shot Yves a hostile glance. "Do I hear you correctly? Do you imply that the time will come when we must kill two English girls to protect the secrets of *L'Ange Noir?*"

Suddenly the irritation faded from Yves's face, leaving him looking drawn and haggard. "You know I would never raise a weapon to a woman."

Yves looked away, at the couples scattered across the

grass, some laughing, some kissing. His loneliness was a cross he had chosen to bear, but the weight of it had to be brutal. When Yves turned his face back to Alexandre, the sorrow there looked bone deep.

"I am sorry for the tragedies that have beset you, *mon ami*. None knows better than I what those events cost you. Another calamity waits on our horizon." He stood up and brushed the dirt and grass from his breeches. "Never has it gone so far before, Alexandre. No matter what happens next, whether or not you choose to admit it, bringing Lady Hanshaw here means the end of *L'Ange Noir*."

"Yves! *Morbleu!* Am I to have no peace at all, from her or from you?"

"If it was peace you wanted, *mon capitaine,* you should have left her to Vasquez."

"Non!"

Alexandre sprang to his feet. That would have become his latest nightmare, Rosalind's voice crying out to him as her long golden hair vanished beneath the waves. That anguish woke the greater sorrow within him always waiting to flood his soul.

"I want *her!*" he cried. "England owes me, Yves. More than it can ever repay! This one I keep!"

"Here?"

"Here!"

"For how long?"

"For as long as I please!"

Yves bowed his head in mocking submission. "As you will, *mon capitaine*. You have forgotten one small detail."

"And what would that be?"

"La petite Anglaise. Is she to be yours as well?"

"Sister Beatrice? No, of course not."

"Then what are we to do with her?"

"She stays until she is fully recovered. Then we will take her to Jamaica and see to it she reaches her destination."

"So." Yves shook his head. *"L'Etoile du Matin* and *Chez Jardin* have both become a refuge for waifs and castaways."

Alexandre's fists clenched. He took a slow, deep breath, then let it hiss out between his teeth. "You are the best friend a man could ask for, *mon ami,* but I warn you, even you can go too far."

Yves bowed his head, but his scowl remained fixed. *"Très bien, mon capitaine.* It will be as you say."

Chapter Twenty-two

Rosalind's bedroom was as grand as any in London. The four posts of the bedframe were carved from mahogany, scrolled about either end with the shapes of fruit, apples, grapes, pomegranates. The bed linens were finely made, the sheets cream colored beneath a blanket of rosy wool. An armoire stood ready to hold her clothing beside a vanity table and its matching bench. The single bookcase held a variety of books, monographs, and pamphlets. In the sitting room through the eastern door there were wingback chairs and a settee, a chess set laid out on its black and white marble board ready for play. Vases of fresh flowers stood here and there about the two rooms, giving them a less stuffy and more welcoming feel. If it wasn't for the cloud Alexandre had cast across her mood, Rosalind would have been quite pleased with her new surroundings.

One of the maids coughed. "Mademoiselle, *le capitaine* has said we are to draw a bath for you. When shall you require this?"

"Now, please. I've been at sea for almost three weeks. I would be delighted to wash the salt from my skin."

The other maid, Adele, looked her over. "Mademoiselle does not care for the sea?"

Rosalind returned her appraising stare. "I care for it quite well in its proper place. That place is not my hair, my skin, nor my clothing."

The maid Sophie smothered a giggle behind her hand. Adele continued to regard Rosalind with that impertinent stare.

"*Très bien,* mademoiselle. It is well when all things are in their proper places."

"I am so glad you think so, Adele. Such understanding is most becoming to one of your station."

Adele's mouth tightened. Her eyes narrowed. She said nothing. Sophie prodded Adele with a discreet elbow and murmured something to her, then opened the armoire. Rosalind's gowns, petticoats, and other linen were neatly arranged on the wooden hangers and shelves. The scent of lavender wafted out of the armoire. Rosalind breathed it in and sighed, thinking of home.

"*Merci, mesdemoiselles.* If you would be good enough to lay out the peach gown, I shall wear that to dinner."

Sophie looked puzzled. "*Pardonnez-moi,* Mademoiselle. Would you not prefer something darker to suit the evening hour?"

"No, thank you. I shall wear the peach." Rosalind gave Adele a pointed smile. "It is *le capitaine's* favorite."

Rosalind took particular care with her bath. This was no mere cleansing of the flesh. This was preparation for battle. If Alexandre insisted on denying her permission to contact Thomas, she would resort to every means available to sway his opinion in her favor. The first and most obvious strategy was to woo him into that contented state where he was so enchanted with her he could deny her nothing.

With that in mind she donned her armor, the silk stockings, the garters trimmed in pale pink rosettes, the lacy petticoats, and the peach gown. The maids had worked wonders with it, removing the creases and restoring it to a much fresher condition. The tropical heat made her hair dry quickly. After a thorough wash with an herbal preparation heady with the scent of flowers, the golden waves gleamed. Sophie brushed out Rosalind's hair, clearly enjoying the task. Her nimble fingers arranged artful loops and curls, piling the golden mass atop Rosalind's head.

When every last curl was in place, Rosalind stood up from her seat before the vanity table, held out her arms, and turned a full circle before the maids.

"Am I grand enough for dinner at *Chez Jardin* with *L'Ange Noir?*"

"*Mais oui*, Mademoiselle!" Sophie answered, all but clapping her hands in delight. "*Le capitaine* will be delighted."

"*Merci*," Rosalind replied with a slight nod. She glanced at Adele. "And what do you think?"

Adele put her head to one side and considered Rosalind, one finger pressed to her lips. "I think, Mademoiselle, that you are not like the others."

Others? Rosalind made her voice light, careless. "*Pourquoi?*"

Adele shrugged. "It is not my place to comment on the character of *le capitaine*'s guests."

Sophie was looking more and more distressed. She hissed something in French at Adele, giving her a sharp look.

"*S'il-vous plaît*, Mademoiselle, pay her no attention," Sophie begged. "It can be dull here, with no one new to talk to. Adele sometimes forgets herself."

Rosalind settled herself at the escritoire, a perfect match to the one in Alexandre's cabin. She located paper, pen, ink, and the blotter. These tasks kept her hands busy and hid their shaking.

"Come, Sophie." Adele began to herd Sophie toward the door. "*Le Capitaine* requires Mademoiselle to retire in perfect quiet."

Rosalind stood up. "One moment." She smiled at Sophie. "Where is *ma petite soeur*, the other *Anglaise?*"

"Since she was not with you, Mademoiselle," Sophie replied, "*Maman* must have taken her to the kitchens."

" 'Maman'?"

"Madame LeFevre," Sophie said. "She is so much like a mother to us all she prefers everyone to call her *Maman*. She says it makes things simpler."

Rosalind silently thanked heaven for that much good luck. She had done what she could for Beatrice, but what the girl really needed was a mother.

"Be good enough to call me to dinner at least a quarter of an hour before *le capitaine* himself is expected. I have found it does not do to keep him waiting."

Both maids dropped far more respectful curtsies and closed the door behind them. Rosalind took up the pen.

My dearest Thomas,

Believe me when I tell you I am alive and well. The Bird of Paradise *was taken by pirates. Beatrice Henderson and I have done all we could to remain together during this misadventure. Please get word to her family and the Lawrences of Kingston that she is also well, recovering from a fever but in good health and spirits.*

Do not try to find me. Just get to London as fast as you can. Bad news awaits you. Mother needs you now more than ever. Give her my love and tell her I'll be home as soon as I possibly can.

Your loving sister,
Rosalind

Rosalind considered the message. She wanted to lay her head down on the paper and weep until the ink ran. She held herself together, calling on the same newly discovered fortitude that got her through that first hideous night aboard *La Fortuna*. Even if her luck ran out, she was on dry ground, with some kind of civil authority only a few hours away. That authority might be French, but if this bizarre adventure had taught her nothing else, it had taught her to lie well.

Rosalind blotted the message and folded it neatly. She'd seal it after Alexandre had given his approval. He could hardly refuse to send such a vague and harmless note. It was not as if the British navy was waiting to intercept every piece of mail coming into Jamaica from Martinique. She sat at the escritoire, head bowed and brooding, watching the shadows shift along the windows until the swish of skirts behind her made her turn.

Sophie stood in the doorway. She bobbed a nervous curtsy. "Come, Mademoiselle. It is time."

Chapter Twenty-three

Sophie led Rosalind out into the covered verandah. Alexandre sat there in a wickerwork chair, smoking his pipe and looking troubled. When Sophie opened the door, he didn't so much as look up.

"Mon capitaine," Sophie said softly. "I have brought Mademoiselle."

"Merci."

Still Alexandre didn't move. Sophie backed out the door and closed it without a sound.

Rosalind stood regarding Alexandre's profile. His brows were drawn together, his full lips pulled down at the corners as he puffed on his pipe.

"Yves still thinks I should have left you to Vasquez." Alexandre stood up, smoke wreathing his head like a tarnished halo. "I don't know what you did to offend him, mademoiselle, but there's no making it right."

"Perhaps you should ask Monsieur Yves that very question, *mon capitaine*. I too would like to know why he hates me."

"He doesn't hate *you*, mademoiselle. That would be too great a compliment to you. He hates your presence here."

"Why? Does Monsieur Yves think I will do all I can to bring every British naval ship in the Caribbean to your door the instant I have the slightest opportunity?"

Alexandre stared at her through the thinning swirls of smoke. "*Exactement*, mademoiselle. He thinks you live for nothing but the joy of seeing me hang."

"He has every reason to think so."

"Does he?" Weariness blunted Alexandre's sharp tone. In the growing twilight he looked not so much angry as sad. "Do you still feel that way, *ma belle?*"

Rosalind sighed. She could hold out against his anger, his sarcasm, and his pride, but she was helpless in the face of this strange vulnerability.

"*Non*, Alexandre. I do not." She went to him and wrapped her arms around his waist, hiding her face against his chest. It suited her strategy, true, but it was also the simple truth.

Alexandre's arms closed around her. He rubbed his cheek against her hair. "Ah, *ma belle*. It is good to hear you say that."

Rosalind sensed something still distracting him. "What is it, Alexandre? What grieves you tonight?"

"Grief, *mais oui*, that is the word. I find a woman unlike any other I have ever met, and it is my misfortune to have her constantly at odds with the one man I know I can call my friend."

"If he is truly your friend, then he wants only what is best for you."

Alexandre nodded. His arms tightened around her. "He is certain you are not what is best for me."

Rosalind leaned back to look up into Alexandre's eyes. "You disagree?"

Alexandre brushed his lips across her forehead. "I do. I think I will never again see a woman so beautiful, so brave, so stubborn, or so passionate."

The splendor of his eyes captured Rosalind, drawing her deep into their tigerish depths, showing her something so fragile, so sweet, she scarcely dared to breathe.

"Rosalind," Alexandre whispered. *"Ma petite fleur, ma belle divine. . . ."*

A great clatter of footsteps and shouts came around the corner of the house. The master gunner and the bosun banged on the door.

"Mon Capitaine!"

"Vive la France!"

"Vive L'Ange Noir!"

Alexandre sighed. He took Rosalind's face in his hands and pressed a tender kiss to her lips. "We will continue this most intriguing conversation after dinner. Perhaps then you would be good enough to tell me what changed your mind."

"About what, *mon capitaine?*"

"About seeing me hang."

Before Rosalind could speak, Alexandre turned her around to face the door. It swung open, held by the grinning bosun.

"Bonsoir, mademoiselle."

"Bonsoir, le Maître d'Equipage. How are you feeling?"

"Quite fit, mademoiselle. Thank God!"

Outside a great crowd of pirates and servants milled and jostled and waited with good-natured impatience. Alexandre surveyed all this with a grin. He offered Rosalind his arm and set off at a brisk pace, pulling Rosalind along with him. They circled halfway around the house, followed by the shouting, whistling mob. Behind the house was a vast flattened area set with all manner of tables and chairs.

Alexandre led Rosalind toward their places at the center of one long table. Fine porcelain dishes and proper silverware adorned each place. Wineglasses, too fragile for shipboard use, sat beside each plate like delicate crystal flowers. Alexandre held her chair while Rosalind arranged her skirts about her. When she was settled comfortably, Alexandre took his own seat beside her. The officers fanned out to either side, taking their own seats. In a clear wave of diminishing seniority the various ranks and watches took their places at the tables, one after another down to the youngest ship's boy who perched on the lap of a serving woman most likely his mother. The chair to Rosalind's left sat empty. Who was to have this place of honor?

"Now, *ma belle*," Alexandre said. "You will taste all that is finest in the culinary arts of this region. Madame LeFevre is an expert at her craft."

"Cooking as well as curing, *mon capitaine?* Madame is a lady of many talents."

Alexandre grinned. "Madame LeFevre has some excellent skills when it comes to healing all sorts of wounds." He looked back toward the mansion, then nodded his head that way. "You will see for yourself. Your *petite amie* comes even now."

Escorted by Dr. Gingras, Beatrice approached the table. Dr. Gingras directed her to the seat just beside Rosalind. Beatrice's eyes were bright, her cheeks pink, her smile demure yet lively with genuine happiness.

"Beatrice!" Rosalind rose and hugged her. "You look much improved!"

"*Maman* is very kind," Beatrice said. "She gave me something to drink that made me feel so much better."

"There, you see?" Alexandre had also risen at Beatrice's approach. He laid an arm around Rosalind's shoulders and pressed a kiss to her temple. "And you thought I was carrying you off to some filthy cave lit by a bonfire and stinking of spilled rum."

A startled laugh burst from Rosalind. She clapped one hand over her mouth, blushing furiously.

Alexandre stared into her eyes. "I wonder, *ma belle*, if you are not perhaps the least bit disappointed to learn we are not the blackguards you thought us."

Rosalind smiled, stroking his cheek. "Do you know what I think, *mon capitaine?* I think you could never disappoint me."

A look of wonder came into Alexandre's dark eyes, the dawning of some new and happy emotion. Rosalind had caught only the briefest glimpses of it before now, in those unguarded moments when Alexandre let her see beneath the face of the Black Angel to the man he really was. Alexandre returned her caress, stroking her cheek and rubbing his thumb along her lower lip. Just as he drew breath to speak, something crashed down on the table before them.

Adele stood there. The platter she'd been carrying sat on the table. The prawns rich with butter and seasonings that had been so carefully arranged now lay in a jumbled heap. The moment Alexandre turned toward her, Adele put on a look of pretty confusion.

"Pardonnez-moi, mon capitaine. I stumbled."

Alexandre waved her away with a brief gesture of irritation. Adele hurried off, casting a poisonous glare at Rosalind over her shoulder.

"Clumsy cow," said the bosun Gaston from where he sat on Alexandre's left. "She might dress like a maid, but there's only one thing she's good for."

"Forget her, Gaston," Alexandre said. "I want no bad feelings tonight."

"Where is Monsieur Yves?" Rosalind asked.

"Keeping watch in the cove," Alexandre replied.

He served Rosalind himself, piling her plate with the prawns, some deep orange mush he called "sweet potatoes," a variety of vegetables, and a lovely filet of sole. The sole had a light, delicate flavor, set off by a sprinkling of lemon juice. Dr. Gingras saw to Beatrice's plate, choosing for her the milder dishes. As Rosalind savored a bite of shrimp, rich with spices, she was glad Beatrice had a guardian to safeguard her delicate stomach.

Despite being preoccupied with their food and boisterous conversations, many of the men and women present still cast curious glances at Rosalind.

Rosalind leaned over to whisper in Beatrice's ear. "Look

at how they stare at us! You'd think they'd never seen English people before!"

Beatrice shook her head. "Not us, Rosalind. You. They want to know all about you. I heard some of them talking while *Maman* kept me with her in the kitchen."

"Did you indeed? How did you know what were they saying?"

"*Maman* translated for me." Beatrice smiled. "The ones who hadn't seen you yet wanted to know what you looked like, how you were dressed, even how you carried yourself."

"And what were they told?"

Beatrice smiled. "They are amazed you are English, for one thing. It surprises none of them that you are so beautiful. The captain wouldn't bring home just any woman."

Rosalind's pleasure dimmed a little. "Ah, but I am. I'm just the one he fancies at the moment."

Beatrice bit her lip, shaking her head. "I don't think so, Rosalind. The way the maids were talking, it's nothing short of amazing that he brought any woman here, much less an Englishwoman."

Rosalind laid her fork down and dabbed at her lips with her napkin. That gave her a moment to steady her voice. "Why, Beatrice? What made you think that's what they meant?"

Beatrice nibbled at a bite of fried plantain. "*Maman* said the captain comes home so rarely everyone here can recall each visit on one hand. Never before has he brought a woman home with him."

"You're sure of this? Someone actually said as much?"

"Oh yes. *Maman* was delighted to see you with him. She said the captain broods too much. It's bad for a man like him to go too long without a woman." As if suddenly realizing the meaning of Madame LeFevre's words, Beatrice blushed deeply. "I—I am sure she meant no harm, Rosalind."

Rosalind patted her hand. "Of course not, Beatrice. Madame LeFevre is very kind."

Yes, the mulatto cook was the soul of kindness, but it was plain Adele was not. *"Mon capitaine,"* Rosalind said. "Tell me, do you entertain guests very often? This is such a wonderful celebration your servants must have a great deal of practice."

Alexandre shook his head. "Not at all, *ma belle*. They are lucky to see us more than twice in the year. When we do come home, it is like a holiday for them all. More work, yes, but more happiness also."

"I'm sure." Some more than others, to judge from the wistful looks aimed at Alexandre by more than a few of the serving women. Some strange impulse prodded Rosalind to ask another question. "The maids you gave me are quite well practiced in attending to a lady's needs. Very considerate, to have such servants available for your female guests."

Alexandre turned a wary look on Rosalind. "What are you getting at, *ma belle*? This much civil conversation from you begins to make me nervous."

As much as she hated the thought of the answer she might receive, Rosalind kept smiling and spoke lightly. "This is the ideal setting for keeping a mistress, is it not? Or a harem, for that matter. I've heard very odd tales of what the sultans and caliphs in the East consider a proper marital state."

Alexandre cocked one eyebrow at her. "You continue to astonish me, mademoiselle, with this strange worldly attitude. You say such things as if they make no difference to you at all."

Rosalind shrugged. "Only because I am not the kept woman, nor am I the slave in the harem. I am an Englishwoman, proud to be one of His Majesty's subjects."

"Dangerous words under a French roof, *ma belle*."

"But we are not under a French roof. We have the sky and the stars and the bowl of the heavens above us."

Alexandre stared at her for a long moment. "Now I know you have something on your mind." He set his wineglass aside and turned his chair toward her. "Out with it, *ma belle*. Tell me what distress forces you to play your part so lightly."

Rosalind barely concealed her surprise. How had he known? How had he known that beneath her blithe exterior, she longed to be certain of what she hoped was true?

"Very well, *mon capitaine*. This is quite a lovely setting for an amorous dalliance. I'm sure a number of fortunate ladies have enjoyed their stays here."

Alexandre continued to stare at her with a look of blank incomprehension. Then understanding dawned. For a moment he looked relieved, even amused. A frown clouded his brow.

"Someone has been cruel to you, *oui*? Someone has been telling you all about *le capitaine*'s conquests? How I never go to bed with less than three women, that I'm such a savage I ruin a woman for all other men, all of that nonsense?"

Rosalind's cheeks stung with the force of her blush. "*Non! Non, mon capitaine*. Nothing like that!"

Alexandre nodded. "*Mais oui*, something like that." His jaw tightened with his growing anger. Alexandre sprang up, searching every face before him.

"*Ecoutez-moi!*" he snapped. "*Immédiatement!*"

Voices died away all over the garden. Alexandre leveled an accusatory finger at Adele.

"You. Come here."

Adele's hostile expression gave way to sudden fright. She stumbled forward to drop an awkward curtsy in front of Alexander.

"*Oui, mon capitaine?*"

"What have you been saying to Mademoiselle?"

"N-nothing, *mon capitaine!*"

Alexandre walked around the table and stood towering over Adele, glaring down into her eyes. "Tell me the truth, Adele. Tell me *now*."

"She is *Anglaise, mon capitaine!*" Adele cried. "The English tell their women what a monster you are! You have told us so yourself!"

"Clever Adele." Alexandre shook his head. "Always a little too clever." He paced a circle around Adele, his glare taking in the entire assembly. "Mademoiselle is my guest! She is here at my special invitation! She is not a whore." He shot Adele a look of icy contempt. "Neither is she a stupid, empty-headed, spiteful little slut from the worst of Paris's gutters!" Once again he raked the entire assembly with his glare. "Do you hear me? Am I understood?"

"Oui, mon capitaine!" The reply came from all sides.

"It disgusts me to see I have to make that clear to all of you. So you will remember this, and show Mademoiselle nothing but the greatest courtesy, Adele here will pay for her spite with ten lashes!"

Adele screamed, falling to her knees before Alexandre, pleading with him through her tears in broken French. For every gasp of horror in the crowd, Rosalind saw the small smiles and slight nods of satisfaction. Adele had few friends here.

"Gaston!" Alexandre said.

The bosun stood up. *"Oui, mon capitaine?"*

"Rig me a grating. This is an excellent opportunity to show the land crew what it is to be flogged."

"Oui, mon capitaine." Gaston drained his wineglass and started off, waving his mates to him.

Adele cowered at Alexandre's feet, her arms wrapped around herself, shaking with the fear that made more tears stream down her cheeks. Beatrice clasped Rosalind's hand in a frantic grip.

"The captain is going to whip her, isn't he?"

Rosalind was speechless with horror. She had to stop this. Alexandre's present temper made challenging his judgement sheer madness, but she couldn't just stand idly by and witness the agony about to be inflicted on Adele.

Alexandre turned to Rosalind. He reached across the table and took her wrist, pulling her up out of her chair. His face was a glowering mask, dark eyes narrowed, full lips pressed into a thin line.

"Does that satisfy you, mademoiselle? Shall I make it fifteen?" He raised his voice. "Perhaps *twenty*?"

Adele cried out in anguish.

"*Mon capitaine.*" Rosalind spoke in a soothing tone. "I bow to your authority. I respect your need to maintain order among your crew. But please, have mercy. She did nothing more than try to get the best of what she no doubt considers one silly Englishwoman."

"You are my guest, *ma belle*, and I will not see you insulted."

The heat in his eyes, the ardor in his voice . . . For a moment Rosalind let herself believe they arose from feelings more refined than just the Black Angel's determination to rule his crew with an iron hand. He was defending her, protecting her, impressing upon everyone present the high regard in which he held her.

"*Merci, mon capitaine,* but don't you see? Adele has done nothing but follow your example. As you loathe the English, so does she. So do all your people."

For a moment Alexandre looked affronted. He let out a long sigh. "Perhaps you are correct. But the order is given. The punishment will be carried out."

"You are *le captaine*," Rosalind said. "Delay the order. Blame me if you must. Say the poor delicate Englishwoman can't stand to see a proper flogging. It would make me ill." She looked Alexandre in the eye. "That is nothing but the simple truth."

Alexandre scowled. Rosalind withdrew her hand and stepped back beside Beatrice. She stroked Beatrice's hair, giving Alexandre a look whose meaning he could not miss. If he carried out this barbaric act right in front of a child like Beatrice, then he had no right to call himself a gentleman.

Gaston and his men returned, carrying between them a grating made of wooden planks hastily nailed together. They propped it up against a large palm tree in the middle of the garden. Alexandre looked it over, nodding.

"*Très bien.*" With one last glance at Rosalind, he caught

Adele by the arm, hauled her up onto her feet, and sent her stumbling toward Gaston. "Now make her fast to the grating."

Gaston barked out the orders. Two of his men seized Adele by the arms and dragged her to the grating, where they lashed her wrists to the boards high over her head. Gaston himself brought Alexandre the red velvet bag that held the dreaded cat-o'-nine-tails. Alexandre pulled out the coiled whip. With a snap of his wrist he shook the cat out to its full length, then paused for a long moment, prolonging Adele's terror and suspense.

"By the gracious wish of *L'Anglaise*," he said, "I am reducing the sentence. Mademoiselle cannot bear to see a proper flogging, one suited to the offense committed here. Therefore Jacques will lay on just one lash, to satisfy honor."

One of the bosun's mates stepped forward. Alexandre handed him the whip. Adele whimpered, huddling tight against the grating. Jacques drew back him arm and wielded the cat-o'-nine-tails with remarkable skill, rending only the cloth of the girl's blouse. Adele screamed. The mere sight of the torn blouse, the thought of the damage the whip could have inflicted, made Rosalind's stomach churn. She pressed her napkin to her lips.

"Take her away," Alexandre said. "And remember! All of you! *L'Ange Noir* is *L'Ange Noir*, by land or by sea!"

"*Oui, mon capitaine!*"

Chapter Twenty-four

"And now, no more long faces! This is a celebration!"

Alexandre clapped his hands together twice. The ship's musicians scurried into position a few yards in front of the head table. Their instruments included a fiddle, a concertina, a flute, and a curious set of drums Henri had found in the Kingston marketplace. They waited for Alexandre to return to his seat and give them the nod to begin. After a few moments tuning up, the quartet began to play. Their music worked its slightly flat charm on the assembled pirates and servants, lightening the mood. Couples sprang up to circle around the musicians in some mad processional dance. Alexandre let himself relax a little more. His crew had earned their liberty. He was glad to see them enjoying themselves.

Alexandre drank, then glanced over at Rosalind. She still stood there, cuddling little Beatrice like her pet cat. It was time to put an end to Rosalind's role as nursemaid.

"Are you distressed, little one? Do you wish to retire?"

Beatrice nodded. "If you please, Captain. I don't feel at all well."

Alexandre looked to Gingras for his opinion.

"*Oui*," Gingras said. "That might be for the best."

Alexandre nodded. "See her to her room then."

Gingras rose and held Beatrice's chair for her while she got to her feet. As they moved off toward the house, Rosalind started after them. Alexandre sprang up to catch her elbow.

"*Non*, mademoiselle. I asked only *monsieur le docteur* to escort little Beatrice. Madame LeFevre will tend her, so you need have no fear for her on that account."

Alexandre smiled, but he regarded Rosalind with a look so direct and unyielding she took an involuntary step backward. She tried to maintain her dignity, making it look as if she merely meant to take her seat again.

"Of course, *mon capitaine*."

"Your beauty shames the very stars, *ma belle*." He sat beside her and took her hand, bringing it to his lips. "Never have I met your equal."

Her blue eyes wide, her full lips trembling, Rosalind regarded him with an expression caught somewhere between surprise and alarm.

"*Merci, mon capitaine*." She bit her lip and looked away.

Alexandre reached over to touch her chin and turn her face back to his. "What distresses you, *ma belle*? Have I given some offense?"

"No! That is, *mais non, mon capitaine*."

"Then why are you so agitated?"

He watched her gather her composure, working hard to contain whatever strong emotion moved her now.

"It's hardly believable, *mon capitaine*. You, the great *L'Ange Noir*, saying such extravagant things to one ordinary English schoolteacher." She looked down at her hands. "You could have the most beautiful women in the world."

"I have that woman here beside me now." Alexandre touched her chin again to lift her face to his. He leaned forward and pressed a gentle kiss to her lips. She tasted so sweet, from the wine, from the juice of the fruit she'd eaten, from her own special sweetness. "As there is only one *L'Ange Noir,* so there can be only one of you, *ma belle divine.*"

Rosalind drew back just enough to speak. *"Merci beaucoup, mon capitaine."* Her breath teased his lips, rousing his desire.

"For what, *ma belle?* For nothing more than the plain truth?" Alexandre smiled. It promised to be a long and glorious night. If he could just remember how to bring that particular look of wonder to her eyes once they retired for the evening. . . .

Rosalind dipped one hand into the neckline of her gown and brought out a folded piece of paper. She held it out to Alexandre. He took it, wondering at her sudden silence. The paper held a trace of her scent, a heady perfume like a faint breath of jasmine. Alexandre unfolded the paper. As he began to read, his brows drew together in a frown.

"What is this? Are you so sure of your power to charm you've all but sealed this and called for the messenger?"

Rosalind sighed. The light seemed to go out of her. She sat back in her chair, shoulders slumped. *"Mon capitaine,* I offer it to you so that you might read it and give it your approval. If you will permit, it can be sent to my brother in the morning. All I ask is this one small favor, this single opportunity to reassure my family I have not been murdered, marooned, or sold into slavery."

Alexandre studied her. Rosalind had fought so hard to maintain her facade of strength, of resolution, no matter what had happened to her. She kept up that facade not just for her own sake but for that of little Beatrice. Now, just when any other woman would have done her best to seduce and persuade him, Rosalind unknowingly allowed just enough of her fear and sorrow to be seen. Alexandre could have refused any amount of coquetry. Anger and spite would not have moved him. But this weariness, this determination to keep trying no matter how desperate the situation became, those Alexandre found impressive.

He read over the message. True to her word, Rosalind had not written anything that might be taken as a hint, a clue, a suggestion of her whereabouts. Instead, she made passing mention of Beatrice, then, instead of pleading for her own rescue, she urged her brother back to London to protect their mother from Murdock's latest schemes. It was Rosalind's love and care for her family, for people who could not possibly know yet what had happened to her, that impressed Alexandre most of all. Rosalind planned for the care and comfort of those who would survive her, giving no thought to the blame they deserved for allowing her to fall into the hands of pirates.

"Remy!" he called.

From wherever he had been amusing himself, Remy appeared. *"Oui, mon capitaine?"*

"Take this message to the ship. Tell Yves I want it sent to Kingston at once. The messenger will see it put into the hand of the man to whom it is addressed. *Comprenez-vous?"*

"Oui, mon capitaine."

Alexandre folded the message again, took up a nearby candle, dripped wax onto the message, then stamped it with the bottom of the candlestick. The result was a smooth, flat oval, utterly blank. Perfectly anonymous. Alexandre grinned to himself, then handed the message over. Remy took it and turned to rush off into the night.

"Remy!" Alexandre called again. "The messenger will wait for a reply!"

Saluting, Remy dashed into the darkness, back toward the cove where *L'Etoile du Matin* lay at anchor.

"That will take a day or two, perhaps as many back again," Alexandre said. "With any luck, we shall hear from your brother within the week."

He turned to find Rosalind staring up at him, her blue eyes wide with disbelief.

"A—a reply?" she asked. "You will allow Thomas to send me a reply?"

"But of course, *ma belle.* You must be assured that your

message arrived and was understood. Otherwise, why should I bother to send it at all?"

Rosalind stood up. She took a slow step forward, then put her arms around Alexandre's waist and rested her cheek against his shoulder. When she spoke, her voice was a choked whisper.

"Thank you, Alexandre. Thank you."

The depth of Rosalind's evident relief startled Alexandre. He offered up a small prayer of thanks that she had been sincere about revealing nothing in her message to her brother. That alone allowed Alexandre the freedom to grant this request. How strange, that his semblance of honor should depend so greatly on how well Rosalind fought to maintain hers. He wrapped his arms around her, rubbing his cheek against her hair.

"You have surely earned some consideration from me."

Her arms tightened around him for a brief, precious moment. "*Mon capitaine,* with your leave I should like to retire."

He wondered if she might perhaps be trying to drop a subtle hint, encouraging him to follow soon after. But that was not Rosalind's way.

"You can't go now, *ma belle.* The celebration has just begun!"

Rosalind arched one pale brow at him. "Do you mean to keep me here all night and display me like some trophy?"

"And why should I not?" Alexandre imitated her playful tone. "After all, never yet have I seen such splendid gold." He stroked her hair. "Nor jewels as dazzling." He kissed her eyelids. "Nor silk, satin, or velvet to match the color and texture of your skin." He ran one fingertip along the curve of her lower lip. "No wine can leave me as intoxicated as one kiss from these lips." He smiled down at her, feeling the welcome heat of desire singing through every vein. "You are a treasure, Rosalind. A treasure beyond price."

"As you wish, *mon capitaine.* If you will not let me go, then will you at least come with me, somewhere away from here?"

She did want to be alone with him! Alexandre looked around them. The twilight deepened, prompting the crew to light torches around the perimeter of the garden. They also lit their pipes, adding to the smoke from the torches. The dancing continued, the garden filling with laughing, sweating bodies. It was an excellent time to slip away.

"You do not care for the festivities, *ma belle?*"

"*Pardonnez-moi, mon capitaine,* if I find it difficult to celebrate my own abduction."

Alexandre grinned. Rosalind's arch tone didn't fool him for a moment. He leaned over to murmur in her ear. "Can you tell me you are still as unhappy to be with me as you were that first afternoon?"

Rosalind looked at him, blushed. "*Non, mon capitaine.* I am not unhappy to be with you now."

She spoke softly, with that simple sincerity that touched his heart. A feeling swelled within Alexandre, a need so strong it drove him up onto his feet. He pulled Rosalind up out of her chair and gathered her against him. He stood there, holding her, breathing in the sweet perfumes of the tropical night. The nightmares were far from him now. Rosalind's radiant beauty held them at bay.

"Perhaps, *ma belle,* you might enjoy a walk along the cliffs? The view should be most appealing tonight."

"The cliffs, *mon capitaine*? That sounds rather dangerous."

Alexandre laughed. "Here at *Chez Jardin* there is only one danger. *C'est moi.*"

Rosalind looked at him with a trace of wariness in her eyes. "You are still a danger to me, *mon capitaine*. But of what sort?"

Alexandre smiled down at her, smoothing her golden hair back from her forehead. "Perhaps I will steal your heart, *ma belle*. Then you must remain with me until I give it back to you."

Rosalind looked up at him. For a moment he thought he

saw a flash of hope in the azure depths of her eyes. Then her customary primness returned.

"*L'Ange Noir* is not known for making restitution," Rosalind said. "Should you succeed in stealing my heart, you would never return it to me."

Alexandre nodded, grinning. "*Exactement, ma belle.* And so you have your answer."

Chapter Twenty-five

Rosalind allowed Alexandre to draw her hand into the curve of his arm. They set off along a trail that took them out of the cultivated tidiness of the garden and into the wilder terrain of the jungle itself. They walked along together in silence, listening to the songs of the night birds and the slight rustlings of small creatures moving through the undergrowth. At last Alexandre spoke.

"Rosalind, I have a question for you. I ask it in all seriousness, therefore I hope you will reply in the same spirit."

Rosalind glanced up at him. Indeed he did look serious, and yet the stern, forbidding mask of *L'Ange Noir* was not in place.

"You have told me of this life that awaits you back in London. If you will forgive me a candid observation, I think the worst thing you could do is return there and submit to marrying this man."

Rosalind stiffened. *"Mon capitaine—"*

"Hush now, until you've heard the question." Alexandre guided her around some tangled tree roots. "I understand your need to marry well and secure your family's future. You cannot imagine how well I sympathize with that concern."

He was silent again, apparently gathering his thoughts. Rosalind felt a strange sense of unease creeping over her. It was not like Alexandre to show any sign of uncertainty or indecision.

Alexandre looked up at the night sky. The trees were thinner here, allowing the moonlight to bathe his face. Once again it showed Alexandre to her at his finest, more beautiful than any pagan god wandering in his own private domain.

"I too must think about the future," he said. "I am not a young man aboard his first ship. It's said of me that I get my luck from the Devil himself." He shrugged. "That may be so. If it is, then I can expect that luck to run out at a most inconvenient moment."

Rosalind's sense of unease deepened, bordering on genuine fear. What was Alexandre leading up to?

Alexandre reached back to pull the ribbon from his hair, making the long black waves spill down around his shoulders. He raked an impatient hand through them once, twice, then once more.

"I was not made for pretty speeches," he said. "I can only speak the plain truth. I want you, Rosalind. I want *you*. Never have I met a woman like you. You are a delight in so many ways, and I cannot imagine a better mother for my sons."

Rosalind stared up at him. Her heart seemed to stop for a moment, then went on pounding all the harder.

"You flatter me, *mon capitaine*," she stammered. "Knowing how vast your experience must be, I take this as the greatest of compliments."

"You are more than welcome, *ma belle*." Alexandre laid his hands on her shoulders. "Now tell me, will you stay here with me? Will you be mine and mine alone?"

Rosalind put her hands to her cheeks, tempted to pinch

herself. Surely this had to be a dream. Was this notorious
French pirate, this beautiful entrancing man, actually pro-
posing marriage to her? Moonlight illumined those stormy
eyes, throwing all of Alexandre's darkness into contrast.
Rosalind longed to fling her arms around him and cry out
her acceptance. Yet it was impossible. No matter how much
she yearned for such deliverance, this was not the moment
to obey the promptings of her wild streak. She had to think
calmly and clearly.

"*Mon capitaine,*" she said gently, hoping the formality
would establish a little necessary distance. "You know my
situation. My widowed mother awaits my return. My
brother will need the benefit of my husband's business connections to reestablish our family's fortunes. I am not allowed to do as I would like."

"Then you would like it? You would accept, if not for
these obligations you feel?"

"I do not merely 'feel' them, *mon capitaine.* They are
facts. You understand what duty is. I must and shall do
mine."

Alexandre drew her onward, across the little clearing to a
sheltered spot near the edge of the cliff. The ground was
covered with palm fronds, leaves, and smaller vines, making
a comfortable cushion for sitting. Alexandre seated himself
cross-legged and held out his hands to Rosalind. She put
her hand in his and settled down beside him. He gazed at
her as if seeking to memorize every detail of her features.

"What can I say to convince you? What can I do? Tell me
and it will be done."

Rosalind leaned her head against his shoulder and sighed.
"Can you replace the *Dover Lady*? Can you bring my father
back to life? Only then would I be free to do as I pleased."

Alexandre laid his arm around her shoulders. "Would
you? Would you take me home to them in London and say,
'Here he is, Mama, Papa. This renegade, this pirate, this
Frenchman will be the father of my children.'"

Despite herself, Rosalind laughed. "Your being French

would not matter so much. I do think we would have to be very vague as to exactly how you came by your wealth."

Alexandre nodded. "That's easily done. I have a considerable amount set aside for investment. I suspect the bankers in London would be delighted to see it returned."

Rosalind smiled. "No doubt."

Alexandre planted a kiss on her forehead. "I am serious, *ma belle*. I could help your family rebuild its fortunes."

For a moment the very heavens seemed to open, offering Rosalind another solution, one that did not include Mr. Murdock. To be with Alexandre, here in this lovely place, far from London and all its painful memories. . . . Rosalind forced herself to call to mind the memory of the *Bird of Paradise* under attack, of the sailor who fell sprawling across Beatrice's lap. Perhaps she was privy to Alexandre's gentler side, but to the world at large he was still *L'Ange Noir*, mortal enemy of every British sailor. An echo of her earlier outrage stirred, making her pull away from his embrace.

"Thank you, *mon capitaine*, but no thank you. While beggars can't be choosers, my family is not so desperate we would sink to accepting the loot *L'Ange Noir* stole from other English ships."

Rosalind started to rise. Before she could get to her feet, Alexandre pulled her down across his lap. He turned his face away. His teeth were clenched, making a muscle flex in his cheek. At last his breath eased out. He looked down at Rosalind, stroking her cheek, tracing the curve of her lower lip with his thumb.

"Think of it as my way of making amends."

Rosalind closed her eyes. He was serious. Wanting her was one thing, but to talk of putting part of his fortune into Hanshaw Shipping, aiding its recovery. . . . This couldn't be possible. It simply was not possible that Providence should hand her the answer to all her hopes and dreams in the person of the Black Angel.

"We should think of your family," she said. "How will they receive me, *Anglaise* that I am?"

"If you are the reason I come home, so I can present you to them, they will love you like their own daughter."

"How can you be so sure?"

"It would make them very happy to see me give up this life."

That look of pain, of old sorrow, crossed Alexandre's face again, lending his features such a tragic beauty Rosalind could only stare in wonder. He spoke from the depths of his heart, allowing her to glimpse the pain inside him.

"But what of Monsieur Yves?" Rosalind spoke lightly. "He doesn't like me."

"True." Alexandre laughed. "He doesn't like me either, half the time. Poor Yves. He loved a woman once, but she broke their engagement and his heart. No other woman will ever win his love, so they all call out his scorn."

"You know him very well."

"He is more than a friend. He is my brother, the only one I have ever had."

"Then you were the only child?"

Alexandre shook his head. "I have sisters. A multitude of sisters. I am the only son."

Without thinking, Rosalind sat up and pulled his head down to her shoulder. "Poor Alexandre. Here we are, two castaways, lost to the lives we were meant to live in ordinary society."

Alexandre's arms slipped around her. He buried his face against her neck. Rosalind stroked his hair, trailing her fingers down through the silky black tresses. If only she truly were nothing more than a spinster schoolteacher. Then they could do as they pleased.

Alexandre turned his head just enough to whisper in her ear. "You haven't answered me, *ma belle*. Twice now I have saved you from death. Shall I save you a third time, from this living death you call your future?"

Rosalind flinched. A living death. The accuracy of that bleak phrase left her shaken. Alexandre sat back, keeping his arms around her waist.

"Do I frighten you, Rosalind?"

"*Mais oui*. What frightens me even more is the thought of the day you don't come back. One precise cannonball, one violent storm, or one attractive woman. Any of these things could take you away, at any time." Rosalind gathered her courage, then spoke from the depths of her own private pain. "You call me brave. I am a coward. It is easier for me to face an empty future, than one so full of—of—"

"Of what?"

"You."

Alexandre closed his eyes. He rested his cheek against the top of her head. He drew a long, slow breath, then released it. When he leaned back to look down at her, Rosalind saw a new heat glimmering in his eyes, a new intensity so much greater than any previous feeling he'd shown her. She wasn't sure what it meant, but she did know what it would lead to.

"Please, *mon capitaine*. We should go back. I have said far too much. I cannot imagine what you must think of me."

Alexandre allowed her to rise to her knees. Before she could stand, he pulled her up against his chest. His free hand slid up under her hair, caressing the nape of her neck.

"I think, *ma belle*," he breathed against her lips, "that what you truly fear is admitting to yourself how wild you really are. You long to escape this life you dread. Why else would you run off to the Caribbean?"

"*Non!* I came here to see my brother!"

Alexandre brushed his lips along her cheek, whispering into her ear. "And so you can, *ma belle*. My lady will want for nothing. Your brother will be happy to see you settled."

His "lady." Not the same as his "wife." He had not said the traditional words, asking her to marry him. Then why even speak of taking her home to meet his family? Perhaps that was the way one did things, even in pirate circles. Neither had he once used the word "love" to describe his feelings for her. He wanted a mistress, a trophy, a toy. The enormity of her own folly crushed her, leaving Rosalind both heartsick and furious.

"How dare you!" She planted her hands against Alexandre's shoulders and shoved back against his iron grip. "How dare you presume to think you know who I am and what I really want!"

Alexandre held her easily, despite the fury animating her. "I know only what you've told me, Rosalind. You are a spinster schoolteacher. Or so you claim. Perhaps there is more? Please, do enlighten me."

Fear stabbed through Rosalind, adding to her temper. She spoke through clenched teeth. "The family of any decent Englishwoman would be most displeased to know she'd become nothing more than the latest doxy of a notorious French pirate!"

Alexandre smiled, thin and cold. "Tell me, my dear mademoiselle, what is the name for a woman sold into marriage to pay her family's debts?"

Rosalind's mouth fell open. Anger surged ahead of fear. The back of her hand cracked against Alexandre's cheek. All humor vanished from his expression. His brows drew together as he scowled.

"I warned you, mademoiselle."

Rosalind lifted her chin. Her voice shook only a little. "Do your worst. I have expected nothing better from the first moment I saw you leering at me from your ship."

Alexandre stared down at her, that new heat blazing in his eyes. "Such courage, such defiance, when any other woman would be pleading with me or sobbing in hysterics." He nodded. "*C'est merveilleux.* I accept your challenge."

Expecting violence, Rosalind tensed in his arms, hands up to ward him off. Alexandre chuckled, shaking his head.

"But on my own terms. You call for my worst? Oh no, *ma belle.* Such an admirable adversary deserves nothing less than my absolute best."

He captured her mouth with a fiery kiss, his tongue plunging between her lips again and again, seeking out the hidden depths of her velvety softness. Rosalind stiffened, tried to turn her head away. His hand on her neck held her still, forcing her to submit to his passion. Just when Rosalind feared she might faint, Alexandre tore his mouth from hers and bent his head to her throat. The sting of his bite added to the frenzy of sensations sweeping through Rosalind.

"You want me," he growled. "Tell me, my pretty little milkmaid. Tell me how much you want me inside you."

Rosalind shook her head. "No!"

"Oh yes." Alexandre held her pinned against him with the strength of one arm around her. His free hand was busy at his belt. "You think I offer you nothing more than a place in my bed for a few weeks, perhaps months? Do you really believe I would treat you, *ma belle divine,* like a common whore?"

There was passion in his voice, and anger, and something more. His previous tempers had been nothing to the mood that moved him now. She had insulted him, and he would make her pay.

"Perhaps I should show you how I'd treat a whore, so you may at last realize the difference."

Alexandre fell backward, pulling Rosalind down on top of him. Reflex made her fight to sit up. With a loud gasp, she realized she straddled his hips, which had somehow been freed of the barrier of his breeches. His desire for her, as hot and rampant as his voice, pressed her there, at her center, where her traitorous blood throbbed.

Alexandre's hands slid up her calves, lifting her skirts, pulling them out from beneath her legs and leaving her naked thighs in direct contact with his hips.

"I expect a woman I pay for to do exactly as she's told. I expect to hear nothing from her but the sounds that tell me she enjoys what we do together. And then I expect her to leave when that time arrives."

Shame stung Rosalind's cheeks. She clapped her hands over her ears. Alexandre caught her wrists and jerked her down across his chest. He stared straight into her eyes. The heat there made them burn like dark stars, seething with furious light.

"Most of all, I expect to feel nothing for her, because it is not my heart but another part of me she must satisfy."

Rosalind hid her face against his chest as the sobs began to shake her. This, then, was the Black Angel. This was the man she'd heard so much about. This was the legend, the terror, and the truth.

Alexandre released her wrists and slid the fingers of both hands up under her hair, lifting her face up so he could stare again into her eyes. Weak tears trickled down Rosalind's cheeks. She met his gaze squarely, fully prepared to endure the rape she knew she was about to suffer.

Alexandre contemplated her in cold silence. At last he spoke. "When have I ever treated you with so little thought? So little consideration?"

"When you attacked the *Bird of Paradise*."

"Not true. I had no idea you were aboard."

"When you mocked both me and Beatrice before your entire crew. You forced me to give myself to you so Beatrice would be spared."

"Again, not true. It was you who set your own terms, mademoiselle. I merely accepted them."

"You knew what I expected from you. I had no way of knowing you were the most gallant cutthroat in the history of piracy!"

Alexandre laughed, letting his head fall back against the carpet of leaves and vines. "I must concede that point, *ma belle*. You went to your doom with all possible dignity." He grinned. "And to think all I wanted to do right then was eat my dinner in peace."

Rosalind seethed. "You are not what I was led to expect."

"And you are not what I had learned to expect from English ladies beset by pirates." He stroked her cheek. "How could I know the heart within that tempting bosom beat more fiercely than any Englishman who'd crossed my path?

How could I know I would find in the fragile vessel known as woman a sense of honor, of duty, that eclipses many stalwart men?"

"More mockery."

"*Mais non,* Rosalind. Only the truth." Alexandre searched her face as a look of distress crossed his. "I never thought to find a woman with such qualities. I most certainly did not think to find her among the very people I have learned to hate."

Rosalind rested her cheek against his shoulder. Something strange was creeping into her weary heart. Something she hadn't felt in ages. Happiness. Relief. Perhaps even hope.

"And I never dreamed of meeting *L'Ange Noir* himself, only to discover the monstrous bloodthirsty pirate is a gentleman after all."

Alexandre's hands combed through her hair, loosening the careful arrangement until the heavy golden mass spilled freely through his fingers. Rosalind lay still, listening to the strong, steady beat of his heart.

"Do you believe in fate, *ma belle?*"

"*Non.* But I do believe in luck."

Alexandre nodded. "Here now, sit up."

Rosalind pushed herself back up to a sitting position. She was about to swing one leg over and stretch out at Alexandre's side. His hands on her waist stopped her.

"*Ma belle,* would you leave me in such distress?" He flexed his hips, pressing the length of his hard shaft against her.

Rosalind sucked in her breath, caught between the sudden pleasure and the acute awareness of being out in the middle of the jungle.

"This is not the time or place!"

"No one knows where we are, and by this time the crew will be too drunk to care." Alexandre slid his hands up over her breasts, caressing them. "Where is that wild streak, *ma belle?* You cannot tell me you do not want this."

Rosalind pushed her hair back over her shoulders. "I have already told you once, *mon capitaine,* I am not some animal to rut whenever and wherever it suits you."

She drew breath to continue, only to have it gust out of her as Alexandre moved his hips under her, rocking her in a rhythm that could only be called seductive.

"Rosalind," he chided softly. "Are you not curious to know how it will feel this way? See, even now I play the gentleman. With you astride me, you will not damage your gown."

He slipped one hand under her skirts again, stroking the sensitive skin of her inner thigh, moving up until his fingers brushed the golden curls there. Rosalind bit her lips against a groan. She rose up onto her knees, trying to gain some respite from this delicious torture. Her mouth opened. Out of her arose a groan so profound Alexandre growled in response. Balanced on the brink of her soft, wet, aching depths, Alexandre took hold of her hips and pushed her down. He sank into her, filling her, pushing on to greater depths than ever before.

"Oh, Rosalind," he groaned. "Ah. . . . *Oui, ma cher, ma fleur, mais oui. . . .*"

Rosalind's body took over, swaying and rocking against him in the patterns of an ancient dance. She looked down at Alexandre. He lay beneath her, trapped under her weight, at her mercy and more than willing to be so. It delighted her to see him rendered helpless by desire. She braced her hands on his shoulders and moved harder against him, taking him as deep as she could. Those dark eyes fluttered closed as Alexandre gave himself up to her. A sense of triumph flooded Rosalind, making her move against him slowly, langorously, savoring every moment.

Alexandre smiled, that lazy smile of pure pleasure. "You are a she-demon, *ma belle,* come to steal my soul. Very well. Take it! Just promise me you'll come back every night."

Rosalind laid down on him, belly to belly, breast to breast, and pressed her lips to his. Alexandre met her, devouring her mouth with an urgent kiss. His arms came around her, holding her tight, giving him the leverage he needed to take over their lovemaking. Rosalind moved with him, her very soul afire, streaking like a comet toward the moment of supreme fulfillment.

Alexandre groaned aloud, his back arching and hips heaving as he plunged into her again and again. "Tell me, *ma belle*. Tell me! Tell me how much . . ."

"Alexandre," Rosalind gasped. *"S'il-vous plaît, mon chevalier du mer. . . ."*

"Ma belle Anglaise, ma belle tempétueux—"

Alexandre moved with such strength, such abandon. With another lithe twist, he rolled her onto her back. Chest heaving, long hair mussed, eyes ablaze, again he resembled a pagan god at the peak of his revels. He withdrew, remaining poised for his next thrust. Her hips worked against his, seeking more of that breathtaking bliss.

"Speak to me, Rosalind. Tell me how much you want me!"

Rosalind cried out, a wordless plea for satisfaction. Still Alexandre held back. She grasped the front of his shirt in both hands, lifting herself up toward him.

"Now, Alexandre! *Now,* or I shall die!"

Rosalind braced herself, expecting to feel the full force of his strength as Alexandre thrust into her. Instead, his slow, gliding motion made new waves of bliss wash over her. He moved slowly, gently, prolonging her pleasure, expanding it. She trembled beneath him, fearful that her body could not contain the ecstasy building within her. Alexandre's arms tightened around her. He buried his face in her neck, his hips moving in short, sharp thrusts. Rosalind abandoned herself to the pleasure bearing her upward on a golden spiral of delight.

"Rosalind. . . ." Her name hissed out between Alexandre's teeth, his voice tight with strain. "Now. Come with me! *Now!*"

As one they cried out, caught up in the same overpowering rapture.

"Rosalind!" Alexandre's passion broke the last of his control. Again and again and again he drove himself into her. *"Mon amour. . . . Mon amour unique. . . ."*

At last he subsided, his head resting against her shoulder. Rosalind looked up at the stars, tracing their patterns as her father had taught her long ago. Drowsiness claimed her, leaving her too tired to move. That was just as well. If she had any strength left, she'd waste it weeping.

"Mon amour unique," Alexandre had called her. My only love. If only that were true.

Chapter Twenty-six

Alexandre looked up at the fading stars. The eastern horizon showed a lighter band of color that heralded the coming sunrise. He gathered Rosalind's limp, exhausted form into his arms. How she had cried out to him, first begging and then demanding more, all that he could give her, all the strength he possessed. It was exactly what he needed from her, the only thing that could satisfy the desperate longing within him to hear Rosalind admit how much she wanted him. If only he could be sure such peace would be his every night, he would gladly give up the sea and all that went with it.

He carried Rosalind back to the house. Madame LeFevre herself waited up, sitting in the spotless kitchen by the light of a single beeswax candle. She opened the back door just as he reached the doorstep.

"Bonne nuit, mon seigneur?" she asked softly.

Alexandre grinned at her inquisitive tone. *"Mais oui, Maman."*

"And now?"

"To bed."

"Yours or hers, *mon seigneur?*"

Alexandre's first impulse was to carry Rosalind to his own bed, there to wait until she wakened and give her cause to sleep again. Recalling other mornings when she had awakened to the sure knowledge of her own abandon, Alexandre thought perhaps a little privacy and some time to herself would do much to restore Rosalind's composure.

"Her room, I think."

Madame LeFevre picked up her candle and guided Alexandre through the hallways to Rosalind's suite. Madame LeFevre went ahead to open the doors, then stood by in silence while Alexandre laid Rosalind on her bed.

"Shall I see to her?" Madame LeFevre asked in a murmur.

Alexandre shook his head. "Leave her to me. I shall put her into a nightgown and tuck her in, nothing more."

Once he had accomplished his task, he sat beside Rosalind, staring down at her. Madame LeFevre came to him and laid a hand on his shoulder.

"You are not entirely happy, *mon seigneur*. Why is that?"

Alexandre hung his head and sighed. "Yves doesn't like her."

"Why not?"

"He thinks she'll be the end of me. The end of all of us."

"One little English girl?"

"Non." Alexandre shook his head. "This is Lady Rosalind Hanshaw, affianced to Edward Murdock."

"Mon Dieu!" Madame LeFevre's hand flew to her mouth, quieting her own cry, then dropped to her bosom where she clutched the tiny cloth charm bag she wore around her neck. "He is the Devil's own brother."

Alexandre rose and took Madame LeFevre by the elbow, leading her into the sitting room. "I sent Murdock's agents in Kingston a message, offering to ransom her."

"What did they say?"

"I'd best return her at once or he'll have every British vessel from man-of-war to river barge out combing the sea lanes for me."

"Is this his love for his fiancée speaking?"

Alexandre shook his head. "It is his pride, his arrogance, his outrage over knowing his woman is in my hands."

Madame LeFevre studied him. "You mean to keep her, then?"

Alexandre paced the floor, raking his hair back and binding it with the length of black ribbon. "That is my hope, but it will only be realized if she chooses to stay with me. She has obligations she insists she must fulfill."

"Such as marrying that *cochon* Murdock?"

"*Oui.*"

"Why would any sane woman marry that man?"

"To restore her family's fortunes. He has money enough to do that, money I've made for him by ruining his business rivals."

Madame LeFevre suddenly fixed him with an uneasy look. "This English lady, what business is her family in?"

"Shipping. Hanshaw Shipping."

"And what ruined their business?"

"A run of very bad luck, which ended when the finest ship of their line was taken by pirates."

Madame LeFevre nodded. "And what was the name of that ship?"

Alexandre squeezed his eyes shut, searching his memory. The hour was late and Rosalind had taken all the wind out of his sails. A pleasant enough activity, but he was now too tired to think. He shook his head.

"I don't recall. Those English ships with their English names . . . I forget them as soon as I'm done with them."

"Was it the *Dover Lady*?"

That name . . . It called to mind that night out on deck with Rosalind, the night they shared their painful secrets. Had she not said something like that again, just a few hours ago? "That does sound familiar."

Madame LeFevre muttered to herself in the patois of the islanders. Her look of unease settled into dead certainty.

"You don't remember, do you, *mon seigneur?* Of course not. You take so many ships, what would one more be to you?"

"What are you saying, *Maman*?"

"You sank that ship, *mon seigneur*. You stripped it, cast the crew adrift in their boats, and sent it straight to the bottom. I remember, because you sent me three bolts of fine *Anglais* linen taken from that ship."

"Now why did I feel the need to be so thorough about that particular ship?"

"Because, *mon seigneur*, that was a ship Murdock wanted you to take."

As the memory came back into focus, Alexandre let out a strangled curse. Murdock had sent him word about a fine fat English merchant vessel bound for Kingston. A rich cargo, lots of investors, plenty of loot for all hands. The ship itself had to be destroyed. As for the crew, Murdock made no specific suggestions, which left Alexandre with the distinct impression that Murdock didn't care if those sailors lived or died. So *L'Etoile du Matin* and the *Diabolique* had set a course for the *Dover Lady*. It had been a glorious and profitable victory.

That victory now left the taste of ashes in Alexandre's mouth. *L'Ange Noir* had ruined Rosalind's family. He had taken the ship that caused the final strain and then her father's collapse. In robbing her of her father, *L'Ange Noir* had left Rosalind at the mercy of that loathsome snake, Edward Murdock. Alexandre staggered to one side. His hand closed on the back of a chair. He dropped into it, then put his head in his hands.

Madame LeFevre hurried out. When she returned, she tugged at his wrist. "Here, *mon seigneur*. Drink this."

Alexandre obeyed, accepting the glass of brandy she offered him. It did little to warm him, merely adding to the sickness that crawled through him, deepening with every moment.

"My fault. My fault!" He slammed one fist down on the arm of his chair. "She is here, at the mercy of pirates, all be cause of me. Because I chose to work off my exile making those *Anglais bâtards* pay."

"Mon seigneur." Madame LeFevre spoke quietly. "Why does this distress you so? She is just one more English subject. Just one more native of that island you despise."

"No!" Alexandre cried. "She is everything beautiful, and good, and kind, and full of courage. She is everything. . . ."

"Still, what is it to you that this English girl will be forced to marry this English man? Why does *L'Ange Noir* spare that a single thought?"

"How can I let Murdock have her? How could I possibly send that magnificent woman back to the very depths of Hell?"

"And yet, *mon seigneur,*" Madame LeFevre said. "You owe her nothing. She is merely one more English victim to suffer your revenge."

Alexandre leaped up out of his chair, chest heaving with the force of his breath. "Never! Never has she been my victim in any sense. I saved her from drowning, I saved her from Vasquez, and by *le bon Dieu* I will save her from Murdock!"

Madame LeFevre came to him and took his hand between hers. *"Mon cher capitaine,* do you know what you are saying? Do you understand why you feel compelled to make this right?"

Alexandre stared at her, confused. His mind was in a turmoil, so many thoughts, memories, emotions. "She—she is everything . . . to me."

"And what does that mean?"

Alexandre stood there, brooding. Comprehension dawned, bringing with it a joy that transfigured his very soul.

"I love her. I am in love with that infuriating little minx!"

He sprang up and strode toward the door. Madame LeFevre hurried after him to catch his arm.

"Oui, oui, mon seigneur, I know. You want to tell her right now. Let her sleep. There will be all the time in the world."

Alexandre took a deep, steadying breath, then nodded. He eased the door open and made his way silently to Rosalind's side. He knelt there, studying her face as if he'd never seen it before. She was his. By every law he still acknowledged, by every tradition he knew, Rosalind belonged to him. He admired her loyalty to her family. Once he'd won her over completely, that loyalty would encompass him. The mere idea of Rosalind devoted to him, fighting on his side, defending him like the tigress she was, filled his heart with a lightness he hadn't felt in years. She had brought him joy. How could he ever let her go?

"Mon amour," he whispered. *"Mon amour unique."*

Chapter Twenty-seven

Rosalind's mind was so full of thoughts and feelings, so overwhelmed by the sheer intensity of the situation, she dressed quickly and sought out the farthest corner of the garden. It took some time to walk all the way out there. With every step she hoped the distance she gained physically would translate into some kind of emotional and mental distance, allowing her to consider the entire situation dispassionately and bring all her conflicting emotions under control.

At last Rosalind found a stone bench in the shade of a cluster of palm trees. She sat down and steeled herself to the task at hand. She must work out the right strategy to persuade Alexandre to send Beatrice to Kingston at once. Then she must see to it she grew no more attached to Alexandre than she had already allowed herself to become. "Attached" was the strongest word she would permit herself to use. To go any further, to name the feeling that swelled within her every time she met the steady gaze of those eyes like dark jewels. . . . Such restraint would hurt, but in time that would pass. Better the lesser pain now, than the greater anguish of allowing herself any more foolish dreams.

Rosalind had awakened to discover herself in bed, clad in her nightgown, safe and sound beneath the roof of *Chez Jardin*. Her last memory of the preceding night involved Alexandre pointing out a particular cluster of stars to her and explaining their navigational significance. So. She had fallen asleep in his arms, and he had seen her safely back again, to the extent of putting her in her nightgown and tucking her into bed.

Out there in the jungle, beneath the moon and the stars, Alexandre had made love to her again and again, in ways that left her blushing at the memory. Alexandre had called her his only love. Rosalind smiled through the tears welling up in her eyes. Could she credit such words, spoken by a man in the heat of passion? Could she believe the Black Angel would allow himself to fall in love with one little English milkmaid? Impossible.

She was doomed to be the plaything of the London gossips no matter what happened, so she'd be wise to take what steps were available toward achieving some kind of respectability. The very fact that Mr. Murdock had made public their engagement meant she had even fewer options open to her. To protest the supposed engagement openly, to insist she never agreed to any such thing, was to pile scandal atop scandal. Having just returned from a sojourn among Caribbean pirates, Rosalind could ill afford any further damage to her own reputation. More important, the marriage would do much to restore her family's standing, without the awkward complication of explaining where the new wealth had originated. Duty to her family must come first. Her mother would need all the comforts Rosalind could provide to help her bear the coming years without Father's hearty presence.

The faint scent of pipe tobacco alerted Rosalind to Alexandre's presence only moments before he himself stepped out from the surrounding jungle. He wore plain dark brown trousers, black boots, and one of his full white shirts. His hair was bound back, and he looked quite mild and content.

"Are you well, mademoiselle?" he asked.

"*Oui, mon capitaine.* What made you think I wasn't?"

"I asked Madame LeFevre if she'd seen you. She told me you looked to be in some distress, having just made off for some far corner. And here I find you, looking as if you face execution."

Rosalind smiled bitterly. "You speak truer than you know, *mon capitaine.* There was a time when I had so many choices, and now I have precious few."

Alexander sat down beside her. "I am familiar with that feeling, *ma belle.* If you will hear a word of advice from a notorious blackguard, I can tell you something that will ease the pain."

"I would be most grateful."

Alexandre sighed. He puffed on his pipe for a moment, then looked Rosalind in the eye. "We are taught to do what society requires of us. We are told we must not dishonor our families, ourselves, our name. And yet we know those requirements are flouted whenever it suits the people who control society."

Rosalind nodded. She had to agree. It was nothing but the cold truth.

"There comes a time when society's regard must become less important than one's own regard for oneself. It may be considered the proper thing to do, in bowing to society's wishes, but is it the *right* thing to do?"

Rosalind smiled a more genuine smile. "Why, *mon capitaine*, I had no idea you were such a philosopher."

Alexandre shrugged. "My point is this. You can go on being a slave to society's idea of what's proper, or you can seize control of your life and do what you know is not merely proper but right. Right for you, right for your family, and right for anyone else who truly matters to you."

Rosalind knew full well what Alexandre wanted her to

do. And yet, instead of telling her outright, or demanding her capitulation, he offered her what he clearly considered an honorable choice.

"*Merci, mon capitaine.* You have given me much food for thought." Rosalind almost wished Alexandre would go away and leave her in peace. His presence alone was enough to rouse those feelings in her that were the most troublesome. She had too much to think about without Alexandre's clever ways of justifying whatever he wanted to do. Or, in this case, what he wanted her to do.

Alexandre blew out a thin, elegant stream of tobacco smoke, then knocked out his pipe against the edge of the bench. "The time has come to give you not merely food for your thoughts, *ma belle,* but a few words that I hope you will consider a feast for the spirit." He glanced around, then shook his head. "This is not the place. A kitchen garden does not suit you, *ma belle.* I shall lay the feast before you amid my own small portion of Paradise."

Alexandre stood up and held out his hand to her. He led her along pathways that brought them out on the southwestern side of the grounds. Before her blossomed roses so sweet, so vibrant, she could almost taste their colors. Their scents rose up through the warm afternoon air, perfuming the entire scene. At the center of the rose garden stood a bush with dark green leaves and white blossoms. The sweet scent of the blossoms dominated that of the roses, adding a stronger tropical presence to the floral bouquet.

"These are magnolias," Alexandre said. "Their petals are like velvet, creamy white, quite delicate. One touch will bruise the petal, leaving a brown stain that withers."

"How sad," Rosalind murmured.

"Not at all. This is the price of its beauty. Left alone, it will blossom in its full splendor, requiring only the right amount of attention to keep it healthy. Should the magnolia fall into the wrong hands, careless, thoughtless hands, the offender will lose both the beauty and the fragrance."

Rosalind smiled. "Is this your feast of words, *mon capitaine?*"

"Merely the *hors-d'oeuvre, ma belle.*" Alexandre bent to take one magnolia blossom by its stem and break it off. Careful to never touch the petals, he tucked the magnolia into Rosalind's hair, just above her temple. "You are much alike, *ma belle*. Stronger than you seem, and capable of repaying harsh treatment."

"Shall I thank you for that, *mon capitaine?* I'm not entirely sure you meant it as a compliment."

"I am sure, Rosalind. For the first time in four long, cold, lonely, agonizing years, I am absolutely certain of what my future must hold for me." Alexandre took both her hands in his. "*Ma Belle Tempétueux*. Never in my life have I ever imagined I'd have England to thank for the woman who is everything I want, and everything I need."

Rosalind's heart began to pound. She felt dizzy, lightheaded, intoxicated by the scent of the flowers and the heat that shimmered in Alexandre's dark eyes. She had to be dreaming.

"Rosalind?"

Alexandre's hands slid round her waist and held her pressed against his chest. He touched her chin to make her look up at him.

"*Ma belle*, what is it? Why do you look so faint?"

It took Rosalind a moment to find her voice. "Say it, Alexandre. Say these words you claim will be a feast for my spirit. Until I met you I didn't even know my spirit had been starving."

Alexandre's look of concern vanished into a brilliant smile. "You know, don't you? You know what I want to tell you."

Rosalind nodded. "You have already said it." The memory brought the blood rushing to her cheeks. "Perhaps you cannot recall doing so. It was a very . . . *intimate* moment."

Alexandre laughed. His arms tightened around Rosalind

and he kissed the top of her head. "I do remember, *ma belle*. I called you *mon amour. Mon amour unique.*"

Rosalind nodded against his chest. She bit her lip, willing her voice to remain steady. "Do—do you mean it, Alexandre?"

"I have never said anything I meant more." He held her at arm's length. "Hear me, *Anglaise. Je t'aime*. With all my black heart and fiendish soul. With every breath, every drop of blood in this French body, I adore you."

Rosalind clung to him, torn between the radiant joy of hearing Alexandre speak the words she'd longed to hear from him and the bitter sorrow of knowing how impossible it was for this to be. She closed her eyes and bowed her head against the weight of the unavoidable truth.

"Speak, Rosalind." A note of perplexity, of discomfort, crept into Alexandre's voice. "Will you give me no words in return?"

With grief deeper than any she'd yet known, Rosalind raised her head to look Alexandre in the eye. "*Merci beaucoup,* Alexandre. I cannot tell you how much those words mean to me. But I am compelled to tell you this. You don't know who I really am. You don't know me well enough to realize I cannot be yours."

Something changed behind Alexandre's eyes, not the thunderous darkness of temper that Rosalind feared, but something lighter, confident, almost amused.

"And neither, *ma belle*, do you know me, if you think I will allow anything to take you from me. You are the first woman I have ever loved, and you will be the only one. You say you cannot be mine, yet I am already yours, body and soul."

Scarcely daring to believe her ears, Rosalind took refuge in cold practicality. "Will you marry me, then? How can *L'Ange Noir* possibly take a wife?"

"That is a most serious question, *ma belle*, and I have already given it considerable thought. You may leave those details to me."

"Then you have a plan for this as well? Are you never without some strategy, *mon capitaine?*"

"Never. Although I will confess you are a most challenging adversary." He kissed the tip of her nose. "In the meantime, there must be some way I can prove to you my feelings are as true as could possibly be."

Rosalind seized the moment. "Send Beatrice to Kingston, to the very door of the Lawrence family's estate. See to it that family receives an explanation of her delay that leaves no possible stain on her character. Succeed in this, *mon capitaine*, and I will be forced to mend my somewhat tattered opinion of you."

Alexandre smiled, those full lips curving and his eyes sparkling with devilish amusement. "Ah, I see it all now. You wish to see Sister Beatrice on her way. Then you will be free to display that wild streak without scandalizing your *petite amie.*"

Rosalind blushed scarlet. "You rogue! How dare you! Carry on like this and all I will show you is the flat of my hand!"

Alexandre threw his head back and let out a shout of laughter. "I see through you, *ma belle!* You want me to tame you the way I did last night!"

Seeing that familiar flame of passion ignite within the depths of his eyes, Rosalind shook her head. *"Mais non, non capitaine!* I am perfectly serious!"

"Rosalind, *ma belle, mon amour,* the charade is over. You might have been a proper English schoolgirl once, but those days are gone. Now they will tell the most glorious stories about *L'Ange Noir* and his one and only love, *La Belle Tempétueux!*"

"You've gone mad!" Despite herself, Rosalind had to laugh. His good humor caught her up. "How can we possibly stay together?"

"As I said, *ma belle,* leave it to me. I have certain resources I have not yet displayed."

"Now that sounds ominous."

"Not at all. In fact, once the necessary messages have been sent, I believe there will be considerable rejoicing."

Rosalind wanted to believe him. She wanted it so desperately she clung to him, hiding her face against his broad chest. There had to be a way. There had to be. Surely Providence would not grant her such total happiness, only to snatch it away again.

"Then you will send Beatrice to Kingston?"

"Still setting terms, *ma belle?*" Alexandre shook his head, laughing. "Very well. I will do this, but not until the messenger returns with your brother's reply. I expect him in two days' time."

"Why must it wait until then?"

"I have only a handful of men I trust so completely I allow them to come and go between Martinique and Kingston. Were any of them captured, he would die before revealing the secret of my estate. All things must be timed with great care, to prevent any possible attempt to follow my men back here."

"I see."

"Do you, *ma belle?* Do you truly understand how much is at stake here, should any of my people betray me?"

Rosalind nodded. *"Oui, mon capitaine.* Innocent lives would be lost, families scattered, and good men killed for the wrong reasons."

Alexandre studied her, eyes narrowed. "That is the most sympathy I have had from you, Rosalind. What brought that about?"

Rosalind put her head to one side, considering him. "It must be a terrible strain on you, *mon capitaine*, pretending to be this fiendish cutthroat, when in fact you are a man of quality."

"Have I at long last succeeded in convincing you of that, *ma belle?*"

"Mais oui, mon capitaine. All that remains is for you to tell me who you really are."

Alexandre regarded her in silence. At last the corner of

his mouth quirked in a wry smile. "Consider that my engagement gift to you, when the time comes for exchanging such things."

"So you will tell me?"

Alexandre nodded. "When the time is right, *ma belle*, you will know all."

For one splendid, precious moment, Rosalind allowed herself to believe it might all really happen. She threw her arms around Alexandre's waist and held him tightly, wishing with all her heart she could tell him her true name, hear his, then be married at once before any other turn of events arose to destroy the perfection of this moment.

Alexandre's arms closed around her. "Do not be afraid, Rosalind. There was a time when you were right to fear me, but that time is past. Now I will stand between you and anything that might do you harm."

Chapter Twenty-eight

When Thomas's reply arrived, Alexandre himself delivered it to Rosalind where she sat out in the garden with Beatrice. Rosalind held the envelope in shaking hands. The sight of Thomas's lazy penmanship spelling out her name made her eyes mist over with tears. She tore open one end of the envelope and took out three sheets of high-quality writing paper, all covered with Thomas's hasty handwriting.

My dearest Rosalind,

Thank God you're alive! Word had reached us here in Kingston of the latest attack by that scoundrel the Black Angel. We were sure you were lost. And yet, miracle of miracles, I received your note! You are alive and well, although plainly still in the hands of the enemy. Tell the blackguard he can name his price as long as he returns you safe and sound.

You may think that an extravagant pledge in light of our family's recent financial difficulties. It will amaze you to know your doting fiancé arrived in Kingston just the day before I received your note. He'd taken one of

*his fastest sloops, determined to reach Jamaica ahead
of you. Having made the arrangements for your passage to Jamaica, he holds himself singularly responsible for your safety. Hence our willingness to meet the
Black Angel's demands. While this is not the best moment, allow me to congratulate you on your engagement. Had you not already been abducted by pirates,
that would have surely been the most surprising news I
could have received.*

*I beg you, send word immediately telling us how and
when and where we may pay the Devil his due and see
you safely housed in Jasmine Court. My greatest hope
is that we will regain you with no word reaching
Mother. She has endured too much strain of late to be
presented with the horrible spectacle of her only daughter being carried off by pirates.*

I am, as always

*Your loving brother,
Thomas*

*P.S. Mr. Jameson sends his best, and hopes you and
the little sister are in good health and spirits.*

Rosalind read and reread the letter, devouring every
word. Now even Thomas believed she had consented to
marry Mr. Murdock! The postscript was puzzling. Rosalind
knew of no Jameson among their London acquaintance.
Perhaps he was one of Thomas's local friends. She held the
letter out to Alexandre.

"Be my guest, *mon capitaine*. My brother is willing to
meet any and all demands."

"Rosalind." Instead of the letter, Alexandre took Rosalind's hand and led her into the shade of the apple tree. "I
have made the only demand I intend to make. I want your
love, and I offer mine in return. If there's a question of ransom, *ma belle*, you are the one to set the terms, for you have
stolen my heart as surely as I took you back from Vasquez."

Rosalind closed her eyes and rested her head against

Alexandre's shoulder, lulled by the steady beat of his heart and the gentle rhythm of his fingers stroking her hair.

"What am I to tell him?" she asked.

"For now, nothing. I also await replies. Once I have received the news I hope for, then all will be well." Alexandre touched her chin and made her look up at him. "I swear to you, Rosalind. The time is coming when there will be no secrets between us."

"Who have you written to? Can you at least tell me that much?"

Alexandre smiled. "I have sent word to my mother and father. You cannot know how happy they will be to learn that I have at long last found the woman I will call my wife."

Rosalind buried her face against his chest. The irony! When Mr. Murdock had the presumption to announce their engagement without her consent, Rosalind had been furious. Now, upon hearing that Alexandre had done more or less the same thing, she was filled with a radiant happiness.

"I take it you approve?" Alexandre asked, muted laughter in his voice.

Rosalind nodded against his chest, pressing her cheek tight against the solid warmth of his flesh. It couldn't be as easy as he made it sound. It couldn't possibly be that easy. Not when Mr. Murdock was so near, knowing as he did the fate of the *Bird of Paradise*.

"I hope *Chez Jardin* is as safe and protected as you claim, *mon capitaine*."

"What makes you say that?"

"Your family may be delighted to receive me, but I cannot imagine mine will be as enthusiastic about you."

Alexandre laughed aloud. "I am somewhat colorful for your stuffy English tastes. All the better. Our children will have your beauty and my panache."

"Children . . ." Rosalind's heart swelled with sudden tenderness. "You look forward to having children?"

"Of course, *ma belle*. At least three sons, with as many daughters as come along until all three are born."

Rosalind's heart brimmed and overflowed. She flung her arms around him. Her shoulders shook with sobs.

"*Ma belle,* what is this? Why do you cry so?"

Rosalind shook her head. "I don't know. Part of me is so happy, but the rest so sad. My father would have liked you, I think. How I wish he could see our sons."

"Here is something to brighten your eyes, *ma belle,*" Alexandre said. "Go and tell little Beatrice she will soon reach her destination."

Rosalind leaned back to look him in the eye. "You mean it? She can start packing?"

Alexandre nodded. "I mean it, *ma belle.* It's time the little one got on with her life as well."

"Oh, Alexandre." Rosalind kissed him soundly on the lips, then slid from his embrace before he could trap her into a longer dalliance. "Thank you! I will tell her at once."

Chapter Twenty-nine

An hour later Rosalind and Beatrice sat in Beatrice's room, another lovely and well-appointed suite. They were happily employed in sorting out which of Beatrice's garments had survived the journey in more or less respectable condition.

"I will forever be in your debt, Rosalind. I brought this on you. Had it not been for my weakness, my inability to swim, my . . ."

"Oh hush now!" Rosalind pulled Beatrice into a fond embrace. "I'll hear none of that. If it weren't for you, I might well have given up and drowned. You have been the source of my courage and ingenuity."

Beatrice smiled. "You say that to be kind. Thank you, Rosalind. You are a good and decent woman, and nothing can take that from you. Not weeks among pirates, not the gossip of unkind and small-minded people."

Rosalind smiled. "What shall I do without you?"

"Oh, Rosalind." Now Beatrice looked troubled. "The British naval authorities will demand to know everything about the Black Angel and this place. I'll have to tell them. It is my duty as a subject of the British Crown." She sighed, fretting at her collar. "And yet if I do so, I put your happiness at risk. I cannot see the lesser evil to choose it, can you?"

"No, I can't. Of course I would never ask you to go against your conscience. Perhaps I could ask you to delay as long as possible?"

"They can hardly interrogate me like some criminal when I've just escaped while suffering from a fever."

"That's the spirit!"

"But there is one final question I would put to you. And this one, I think, matters most of all."

Rosalind nodded, waiting attentively.

Beatrice took a deep breath. "Rosalind, this man wants to marry you. He has told you he's in love with you. That's wonderful for him, but do you feel the same? Do you love him in return?"

Rosalind thought of Alexandre, of his beauty, his fierce loyalties, his nightmares and his dreams. She thought of the rage in his voice as he fought his way toward her across the deck of *La Fortuna*. She thought of the way he liked to tease her, the heat of his kisses, and the passion that simmered in his eyes. He was intimidating and endearing and infuriating and breathtaking. Never could there be another man like him. She nodded, feeling true joy chase the fear out of her heart.

"Yes. I believe I do."

Beatrice smiled. "Good for you, Rosalind. Good for you!"

"You really think so? He is, after all, the Black Angel."

"You and I know he is much more than that. He is a good man, no matter how hard he tries to do wrong."

Rosalind stared at Beatrice in complete astonishment. "Now how did you come to that conclusion?"

"It's obvious. While the captain fancies himself all too clever with words, he never once allowed any real harm to come to either of us, nor even to poor Mr. MacCaulay."

"I wish I had your disposition, Beatrice. I believe you could find virtue in the Devil himself."

"It's easy to think the worst of people. Once they realize

that's all you expect, they're happy to oblige. But if they know you think of them as kind and good, they'll try even harder to live up to that opinion."

"If only it were that simple."

Rosalind sighed, thinking of Mr. Murdock and the trouble he was sure to cause. Mr. Murdock was not one to willingly change his plans. He was far more accustomed to everyone around him simply doing as they were told.

Once the pile of salvaged clothing was complete, Rosalind rang for the maid. Sophie appeared in the doorway. She made a nervous curtsy.

"Oui, mesdemoiselles?"

"Is there a seamstress among the household staff?" Rosalind asked. "We have some mending to be done."

"Oui, mademoiselle. I will tell Celeste she is wanted."

"One moment, Sophie." Rosalind stood up and walked over to the doorway, looking at Sophie in the better light. "Are you well? You look so pale."

"I am fine, mademoiselle. *Merci.*"

"Where is Adele?"

"I don't know, mademoiselle." Sophie shrugged. Her thin hands knotted the hem of her apron. "She said she was ill, mademoiselle. I could not doubt her, not after—" Sophie ended with another slight shrug, keeping her eyes down.

"Oh." Rosalind nodded. "I see."

"Rosalind?" Beatrice turned from folding another pile of handkerchiefs. "Is something wrong?"

"Sophie says she doesn't know where Adele is. I find it strange that Adele should be so completely absent."

"What's strange about that?" Beatrice asked. "She doesn't dare come near you after the captain got so angry with her."

Rosalind nodded. Still, something rankled. She'd feel much more comfortable knowing exactly where Adele might be.

"Go, Sophie. Find this Celeste and send her to us. Please tell Madame LeFevre I'd like a word with her."

Sophie curtsied and scurried out.

"I'm afraid the Lawrences will find me no more imposing than a church mouse," Beatrice said. "I shall arrive on their doorstep little better than a beggar in my rags."

"Oh, Beatrice, do stop being so melodramatic," Rosalind teased. "Once word gets out that you survived shipwreck and pirate attack, everyone will be longing to meet you and hear of your adventures."

The door opened to admit Madame LeFevre and a younger woman whose skin was the shade of coffee mixed with cream.

"*Bonjour, mesdemoiselles.* I have brought you Celeste, my finest seamstress. What would you have her do?"

"*Merci, Maman,*" Rosalind said. "I fear our adventures have been rather hard on poor Beatrice's wardrobe." She gestured to the pile of salvaged clothing.

"Nothing could be simpler." Madame LeFevre spoke rapidly in the island patois. Celeste gathered up Beatrice's clothing and hurried out. Madame LeFevre turned to Rosalind. "You wanted a word with me, mademoiselle?"

"*Oui, Maman. Merci.*" Rosalind considered her words carefully. "Have you seen Adele today?"

"*Non,* mademoiselle, I have not."

"Did you see her yesterday?"

Madame LeFevre shook her head. "Sophie always comes in first. I give her the work for the day. She and Adele work together."

"Then where is Adele today? Only Sophie came when I rang the bell. Have you sent her to some other part of *Chez Jardin?*"

"*Non.* I have made no changes in the household staff for over a month now."

Rosalind tried to control her growing sense of alarm. "Tell me, *Maman,* when was the last time you remember seeing Adele?"

"The night after the feast. She came to me, complaining of the pain across her back. It was nothing, maybe a slight bruise. The way Adele carried on, you'd think she was dying."

"What did you do?"

"I gave her some ointment to put on it and told her she'd do well to be quiet and not cause any more trouble."

"Would you be good enough to show me to Adele's room, *Maman*? Please believe me when I tell you it is of the greatest importance."

"As you wish."

Rosalind turned to Beatrice. "I think it might be best if you got on with your packing. This won't take long. I'll come back as soon as I can."

Beatrice's face grew troubled. "Something *is* wrong, isn't it? And you know what it is."

"I can't be sure, not yet. But I soon will be."

Rosalind followed Madame LeFevre through the hallways to a less ornate part of the house. Madame LeFevre bustled up to one particular door and knocked. No answer came. She knocked again.

"Sophie? Adele?"

Madame LeFevre waited another long moment, then with a sigh she reached for the knob and opened the door. There were two beds in the room. On one side the bed was made, the dresser tidy, the floor clear, and the general air one of order and purpose. The other side of the room was a jumble of clothing, used candle ends, rumpled sheets, and a smell of neglect. Madame LeFevre stepped back.

"She is not here."

Rosalind made her way through the mess to the closet. The two dresses hanging there were little more than rags, stained with soot and tar and other things. A clean patch showed among the dust and clutter on the dresser where some object had lain.

"She took with her only what she knew she'd need," Rosalind said. "Her best gowns, her jewelry, and her cosmetics."

"But why?" Madame LeFevre asked. "Where would she wear them?"

"In the main port of Martinique, where a whore and a pickpocket could find plenty of work."

Madame LeFevre's eyes widened in horror. "You think she has run away?"

"I don't see what else we can think. Everything points to it."

"Mon Dieu! We must tell *le capitaine!"*

Rosalind nodded. "Indeed we must. Where can we find him at this hour?"

"Le capitaine and Monsieur Yves had planned to visit the ships today, to see that all was kept in order. I do not think they have started off yet."

Rosalind ran back through the hallways to the kitchen, looking out every window in turn until she caught a glimpse of Alexandre's glossy black mane among the bright colors of the garden. He was sitting in the shade with Yves and Gaston.

"Mon capitaine!"

She ran toward him, all too aware of the heads turning to follow her. Alexandre sprang to his feet and met her halfway, catching her in his arms.

"What is it, *ma belle?* Is Beatrice ill again?"

"Non, non, mon capitaine. It's worse. I think Adele has run away."

"Run away? *Pourquoi?"*

"How can you even ask me that? You humiliated her, then sent her away like she was nothing, and all on my account. How could she stand to live here another day with everyone either laughing at her or pitying her?"

"Why do you take her side? She brought her punishment upon herself."

"I am not 'taking her side'! Don't you see? She is in pain. She will be angry, thinking vengeful thoughts. It is within her power to hand you and every single one of your people over to the authorities!"

Alexandre set his jaw, then nodded. "How long do you believe she has been gone?"

"Since the night after the feast, at the earliest. Madame LeFevre gave her some ointment for the mark of the lash."

"Calm yourself, *ma belle.* All is not as desperate as you

believe. Even if Adele were to reach the main port, she will not find the vengeance she is seeking there. She will have to reach Kingston before she can do *Chez Jardin* any serious harm."

"How can you be sure?"

Alexandre laughed and kissed Rosalind on both cheeks. He hugged her tightly, whispering into her ear. "Because, *ma belle,* the officer in charge of the French naval forces here is a cousin on my mother's side."

"Then you're safe? Everyone here is safe?"

"Not merely safe, but protected." Alexandre's humor vanished into a frown. "Adele is worse than a fool to give up that protection. She knows there is nowhere on Martinique she can hide from me."

Taking Rosalind by the hand, Alexandre strode back to Yves and Gaston.

"Adele has run off," he said. "Yves, you will have the house and grounds searched. By now she is long gone, but we must be thorough."

"Oui, mon Capitaine."

"Gaston, gather as many men as you like and take the overland route to the other side of the island. It is entirely possible Adele has fallen by the wayside. One can travel only so far on hatred and vengeance."

"Oui, mon Capitaine," said Gaston. "And when we find her? What would you have us do with her?"

Alexandre started to speak. He glanced down at Rosalind and sighed. "Bring her back. I will deal with her when the time is right."

Rosalind looked from one man to the next. Not one of them seemed even a little alarmed.

"Does this mean nothing to you? Adele could tell anyone about *Chez Jardin*! I have no doubt that is exactly what she intends to do!"

"Rosalind, calm yourself!" Alexandre took her by the shoulders and gave her a gentle shake. "Adele can do us no harm at all. My cousin and I have an understanding. Should any of my crew or household staff fall into the hands of the authorities here on Martinique, they send word and that person is returned to me."

"Does Adele know about this arrangement?"

"Of course not. Only the three of us, and now you, know of it. I trust you will keep this to yourself?"

"Mais oui, mon capitaine." Rosalind still fretted. "Still, Adele is a loose cannon in every sense!"

Alexandre studied her. "Rosalind, what is it that you fear? Surely the welfare of this den of pirates cannot be causing you such distress."

Rosalind looked away. There was fear in her heart, fear that threatened to become genuine panic. Perhaps Adele could do no harm to *Chez Jardin*, but she could very easily tell the world where the missing Lady Hanshaw was now being held.

"Adele hates me, *mon capitaine*. She can use me to hurt you, by telling the right people where I am. Your cousin might shield you, but he cannot simply ignore my presence here."

"Why not?" Alexandre asked. "Who are you that your presence here is of such importance?"

He smiled as he said it, but Rosalind sensed the sudden alertness behind his question. In her need to save herself and him, she had almost given herself away. How could she make the danger clear to Alexandre, yet keep him from seeing her deception as outright betrayal?

"I am a subject of the British Crown, brought here against my will. As is Beatrice. Surely France would not wish to provoke England by turning a blind eye to our abduction."

Alexandre laughed. There was a wicked gleam in his eye. "You astonish me, mademoiselle. For days now you have told me you are nothing, of no consequence, no one at all. Yet now you seem to think two English schoolteachers make so much difference to world events."

The desperation growing in Rosalind made her fall back on the naked truth. "They will take me from you, Alexandre! And then they will use me to destroy you!"

"Ma belle." Alexandre hugged her to him, smoothing her hair. *"Ma petite fleur.* Have no fear."

Alexandre led the way to the house, to his own library, rich with French nautical items and portraits of both ships and naval officers. He seated himself at the desk and took out writing paper, a pen, and an inkwell.

"Yves. I will send *mon cousin* a brief note making him aware of Adele and her likely course of action." Alexandre blotted the note, then sealed it with a blob of blank wax. "Once you have finished searching the house and grounds, then we will go down to the cove and inspect the ships."

"Oui, mon Capitaine." Yves tucked the message inside his jacket and hurried out.

Alexandre gave the bosun a nod.

"Go, Gaston. Make the most of the daylight remaining."

Gaston departed on his errand.

Rosalind could not shake off a sense of impending disaster. She paced around the room.

"Something is coming, Alexandre. I feel it as surely as you might see a storm front moving in."

"Your recent run of bad luck has colored all your thinking, *ma belle.* You believe that because nothing bad has happened for a few days, something all the more terrible must be about to strike."

"That is what I think, *mon capitaine,* and rightly so. How will Adele's disappearance affect your plans to send Beatrice to Kingston?"

"Why should that have any effect at all?"

"Too many people coming and going from *Chez Jardin* is dangerous."

"Oui, along the same route, but that can be avoided."

"You're certain, *mon capitaine?"*

Alexandre let out a gusty sigh. "As sure as a man can be of anything, *ma belle."* He stood up and crossed the room to take her in his arms. "You are safe here, Rosalind. I know you have had very little safety of late. All your security was torn from you when your father died."

Rosalind leaned against him, taking comfort in the strength of his arms around her. "I am so tired, Alexandre. So tired of living in fear of what might happen next."

"Let me take your mind off these worries, *ma belle*." His hands slid down her back to her hips. "What you need is rest, and I have just the place for that."

He led her through the far door. It opened onto his sitting room. The next door led to his bedchamber.

Chapter Thirty

A furious hammering at the door woke Rosalind. A voice shouted something urgent in hasty French, prompting Alexandre to lunge out of bed and throw on his clothing.

"Damnation! Yves was right again."

"Alexandre?" Rosalind asked. "What is it?"

A sound like thunder rumbled somewhere in the distance. The thunder rumbled again and again, several sharp bursts of it. Rosalind knew that sound. She'd heard it the morning that Vasquez had taken Captain Bellamy's ship. Cannon fire, close enough to be heard in the valley. Sudden icy dread gripped Rosalind, making her catch her breath in a painful gasp.

"The ships!" she cried.

"*Mais oui.*" Alexandre stamped into his boots. "The ships. We are under attack." He bent to plant a swift kiss on her lips. "Stay here, *ma belle.* Do not leave this house. I'll be back as soon as I can."

Rosalind flung her arms around his neck. The moment had come. Cruel Fate had caught up with her again, and yet another disaster was about to strike.

"Rosalind!" Alexandre tugged at her arms. "I must go!"

"No matter what happens," she said, "know that I love you. With my whole heart, I love you."

Alexandre looked down at her. "The sweetest words I have ever heard." He brushed his lips across her brow. "Do not be afraid, *mon amour.* Now that I have found you, nothing and no one will take you from me."

With that he was gone, out the door and running down the hallway after whoever had been sent to summon him.

Rosalind flung back the sheet and hurried into her own garments, her heart pounding with dread. Could the British naval authorities have somehow discovered the hiding place of *L'Etoile du Matin* and the *Diabolique*? Were they even now delivering broadside after broadside, smashing both ships to splinters before gathering up the survivors to be hanged?

As Rosalind hurried through the hallways toward the kitchen, she met no one, heard no one. An eerie quiet hung over *Chez Jardin*, broken only by the distant sounds of cannon fire. If the battle was being waged on the open seas, Rosalind wouldn't have wasted a moment in worry. But trapped as *L'Etoile du Matin* was in such a small cove, the likelihood of the Black Angel's usual effortless victory was slight indeed. By the time Rosalind reached the kitchen she was nearly running. She burst in through the door, then staggered to an abrupt stop.

A dozen servants huddled around Madame LeFevre. All heads turned toward Rosalind as she made her abrupt entrance. Madame LeFevre cried out. She took a step toward Rosalind, hands outstretched.

"Mademoiselle! Hide yourself! The *Anglais*—"

The garden was suddenly full of men running and shouting. Pistols fired. Women screamed. Rosalind turned toward the door that led out to the garden. It burst inward ahead of her reaching hand, making her stumble backward. Five ruffians in the elegant attire of English gentlemen crowded into the kitchen, all armed and looking more than ready to shoot.

Another man moved forward through their ranks. He held a young mulatto girl against his chest, his arm around the girl's throat and a pistol pressed against her temple.

"Chloe!" Madame LeFevre cried out. *"Ma fille!"*

"Good afternoon, my lady," said the man who held Chloe captive. "Please be good enough to tell the darkies that if they try anything clever, I will kill this girl."

Rosalind took one look at the anguish on Madame LeFevre's face and considered any such translation redundant. "Who are you?"

"That's Mr. Hastings. A very useful sort of fellow."

The crowd of Englishmen gave way again as another man stepped forward. Rosalind could scarcely believe her eyes.

"Edward Murdock? Can it really be you?"

"Ah, Rosalind, my dear. There you are."

Mr. Murdock smiled. His fawn-colored coat and breeches were without wrinkle, his jabot and cuffs spotless, his pistol held loosely in his hand. His weeks aboard ship had done him good, lending color to his pallid cheeks and giving him a general air of robust good health.

"I am relieved to see you looking so well." Mr. Murdock made her a slight bow. "I have come to fetch you home safe and sound."

"But—how could you possibly have known where to find me, in such a remote corner of one small tropical island?"

Mr. Murdock's only answer was a satisfied smile.

Rosalind groaned. "Adele. You found Adele, or she found you."

"It was the least I could do, my dear."

The helpless panic of her nightmare flooded Rosalind, threatening to steal the last of her composure. She retreated behind a shield of frosty courtesy. "First things first, Mr. Murdock. Kindly tell your associate to take his hands off that girl."

Mr. Murdock nodded. "Hastings, let her go. Now that Lady Hanshaw has been kind enough to spare us the task of searching the premises for her, we really have no further need of the darkies."

The man called Hastings let his arm drop from around Chloe's neck. She fled to Madame LeFevre and huddled sobbing in her arms.

"Thank you, Mr. Murdock." Rosalind drew a steadying breath. "I have business in this part of the world, business which is as yet unfinished. I cannot and will not return to London until I have attended to those matters."

"Ah yes, your visit to your brother Thomas. I will be happy to escort you to the very door of Jasmine Court. Now come along. I'm sure you're as anxious as I am to see yourself safely out of the Black Angel's clutches."

To hear Alexandre's elegant hands described by so coarse and inappropriate a term so soon after the ecstasy of their lovemaking made Rosalind absolutely furious.

"Really, Mr. Murdock. Open your eyes! I am not chained up in some horrible torchlit cavern. That might suggest to you that I'm here of my own free will."

"'Of your own free will'?" Mr. Murdock's smile faded. "You must be joking."

"Things are not always as they seem, Mr. Murdock. For example, you yourself presently labor under the mistaken belief that I have already agreed to marry you."

"There's no mistake about it, my dear. All the necessary preparations are already under way."

"Are they?" Rosalind's outrage boiled up within her, making it difficult to speak. "Is my wedding gown already chosen, with the fabric, lace, and every last seed pearl mapped out according to your specifications?"

"Really, Rosalind," Mr. Murdock said. "I find your entire manner remarkably lacking in gratitude. Few men would be so understanding as I am about the consequences of this little misadventure."

"How dare you speak to me of courtesy!" Rosalind slapped Mr. Murdock right across his smug smile. "What a pity *you* didn't have the common courtesy to wait for your proposal to be accepted by the object of your self-serving affections!" She stepped back to stand beside Madame LeFevre, linking arms with her. "Here's your answer, Mr. Murdock. No, no, and a thousand times *no!*"

Mr. Murdock stood glaring at her. The marks of her fingers showed white against his reddened cheek. When he spoke, his tone was cold and direct, as if he spoke to some simpleminded housemaid.

"My dear Rosalind, we are here to take you home. Home, to your devoted mother, who even now languishes in an agony of uncertainty, wondering if her dear sweet daughter is alive or dead."

Rosalind returned his glare, wondering how she could have ever entertained the idea of marrying him. "Mr. Murdock, you will kindly take your men and get out of here. I am *not* leaving this house."

"You cannot see where your best interests lie, my dear. That is unfortunate." Mr. Murdock reached into his jacket and withdrew a folded sheet of writing paper. "I think, my dear Lady Hanshaw, you should look at this. You'll find it most enlightening."

Rosalind snatched the paper out of his hand and glanced at the few lines of meticulous handwriting. She gasped, unable to draw a proper breath. Her heart turned cold and leaden within her.

M. Murdock,

You will be pleased to know a lady of your acquaintance has narrowly escaped a brutal death at the hands of Ricardo Vasquez. I had reason to engage La Fortuna *in combat. Proving victorious, I stripped her of all her valuables. First among them proved to be Lady Rosalind Hanshaw. I will be happy to return her to you for double my usual fee.*

L'Ange Noir

Rosalind's hands shook so badly she could scarcely hold the paper. She turned it over. There was Alexandre's seal, a perfect circle of smooth, blank wax, broken across its middle.

"He knew." She stared unseeing at the broken seal. "He knew who I am. He's known all along."

"Indeed, my dear. He has." Mr. Murdock stepped forward to lay his hand on her shoulder. "I don't know what pretty lies he's been telling you, but to the Black Angel you are nothing more than a particularly valuable hostage dropped into his hands by a perverse twist of Providence."

Rosalind's head was spinning. Alexandre had lied to her, playing a cunning game of deceit with her for very nearly the entire time she'd been his captive. He continued to play the game even after seducing her, even after hearing from her own lips how bitter and desolate a future she faced as the wife of Edward Murdock. Alexandre. Her beloved Alexandre. How could all of it have been a lie? And yet here in her own hands she held the proof. Grief washed over her, drowning her in its black depths.

"Mademoiselle!" Madame LeFevre snatched the message out of Rosalind's hand and looked it over. "Listen to me, I beg you! *Le capitaine*, he did mean to ransom you at first, but he changed his mind!"

Rosalind shook her head. She no longer knew what to believe.

"Mademoiselle, *s'il-vous plaît! Le capitaine* loves you with everything in him!"

Rosalind tried to shut out the unbearable agony by forcing herself to think in practical terms. "What of Miss Henderson? Surely you intend to take her along with us as well?"

Mr. Murdock frowned. "She is not my concern."

"What greater trouble is it to take two women when you've come all this way just for one? She is English, Mr. Murdock. You cannot mean to leave her here, to abandon her to this den of thieves and cutthroats."

"My lady—"

"You said you would take me to see my brother Thomas. Very well. Beatrice is also bound for Kingston. Take her with us and we can put her into the keeping of the proper people there."

Clearly taking Rosalind's reference to "us" as a sign of surrender, Mr. Murdock smiled. "Very well, my dear. Where is she?"

"Let me run and fetch her. I'll only be a moment." Rosalind turned toward the hallway door.

"Hastings!"

Mr. Hastings lunged forward to catch Rosalind around the waist and haul her up over his shoulder. Rosalind fought Hasting's grip, trying to thrash free of his arm around her waist. Mr. Murdock stepped up to her and caught a fistful of her hair.

"I've had quite enough of your prissy little temper, my dear Lady Hanshaw. You will kindly shut your mouth and do as you're told!"

Now Mr. Murdock looked much as he had in her nightmare, lacking only Vasquez's redingote. Vasquez was dead. Unless Mr. Murdock counted necromancy among his many interests, the second half of her nightmare could not come true. That left a world of possibilities just waiting to happen. The open sea was the Black Angel's domain. To the open sea she would go.

"Very well, Mr. Murdock. If you insist."

Chapter Thirty-one

Alexandre and Yves made their way down the cliff, running hard across the beach to reach the ship's boat. Cannon fire tore through the air, the balls splashing some hundred yards off *L'Etoile du Matin*'s starboard bow. *L'Etoile du Matin* was under attack from a frigate that flew no colors.

"*Mon capitaine.*" Yves put his back into it, helping Alexandre and the two rowers push the boat out into the surf. "Something is wrong here. This frigate, it only toys with us. It has the weather gauge, and its guns are enough to sink us. And yet it holds back."

"Are they trying to take us alive?"

"I don't know, *mon capitaine.* I begin to doubt that they are trying to take us at all."

"Then why attack?"

Yves shook his head. "This is all too convenient, *mon capitaine.* That *coquine* Adele vanishes. We scatter ourselves to search for her, and then this attack comes from out of the blue."

Alexandre nodded. "*Mais oui.* I see your point. For now

we must make short work of that swine before *L'Etoile du Matin* takes any serious damage."

The rowers brought them alongside *L'Etoile du Matin* well astern of the guns. Alexandre caught a line and clambered up the hull, landing lightly on the deck. Remy stood on the quarterdeck. Upon sighting Alexandre, he crossed himself with a look of deep relief and came down in a breathless rush, holding Alexandre's spyglass in his hand.

"*Mon capitaine,* one moment all was quiet, the next, this *Anglais bâtard* comes in firing most of a broadside. Then he runs out again, as if teasing us to follow him! What shall we do?"

Alexandre took the spyglass and studied the frigate. "He's found our cove. We have no choice. Fly the red."

Remy nodded. He turned to rush off again, but Alexandre caught him by the shoulder.

"What makes you think this ship is *Anglais?*"

"Only the *Anglais* would be stupid enough to attack us here, in French waters. And the only *Anglais* angry enough to be that stupid is Murdock. You sank his ship and stole his woman. He will feel the need to teach you some respect."

Alexandre looked to Yves, who nodded.

"I would not have thought Murdock so impetuous," Yves said, "but Remy makes a good case. This is the perfect opportunity for Murdock to rid himself of you once and for all."

Alexandre smiled, cold and wolfish. "Then Monsieur Murdock is in for even greater disappointment. He is the one who shall be taught the lesson in respect!"

With Yves and Remy working together like his right and left hands, Alexandre soon had *L'Etoile du Matin* rounding on the frigate, aiming to cut her wind and leave her dead in the water. One or two broadsides timed properly, followed by the right amount of fire from the deck guns, and all serious resistance would be at an end. Even as Alxandre brought the ship about and prepared to make his first run at the frigate, the frigate itself laid on sail and ran out of the cove toward the open sea.

"Are they mad?" Alexandre said. "In open waters I have every advantage. The *capitaine* is either far too confident or as yellow as can be!"

Yves frowned. "You see, *mon capitaine?* The tactics here make no sense. Again and again, he tries to draw us away from shore, out into the currents."

Suddenly Alexandre understood. He spun around, clapping his spyglass to his eye and training it on the signal tower high above *Chez Jardin*. Just as he did so, the lookout in the crow's nest hailed him. Colored flags rose one after another up the signal tower's flagpole. The British flag, identifying the enemy. The green flag, broken by a red bend. Invasion, with wounded. The blue flag, on its field a single white diamond. The treasure. And finally, the black flag, marked with a skull. British agents had invaded *Chez Jardin* and stolen the treasure. The treasure could be none other than Rosalind herself. Every curse Alexandre had ever heard rose to his lips in a scalding torrent. He turned to Yves.

"Run for open water. Set course for Kingston."

Yves and Remy both turned to stare at him, their shock plain on their faces.

"Kingston, *mon capitaine?*" Yves asked.

"You heard me! *Allons!*"

"*Oui, mon capitaine.*"

Alexandre turned to Remy. "Get a man up to the crow's nest with the flags. Signal the *Diabolique* to sail north by northeast around the island, then make for Kingston with all speed. Stop any ship encountered on route."

Remy saluted. "*Oui, mon capitaine!*"

Alexandre stepped up to the ship's bell, grasped the rope and rang it until his arm ached.

"My brothers-in-arms! *Ecoutez-moi!*"

Once he had the crew's attention, he held up his hands for silence.

"The *Anglais* stole our lives from us! They took our future and gave us nothing in return! Now they mean to do the same again!"

Angry voices rose on all sides, shouting questions and threats. Alexandre nodded.

"Hear me! We sail not just to avenge the honor of France. We sail to strike down these *Anglais* dogs who have the gall to trespass on our sanctuary. They know where we live. Not a single man among them can be allowed to escape. Every life at *Chez Jardin* now hangs in the balance."

That thought brought Alexandre's blood to a boil. The crew's outrage grew even more passionate, more furious.

"This silly little skirmish was nothing more than a diversion to draw us away so Murdock's men could invade *Chez Jardin* and seize *La Belle Tempétueux*. She will surrender rather than risk any harm to the innocent lives of *Maman* and her staff. Think of how she defended *la petite* Beatrice at every turn!"

"*Mais oui!*" cried Eric. "*Vive la Belle Tempétueux!*"

"Death to the English swine!"

Alexandre nodded. A fitting battle cry.

"We sail not just to restore our proper lives, but to protect lives yet to come. *La Belle Tempétueux* shall be my bride! Mother to future sons of France!"

The crew whistled and cheered.

"The time has come to tell you this will be *L'Ange Noir*'s last battle. We will take back my woman from the *Anglais*, and then we sail for France. My brothers, it's time to go home."

There was a moment of awestruck silence, then as one man the French crew roared with delight. He knew how they suffered for their loyalty to him. It was time he paid a number of debts.

Alexandre rang the "all hands" alarm. The last of the crew who weren't already on deck came swarming up from below. Every man took his station on deck or aloft in the rigging. Alexandre could hear the master gunner below, bellowing orders with gusto.

"Yves!" Alexandre shouted. "Fly the *fleur-de-lis!* Today we sail for the glory of France!"

Yves snapped out the necessary orders and the men jumped to obey. As the French flag rose up into the air, rippling and snapping in the breeze, one of Yves's rare smiles flashed across his face.

Alexandre glared out at the frigate, still playing its coy little games. As the *Diabolique* cleared the mouth of the cove, her *capitaine* Etienne Duchard turned her head to the northeast and laid on all possible sail. Alexandre turned *L'Etoile du Matin* southwest and ran ahead of the obliging wind, dismissing the frigate as though she were nothing more than so much seaweed

"On deck!" cried the lookout. "She's rounding on us, *mon capitaine!* The *Anglais* ship is now pursuing us!"

Alexandre laughed. "Now we shall see what the game truly is!"

Adolphe stood at the helm. "Your orders, *mon capitaine?*"

"We must reach the boundary between French and *Anglais* waters before they do. Make for Kingston until I say otherwise."

"Before the frigate, *mon captaine?*"

"*Non.* We must get there ahead of the ship that now carries Mademoiselle Rosalind."

"*Oui, mon capitaine.*"

Alexandre stood on the quarterdeck, his glass trained on the frigate. That ship was heavy in the water, making a large wake. The gunports along its starboard side had opened, revealing ten twenty-pound cannons. Now came the worst part, the waiting. Did the frigate mean to sink him, or merely harry him onward?

As the minutes passed, Alexandre noted with grudging admiration the closing distance between the frigate and *L'Etoile du Matin*'s stern. The *Anglais capitaine* hoped to get within range of his own cannon, perhaps even the deck guns as well. The purpose was capture, not destruction. Alexandre smiled. He had no such niceties holding him back.

"On deck!" The lookout hailed Alexandre again. "A ship to starboard, *mon capitaine!* Another *Anglais,* a merchantman by her lines!"

"Where is she bound?" Alexandre asked.

"I think she simply waits, *mon capitaine.* She looks to be pacing the boundary line itself."

"Can you describe to me the people aboard? The *capitaine?* Any of the mates?"

The lookout squinted through his own spyglass. "Two men on the quarterdeck, *mon capitaine.* One older, with gray sidewhiskers. The younger man is fair, no beard, his hair a bright yellow."

"Are they British navy?"

"No way to tell, *mon capitaine.* Perhaps the owner of the ship and his *capitaine?*"

Alexandre shook his head. "*Mais non.* They'll be more than that. They are waiting for whoever makes it around the island first."

Cannon fire from the frigate made Alexandre jerk around to watch where the balls landed. Two, only a few hundred yards off the stern on the portside. Moments later two more cannons roared. The balls hurtled through the air, striking the water more directly behind the ship.

One of the master gunner's mates came thundering up from below and saluted. "*Mon capitaine, Monsieur Maitre d'Cannonier* presents his compliments and asks for your orders."

"Offer him mine in return, and tell him to keep the main guns quiet until we are engaged within the range of a full broadside. The deck guns may be loaded and readied as he sees fit."

The mate saluted again and vanished below. Minutes later many feet came pounding up the ladders as the gun crews diverted to the deck guns rushed up to prepare their weapons. Alexandre watched them with a rush of almost fatherly pride. They looked like pirates, in their lace and velvet and mismatched jewels, but they were the best crew the French navy could boast.

"Yves." Alexandre beckoned him. "Take us in close to that *Anglais* ship on the boundary. I think I might know one of the gentlemen aboard."

"Vraiment, mon capitaine? Who could that be?"

"We shall shortly know, *mon ami.* If he is in fact who I suspect him to be, we are in for a most invigorating evening."

Rosalind sat in the captain's cabin of the *Jamaica Pearl*. She was the picture of propriety in all the required layers of plain muslin, pink batiste, white satin, and emerald taffeta appropriate to an English lady, even here in the tropics. Her hair was braided and bound into a demure bun. Her hands were free, she was not tied to her chair, and yet she felt as if the heaviest chains bound her to the very earth itself. She had only one slight measure of hope, a single solitary fact that kept her from sinking into utter despair. *L'Etoile de Matin* had traveled eastward to Martinique. The *Jamaica Pearl* now traveled west, against both the trade winds and the currents. That would slow their progress, perhaps enough to allow Alexandre to overtake them.

Rosalind stared at her hands, the fine, soft, well-kept hands of an English lady. The hands of a woman who didn't have to cook her own meals or wash her own clothing. The hands of a woman who was largely ornamental. Madame LeFevre's hands were rough with years of washing up, of cleaning and dressing fowl for the table, of bathing babies and wringing out clothes. Her hands were the outward proof of the character and honor she possessed.

Rosalind stood up. It was high time she took matters into her own hands, hands that now had some experience of the real world and its perils. Alexandre had said the people of the Caribbean would tell stories about *L'Ange Noir* and his one true love, *La Belle Tempétueux.* If she could best Ricardo Vasquez, then she would not be defeated by the likes of Edward Murdock.

Rosalind marched out on deck. The sailors going about their work dodged around her with many a polite bob of the head and muttered "my lady." Other than avoiding her like any other obstacle, they treated her like she wasn't even there. She found Captain Anderson beside the helmsman at the wheel.

"Tell me, Captain, are we making good headway?"

Captain Anderson was a man of average height, built like a barrel, his red hair and beard gone to gray. He glanced at her, startled. He took his pipe out of his mouth, removed his hat, and smiled. "Good evening, my lady. Oh yes, she's doing quite well."

"Isn't that strange."

"What's that, my lady?"

"We sail against the trades, Captain. I'm sure you know that. How can we be doing well against them?"

The captain gave her a puzzled look, as though he hadn't heard right. "Don't you fret, my lady. We'll be in Kingston in no time at all."

"I would guess it more likely to be three or four days, Captain. But of course you know best."

The captain went on smiling at her as though she was daft. She felt a twinge of what was almost nostalgia for the crew of *L'Etoile du Matin*. They also treated her as if nautical matters were beyond her grasp, but they knew better than to underestimate her once she was good and angry.

"Might I have a look around the ship, Captain?"

Captain Anderson nodded. "By all means, my lady. Just have a care where you step. We don't want you dirtying that lovely gown."

"Thank you, Captain. I shall be careful."

Rosalind turned and surveyed the deck. There were a few cannons up here, lightweight sixteen pounders. Each had a little pyramid of cannonballs piled neatly beside it. She wondered where the powder was kept. Somewhere below, probably down near the orlop deck. She'd never make her way down that far, so she'd have to work with what was close to hand.

"Rosalind!" Mr. Murdock appeared, pushing his way through the sailors as he hurried toward her from the bow. "My dear, what are you doing out here in the sun?"

"Just getting some air." It was all Rosalind could do to hold her temper in the face of his falsely solicitous tone of voice.

"Really, my dear, it would be for the best if you went back inside."

"Why? It's such a lovely evening."

"It's just that sailors tend to be such a coarse lot. I would not have your pretty ears sullied with their language."

Rosalind bit her lips against a burst of scornful laughter. What little she'd heard from the mouths of this English crew was nothing compared with the uproar that had greeted her that first evening on the main deck of *L'Etoile du Matin*.

"On deck!" called the lookout. "Ship on the horizon! Off the starboard stern!"

"What colors does she fly?" asked Captain Anderson.

"France, skipper! A sloop by the look of her, and she's making for us with full sail!"

Mr. Murdock took Rosalind by the arm and drew her with him up to the quarterdeck alongside Captain Anderson.

"Any cause for concern?" Mr. Murdock asked.

Captain Anderson pursed his chapped lips. "Too soon to tell. Could be nothing more than some naval nonsense."

"We'd be expecting any pursuit from the southwest, correct?"

"Aye, that we would. Nothing showing so far."

"Good." Mr. Murdock nodded. "The frigate must be doing its work."

"Frigate?" Rosalind asked. "What do you mean?"

"Now, my dear," Mr. Murdock said, "this ordeal is over. Leave these last few details to me."

"What 'last few details'? What is this about a frigate? What have you done?"

"Rosalind, lower your voice."

"I will not! I have asked a simple question, and I deserve a civil answer!"

"I drew that arrogant fool away from you by attacking the one thing he loves above all else, his precious ship. Even now an English frigate will be cutting off any retreat and driving him toward British waters."

Rosalind's mouth went dry. A dull pain shot through her. "You're using me as bait. You mean to have him captured."

"And hanged. The rogue needs to be taught a permanent lesson."

Rosalind turned away, fighting back the tears that stung her eyes. So far there was no sign of an actual naval vessel. Alexandre was still free. If Rosalind could do nothing else for him, she would see to it he remained free. The forces of nature were working in her favor. Perhaps she could convince Providence itself to yield.

"Might I go forward to the bow? I'm told dolphins like to ride the bow wave of ships. That would be such a wonderful sight to see."

Mr. Murdock and the captain both beamed at her, satisfied with a request they clearly considered altogether feminine.

"By all means, my dear," Mr. Murdock said. "I'll join you shortly."

Holding her skirts daintily to the side, Rosalind went down the little stairs to the main deck and wandered forward, looking around her with wide eyes and little squeaks of surprise and pleasure. The sailors eddying around her passed by with smiles and nods. Affecting to drop her handkerchief on the deck, Rosalind bent to pick it up. Her other hand closed around the bottom cannonball that made the corner of one pyramid. She yanked at it, pulling it free. The balls tumbled down, rolling back and forth across the deck. Sailors cried out in alarm as they stumbled over the balls, colliding with each other. Curses and shouts multiplied as more and more crewmen became involved in the spreading confusion.

Rosalind hurried out of the way. She eyed the multitude of ropes before her, all running up into the complicated works of the mainmast rigging. Ignoring the continuing chaos behind her, Rosalind stepped up to a likely looking belaying pin currently not in use. She pulled it free and carried it in one hand as she might carry a parasol. Next she spied a line that looked promising. Using the end of the belaying pin, she hammered at the bottom of another pin until that pin came free and the line knotted around it went flying upward. Now there were shouts above her as well. Rosalind made her way forward. The ship's cook might have exactly what she needed, if events called for more desperate measures.

Alexandre trained his spyglass on the English merchantman. He could read her name now, painted along her bow. The *Elegance*. A good name for a ship, particularly if her master chose to trade in luxury goods—such as fine English linen. Alexandre closed his eyes for a moment, feeling a rare pang of regret. He had been given the opportunity to make it right. It was up to him to make the best of that opportunity.

"Mon capitaine!" called the lookout. "To the north! Another *Anglais* ship!"

Alexandre turned to scan the horizon. White sails flew from the masts of a sturdy English schooner. The way it sliced through the waves, as if defying nature to slow its progress, told him it was the ship he sought. Only Murdock could drive a good vessel that hard.

"Yves! Here comes *La Belle*'s ferry now!"

Yves clambered down from the mizzenmast. *"Mon capitaine*, we are now at the center of a triangle made up of three *Anglais* ships. A schooner, a merchantman, and a frigate, the last fully armed and all too willing to sink us!"

Alexandre scowled. "There is nothing wrong with my eyes nor my mathematical skill."

"*Certainement, mon capitaine.* I thought perhaps the word 'trap' might have crossed your mind."

"This is no trap, *mon ami.* These ships, they do not work together. They do not signal each other. They do nothing but converge. That is not proper strategy."

"In perhaps a quarter of an hour, it will not matter!" Yves stepped up, close enough for his undertone to still be heard. "Alexandre, *s'il-vous plaît!* You said we were going home. You did not say we would do so in our coffins!"

"Have you no faith in me, *mon ami?*" Alexandre sighed and shook his head. "Even after all these years?"

"On deck!" roared the lookout. "The *Diabolique* is closing on the *Anglais* schooner!"

"You see?" Alexandre smiled at Yves. "The tide is turning in our favor. Time now to give it an extra push."

L'Etoile du Matin glided into broadside range of the English merchantman. Alexandre climbed from the quarterdeck up into the shrouds, giving himself a better view of the merchantman's deck.

"Good afternoon, my friends!" he called out in English. "Is there one among you named Thomas Hanshaw? I have a message for him!"

The young blond man at the wheel stepped forward. "Good evening. What is your message?"

"Your sister Rosalind is now a prisoner aboard the ship to the north that makes its way toward Kingston. Would you care for any assistance in taking her back from the swine who has abducted her?"

Thomas Hanshaw's fair face flushed a deep red. "That's a most serious accusation, sir! What proof have you to offer?"

Alexandre laughed. "Ask the man who stands behind you. I think he and I sailed together once."

Behind Thomas stood the grizzled figure of Mr. MacCaulay.

"It is good to see you upright and well," Alexandre called to him. "We feared the worst when we found you lying halfdead, shot up with Spanish pistol balls!"

"You have my thanks for you mercy and kindness, Captain," Mr. MacCaulay replied. "Is Lady Hanshaw truly in danger?"

"She is, at the hand of that vicious animal Murdock himself!"

"Murdock? Edward Murdock?" Thomas looked from Alexandre to Mr. MacCaulay and back again. "But—he's ashore, in Kingston!"

"He's aboard that ship," Alexandre said, "making for Kingston as fast as he can."

Thomas looked thoroughly confused and not a little angry. "Why is this of any interest to you, sir?"

"That is a very long story," Alexandre said, "one better told at another time. For now, know that I will do everything in my power to deliver your sister from Murdock."

"Who *are* you?" Thomas snapped.

Alexandre bowed with a flourish. "I am the captain who came upon your sister while she was floating among the wreckage of the *Bird of Paradise*. I am the man who pulled her and her little friend Beatrice from the sea before the sharks could devour them. I am the man whom your dear sister has sworn to love no matter what the future brings."

"Your name, sir!"

"I am known as *L'Ange Noir*. In English, the Black Angel."

As deeply as Thomas had reddened earlier, so now he paled nearly white. He snatched the pistol from his belt. Before he could take aim, Mr. MacCaulay grabbed his arm and pulled it down.

"Captain, why is that frigate chasing you?"

"Another ploy of Murdock's to drive me across the boundary and into the clutches of the British navy."

"Indeed. How ironic." Mr. MacCaulay turned to a sailor standing at attention behind him and gave him some orders Alexandre couldn't overhear. The sailor saluted and hurried off. "Tell me, Captain, is your offer of assistance sincere?"

"Completely. I want nothing more than to deliver Rosalind from that fiend's evil designs."

"Will you promise me to take Murdock alive, and hand him over to me once you do so?"

"And why should I do such a thing? Who are you to command such a promise from me?"

"My full name and rank may persuade you. I am Sir Lionel Jameson, post captain under the Admiral of the Blue in His Majesty's Royal Navy."

Alexandre stared at the man revealed as his deadliest enemy. "Oh, this is too good! I had you aboard, in chains, and I never knew!" He threw his head back and roared with laughter. "Tell me, were you hoping to cross paths with *L'Ange Noir*?"

"No, actually, I was after someone a bit closer to home. It was just some strange twist of fate that put me into your hands." Captain Jameson's expression darkened. "Now your answer, if you please. Will you swear to hand Edward Murdock over to me as soon as he's taken, with no undue harm done to him?"

"Tell me why."

"Because he is the one I am after."

Now Alexandre was truly surprised. "Can it be that someone in the British navy has finally guessed why it is that *L'Ange Noir* can strike so often and so accurately?"

"We have. We knew you must be receiving information from someone with contacts at high levels."

"And so you will use me to capture him!" Alexandre laughed again. "Oh, this is a day I will long remember. I would ask you one thing more."

"What is it?"

"How did you know to be here at this time and place? Surely it is no coincidence?"

"None at all. I believe you once employed a housemaid calling herself Adele. When she left your service, she ran afoul of Murdock's spies. They beat every last detail out of her. They know all about you and your hideaway."

"Is she still alive?"

"She is. It was a very near thing, but we found her in time to get her to a doctor."

Alexandre bowed his head. Because of his temper, he had driven Adele away, and she had almost been the death of *Chez Jardin* and everyone who dwelled there. Only God's own mercy had saved him from Adele's vengeance. It was now his duty to show mercy as well.

"Very well, Captain Jameson, you have my word as an officer and a gentleman. Murdock will be delivered to you without the beating he so richly deserves."

"Done!" Captain Jameson cried. "You see to Lady Hanshaw. I'll set this frigate to rights."

Alexandre called down to Yves. "Make for the schooner! If the *Diabolique* cannot cut off her wind, then we shall!"

Alexandre lingered in the rigging, watching the signal flags run up aboard the *Elegance*. In minutes the frigate answered. It took another two exchanges of flags to force the frigate's captain to yield to Captain Jameson's authority. Much to his growing delight, Alexandre watched as the frigate took up a position off the *Elegance*'s stern. He swung down to the deck, feeling the breeze combing through his hair and the thrill of the chase stirring his blood. In mere minutes the odds had changed from two against three to four against one. He needed no further sign from Heaven that Rosalind was meant to be his.

Chapter Thirty-two

Aboard the *Jamaica Pearl,* Rosalind watched with growing dread as the three ships maneuvered to port. She knew *L'Etoile du Matin* well enough, with its crew dressed in gaudy splendor. The larger ship firing cannonballs at *L'Etoile du Matin's* stern had to be the frigate Murdock mentioned. But who was aboard that third ship, the one Alexandre drew alongside and seemed to be conferring with? Could that be some ally of his, some ship under the command of his cousin in charge of Martinique's naval forces? Rosalind could only pray that was true. *L'Etoile du Matin* and the *Diabolique* made a fearsome pair, but even they might not be enough to stand against the combined guns of both the frigate and the *Jamaica Pearl.*

"Rosalind!" Mr. Murdock came thundering toward her. His expression of high good humor was positively obscene. "Get below, my dear! Things are about to get a bit busy!"

"Whatever do you mean?"

"That fine French fool has fallen neatly into my trap!" He threw an arm around her shoulders and pointed toward the mysterious third ship. "That's an English merchantman. I'll wager all the guineas I own that she's really a British naval vessel, on the lookout for French smugglers and pirates."

Rosalind's heart thudded painfully. The one danger Alexandre had always been careful to avoid was the British navy. Now she had become the instrument of his capture, and very likely his death. What bitter irony, to recall the days when she had joyfully contemplated seeing the Black Angel hang. Now that thought was a dagger in her heart.

"You look rather distressed, my dear." Mr. Murdock smiled. "Can it be you'll miss your French playmates?"

Rosalind shook off his arm, and turned to glare at him. "I think, my dear Mr. Murdock, you'd do well to save your breath. You'll need it when the time comes to beg the Black Angel for mercy."

Mr. Murdock's face darkened with displeasure. "I am so relieved to know just what a spiteful little harridan you really are, Lady Hanshaw. That will make it so much easier to see you shut away!"

Rosalind stared at him. "What—what are you saying?"

He seized her arm in a bruising grip and dragged her closer to the rail. "Your father really was entirely too stupid, blaming everything that has happened in the last six months on chance and circumstance. I will soon turn its luck to the good, just as I created all the bad."

"You? You were behind all of this? You deliberately ruined my father?" A wave of dizziness swept over Rosalind. Her stomach lurched within her. For a moment, there was only one clear thought in her mind. "Thomas is master of Hanshaw Shipping!"

"Oh, I have plans for Thomas, indeed I do. By then you will have been my wife for some months, long enough to satisfy the courts. Hanshaw Shipping will then belong to me."

Rosalind swayed on her feet, sick and terrified and on the very brink of fainting dead away. She fumbled in her skirt pockets, her fingers closing around the hard smooth shape of the belaying pin.

Mr. Murdock smiled his revolting smile. "How's that for

an engagement present, my dear? There's nothing like the cold, hard truth."

Here before her stood the man responsible for every hour, every minute of the suffering she had endured, the ruin of her family, the death of her father, her ordeal aboard both *L'Etoile du Matin* and *La Fortuna*. All the grief and terror and humiliation and anguish. Rosalind snatched the belaying pin out of its hiding place and struck Mr. Murdock backhanded across the face. He reeled back from her, his nose streaming blood.

"You mad bitch!" he bellowed.

Rosalind stuffed the belaying pin back in her pocket and ran past the faces of the startled sailors. She dashed into the galley and grabbed an apron hanging on a peg nearby, then wound the apron around her hand and plunged it into the bucket of lard sitting to one side. She held the greasy cloth to the fire burning beneath a bubbling pot. The cloth caught, burning with an evil stink. Out on the main deck Rosalind made for the nearest deck gun and the small keg of gunpowder that sat beside it. She yanked the plug free and kicked the keg over. It rolled with the motion of the ship, leaving a fat black trail across the deck. Shielding her face with one arm, Rosalind threw the flaming rag down onto the black trail. The gunpowder caught, rushing along the deck like a snake all bright red and hissing. Amid cries of "Fire!" the sailors tried to stamp out the blazing line of gunpowder. More sailors ran for buckets of sand and others of seawater.

"Rosalind!" Mr. Murdock charged toward her, one hand holding his bloodied handkerchief over his broken nose.

Rosalind fled toward the quarterdeck, stumbling over coils of rope and other items dropped by the sailors trying to douse the gunpowder. To her left she heard that ominous hissing. A glance that way showed her the red tail of the snake racing toward one of the deck guns. The small keg of gunpowder had fetched up against the larger keg, right beside the pile of cannonballs. Rosalind hurried onward, trying desperately to put the mainmast between her and the deck gun before both kegs ignited.

"Captain!" Rosalind threw herself into Captain Anderson's arms, sobbing on his shoulder. "Captain, Mr. Murdock has gone mad! He thinks you are an English privateer, meant to wage war on any French ship you see!"

"What's this?"

Captain Anderson and the helmsman both stared at her.

"Please, Captain, he's abandoned all reason! He thinks we must make for that ship to port, the brigantine. You see it there, between the frigate and the merchantman?"

"You have good eyes, my lady." Captain Anderson pulled out his spyglass and looked the three ships over. "I'll be damned! The frigate and the merchantman are signaling each other!" He called to his lookout. "Peterson! What are those signals? Can you tell?"

The first mate came running. "Captain, sir! Get down! There's a keg of powder loose on deck!"

His last words were drowned out in the sudden thunderous boom of the explosion. The force of it threw everyone on the quarterdeck flat. Though winded and bruised, Rosalind was grateful for the additional cover of the captain and his mate protecting her from the blast. She tried to shut her ears to the cries of pain from the wounded. Worse bloodshed was on its way if she couldn't stop the coming battle before it started.

Flaming wreckage from the explosion of the first gun rained down on the deck, igniting small fires and touching off more of the gunpowder lined up beside the deck guns. Another explosion near the bow tore some of the smaller sails away from their clews, shredding them with bits of flying metal.

Hands pulled the captain and the first mate up onto their feet. More hands reached down to jerk Rosalind upward.

"You demented little witch!" Mr. Murdock snarled. "What kind of sabotage was that?"

"Take your hands off her, sir!" Captain Anderson snapped. "I don't know what possesses you, but I will not see a lady treated so roughly aboard my ship!"

"This is no lady!" Mr. Murdock snapped. "This is the whore of a French pirate who has killed more good English sailors than any other of his scabrous brethren!"

"How *dare* you!" Rosalind tried to fight free of Murdock's brutal grip on her arms. "Captain, I beg you! Make him stop saying such horrible things!"

The captain barked three names. The sailors he'd summoned appeared out of the smoke and wreckage on the main deck. Each was a head taller than Mr. Murdock and far more brawny.

Mr. Murdock glared at the three sailors. "Don't you understand? I'm not your enemy! He is!" He jabbed a finger to port, where *L'Etoile du Matin* was coming toward them, slicing through the water with terrible intent. "That's the Black Angel! We have to catch him! Just imagine, being the men who brought the Black Angel to justice!"

"Don't be daft, man," said Captain Anderson. "The Black Angel took the *Bird of Paradise* not three weeks ago. He knows every spare vessel the British navy has will be out combing the currents for him!"

"You know that's the Black Angel's ship!" Murdock shook Rosalind. "Tell him! Tell the captain who that is!"

Rosalind smiled. Now it was her turn to speak to him as if he were a simpleminded housemaid. "Oh, Edward! This obsession has got to stop! Look at what it's done to you!"

"You traitorous slut!" If Murdock had been furious before, he now turned a shade of purple that bordered on apoplectic. "I'll see you hang right beside him!"

"Ahoy, *Jamaica Pearl*!" roared an English voice. "Heave to! Heave to, in His Majesty's name!"

Murdock squinted at the English merchantman bearing down on them. He snatched Captain Anderson's spyglass out of his hand and took a better look. "I'll be damned! It's the *Elegance*!"

"The *Elegance*?" Rosalind's heart started pounding with hope and fear. "Thomas's flagship?"

"The very same!" Murdock handed the spyglass back to Captain Anderson. "That's Thomas Hanshaw's ship. He must have been conscripted by the British navy to help hunt that French bastard down!"

Captain Anderson looked out at the *Elegance* and *L'Etoile du Matin*, both closing in on the *Jamaica Pearl*. Behind the *Elegance* came the frigate, and to the *Jamaica Pearl*'s starboard there hovered the *Diabolique*. Rosalind watched Captain Anderson mull over the implications.

Murdock cupped his hands around his mouth. "Hullo! Thomas! It's me, Edward Murdock! Tell the naval officer who I am!"

"Ahoy there, *Jamaica Pearl*!" The voice that answered left Rosalind's eyes wide open and her mouth agape. "I know who Edward Murdock is! And I know what he's been up to these last six months, setting the Black Angel on every honest English ship to enter these waters!"

Rosalind fixed Murdock with a look of absolute horror. "You? It was you, all this time? You told him where to find our ships?"

"Business is business, my dear. A good businessman uses all the tools that come to hand."

"That's not business. That's piracy!" Captain Anderson turned to the helmsman. "Heave to, cheerily now! Do as you're told by His Majesty's officer!"

"Aye, Captain!"

Captain Anderson scowled at Mr. Murdock. "By my authority as captain of this vessel, I hereby order you, Edward Murdock, to surrender yourself to my mates and suffer yourself to be put in chains until such time as the naval officer arrives and gives me further orders."

Murdock's jaw clenched. His face colored a deep red. He snatched the marlinspike from the belt of the sailor closest to him and jerked Rosalind up against his chest, holding the point of the marlinspike to her throat.

"You'll sail on to Kingston, or I'll cut Lady Hanshaw's throat!"

Rosalind stood still, wincing each time the motion of the ship made the point prick her throat. Murdock backed up, moving toward the stern. At the captain's jerk of his head, the three big sailors cleared out of Murdock's path. Once he stood with his back to the stern rail, Murdock hurled his voice toward the *Elegance.*

"To Kingston, damn you! Let us continue or Lady Hanshaw feeds the sharks!"

Rosalind looked wildly toward the two oncoming ships. *L'Etoile du Matin* would reach the *Jamaica Pearl* first, blocking any cannon fire from the frigate. The *Elegance* was scant yards behind, closing in off the *Jamaica Pearl*'s bow. A figure clung to the shrouds at *L'Etoile du Matin*'s bow as the brigantine came alongside. That streaming black hair could belong to only one man.

"Rosalind!" Alexandre shouted. "*Ma belle*, over the side! Jump before the whole ship explodes!"

"He doesn't give a damn about you!" Murdock roared. "I'll prove it." He raised his voice and hurled it at *L'Etoile du Matin*. "The Black Angel sank the *Dover Lady*!"

Rosalind tried to clap her hands over her ears. "Liar! I shall marry him and he shall share in Hanshaw shipping!"

"Over your dead body!" Murdock roared. "Your precious Frenchman might as well have driven his knife through your father's heart!"

Rosalind screamed, part fury and part fright. She struggled against Murdock's grip, looking to Alexandre in mute appeal. The chagrin darkening his handsome face threatened to confirm her worst fears.

"You lose, Frenchman!" Murdock laughed, a sound more like an animal's snarl. "The gold, the lady, and your miserable life!"

He drove his point home, jabbing the air between himself and Alexandre with the marlinspike. Rosalind seized that moment of partial freedom and yanked the belaying pin out of her pocket, driving one end of it into Mr. Murdock's groin. As he doubled over in agony, Rosalind struck him full across the face, sending him sprawling across the deck. She dropped the belaying pin and ran to the portside rail. *L'Etoile du Matin* was too far away to risk a jump, yet if she dove into the water, she might easily be crushed between the ships' hulls.

"Rosalind!" Alexandre ran along his own deck, keeping even with her. "Take a line, *ma belle!* Anything!" His voice was harsh with rising panic. "Get off that ship before the powder room goes!"

Hands grasped a line knotted to the rail right before Rosalind. She looked back to see Captain Anderson himself freeing the line.

"Go, Lady Hanshaw! We'll see that traitorous bastard straight to Hell!"

Rosalind planted a swift kiss on his cheek, took the rope in both hands, and clambered up onto the rail. *L'Etoile du Matin*'s stern was even with the *Jamaica Pearl*'s bow, sliding past at an alarming rate.

"Alexandre!" Rosalind cried. *"J'arrive!"*

She leaped off the rail, swinging out into space above the watery gap between the ships. A dozen hands grabbed at her skirts and hauled her in over *L'Etoile du Matin*'s rail. She had eyes for no one but Alexandre. He caught her up against him, holding her tightly and raining kisses on her hair. She pushed back from his embrace and looked him squarely in the eye.

"Mon capitaine, tell me this. Did you attack the *Dover Lady?"*

Alexandre's eyes closed. He bowed his head. "I did."

"Did you know that was my father's ship? Did you know how much financial trouble my family was already in?"

"Non. I knew nothing of that. All Murdock told me was where and when to find that ship." Alexandre gazed down at her, those dark eyes tragic with weariness and pain. *"Ma belle*, can you still love me, even knowing that?"

Rosalind gazed up at him, her heart spilling over with that very love. "This is what you were referring to, when you said you were more than willing to make amends."

Alexandre nodded. "With your permission, I will devote the rest of my life to ensuring the happiness of you and your family."

"Who are you? Tell me this instant."

"I am Alexandre de Marchant, only son of Philipe, the Marquis de Marchant."

"And you know who I am. You've known all along."

Alexandre smiled. "*Mais oui*. You are my little milkmaid."

While they watched from a safe distance, the fires aboard the *Jamaica Pearl* were extinguished. The bosuns piped Captain Jameson across, where he saw Murdock shackled and removed to the *Elegance*.

"I suppose I should thank him," Rosalind said softly.

"Murdock? That swine? Whatever for?"

"For bringing us together." Rosalind smiled, her eyes shimmering with unshed tears. "This is the third time you and I have come to terms, *mon capitaine*. As we both know, the third time is the charm."

Laughing, Alexandre swept Rosalind up into his arms.

RIDE THE FIRE
PAMELA CLARE

There is only one rule on the frontier—survival. So when a wounded, buckskin-clad stranger appears at the door of her isolated cabin, Elspeth Stewart feels no qualms about disarming him and then tying him to her bed. Nicholas Kenleigh threatens not only her safety, but her peace of mind. Bethie has every reason in the world to distrust men; the cruelty she has suffered at their hands has marked her soul, though her blonde beauty shows no sign of it. But she finds herself believing in Nicholas, in his honor, his strength. As he brings her baby into the world, then takes both mother and daughter into his care, she realizes this scarred survivor can heal her wounded spirit, and together they will…